The Black Eagle

Or, Ticonderoga

by

G. P. R. James

Double 9
BOOKS

The Black Eagle
Or, Ticonderoga
by G. P. R. James

ISBN: 978-93-69079-31-5

Published by

DOUBLE 9 BOOKS
2/13-B, Ansari Road
Daryaganj, New Delhi – 110002
info@double9books.com
www.double9books.com
Tel. 011-40042856

This book is under public domain

ABOUT THE AUTHOR

George Payne Rainsford James, a London-born novelist and historian, was born on August 9, 1799, and died on June 9, 1860. He served as the British Consul for a long time in a number of locations across the continent and in the United States. During the final years of William IV's reign, he was the honorary British Historiographer Royal. In 1799, George Payne Rainsford James was born in London's Hanover Square on St. George Street. His father was a doctor who had been in the navy and had fought alongside Benedict Arnold in the Battle of Groton Heights in America during the Revolutionary War. He became passionate in learning new languages, such as Arabic, Persian, Greek, and Latin. When he was younger, he also studied medicine, but his preferences took him in a different way. His father, who had served in the navy himself, opposed his desire to enlist, which ultimately led to him being able to enlist in the army. James was injured in a minor battle after the Battle of Waterloo and remained in the army for a brief period of time during the Hundred Days as a lieutenant.

CONTENTS

CHAPTER I

"Among the minor trials of faith, few, perhaps, are more difficult to contend against than that growing conviction, which, commencing very soon after the holiday happiness of youth has been first tasted, becomes stronger every year, as experience unfolds to us the great, dark secrets of the world in which we are placed--the conviction of the general worthlessness of our fellow-men. A few splendid exceptions, a few bright and glorious spirits, a few noble and generous hearts, are not sufficient to cheer and to brighten the bleak prospect of the world's unworthiness; and we can only reconcile to our minds the fact that this vast multitude of base, depraved, tricky, insincere, ungrateful beings, are the pride of God's works, the express images of his person, by a recurrence to the great fundamental doctrine of man's fallen state, and utter debasement from his original high condition, and by a painful submission to the gloomy and fearful announcement, that *strait is the gate, and narrow is the way, and few there be that find it.*'

"If man's general unworthiness be a trial of our faith and of our patience, the most poignant anguish of the torture is perhaps the keen conviction of his ingratitude and his injustice--not alone the ingratitude and injustice of individuals, but those of every great body--of every group--of so-called friends, of governments, of countries, of people. Vainly do we follow the course of honour and uprightness; vainly do we strive to benefit, to elevate, to ennoble our fellow-men; vainly do we labour to serve our party, or our cause, or our country. Neither honour, nor distinction, nor reward, follows our best efforts, even when successful, unless we possess the mean and contemptible adjuncts of personal interest, pushing impudence, crooked policy, vile subserviency, or the smile of fortune.

"Here am I, who for many arduous years laboured with zeal, such as few have felt, at sacrifices such as few have made, and with industry such as few have exerted, to benefit my kind and my country. That I did so, and with success, was admitted by all; even while others, starting in the career of life at the same time with myself, turned their course in the most opposite direction, pandered to vice, to folly, and even to crime, and trod a flowery and an easy way, with few of the difficulties and impediments that beset my path.

"And what has been the result? Even success has brought to me neither reward, nor honour, nor gratitude. On those who have neither so laboured, nor so striven, whose objects have been less worthy, whose efforts have been less great, recompenses and distinctions have fallen thick and fast--a government's patronage--sovereign's favour--a people's applause. And I am an exile on a distant shore; unthought of, unrecompensed, unremembered."

He paused with the pen in his hand, and the bitter and corroding thoughts of the neglect he had endured still busy in his mind, spreading into a thousand new channels, and poisoning all the sources of happiness within him. An old newspaper lay on the table. Newspapers were scarce in those days, and it had reached him tardily. Some accidental traveller through the wilderness had brought it to him lately, and he had found therein fresh proofs of the forgetfulness of friends--fresh evidence of the truth of the old axiom, "out of sight out of mind."

The perusal of this journal had given rise to the dark view of his own fate, and of human nature which he had just put upon record. His was not, in truth, a complaining spirit. It was not his nature to repine or to murmur. He had a heart to endure much, and to struggle on against obstacles: to take even bright and happy views: to rely upon friendship, and trust in God. It was only when some fresh burden was cast upon the load of ingratitude and falsehood he had met with, that a momentary burst of indignation broke from him--that the roused and irritated spirit spoke aloud. He had been a good friend, faithful, and true, and zealous. He had been a kind master, looking upon all around him as brethren, seeking their welfare and their happiness often more than his own. He had been a good subject, honouring and loving his sovereign, and obedient to the laws. He had been a good patriot, advocating by pen and voice (without fear, and without favour) all those measures which, from his very inmost heart, he believed were for his country's welfare, and grudging neither time, nor exertion, nor labour, nor money, to support that party which he knew to be actuated by the same principles as himself.

But, with all this, no one had ever sought to serve him; no one had ever thought of recompensing him. Many a friend had proved false, and neglected the best opportunity of promoting his interests: many, who had fed upon his bounty, or shared his purse, had back-bitten him in private, or maligned him in the public prints; and, though there were a few noble and generous exceptions, was it wonderful that there should be some bitterness in his heart, as he sat there in a lowly dwelling, in the midst of the woods of America, striving to carve a fortune from the wilderness for himself and his two children?

Yet it was but for a moment that the gloom was suffered to remain--that the repining spirit held possession of him. Though his hair was very many checks; while France, from her much larger population, can pour a continuous stream of troops into her colonies."

"Not for long," answered his host. "The fabric of her power is undermined at the foundation; the base is rotten; and the building, though imposing without, is crumbling to decay. It is well, however, to see as you do the utmost extent of a danger--perhaps, even to overestimate it, in order to meet it the more vigorously. Depend upon it, however, the present state of things in France is not destined for long duration. I judge not by the feebleness she has shown of late years in many most important efforts. Beset as she is by enemies, and enemies close at her gates, distant endeavours may well be paralyzed without there being any real diminution of her power. But I judge from what I myself saw in that country a good many years ago. The people--the energetic, active, though volatile people, in whom lies her real strength--were everywhere oppressed and suffering. Misery might drive them into her armies, and give them the courage of despair; but, at the same time, it severed all ties between them and those above them--substituted contempt and hatred for love and reverence, in the case of the nobility, and fear, doubt, and an inclination to resist, for affection, confidence, and obedience, towards the throne. Corruption, spreading through every class of society, could only appear more disgusting when clad in the robes of royalty, or tricked out in the frippery of aristocracy; and nations speedily learn to resist powers which they have ceased to respect. A state of society cannot long endure, in which, on the one side, boundless luxury, gross depravity, and empty frivolity, in a comparatively small body, and grinding want, fierce passions, and eager, unsated desires on the other side, are brought into close contiguity, without one moral principle, or one religious light--where there is nothing but the darkness of superstition, or the deeper darkness of infidelity. Ere many years have passed, the crown of France will have need of all her troops at home."

The stranger mused much upon his companion's words, and seemed to feel that they were prophetical. The same, or very nearly the same, were written by another; but they were not given to the world for several years after, on the eve of the great catastrophe; and in the year one thousand seven hundred and fifty-seven, few seemed to dream that the power of France could ever be shaken, except by an external enemy. Men ate, and drank, and danced, and sang, in the Parisian capital, as gaily as they did in the palace of Sardanapalus, with as great a fall at hand.

The conversation then assumed a lighter tone. Each asked the other of his travels, and commented on many objects of interest which both had seen on the broad high-ways of the world. Both were men of thought, according to their several characters--both men of taste and refinement; and the two young people, who had sat silent, listening to their graver discourse, now joined in, from time to time, with happy freedom and unchecked ease. Their father's presence was no restraint upon them; for, in all that they had known of life, he had been their companion and their friend--the one to whom their hearts had been ever opened--the one chiefly reverenced from love. The stranger, too, though he was grave, was in no degree stern, and there was something winning even in his very gravity. He listened, too, when they spoke--heard the brief comment--answered the eager question; and a kindly smile would, ever and anon, pass over his lip, at the strange mixture of refinement and simplicity which he found in those two young beings, who passed many a month of every year without seeing any one, except the wild Indians of the friendly tribes surrounding them, or an occasional trader wending his way, with his wares, up the stream of the Mohawk.

More than an hour was beguiled at the table--a longer period than ordinary--and then the bright purple hues, which spread over the eastern wall of the room, opposite to the windows, told that the autumnal sun had reached the horizon. The master of the house rose to lead the way into the other room again; but ere he moved from the table, an additional figure was added to the group around it, though the foot was so noiseless that no one heard its first entrance into the chamber.

The person who had joined the little party was a man of the middle age, of a tall, commanding figure, upright and dignified carriage, and fine, but somewhat strongly-marked, features. The expression of his countenance was grave and noble; but there was a certain strangeness in it--a touch of wildness perhaps I might call it--very difficult to define.

It was not in the eyes; for they were good, calm, and steadfast, gazing straight at any object of contemplation, and fixed full upon the face of any one he addressed. It was not in the lips; for, except when speaking, they were firm and motionless. Perhaps it was in the eyebrow, which, thick and strongly marked, was, every now and then, suddenly raised or depressed, without any apparent cause.

His dress was very strange. He was evidently of European blood, although his skin was embrowned by much exposure to sun and weather. Yet he wore not altogether either the European costume, the garb of the American back-woodsman, or that of the Indian. There was a mixture of all, which gave him a wild and fantastic appearance. His coat was evidently English, and had stripes of gold lace upon the shoulders; his knee-breeches and high riding-boots would have looked English also, had not the latter being destitute of soles, properly so called; for they were made somewhat like a stocking, and the part beneath the foot was of the same leather as the rest. Over his shoulder was a belt of rattlesnake skin, and round his waist a sort of girdle, formed from the claws of the bear, from which depended a string of wampum, while two or three knives and a small tomahawk appeared on either side. No other weapon had he whatever. But under his left arm hung a common powder-flask, made of cow's horn, and, beside it, a sort of wallet, such as the trappers commonly used for carrying their little store of Indian corn. A round fur cap, of bear-skin, without any ornament whatever, completed his habiliments.

It would seem that in that house he was well known; for its master instantly held forth his hand to him, and the young people sprang forward and greeted him warmly. A full minute elapsed before he spoke; but nobody uttered a word till he did so, all seeming to understand his habits.

"Well, Mr. Prevost," he said, at length, "I have been a stranger to your wigwam for some time. How art thou, Walter? Not a man yet, in spite of all thou canst do. Edith, my sweet lady, time deals differently with thee from thy brother. He makes thee a woman against thy will." Then, turning suddenly to the stranger, he said, "Sir, I am glad to see you; were you ever at Kielmansegge?"

"Once," replied the stranger, laconically.

"Then we will confer presently," observed the new comer. "How have you been this many a day, Mr. Prevost? You must give me food; for I have ridden far--I will have that bear-skin, too, for my night's lodging place, if it be not pre-engaged. No, not that one; the next. I have told Agrippa to see to my horse, for I ever count upon your courtesy."

There was something extremely stately and dignified in his whole tone, and, with frank straightforwardness, but without any indecorous haste, he seated himself at the table, drew towards him a large dish of cold meat, and, while Edith and her brother hastened to supply him with everything else he needed, proceeded to help himself liberally to whatever was within his reach. Not a word more did he speak for several minutes, while Mr. Prevost and his guest stood looking on in silence, and the two young people attended the new comer at the table.

As soon as he had done, he rose abruptly, and then, looking first to Mr. Prevost, and next to the stranger, said--

"Now, gentlemen, if you please, we will to council."

The stranger hesitated; and Mr. Prevost answered, with a smile--

"I am not of the initiated, Sir William, so I and the children will leave you with my guest, whom you seem to know, but of whose name and station I am ignorant."

"Stay, stay," interposed the other, to whom he spoke, "we shall need not only your advice but your concurrence. This gentleman, my lord, I will answer for, as a faithful and loyal subject of his Majesty King George. He has been treated with that hardest of all hard treatment--neglect. But his is a spirit in which not even neglect can drown out loyalty to his king and love to his country. Moreover, I may say, that the neglect which he has met with has proceeded from a deficiency in his own nature. God, unfortunately, did not make him a grumbler, or he would have been a peer long ago. The Almighty endowed him with all the qualities that could benefit his fellow-creatures, but denied him those which were necessary to advance himself. Others have wondered that he never met with honours, or distinction, or reward. I wonder not at all; for he is neither a charlatan, nor a coxcomb, nor a pertinacious beggar. He cannot stoop to slabber the hand of power, nor lick the spittle of the man in office. How can such a man have advancement? It is contrary to the course of the things of this world. But as he has loved his fellow-men, so will he love them. As he has served his country, so will he serve it. As he has sought honour and truth more than promotion, honour and truth will be his reward. Alas, that it should be the only one! But when he dies, if he dies unrecompensed, it will not be unregretted or unvenerated. He must be of our council."

Mr. Prevost had stood by in silence, with his eyes bent upon the ground, and, perhaps, some self-reproach at his heart for the bitter words that he had written only a few hours before. But Edith sprang forward, and caught Sir William Johnson's hand, as he ended the praises of her father; and, bending her head with exquisite grace, pressed her lips upon it. Her brother seemed inclined to linger for a moment; but saying, "Come, Walter," she glided out of the room, and the young lad, following, closed the door behind him.

CHAPTER III

"Who can he be?" said Walter Prevost, when they had reached the little sitting-room. "Sir William called him 'my lord.'"

Edith smiled at her brother's curiosity. Oh, how much older women always are than men!

"Lords are small things here, Walter," she said, gazing forth from the window at the stately old trees within sight of the house, which for her, as for all expanding minds, had their homily. Age--hackneyed age--reads few lessons. It ponders those long received, subtilizes, refines, combines. Youth has a lesson in every external thing; but, alas! soon forgets the greater part of all.

"I do not think that lords are small things anywhere," answered her brother, who had not imbibed any of the republican spirit which was even then silently creeping over the American people. "Lords are made by kings for great deeds, or great virtues."

"Then they are lords of their own making," retorted Edith; "kings only seal the patent nature has bestowed. That great red oak, Walter, was growing before the family of any man now living was ennobled by the hand of royalty."

"Pooh, nonsense, Edith!" ejaculated her brother; "you are indulging in one of your day-dreams. What has that oak to do with nobility?"

"I hardly know," replied his sister; "yet something linked them together in my mind. It seemed as if the oak asked me, 'What is *their* antiquity to *mine?*' and yet the antiquity of their families is their greatest claim to our reverence."

"No, no!" cried Walter Prevost, eagerly; "their antiquity is nothing, for we are all of as ancient a family as they are. But it is that they can show a line from generation to generation, displaying some high qualities, ennobled by some great acts. Granted that here or there a sluggard, a coward, or a fool, may have intervened, or that the acts which have won praise in other days may not be reverenced now; yet I have often heard my father say, that, in looking back through records of noble houses, we shall find a sum of deeds and qualities suited to, and honoured by, succeeding ages, which, tried by the standard of the times of the men, shows that hereditary nobility is not merely an honour won by a worthy father for unworthy children, but a bond to great endeavours, signed by a noble ancestor, on behalf of all his descendants. Edith, you are not saying what you think."

"Perhaps not," answered Edith, with a quiet smile; "but let us have some lights, Walter, for I am well-nigh in darkness."

They were not ordinary children. I do not intend to represent them as such. But he who says that what is not ordinary is not natural, may, probably, be an ass. How they had become what they were is another question; but that is easily explained. First--Nature had not made them of her common clay; for, notwithstanding all bold assertions of that great and fatal falsehood, that all men are born equal, such is not the case. No two men are ever born equal. No two leaves are alike upon a tree, and there is a still greater dissimilarity--a still greater inequality--between the gifts and endowments of different men. God makes them unequal. God raises the one, and depresses the other, ay, from the very birth, in the scale of his creation; and man, by one mode or another, in every state of society, and in every land, recognizes the difference, and assigns the rank. Nature, then, had not made those two young people of her common clay. Their father was no common man; their mother had been one in whom mind and heart, thought and feeling, had been so nicely balanced, that emotion always found a guide in judgment. But this was not all. The one child up to the age of thirteen, the other until twelve, had been trained and instructed with the utmost care. Every advantage of education had been lavished upon them, and every natural talent they possessed had been developed, cultivated, directed. They had been taught from mere childhood to think, as well as to know; to use, as well as to receive, information. Then had come a break--the sad, jarring break in the sweet chain of the golden hours of youth--a mother's death. Till then their father had borne much from the world and from society unflinching. But then his stay and his support were gone. Visions became realities for him. What wonder if, when the light of his home had gone out, his mental sight became somewhat dim, the objects around him indistinct? He gathered together all he had, and migrated to a distant land, where small means might be considered great, and where long-nourished theories of life might be tried by the test of experience.

To his children, the change was but a new phase of education--one not often tried, but not without its uses. If their new house was not completely a solitude, it was very nearly so. Morally and physically they were thrown nearly upon their own resources. But previous training had made those resources many. Mentally, at least, they brought a great capital into the wilderness, and they found means to employ it. Everything around them, in its newness and its freshness, had a lesson and a moral. The trees, the flowers, the streams, the birds, the insects, the new efforts, the new labours, the very wants and deficiencies of their present state--all taught them something. Had they been born amidst such things; had they been brought up in such habits; had their previous training been at all of the same kind; or, even had the change been as great as it might have been; had they been left totally destitute of comforts, conveniences, attendance, books, companionships, objects of art and taste, to live the life of the savage,--the result might have been--must have been--very different. But there was enough left of the past to link it beneficially to the present. They brought all the materials with them from their old world for opening out the rich mines of the new. It is not to be wondered at, then, if they were no ordinary children; and if, at fifteen and sixteen, they reasoned and thought of things, and in modes, not often dealt with by the young. I say, not often; because, even under other circumstances, and with no such apparent causes, we see occasional instances of beings like themselves.

They were, then, no ordinary children, but yet quite natural.

The influences which surrounded them had acted differently, of course, on the boy and on the girl. He had learned to act as well as think: she to meditate as well as act. He had acquired the strength, the foot, the ear, the eye of the Indian. She, too, had gained much in activity and hardihood; but in the dim glades, and on the flower-covered banks, by the side of the rushing stream, or hanging over the roaring cataract, she had learned to give way to long and silent reveries, dealing both with the things of her own heart and the things of the wide world; comparing the present with the past, the solitude with society, meditating upon life and its many phases, and yielding herself, while the silent majesty of the scene seemed to sink into her soul, to what her brother was wont to call her "day-dreams."

I have said that she dealt with the *things of her own heart*. Let me not be misunderstood: the things of that heart were very simple. They had never been complicated with even a thought of love. Her own fate, her own history, her soul in its relation to God and to His creation, the sweet and bright emotions produced within her by all things beautiful in art or nature, the thrill excited by a lovely scene or a dulcet melody, the trance-like pleasure of watching the clear stream waving the many-coloured pebbles of its bed, these, and such as these, were the things of the heart I spoke of; and on them she would dwell and ponder, asking herself what they were, whence they came, how they arose, whither they tended. It was the music, the poetry, of her own nature, in all its strains, which she sought to search into; but the sweetest, though sometimes the saddest, of the harmonies in woman's heart was yet wanting.

She had read of love, it is true; she had heard it spoken of, but, with a timidity not rare in the most sensitive minds, she had excluded it even from her day-dreams. She knew that there was such a thing as passion: she might be conscious that it was latent in her own nature; but she tried not to seek it out. To her it was an abstraction. Psyche had not held the lamp to Eros.

So much it was needful to say of the two young Prevosts before we went onward with our tale; and now, as far as they were concerned, the events of that day were near their close. Lights were brought, and Walter and his sister sat down to muse over books--I can hardly say read--till their father re-appeared; for the evening prayer and the parting kiss had never been omitted in their solitude ere they lay down to rest.

The conference in the hall, however, was long, and more than an hour elapsed before the three gentlemen entered the room. Then a few minutes were passed in quiet conversation, and then, all standing round the table, Mr. Prevost raised his voice, saying,

"Protect us, O Father Almighty! in the hours of darkness and unconsciousness. Give us Thy blessing of sleep, to refresh our minds and bodies; and, if it be Thy will, let us wake again to serve and praise Thee through another day more perfectly than in the days past, for Christ's sake."

The Lord's Prayer succeeded; and then they separated to their rest.

CHAPTER IV

Before daylight in the morning, Sir William Johnson was on foot, and in the stable. Some three or four negro-slaves--for there were slaves then on all parts of the American continent--lay sleeping soundly in a small sort of barrack hard by; and, as soon as one of them could be roused, Sir William's horse was saddled, and he rode away, without pausing to eat, or to say farewell. He bent his course direct towards the Mohawk, flowing at some twenty miles' distance from the cottage of Mr. Prevost.

Before Sir William had been five minutes in the saddle, he was in the midst of the deep woods which surrounded the little well-cultivated spot where the English wanderer had settled. It was a wild and rather gloomy scene into which he plunged; for, though something like a regular road had been cut, along which carts as well as horses could travel, yet that road was narrow, and the branches nearly met overhead.

In some places the underwood, nourished by a moist and marshy soil, was too thick and tangled to be penetrated either by foot or eye. In others, where the path ascended to higher grounds, or passed amongst the hard dry rocks, the aspect of the forest changed. Pine after pine, with now and then an oak, a chestnut, or a locust-tree, covered the face of the country, with hardly a shrub upon the ground below, which was carpeted with the brown slippery needles of the resinous trees; and between the huge trunks poured the grey, mysterious light of the early dawn, while a thin, whitish vapour hung amongst the boughs overhead.

About a mile from the house, a bright and beautiful stream crossed the road, flowing on towards the greater river; but bridge there was none, and, in the middle of the stream, Sir William suffered his horse to stop, and bend its head to drink. He gazed to the westward, but all there was dark and gloomy under the thick overhanging branches. He turned his eyes to the eastward, where the ground was more open, and the stream could be seen flowing on for nearly half a mile, with little cascades, and dancing rapids, and calm lapses of bright, glistening water, tinted with a rosy hue, where the morning sky gleamed down upon it through some break in the forest canopy.

While thus gazing, his eye rested on a figure standing in the midst of the stream, with rod in hand, and the back turned towards him. He thought he saw another figure also amongst the trees upon the bank; but it was shadowy there, and the form seemed shadowy too.

After gazing for a minute or so, he raised his voice, and exclaimed--

"Walter!--Walter Prevost!"

The lad heard him, and, laying his rod upon the bank, hastened along over the green turf to join him; at the same moment the figure amongst the trees--if really figure it was--disappeared from the sight.

"Thou art out early, Walter," said Sir William. "What do you at this hour?"

"I am catching trout for the stranger's breakfast," replied the lad, with a gay laugh. "You should have had your share, had you but waited."

"Who was that speaking to you on the bank above?" asked the other, gravely.

"Merely an Indian girl watching me fishing," responded Walter Prevost.

"I hope your talk was discreet," rejoined Sir William. "These are dangerous times, when trifles are of import, Walter."

"There was no indiscretion," returned the lad, with the colour mounting slightly in his cheek. "She was remarking the feather-flies with which I caught the trout, and blamed me for using them. She said it was a shame to catch anything with false pretences."

"She is wise," observed the other, with a faint smile; "yet that is hardly the wisdom of her people. An Indian maiden!" he added, thoughtfully. "Of what tribe is she? One of the Five Nations, I trust?"

"Oh, yes--an Oneida," replied Walter; "one of the daughters of the Stone; the child of a Sachem, who often lodges at our house."

"Well, be she whom she may," rejoined Sir William, "be careful of your speech, Walter, especially regarding your father's guest. I say not, to conceal that there is a stranger with you, for that cannot be; but, whatever you see or guess of his station, or his errand, keep it to yourself, and let not a woman be the sharer of your thoughts, till you have tried her with many a trial."

"She would not betray them, I am sure," said the lad, warmly; and then added, with slight embarrassment, as if he felt that he had in a degree betrayed himself, "but she has nothing to reveal, or to conceal. Our talk was all of the river, and the fish. We met by accident, and she is gone."

"Perhaps you may meet again by accident," suggested the other, "and then be careful. But now, to more serious things. Perchance your father may have to send you to Albany--perchance, to my castle. You can find your way speedily to either. Is it not so?"

"Farther than either," replied the lad, gaily.

"But you may have a heavy burden to carry," rejoined Sir William; "do you think you can bear it?--I mean the burden of a secret."

"I will not drop it by the way," returned Walter, gravely.

"Not if the Sachem's daughter offers to divide the load?" asked his companion.

"Doubt me not," replied Walter.

"I do not doubt you," said Sir William, "I do not. But I would have you warned. And now farewell. You are very young to meet maidens in the wood. Be careful. Farewell."

He rode on, and the boy tarried by the wayside, and meditated. His were very strange thoughts, and stranger feelings. They were the feelings that only come to any person once in a lifetime--earlier with some, later with others--the ecstatic thrill, the joyous emotion, the dancing of the young bright waters of early life, in the pure morning sunshine of first love--the dream--the vision--the trance of indefinite joy--the never-to-be-forgotten, the never-to-be-renewed, first glance at the world of passion that is within us. Till that moment, he had been as one climbing a mountain with thick boughs shading from his eyes the things before him; but his friend's words had been a hand drawing back the branches on the summit, and showing him a wondrous and lovely sight beyond.

Was he not very young to learn such things? O yes, he was very, very young; but it was natural that in that land he should learn them young. All was young there: all is young: everything is rapid and precocious; the boy has the feelings of the young man; the young man the thoughts of maturity. The air, the climate, the atmosphere of the land and the people, all have their influence. The shrubs grow up in an hour: the flowers succeed each other with hasty profusion, and even the alien and the stranger-born feel the infection, and join unresistingly in the rapid race. Well did the dreamers of the Middle Ages place the fountain of youth on the shores of the new world.

The boy, who stood there meditating, had lived half a lifetime in the few short years he had spent upon that soil; and now, at Sir William's words, as with him of old, the scales fell from his eyes, and he saw into his own heart.

His reverie lasted not long, indeed; but it was long enough. In about two minutes, he took his way up the stream again, still musing, towards the place where he had laid down his rod upon the bank. He heeded not much where he set his feet. Sometimes it was on the dry ground, by the side of the stream; sometimes it was in the gurgling waters, and amongst the glossy pebbles.

He paused, at length, where he had stood fishing a few minutes before, and looked up to the bank covered with green branches. He could see nothing there in the dim obscurity; but even the murmur of the waters and the sighing of the wind did not prevent him from hearing a sound--a gentle stirring of the boughs. He sprang up the bank, and in amongst the maples; and, about ten minutes after, the sun, rising higher, poured its light through the stems upon a boy and girl, seated at the foot of an old tree: he, with his arms around her, and his hand resting on the soft, brown, velvety skin, and she, with her head upon his bosom, and her warm lips within the reach of his. What, though a sparkling drop or two gemmed her sunny cheek, they were but the dew of the sweetest emotion that ever refreshes the summer morning of our youth.

Her skin was brown, I have said--yes, very brown--but, still, hardly browner than his own. Her eyes were dark and bright, of the true Indian hue, but larger and more open than is at all common in any of the tribes of Iroquois. Her lips, too, were as rosy and as pure of all tinge of brown, as those of any child of Europe; and her fingers, also, were stained of Aurora's own hue. But her long, silky, black hair would have spoken her race at once, had not each tress terminated in a wavy curl. The lines of the form and of the face were all wonderfully lovely too, and yet were hardly those which characterize so peculiarly the Indian nations. The nose was straighter, the cheek-bones less prominent, the head more beautifully set upon the shoulders. The expression, also, as she rested there, with her cheek leaning on his breast, was not that of the usual Indian countenance. It was softer, more tender, more impassioned; for, though romance and poetry have done all they could to spiritualize the character of Indian love, I fear, from what I have seen, and heard, and known, it is rarely what it has been portrayed. Her face, however, was full of love, and tenderness, and emotion; and the picture of the two, as they sat there, told, at once, the tale of love just spoken to a willing ear.

There let us leave them. It was a short hour of joy; a sweet dream in the dark, stormy night of life. They were happy, with the unalloyed happiness so seldom known even for an hour, without fear, or doubt, or guilt, or remorse; and so let them be. What matters it if a snake should glide through the grass hard by? it may pass on, and not sting them. What matters it if a cloud should hang over the distant horizon?--the wind may waft away the storm. Forethought is a curse or a blessing, as we use it. To guard against evils that we see is wise, to look forth for those we cannot guard against is folly.

CHAPTER V

The hour of breakfast had arrived, when Walter Prevost returned with his river spoil; but the party at the house had not yet sat down to table. The guest who had arrived on the preceding night was standing at the door, talking with Edith, while Mr. Prevost himself was within, in conference with some of the slaves. Shaded by the little rustic porch, Edith was leaning against the doorpost in an attitude of exquisite grace; and the stranger, with his arms crossed upon his broad, manly chest, now raising his eyes to her face, now dropping them to the ground, seemed to watch with interest the effect his words produced, as it was written on that beautiful countenance. I have said with interest, rather than with admiration; for although it is hardly possible to suppose that the latter had no share in his sensations, yet it seemed, as far as outward manner could indicate inward thought, that he was reading a lesson from her looks, instead of gazing upon a beautiful picture. The glance, too, was so calm, and so soon withdrawn, that there could be nothing offensive in it--nothing that could even say to herself, "I am studying you," although a looker-on might so divine.

His words were gay and light indeed, and his whole manner very different from the day before. A cloud seemed to have passed away--a cloud rather of reflection than of care; and Walter, as he came up, and heard his cheerful tones, wondered at the change; for he knew not how speedily men accustomed to action and decision cast from them the burden of weighty thought, when the necessity for thought is past.

"I know not," said the stranger, speaking as the young man approached--"I know not how I should endure it myself for any length of time. The mere abstract beauty of nature would soon pall upon my taste, I fear, without occupation."

"But you would make occupation," answered Edith, earnestly; "you would find it. Occupation for the body is never wanting, where you have to improve, and cultivate, and ornament; and occupation for the mind flows in from a thousand gushing sources in God's universe--even were one deprived of books and music."

"Ay, but companionship, and social converse, and the interchange of thought with thought," said the stranger,--"where could one find those?" And he raised his eyes to her face.

"Have I not my brother and my father?" she asked.

"True," said the other; "but I should have no such resource."

He had seen a slight hesitation in her last reply. He thought that he had touched the point where the yoke of solitude galled the spirit. He was not one to plant or to nourish discontent in any one; and he turned at once to her brother, saying, "What, at the stream so early, my young friend? Have you had sport?"

"Not very great," answered Walter; "my fish are few, but they are large. Look here."

"I call such sport excellent," observed the stranger, looking into the basket. "I must have you take me with you some fair morning, for I am a great lover of the angle."

The lad hesitated, and turned somewhat redder in the cheek than he had been the moment before; but his sister saved him from reply, saying in a musing tone,--

"I cannot imagine what delight men find in what they call the sports of the field. To inflict death may be a necessity, but surely should not be an amusement."

"Man is born a hunter, Miss Prevost," replied the stranger, with a smile: "he must chase something. It was at first a necessity, and it is still a pleasure when it is no longer a need. But the enjoyment is not truly in the infliction of death, but in the accessories. The eagerness of pursuit; the active exercise of the faculties, mental and corporeal; the excitement of expectation, and of success,--nay, even of delay; the putting forth of skill and dexterity, all form part of the enjoyment. But there are, especially in angling, a thousand accidental pleasures. It leads one through lovely scenes; we meditate upon many things as we wander on; we gaze upon the dancing brook, or the still pool, and catch light from the light amidst the waters; all that we see is suggestive of thought,--I might almost say of poetry. Ah, my dear young lady! few can tell the enjoyment, in the midst of busy, active, troublous life, of one calm day's angling by the side of a fair stream, with quiet beauty all around us, and no adversary but the speckled trout."

"And why should they be your foes?" asked Edith. "Why should you drag them from their cool, clear element, to pant and die in the dry upper air?"

"'Cause we want to eat 'em," uttered a voice from the door behind her: "*they* eats everything. Why shouldn't *we* eat *them*? Darn this world! it is but a place for eating, and being eaten. The bivers that I trap eat fish; and many a cunning trick the crafty critters use to catch 'em: the minkes eat birds, and birds' eggs. Men talk about beasts of prey. Why, everything is a beast of prey, bating the oxen and the sheep, and such-like; and sometimes I've thought it hard to kill them who never do harm to no one, and a great deal of good sometimes. But, as I was saying, everything's a beast of prey. It's not lions, and tigers, and painters, and such; but from the fox to the emmet, from the beetle to the bear, they're all alike, and man at the top o' them. Darn them all! I kill 'em when I can catch 'em, ma'am, and always will. But come, Master Walter, don't ye keep them fish in the sun. Give 'em to black Rosie, the cook, and let us have some on 'em for breakfast afore they're all wilted up."

The types of American character are very few--much fewer than the American people imagine. There are three or four original types very difficult to distinguish from their varieties; and all the rest are mere modifications--variations on the same air. It is thus somewhat difficult to portray any character purely American, without the risk of displaying characteristics which have been sketched by more skilful hands. The outside of the man, however, affords greater scope than the inside; for Americans are by no means always long, thin, sinewy fellows, as they are too frequently represented; and the man who now spoke was a specimen of a very different kind. He might be five feet five or six in height, and was anything but corpulent; yet he was, in chest and shoulders, as broad as a bull; and though the lower limbs were more lightly formed than the upper, yet the legs, as well as the arms, displayed the strong, rounded muscles swelling forth at every movement. His hair was as black as jet, without the slightest mixture of grey, though he could not be less than fifty-four or fifty-five years of age; and his face, which was handsome, with features somewhat eagle-like, was browned, by exposure, to a colour nearly resembling that of mahogany. With his shaggy bear-skin cap, well worn, and a frock of deer-skin, with the hair on, descending to the knees, he looked more like a bison or bonassus than anything human; and, expecting to hear him roar, one was surprised to trace tones soft and gentle, though rather nasal, to such a rude and rugged form.

While Walter carried his basket of fish to the kitchen, and Mr. Prevost's guest was gazing at the stranger, in whom Edith seemed to recognize an acquaintance, the master of the house himself appeared from behind the latter, saying, as he came,--

"Let me make you acquainted with Mr. Brooks; Major Kielmansegge--Captain Jack Brooks."

"Pooh, pooh, Prevost," exclaimed the other. "Call me by my right name. I war Captain Brooks long agone. I'm new christened, and called Woodchuck now--that's because I burrow, major. Them Ingians are wonderful circumdiferous; but they have found that, when they try tricks with me, I can burrow under them; and so they call me Woodchuck, 'cause it's a burrowing sort of a beast."

"I do not exactly understand you," replied the gentleman who had been called Major Kielmansegge; "what is the exact meaning of *circumdiferous?*"

"It means just circumventing like," answered the Woodchuck. "First and foremost, there's many of the Ingians--the Aloquin, for a sample--that never tell a word of truth. No, no, not they. One of them told me so plainly, one day: 'Woodchuck,' says he, 'Ingian seldom tell truth; he know better than that. Truth too good a thing to be used every day: keep that for time of need.' I believe, at that precious moment, he spoke the truth, the first time for forty years."

The announcement that breakfast was ready interrupted the explanation of Captain Brooks, but appeared to afford him great satisfaction; and, at the meal, he certainly ate more than all the rest of the party put together, consuming everything set before him with a voracity truly marvellous. He seemed, indeed, to think some apology necessary for his furious appetite.

"You see, major," he said, as soon as he could bring himself to a pause sufficiently long to utter a whole sentence, "I eat well when I *do* eat; for sometimes I get nothing for three or four days together. When I get to a lodge like this, I take in stores for my next voyage, as I can't tell what port I shall touch at again."

"Pray do you anticipate a long cruise just now?" asked the stranger.

"No, no," answered the other, laughing; "but I always prepare against the worst. I am just going up the Mohawk, for a step or two, to make a trade with some of my friends of the Five Nations--the Iroquois, as the French folks call them. But I shall trot up afterwards to Sandy Hill and Fort Lyman, to see what is to be done there in the way of business. Fort Lyman I call it still, though it should be Fort Edward now; for, after the brush with Dieskau, it has changed its name. Ay, that was a sharp affair, major. You'd ha' like to bin there, I guess."

"Were you there, captain?" asked Mr. Prevost. "I did not know you had seen so much service."

"Sure I was," answered Woodchuck, with a laugh; "though, as to service, I did more than I was paid for, seeing I had no commission. I'll tell you how it war, Prevost: just in the beginning of September--it was the seventh or eighth, I think, in the year afore last, that is seventeen fifty-five--I was going up to the head of the lake to see if I could not get some peltry, for I had been unlucky down westward, and had made a bargain in Albany I did not like to break. Just on the top o' the hill, near where the King's road comes down to the ford, who should I stumble upon amongst the trees, but old Hendrik, as they called him--*why*, I can't tell--the Sachem of the Tortoise totem of the Mohawks. He was there with three young men at his feet; but we were always good friends, he and I, and, over and above, I carried the calumet, so there was no danger. Well, we sat down and had a talk, and he told me that the general--that is, Sir William, as he is now--had dug up the tomahawk, and was encamped near Fort Lyman to give battle to You-non-de-yoh--that is to say, in their jargon, the French governor. He told me, too, that he was on his way to join the general, but that he did not intend to fight, but only to witness the brave deeds of the Corlear's men--that is to say, the English. He was a cunning old fox, old Hendrik, and I fancied from that, he thought we should be defeated. But when I asked him, he said no, that it was all on account of a dream he had had, forbidding him to fight, on the penalty of his scalp. So I told him I was minded to go with him and see the fun. Well, we mustered, before the sun was quite down, well nigh upon three hundred Mohawks, all beautiful painted and feathered; but they told me that they had not sung their war song, nor danced their war dance, before they left their lodges, so I could see well enough they had no intention to fight, and the tarnation devil wouldn't make 'em. How could we get to the camp where they were all busy throwing breastworks, and we heard that Dieskau was coming down from Hunter's in force? The next morning early, we were told that he had turned back again from Fort Lyman, and Johnson sent out Williams with seven or eight hundred men to get hold of his haunches. I tried hard to get old Hendrik to go along, for I stuck fast by my Ingians, knowing the brutes can be serviceable when you trust them. But the Sachem only grunted and did not stir. In an hour and a half we heard a mighty large rattle of muskets, and the Ingians could not stand the sound quietly, but began looking at their rifle-flints and fingering their tomahawks. Howsever, they did not stir, and old Hendrik sat as grave and as brown as an old hemlock stump. Then we saw another party go out of camp to help the first; but in a very few minutes they came running back with Dieskau at their heels. In they tumbled, over the breastworks, head over heels any how; and a pretty little considerable quantity of fright they brought with them. If Dieskau had charged straight on that minute, we should have all been smashed to everlasting flinders; and I don't doubt, no more than that a *bee*ar's a crittar, that Hendrik and his painted devils would have had as many English scalps as French ones.

"But Dieskau, like a stupid coon, pulled up short two hundred yards off, and Johnson did not give him much time to look about him, for he poured all the cannon-shot that he had got into him as hard as he could pelt. Well, the French Ingians--and there was a mighty sight of them--did not like that game of ball, and they squattered off to the right and left--some into the trees, some into the swamps; and I couldn't stand it no longer, but up with my rifle, and give them all I had to give, and old Hendrik, seeing how things was like to go, took to the right end too, but a little too fast; for the old devil came into him, and he must needs have scalps. So out he went with the rest; and just as he had got his forefinger in the hair of a young Frenchman, whiz came a bullet into his dirty red skin, and down he went like an old moose. Some twenty of his Ingians got shot too; but, in the end, Dieskau had to run.

"Johnson was wounded too; and then folks have since said that he had no right to the honour of the battle, but that it was Lyman's, who took the command when he could fight no longer. But that's all trash. Dieskau had missed his chance, and all his irregulars were sent skimming by the first fire long afore Johnson was hit. Lyman had nothing to do but hold what Johnson left him, and pursue the enemy. The first he did well enough; but the second he forgot to do--though he was a brave man and a good soldier, for all that."

This little narrative seemed to give matter for thought both to Mr. Prevost and his English guest; and, after a moment or two of somewhat gloomy consideration, the latter asked the narrator whether the friendly Indians had, on that occasion, received any special offence to account for their unwillingness to give active assistance to their allies, or whether their indifference proceeded merely from a fickle or treacherous disposition.

"A little of both," replied Captain Brooks. And after leaning his great broad forehead on his hand for a moment or two, in deep thought, he proceeded to give his view of the relations of the colonies with the Iroquois, in a manner and tone totally different from any he had used before. They were grave and almost stern; and his language had few, if any, of the coarse provincialisms with which he ordinarily seasoned his conversation.

"They are a queer people, the Indians," he said, "and not so much savages as we are inclined to believe them. Sometimes I am ready to think that in one or two points they are more civilized than ourselves. They have not got our arts and sciences; and, as they possess no books, one set of them cannot store up the knowledge they gain in their own time to be added to by every generation of them that come after; and we all know that things which are sent down from mouth to mouth are soon lost or corrupted. But they are always thinking, and they have a calmness and a coolness in their thoughts that we white men very often want. They are quick enough in action when once they have determined upon a thing, and for perseverance they beat all the world; but they take a long time to consider before they act, and it is really wonderful how quietly they do consider, and how steadily they stick in consideration to all their own old notions.

"We have not treated them well, sir; and we never did. They have borne a great deal, and they will bear more still; yet they feel and know it, and some day they may make us feel it too. They have not the wit to take advantage at present of our divisions, and, by joining together themselves, make us feel all their power; for they hate each other worse than they hate us. But, if the same spirit were to take the whole red men, that got hold of the Five Nations many a long year ago, and they were to band together against the whites, as those Five Nations did against the other tribes, they'd give us a great deal of trouble; and though we might thrash them at first, we might teach them to thrash us in the end.

"As it is, however, you see there are two sets of Indians and two sets of white men in this country, each as different from the other as anything can be. The Indians don't say, as they ought, 'The country is ours, and we will fight against all the whites till we drive them out;' but they say, 'The whites are wiser and stronger than we are, and we will help those of them who are wisest and strongest.'

"I don't mean to say that they have not got their likings and dislikings, or that they are not moved by kindness, or by being talked to; for they are great haters, and great likers. Still what I have said is at the bottom of all their friendships with white men. The Dutchmen helped the Five Nations-- Iroquois, as the French call them--gave them rifles and gunpowder against their enemies, and taught them to believe they were a very strong people. So the Five Nations liked the Dutch, and made alliance with them. Then came the English, and proved stronger than the Dutch, and the Five Nations attached themselves to the English.

"They have stuck fast to us for a long time, and would not go from us without cause. If they could help to keep us great and powerful they would, and I don't think a little adversity would make them turn. But to see us whipped and scalped would make them think a good deal, and they won't stay long by a people they don't respect.

"They have got their own notions, too, about faith and want of faith. If you are quite friendly with them--altogether--out and out--they'll hold fast enough to their word with you; but a very little turning, or shaking, or doubting, will make them think themselves free from all engagements; and then take care of your scalp-lock. If I am quite sure, when I meet an Indian, that, as the good Book says, '*my* heart is right with *his* heart;' that I have never cheated him, or thought of cheating him; that I have not doubted him, nor do doubt him--I can lie down and sleep in his lodge as safe as if I was in the heart of Albany. But I should not sleep a wink if I knew there was the least little bit of insincerity in my own heart; for they are as 'cute as serpents, and they are not people to wait for explanations. Put your wit against theirs at the back of the forest, and you'll get the worse of it."

"But have we cheated, or attempted to cheat, these poor people?" asked the stranger.

"Why, the less we say about that the better, major," replied Woodchuck, shaking his head. "They have had to bear a good deal; and now when the time comes that we look as if we were going to the wall, perhaps they may remember it."

"But I hope and trust we are not exactly going to the wall," pursued the other, with his colour somewhat heightened; "there has been a great deal said in England about mismanagement of our affairs on this continent; but I have always thought, being no very violent politician myself, that party spirit dictated criticisms which were probably unjust."

"There has been mismanagement enough, major," replied Woodchuck; "hasn't there, Prevost?"

"I fear so, indeed," replied his host with a sigh; "but quite as much on the part of the colonial authorities as on that of the government at home."

"And whose fault is that?" demanded Woodchuck, somewhat warmly; "why, that of the government at home too! Why do they appoint incompetent men? Why do they appoint ignorant men? Why do they exclude from every office of honour, trust, or emolument the good men of the provinces, who know the situation and the wants and the habits of the provinces, and put over us men who, if they were the best men in the world, would be inferior, from want of experience, to our own people, but who are nothing more than a set of presuming, ignorant, grasping blood-suckers, who are chosen because they are related to a minister, or a minister's mistress, or perhaps his valet, and whose only object is to make as much out of us as they can, and then get back again. I do not say that they are all so, but a great many of them are; and this is an insult and an injury to us."

He spoke evidently with a good deal of heat; but his feelings were those of a vast multitude of the American colonists, and those feelings were preparing the way for a great revolution.

"Come, come, Woodchuck," exclaimed Walter Prevost with a laugh, "you are growing warm; and when you are angry, you bite. The major wants to hear your notions of the state of the English power here, and not your censure of the king's government."

"God bless King George!" cried Woodchuck warmly, "and send him all prosperity. There's not a more loyal man in the land than I am; but it vexes me all the more to see his ministers throwing away his people's hearts, and losing his possessions into the bargain. But I'll tell you how it is, major--at least how I think it is--and then you'll see.

"I must first go back a bit. Here are we, the English, in the middle of North America, and we have got the French on both sides of us. Well, we have a right to the country all the way across the continent--and we *must* have it, for it is our only safety. But the French don't want us to be safe, and so they are trying to get behind us, and push us into the sea. They have been trying it a long time, and we have taken no notice. They have pushed their posts from Canidy, right along by the Wabash and the Ohio, from Lake Erie to the Mississippi; and they have built forts, won over the Ingians, drawing a string round us, which they will tighten every day, unless we cut it.

"And what have the ministers been doing all the time? Why, for a long time they did nothing at all. First, the French were suffered boldly to call the country their own, and to carry off our traders and trappers, and send them into Canidy, and never a word said by our people. Then they built fort after fort, till troops can march and goods can go, with little or no trouble, from Quebec to New Orleans; and all that this produced was a speech from Governor Hamilton, and a message from Governor Dinwiddie. The last, indeed, sent to England, and made representations; but all he got was an order to repel force by force, if he could, but to be quite sure that he did so on the *undoubted* territories of King George.

"Undoubted! Why, the French made the doubt, and then took advantage of it. Dinwiddie, however, had some spirit, and, with what help he could get, he began to build a fort himself, in the best-chosen spot of the whole country, just by the meeting of the Ohio and the Monongahela. But he had only one man to the French ten, and not a regular company amongst them. So the French marched with a thousand soldiers, and plenty of cannon and stores, turned his people out, took possession of his half-finished fort, and completed it themselves. That was not likely to make the Ingians respect us.

"Well, then, Colonel Washington, the Virginian, and the best man in the land, built Fort Necessity; but they left him without forces to defend it, and he was obliged to surrender to Villiers, and a force big enough to eat him up. That did not raise us with our redskins; and a French force never moved without a whole herd of Ingians, supposed to be in friendship with us, but ready to scalp us whenever we were defeated.

"Then came Braddock's mad march upon Fort Duquesne, where he and a'most all who was with him were killed by a handful of Ingians amongst the bushes--fifteen hundred men dispersed, killed, and scalped, by not four hundred savages--all the artillery taken, and baggage beyond count--think of that! Then Shirley made a great parade of marching against Fort Niagara; but he turned back almost as soon as he set out; and, had it not been for some good luck, on the north side of Massachusetts Bay, and the victory of Johnson over Dieskau, you would not have had a tribe hold fast to us. They were all wavering as fast as they could--I could see that, as plain as possible, from old Hendrik's talk; and the French Jesuits were in amongst them day and night to bring the Five Nations over. This was the year afore last.

"Well, what did they do last year? Nothing at all, but lose Oswego. Lord Loudun, and Abercrombie, and Webb, marched and countermarched, and consulted, and played the fool, while bloody Montcalm was besieging Mercer, taking Oswego, breaking the terms he had expressly granted, and suffering his Ingians to scalp and torture his prisoners of war before his eyes. Well, this was just about the middle of August; but it was judged too late to do anything more, and nothing *was* done. There was merry work in Albany, and people danced and sang; but the Ingians got a strange notion that the English lion was better at roaring than he was at biting.

"And now, major, what have we done this year to make up for all the blunders of the last five or six? Why, Lord Loudun stripped the whole of this province of its men and guns, to go to Halifax and attack Louisburg. When he got to Halifax, he exercised his men for a month, heard a false report that Louisburg was too strong and too well prepared to be taken, and sailed back to New York. In the meanwhile, Montcalm took Fort William Henry on Lake George, and, as usual, let the garrison be butchered by his Ingians.

"So, now the redskins see that the English arms are contemptible on every part of this continent, and the French complete masters of the lakes and the whole western country. The Five Nations see their long house open to our enemies on three sides, and not a step taken to give them assistance or protection. We have abandoned *them*. Can you expect them not to abandon *us*?"

The young officer, long before this painful question was asked, had leaned his elbows on the table, and covered his eyes and part of his face with his hand. Walter and Edith both gazed at him earnestly, while their father bent his eyes gloomily down on the table, all three knowing and sympathizing with the feelings of a British officer while listening to such a detail. The expression of his countenance they could not see; but the finely-cut ear, appearing from beneath the curls of his hair, glowed like fire before the speaker finished.

He did not answer, however, for more than a minute; but then, raising his head, with a look of stern gravity, he replied,--

"I cannot expect it. I cannot even understand how they have remained attached to us so long and so much."

"The influence of one man has done a great deal," replied Mr. Prevost. "Sir William Johnson is what is called the Indian agent; and, whatever may be thought of his military abilities, there can be no doubt that the Iroquois trust him, and love him more than they have ever trusted or loved a white man before. He is invariably just towards them, always keeps his word with them; he never yields to importunity or refuses to listen to reason; and he places that implicit confidence in them which enlists everything that is noble in the Indian character in his favour. Thus, in his presence, and in their dealings with him, they are quite a different people from what they are with others--all their fine qualities are brought into action, and all their wild passions are stilled."

"I should like to see them as they really are," exclaimed the young officer, eagerly. And then, turning to Woodchuck, he said--"You tell me you are going amongst them, my friend; can you not take me with you?"

"Wait three days and I will," replied the other. "I am first going up the Mohawk, as I told you, close by Sir William's castle and hall, as he calls the places. You'd see little there; but, if you will promise to do just as I tell you, and mind advice, I'll take you up to Sandy Hill and the creek, where you'll see enough of them. That will be arter I come back on Friday about noon."

Mr. Prevost looked at the young officer, and he at his entertainer; and then the former said--

"When will you bring him back, captain? He must be here again by next Tuesday night."

"That he shall be, with or without his scalp," answered Woodchuck, with a laugh. "You get him ready to go; for you know, Prevost, the forest is not the parade-ground."

"I will lend him my Gakaah and Gischa and Gostoweh," cried Walter. "We will make him quite an Indian."

"No, no!" answered Woodchuck, "that won't do, Walter. The man who tries to please an Ingian by acting like an Ingian makes naught of it. They know it's a cheat, and they don't like it. We have our ways, and they have theirs; and let each keep their own, like honest men. So I think, and so the Ingians think. Putting on a lion's skin will never make a man a lion. Get the major some good tough leggins, and a coat that won't tear; a rifle and an axe and a wood-knife--a bottle of brandy is no bad thing. But don't forget a calumet and a pouch of tobacco, for both may be needful. So now good-bye to ye all. I must trot."

Thus saying, he rose from the table, and, without more ceremonious adieu, left the room.

CHAPTER VI

"How sweet she looks!" exclaimed a man of nearly my own age--a man most distinguished in his own land--as we gazed on a young and lovely girl, near and dear to us both as our own child--soon to become my child-in-law as she already is in affection. "How sweet she looks!"

The words set me thinking. What was it in which that sweetness consisted? Sweetness as of the song of a bird, or the ambrosial breathing of a flower--sweetness as of an entrancing melody, which had its solemn sadness as well as its delight--sweetness which carried the soul on its wings of perfume into the far future, to gather in the land of dreams, with the trembling awe of fear-touched hope, the mystic signs of her future destiny. It consisted not in the lovely lines of the features, in the exquisite hues of the complexion, in the beautiful symmetry of the form. But it consisted in that nameless, unphonetic, but ever lucid, hieroglyph of the heart--expression--expression in form as well as in face--in tranquillity as well as in movement--in the undefined and undefinable beauty of beauties--grace.

"La grace encore plus belle que la beauté."

Grace which no art can ever attain, though it may imitate. Grace which is the gift of God to the body, to the mind, to the spirit. Grace which, in our pristine state, was, doubtless, common to all the three, blending taste, and reason, and religion in one harmony almost divine--breathing forth from the earthly form in the image of its Maker, and which lingers yet, and breathes forth still, in the pure and the innocent and the bright.

Such grace was in Edith Prevost; and hard or preoccupied must have been the heart that could resist it. She was certainly very beautiful, too, and of that beauty the most attractive. Though so young, her fully-developed form left maturity but little to add; and every swelling line flowed into the other with symmetry the most perfect. The rich, warm, glossy curls of her nut-brown hair, unstained and unrestrained by any of the frightful conceits of the day, wantoned round her ivory forehead in lines all in harmony with her figure and her features, and in hue contrasting, yet harmonizing, with her complexion, in its soft, rich warmth; fair, yet glowing with a hardly perceptible shade of brown, such as that which distinguishes the Parian marble from the stone of Carrara. Then her liquid, hazel eyes, full of ever-varied expression--now sparkling with gay, free joy, now full of tender light (especially when they turned upon her father), and now shaded with a sleepy sort of thoughtfulness, when one of her day-dreams fell upon her. There was something, moreover, in her manner--in her whole demeanour--which lent another charm to beauty, and added grace to grace. Yet it was of a kind difficult to define. I cannot describe it; I can only tell how she came by it.

I have shown that, in early years, she had been educated in a land where civilization and refinement were carried to their highest point; but it is necessary to add, that her education there had been conducted in the midst of the most refined society of that land, and by those in whom refinement had been a quality rather than an acquisition. She had it, too, as an hereditary right: it was in her blood and in her nature; and, until she was nearly fourteen years of age, everything that father or mother could do was done to cultivate the rich soil of her mind and her heart--remember, to cultivate, not to alter: it needed no change. Every natural grace remained entire, and many a bright gift was added.

Then suddenly she was transplanted to a scene where all was wild--where there were no conventionalities--where Nature ruled, and was the rule. She came there exactly at the age when, without losing one particle of that which society could confer that was worth retaining, the mind--the fresh, young mind--was ready to receive a peculiar tone from the wild things around her, a freedom, an innocent carelessness of the trifles magnified into false importance in a more artificial state. Feeling, knowing, that she was a lady, that every thought was pure and bright, that every purpose was noble and true, she had no fear of infringing small proprieties; she had no thought of that dread bugbear of the multitude, "*what the world would say.*" Thus, while habit rendered all refined, and while heart and innocence gave dignity and calmness, she had all the free, frank, heartful confidence of untutored nature.

Such was Edith Prevost, and such she appeared to the stranger who had visited her father's house. At first, perhaps, he did not comprehend her fully; but he was a man of keen perceptions and a great and noble heart. Within his breast and hers were those sympathies which are keys to open the doors of character; and he had not been four-and-twenty hours under the same roof before he knew her, and appreciated her entirely. He had seen much of the world, much of society; and perhaps that which is false and wrong therein had been over-estimated by a mind somewhat too clear-sighted for much happiness. At all events, he had passed through life hitherto heart-whole and untouched with love; and he felt fearless and confident from the experience of security. Thus he boldly made the character of Edith a study;

scanned it accurately, watched every little trait, dwelt upon her beauty and her grace, and took pleasure in eliciting all that was bright and lovely. Imprudent man! He had never met any one like her before.

She, too, in unconscious frankness, without thought or design, was led on, by new and fresh association, to open all the treasures of her mind to her new friend, not knowing how they might dazzle; and her brother and her father both aided, unthinkingly, in the same course.

When Brooks had left them, half an hour was spent in one of those pleasant after-breakfast dreams, when the mind seems to take a moment's hesitating pause before grappling with the active business of the day. But little was said; each gazed forth from window or from door--each thought, perhaps, of the other, and each drank in sweet sensation from the scene before the eyes.

Each thought of the other, I have said; and when such is the case, how infinite are the varieties into which thought moulds itself!

Walter paused and pondered upon the stranger's state and objects; asked himself who he was; what could be his errand; how, why, he came thither. Major Kielmansegge he knew him not to be. A chance word had shown him not only his rank and station, but had shown also that there was a secret to be kept--a secret to which his imagination, perhaps, lent more importance than it deserved. He was an English peer, the young man knew, one of a rank with which, in former years, he had been accustomed to mingle, and for which, notwithstanding all that had passed, and lapse of time, and varied circumstances, he retained an habitual veneration. But what could have led a British peer to that secluded spot? what could be the circumstances which, having led him thither, had suddenly changed his purpose of proceeding onward, and induced him to remain a guest in his father's cottage, in a state of half-concealment? Could it be Lord Loudun, he asked himself, the commander-in-chief of the royal forces, whose conduct had been so severely censured in his own ears by the man just gone?

Youth always leaves a thousand things out of calculation, and darts at its conclusions with rapidity that overleaps the real end; and thus, what with the military bearing, the secrecy, a certain degree of reserve of manner, and an air of command, he argued himself into the belief that their guest was certainly the general of whom they had heard so much and knew so little; without at all considering how unlikely it was, that so important a command should be intrusted to one so young. It did not, indeed, raise the stranger in his esteem, or in his regard, to believe him to be Lord Loudun; for this nobleman had not won the goodwill of the people of the province, nor secured their approbation. They had perhaps expected too much from his coming, and had been bitterly disappointed by the result.

Edith thought of his rank and station not at all. Some of his words lingered in her ear, and afforded matter for the mind to work with. They were not such as she had heard for long. They were different even, in some respects, from any that she remembered. There was nothing light in them, nothing frivolous; but, combined with the tone and manner, they gave the impression that they sprang from a mind deep, powerful, self-relying, cultivated and enriched by study and observation, and full of activity and eagerness. She might inquire what sort of heart was united with that mind; she might be doubtful of it; for she had not much experience, and she knew not how often men, in mere sport, or to elicit the shy secrets of woman's heart, or for idle vanity or light caprice, utter that which they do not feel, affect a character they do not possess, and often inferior to their own.

She did not make up her mind hastily, however. Indeed she had not yet sufficient interest in the object of her thoughts to care much about making up her mind at all. She thought him a very handsome and a very agreeable man, sufficiently odd, or different from the common run, to excite some interest, yet with an oddity in no degree offensive; but that was all. She knew that he had only come for a day, and that, though some accidental meeting with Sir William Johnson had induced him to protract his stay, it would probably only be for a day or two longer. Then he would go: his shadow would pass away from the floor, and his memory from her mind-- she thought.

Accident! Who is there that believes in accident? On my life, it requires more faith to conceive such a thing as accident than to believe in the divinity of Juggernaut. The only reason why any man can imagine such a thing, is because he sees not the causes which bring to pass the event which he calls an accident; and yet he perceives the hands of a clock move round the dial, without beholding the springs and wheels, and never dreams it is by accident that the bell chimes noon. Let any man look through the strange concatenation of event with event, through the course of his own life, and dream of accident, if he can.

It was not by accident that Lord H---- and Edith

Prevost met there. It was for the working out of their mutual destiny, under the will of God; for, if there be a God, there is a special Providence.

"This is very lovely, Miss Prevost," said the young soldier, when the long meditative lapse was drawing to a close; "but I should think the scene would become somewhat monotonous. Hemmed in by these woods, the country round, though beautiful in itself, must pall upon the taste."

"Oh, no!" cried Edith, eagerly; "it is full of variety. Each day affords something new; and every morning's walk displays a thousand fresh beauties. Let us go and take a ramble, if you have nothing better to do, and I will soon show you there is no monotony. Come, Walter, take your rifle and go with us. Father, this is not your hour. Can you never come before the sun has passed his height, and see the shadows fall the other way?"

"Mine is the evening hour, my child," answered Mr. Prevost, somewhat sadly; "but go, Edith, and show our noble friend the scenes you so much delight in. He will need something to make his stay in this dull place somewhat less heavy."

The stranger made no complimentary reply, for his thoughts were busy with Edith, and he was, at that moment, comparing her frank, unconscious, undesigning offer to lead him through love-like woods and glades with the wily hesitations of a court coquette.

"Perhaps you are not disposed to walk?" said Edith, marking his reverie, and startling him from it.

"I shall be delighted," he said, eagerly, and truly, too. "You must forgive me for being somewhat absent, Miss Prevost. Your father knows I have much to think of, though, indeed, thought at present is vain; and you will confer a boon by banishing that idle but importunate companion."

"Oh, then, you shall not think at all while you are with me," returned Edith, smiling.

And away she ran, to cover her head with one of those black wimples very generally worn by the women of that day.

CHAPTER VII

Let us see what can be made out of a walk. It began with a bad number, though one that is generally assumed to be lucky. But, on the present occasion, no one felt himself the third; and Walter, and Edith, and Lord H----, conversed as freely as if only two had been present. First came a discussion between Edith and her brother as to what path they should take; and then they referred it to their companion, and he, with a smile, reminded them that he knew none but that by which he had come thither; and so Edith had her own way, and led towards the west.

By dint of labour and taste, aided, in some degree, by accident, not less than fifty acres of ground had been cleared around the house of Mr. Prevost--not partially cleared, with large black stumps of trees sticking up in the fields, and assuming every sort of strange form, all hideous; but perfectly and entirely, leaving the ground (some part of which had, indeed, been free of forest when Mr. Prevost first settled there) smooth and trim as that of the fair farms of England. The fences, too, were all in good order, and the buildings neat and picturesque.

Beyond the cultivated ground, as you descended the gentle hill, lay the deep forest, at the distance of about three hundred yards; and at its edge Edith paused, and made her companion turn to see how beautiful the cottage looked upon its eminence, shaded by gorgeous maple-trees, in their gold and crimson garb of autumn, with a tall rock or two, grey and mossy, rising up amidst them.

Lord H---- gazed at the house, and saw that it was picturesque and beautiful--very different, indeed, from any other dwelling he had beheld on the western side of the Atlantic; but his eyes expressed an absent thoughtfulness, and Edith thought he did not admire it half enough.

Close by the spot where she had stopped appeared the entrance of a broad road, cut, probably, by the Dutch settlers many years before. It could not be called good, for it was furrowed and indented with many a rut and hollow, and roughened by obtrusive stones and rock; but there were no stumps of trees upon it, no fallen trunks lying across, which, for a forest road in America, at that time, was rare perfection. For about a quarter of a mile it was bordered on each side by tangled thicket, with gigantic pine-trees rising out of an impenetrable mass of underwood, in which berries of many a hue supplied the place of flowers. But flowers seem hardly wanting to an American autumn; for almost every leaf becomes a flower, and the whole forest glows with all the hues of yellow, red, and green, from the soft primrose-colour of the fading white-wood and sycamore, through every tint of orange, scarlet, and crimson on the maple, and of yellow and green on the larch, the pine, and the hemlock.

"How strange are man's prejudices and prepossessions!" ejaculated Lord H----, as they paused to gaze at a spot where a large extent of woodland lay open to the eye below them. "We are incredulous of everything we have not seen, or to the conception of which we have not been led by very near approaches. Had any one shown me, before I reached these shores, a picture of an autumn scene in America, though it had been perfect as a portrait, hue for hue, or even inferior in its striking colouring to the reality, I should have laughed at it as a most extravagant exaggeration. Did not the first autumn you passed here make you think yourself in fairy-land?"

"No; I was prepared for it," replied Edith; "my father had described the autumn scenery to me often before we came."

"Then was he ever in America before he came to settle?" asked her companion.

"Yes, once," answered Edith. She spoke in a very grave tone, and then ceased suddenly.

But her brother took the subject up with a boy's frankness, saying--"Did you never hear that my grandfather and my father's sister both died in Virginia? He was in command there, and my father came over just before my birth."

"It is a long story, and a sad one, my lord," interposed Edith, with a sigh; "but look now as we mount the hill, how the scene changes. Every step upon the hill-side gives us a different sort of tree, and the brush disappears from amidst the trunks. This grove is my favourite evening seat, where I can read and think under the broad shady boughs, with nothing but beautiful sights around me."

They had reached a spot where, upon the summit of an eminence, numbers of large oaks crested the forest. Wide apart, and taller than the

English oak, though not so large in stem, the trees suffered the eye to wander over the grassy ground, somewhat broken by rock, which sloped down between hundreds of large bolls to the tops of the lower forest trees, and thence to a scene of almost matchless beauty beyond. Still slanting downwards with a gentle sweep, the woodlands were seen approaching the banks of a small lake, about two miles distant, while, beyond the sheet of water, which lay glittering like gold in the clear morning sunshine, rose up high purple hills, with the shadows of grand clouds floating over them. Around the lake, on every side, were rocky promontories and slanting points of lower land jutting out into the water; and, where they stood above, they could see all the fair features of the scene itself, and the images of the clouds and sky redoubled by the golden mirror. To give another charm to the spot, and make ear and eye combine in enjoyment, the voices of distant waters came upon the breeze, not with a roar exactly, but with rather more than a murmur, showing that some large river was pouring over a steep not far away.

"Hark!" ejaculated Lord H----. "Is there a waterfall near?"

"Too far to go to it to-day," answered Edith. "We must economize our scenes, lest we should exhaust them all before you go, and you should think more than ever that our country wants variety."

"I cannot think so with that prospect before my eyes," replied the young nobleman. "Look how it has changed already! The mountain is all in shade, and so is the lake; but those low, wavy, wood-covered hills, which lie between the two, are starting out in the prominence of sunshine. A truly beautiful scene is full of variety in itself. Every day changes its aspect, every hour, every season. The light of morning, and evening, and mid-day, alters it entirely; and the spring and the summer, the autumn and the winter, robe it in different hues. I have often thought that a fair landscape is like a fine mind, in which every varying event of life brings forth new beauties."

"Alas, that the mind is not always like the landscape!" exclaimed Edith. "God willed it so, I doubt not, for there is harmony in all His works; but man's will and God's will are not always one."

"Perhaps, after all," said her companion, thoughtfully, "the best way to keep them in harmony is for man, as much as may be, to recur to Nature, which is but an expression of God's will."

"Oh yes!" cried Walter Prevost, eagerly; "I am sure the more we give ourselves up to the factitious and insincere contrivances of what we call society, the more we alienate ourselves from truth and God."

The young nobleman gazed at him with a smile almost melancholy.

"Very young," he thought, "to come to such sad conclusions. But do you not, my friend Walter," added he aloud, "think there might be such a thing as extracting from society all that is good and fine in it, and leaving the chaff and dross for others? The simile of the bee and the poisonous flower holds good with man. Let us take what is sweet and beneficial in all we find growing in the world's garden, and reject all that is worthless, poisonous, and foul. But truly this is an enchanting scene. It wants, methinks, only the figure of an Indian in the foreground. And there comes one, I fancy, to fill up the picture.--Stay, stay, we shall want no rifles. It is but a woman coming through the trees."

"It is Otaitsa--it is the Blossom!" cried Edith and Walter in a breath, as they looked forward to a spot where, across the yellow sunshine as it streamed through the trees, a female figure, clad in the gaily-embroidered and brightly-coloured *gakaah* or petticoat of the Indian women, was seen advancing with a rapid yet somewhat doubtful step.

Without pause or hesitation, Edith sprang forward to meet the new comer, and, in a moment after, the beautiful arms of the Indian girl who had sat with Walter in the morning were round the fair form of his sister, and her lips pressed on hers. There was a warmth and eagerness in their meeting, unusual on the part of the red race; but, while the young Oneida almost lay upon the bosom of her white friend, her beautiful dark eyes were turned towards her lover, as, with a mixture of the bashful feelings of youth and the consciousness of having something to conceal, Walter, with a glowing cheek, lingered a step or two behind his sister.

"Art thou coming to our lodge, dear Blossom?" asked Edith, and then added, "Where is thy father?"

"We both come," answered the girl, in fluent English, with no more of the Indian accent than served to give a peculiar softness to her tones. "I wait the Black Eagle here since dawn of day. He has gone towards the morning, with our father the White Heron; for we heard of Hurons by the side of Corlear, and some thought the hatchet would be unburied; so he journeyed to hear more from our friends by the Horicon, and bade me stay and tell you and our brother Walter to forbear that road if I saw you turn your eyes towards the east wind. He and the White Heron will be by your father's council-fire with the first star."

A good deal of this speech was unintelligible to Lord H----, who had now approached, and on whom Blossom's eyes were turned with a sort of timid and inquiring look. But Walter hastened to interpret, saying--

"She means that her father and the missionary, Mr. Gore, have heard that there are hostile Indians on the shores of Lake Champlain, and have gone down towards Lake George to inquire; for Black Eagle--that is her father--is much our friend, and he always fancies that my father has chosen a dangerous situation here just at the verge of the territory of the Five Nations, or their Long House, as they call it."

"Well, come to the lodge with us, dear Blossom," said Edith, while her brother was giving this explanation; "thou knowest my father loves thee well, and will be glad to have the Blossom with us. Here, too, is an English chief, dwelling with us, who knows not what sweet blossoms grow on Indian trees."

But the girl shook her head, saying--

"Nay, I must do the father's will. It was with much praying that he let me come hither with him; and he bade me stay here from the white rock to the stream. So I must obey."

"But it may be dangerous," replied Edith, "if there be Hurons so near; and it is sadly solitary, dear sister."

"Then stay with me for a while," said the girl, who could not affect to deny that her lonely watch was somewhat gloomy.

"I will stay with her, and protect her," cried Walter eagerly; "for, dearest Blossom, should there be danger, my sister must fly to the lodge."

"Yes, stay with her, Walter. Oh, yes, stay with her," ejaculated the unconscious Edith. And so it was settled, for Otaitsa made no opposition, though, with a cheek in which something glowed warmly through the brown, and with a lip that curled gently with a meaning smile, she said--

"Perhaps my brother Walter would be elsewhere? He may find a long watch wearisome on the hill and in the wood."

Well was it that others were present, or the lips that spoke would have paid for their insincerity. But perhaps the Blossom would not have so spoken had they been alone; for woman feels a fear of playfulness, and knows that it needs a safeguard; while deep passion and pure tenderness seem to have a holy safeguard in themselves, and often in their very weakness find strength.

"Let us stay awhile ourselves," said Lord H----, seating himself on the grass, and gazing forth with a look of interest over the prospect: "methinks this is a place where one may well dream away an hour, without the busiest mind reproaching itself for inactivity."

There was no ceremony certainly in his manner, and yet no assumption. Had there been older persons present, women nearer his own age, perhaps the formal decorums of the time might have put upon him a more ceremonious bearing: he might have asked their wishes--waited till they were seated--bowed, and assisted them to a commodious spot. But Edith was so young, that a feeling of her being almost a child was unconsciously present in his mind--a very dangerous feeling, inasmuch as it put him wholly off his guard; and, acting as plain nature taught, he cast himself down there to enjoy an hour of pleasant idleness, in a beautiful scene, with one too lovely, too deep-toned in mind--ay, too mature in heart and in body--to be so treated with impunity.

That hour passed by, and another came and went, while into his thoughts and into his breast's inmost caves were stealing strange new sensations. A dreamy charm was over him, a golden spell around him, more powerful than Circe ever threw, or the Siren ever sung. Oh, the Lotus!--he was eating the Lotus, that sweet fruit, the magic taste of which could never be forgotten--which was destined thenceforth and for ever to draw him back, with irresistible power, to the spot where it grew.

Surely that nectareous fruit, which transformed the whole spirit into desire for itself, was but an image of love, pure and bright, growing wild upon the bank of the sacred river. And the first taste, too, gave no warning of its power. Thus he was all unconscious of what was coming over him, but yielded himself calmly to the enjoyment of the moment, and imagined that in the next he could be free again in every thought.

The reader may ask--"Was he thus early in love? Had the impassioned haste of Italian love--the love of Romeo and Juliet--flown across the wide Atlantic?"

No! I answer, no. But he was yielding himself to thoughts and feelings, scenes, circumstances, and companionships, which were sure to light it up in his heart--yielding without resistance. He was tasting the Lotus-fruit; and its effects were inevitable.

For two hours the four companions sat there on the hill-side, beneath the tall shady trees, with the wind breathing softly upon them--the lake glittering before their eyes--the murmur of the waterfall sending music through the air. But to the young Englishman these were but accessories. The fair face of Edith was before his eyes, the melody of her voice in his ear.

At length, however, they rose to go, promising to send one of the slaves from the house with food for Walter and Otaitsa at the hour of noon; and Lord H---- and his fair companion took their way back towards the house.

The distance was not very far, but they were somewhat long upon the way. They walked slowly back, and by a different path from that by which they went; and often they stopped to admire some pleasant scene; often Lord H---- had to assist his fair companion over some rock, and her soft hand rested in his. He gathered flowers for her--the fringed gentia and other late blossoms; they paused to examine them closely, and comment on their loveliness. Once he made her sit down beside him on a bank, and tell the names of all the different trees; and from trees his conversation went on into strange, dreamy, indefinite talk of human things and human hearts.

Thus noon was not far distant when they reached the house; and both Edith and her companion were very thoughtful.

CHAPTER VIII

Edith was very thoughtful through the rest of the day. Was it of herself she thought? Was it of him who had been her companion through the greater part of the morning? Hardly at all.

Hast thou not heard, reader, in eastern fable, of springs of deep, clear water, covered from the eye of passing strangers by a sealed stone; and how, when he who has the talismanic secret approaches and says the words of power, or makes the sign, the sealed fountain opens its cool treasure, and the bright stream wells forth? Such is woman's love.

No word had been spoken, no sign had been given; no intimation to make the seal on the fountain indicate that the master of its destiny was near. Edith had had a pleasant ramble with one such as she seldom saw--and that was all. That he was different from the common multitude--higher, brighter, nobler in his thoughts--she had gathered from their short acquaintance; and so far she might be led to think of him somewhat more than she thought of other men. But her meditations had another object; her mind was attracted strongly in another direction.

It is strange how clearly and how willingly women look into the hearts of others--how dimly, how reluctantly they see into their own. There had been something in the manner of her brother Walter, a hesitation, and yet an eagerness, a timidity unnatural, with a warmth that spoke of passion, which had not escaped her eye. In the sweet Indian girl, too, she had seen signs not equivocal: the fluttering blush; the look full of soul and feeling; the glance suddenly raised to the boy's face, and suddenly withdrawn; the eyes full of liquid light, now beaming brightly under sudden emotion, now shaded beneath the long fringe, like the moon behind a passing cloud.

They were signs that Edith did not mistake, and they were for her suggestive of thoughtfulness.

It might tire the reader, were we to trace all the considerations that chased one another through her mind, or to tell how, for the first time--when she thought of her brother wedding an Indian girl, linking his fate for ever to the savages of the woods--she realized the consequences of the solitary life her father had chosen, of the removal from civilization, of the life in the wild forest.

For the first time it seemed to her that a dark, impenetrable curtain was falling between herself and all the ancient things of history; that all, indeed, was to be new, and strange, and different. And yet she loved Otaitsa well, and, in the last two years, had seen many a trait which had won esteem as well as love. The old Black Eagle, as her father was called, had ever been a fast and faithful ally of the English; but to Mr. Prevost he had attached himself in a particular manner. An accidental journey on the part of the old Sachem had first brought them acquainted, and from that day forward the distance of the Oneida settlements was no impediment to their meeting. Whenever the Black Eagle left his lodge, he was sure, in his own figurative language, to wing his flight sooner or later towards the nest of his white brother; and, in despite of Indian habits, he almost invariably brought his daughter with him. When any distant or perilous enterprise was on hand, Otaitsa was left at the lodge of the English family; and many a week she had passed there at a time, loved by, and loving, all its inmates.

It was not there, however, that she had acquired her knowledge of the English tongue, or the other characteristics which distinguished her from the ordinary Indian women. When she first appeared there, she spoke the language of the settlers as perfectly as they did; and it was soon discovered that from infancy she had been under the care and instruction of one of the English missionaries--at that time, alas! few--who had sacrificed all that civilized life could bestow for the purpose of bringing the Indian savage into the fold of Christ.

Nor was it altogether rare in those days to find an Indian woman adopting, to a considerable degree, the habits and manners of the Europeans. The celebrated Queen of Hearts, who played so important a part in the conspiracy of Pontiac, went even further than Otaitsa, for she assumed the garb of the French, while the latter always retained the dress of her own nation, and was proud of her Indian blood. And yet it was with a sort of melancholy pride; for she would frankly acknowledge the superiority of the white race, and the advantage of the civilization which her own people did not possess. It was, perhaps, rather like the clinging affection which binds the noble-hearted to the falling and unfortunate than that vainer sort of pride which fancies a reflected light to fall upon ourselves through connection with the powerful and the prosperous.

Whatever she was--whatever was high and bright in her nature--she was still the Indian maiden; and as such only could Edith look upon her when she thought of the love between her brother and Otaitsa, which had become but too apparent to her eyes.

Then again she asked herself, how should she act towards Walter, towards her father. Could she direct his attention to that which was so evident to her? Oh, no! She felt as if it would be betraying a secret intrusted to her keeping. True, no word had been spoken, no confession made; still they had both unveiled their hearts to eyes they believed friendly, and she would not take advantage of the knowledge so acquired. Her father could and would see, she thought, and he would then judge for himself, and act according to his judgment.

But Edith did not know how little and how rarely men see into such secrets--especially men of studious habits. Mr. Prevost judged it quite right that Walter should stay with Otaitsa, and he even sent out the old slave Agrippa, who, somehow, was famous as a marksman, with a rifle on his shoulder, to act as a sort of scout upon the hill-side, and watch for anything bearing a hostile aspect.

After dinner, too, he walked out himself, and sat for an hour, with his son and the Indian girl, speaking words of affection to her that sank deep into her heart, and more than once brought drops into her bright eyes. No father's tenderness could exceed that he showed her; and Otaitsa felt as if he were almost welcoming her as a daughter.

When Mr. Prevost returned to the house, he gave himself up to conversation with his guest, transporting his spirit far away from the scenes before him to other lands and other times. Matters of taste and art were discussed: the imperishable works of genius, and the triumphs of mind; and, from time to time, the musical tones of Edith's voice mingled with the deeper sounds of her two companions. It was a pleasant afternoon to all, for Mr. Prevost was himself somewhat of a dreamer; and he, or Edith, or both, perhaps, had taught Lord H----, for the time, at least, to be a dreamer also.

Nor were higher topics left untouched. Nowhere so well as in wide solitudes can the spirit feel itself free to deal with its own mighty questions. The pealing organ and the sounding choir may give a devotional tone to the mind; and the tall pillar and the dusty aisle may afford solemnity to the thoughts; but would you have the spirit climb from the heart's small secret chamber towards the footsteps of the throne of God, and bring back some rays of brighter light to illuminate the darkness of our earthly being, choose the temple unprofaned of his own creation; stand and contemplate His might and majesty amidst the solemn woods or on the awful mountain-tops: or gaze with the astronomer at the distant stars, resolving filmy clouds into innumerable worlds, and separating specks of light into suns and systems.

Evening had not lost its light, when a shout from Walter's voice announced that he was drawing nigh the house; and in a moment after he was seen coming across the cleared land, with his bright young companion, and two other persons.

One was a tall red man, upwards of six feet in height, dressed completely in the Indian garb, but without paint. He could not have been less than sixty years of age; but his strong muscles seemed to have set at defiance the bending power of time. He was as upright as a pine, and he bore his heavy rifle in his right hand as lightly as if it had been a reed. In his left he carried a long pipe, showing that his errand was one of peace; but tomahawk and scalping-knife were in his belt, and he wore the sort of feather crown or Grostoweh distinguishing the chief.

The other man might be of the same age, or a little older. He, too, seemed active and strong for his years; but he wanted the erect and powerful bearing of his companion; and his gait and carriage, as much as his features and complexion, distinguished him from the Indian. His dress was a strange mixture of the ordinary European costume and that of the half-savage rangers of the forest. He wore a black coat, or one which had once been black; but the rest of his garments were composed of skins, some tanned into red leather, after the Indian fashion, some with the hair still on, and turned outwards. He bore no arms whatever, unless a very long and sharp-pointed knife could be considered a weapon, though in his hands it only served the innocent purpose of dividing his food, or carving willow whistles for the children of the Sachem's tribe.

Running, with a light foot, by the side of the chief, as he strode along, came Otaitsa; but the others followed the Indian fashion, coming after him in single file, while old Agrippa, with his rifle on his arm, brought up the rear, appearing from the wood somewhat behind the rest.

"It is seldom I have so many parties of guests in two short days," said Mr. Prevost, moving towards the door. "Generally, I have either a whole tribe at once, or none at all. But this is one of my best friends, my lord, and I must go to welcome him."

"He is a noble-looking man," observed the young officer. "This is the Black Eagle, I suppose, whom the pretty maiden talked of."

Mr. Prevost made no reply, for, by this time, the chief's long strides brought him almost to the door, and his hand was already extended to grasp that of his white friend.

"Welcome, Black Eagle!" said Mr. Prevost.

"Thou art my brother," returned the chief, in English, but with a much less pure accent than that of his daughter.

"What news from Corlear?" asked Mr. Prevost.

But the Indian answered not; and the man who followed him replied in so peculiar a style, that we must give his words, though they imported very little, as far as the events to be related are concerned.

"All is still on the banks of Champlain Lake," he said; "but Huron tracks are still upon the shore. The friendly Mohawks watched them come and go; and tell us that the Frenchman, too, was there, painted and feathered like the Indian chiefs; but finding England stronger than they thought, upon the side of Horicon, they sailed back to Fort Carrillon on Monday last."

For awhile, Lord H---- was completely puzzled to discover what it was that gave such peculiarity to the missionary's language; for the words and accents were both those of an ordinary Englishman of no very superior education; and it was not till Mr. Gore had uttered one or two sentences more, that he perceived that everything he said arranged itself into a sort of blank verse, not very poetical, not very musical, but easily enough to be scanned.

In the mean while, the Black Eagle and his host had entered the house, and proceeded straight to the great eating-hall, where the whole party seated themselves in silence, Otaitsa taking her place close to the side of Edith, and Walter stationing himself where he could watch the bright girl's eyes, without being remarked himself.

For a moment or two, no one spoke, in deference to the Indian habits; and then Mr. Prevost broke silence, saying,--

"Well, Black Eagle, how fares it with my brother?"

"As with the tamarack in the autumn," answered the warrior; "the cold wind sighs through the branches, and the fine leaves wither and fall; but the trunk stands firm as yet, and decay has not reached the heart."

"This is a chief from the land of my white fathers," said Mr. Prevost, waving his hand gracefully towards Lord H----; "he has but lately crossed the great water."

"He is welcome to what was once the red man's land," said Black Eagle; and, bending his eyes upon the ground, but without any sign of emotion at the thoughts which seemed to lie beneath his words, he relapsed into silence for a minute or two. Then raising his head again, he asked, "Is he a great chief? Is he a warrior? or a man of council? or a medicine man?"

"He is a great chief and a warrior," answered Mr. Prevost; "he is moreover skilful in council, and his words are clear as the waters of Horicon."

"He is welcome," repeated the chief; "he is our brother. He shall be called the Cataract, because he shall be powerful, and many shall rejoice at the sound of a strong voice.--But my brother--"

"Speak on," said Mr. Prevost, seeing that he paused; "they are friends' ears that listen."

"Thou art too near the Caturqui; thou art too near to Corlear," said the warrior, meaning, the river St. Lawrence and Lake Champlain. "There is danger for our brother; and the wings of the Black Eagle droop when he is in his solitary place afar amidst the children of the Stone, to think that thou art not farther within the walls of the Long House."

"What does he mean by the walls of the Long House?" asked Lord H----, in a whisper, addressing Edith.

"Merely the territory of the Five Nations, or Iroquois, as the French call them," answered his fair companion.

"I fear not, brother," replied Mr. Prevost; "the fire and the iron have not met to make the tomahawk which shall reach my head."

"But for the maiden's sake," pursued Black Eagle. "Is she not unto us as a daughter? Is she not the sister of Otaitsa? I pray thee, White Pine-tree, let her go with the Eagle and the Blossom into the land of the children of the Stone--but for a few moons--till thy people have triumphed over their enemies, and till the Five Nations have hewed down the tree of the Huron and the Alonquin; till the war-hatchet is buried, and the pipe of peace is smoked."

"'Twere better, truly, my good friend Prevost," said Mr. Gore. "We have seen sights to-day would make the blood of the most bold and hardy man on earth turn cold and icy to behold, and know he had a daughter near such scenes of death."

"What were they, my good friend?" asked Mr. Prevost. "I have heard of nothing very new or near. The last was the capture of Fort William-Henry, some six weeks since, but as yet we have not heard the whole particulars; and surely, if we are far enough away for the tidings not to reach us in six weeks, it is not likely that hostile armies would approach us very soon."

"Thou art deceived, my brother," answered the Black Eagle. "One short day's journey lies betwixt thee and the battle-field. This morning we crossed it when the sun wanted half an hour of noon, and we are here before he has gone down behind the forest. What we saw chilled the blood of my brother here, for he has not seen such things before. The children of the Stone slay not women and children when the battle is over."

"Speak, speak, my good friend, Mr. Gore," said the master of the house; "you know our habits better, and can tell us more of what has happened. Things which are common to his eye must be strange to yours."

"We passed the ground between the one fort and the other," answered the missionary. "The distance is but seven or eight miles, and in that short space lay well nigh a thousand human bodies slain by every dark and terrible means of death. There were young and old; the grey-headed officer; the blooming youth fresh from his mother's side; women, and boys and girls, and little infants snatched from a mother's breast, to die by the hatchet, or the war-club. We heard that the tiger Montcalm, in violation of his given word, in defiance of humanity, Christianity, and the spirit of a gentleman, stood by and saw his own convention broken, and gallant enemies massacred by his savage allies. But what the chief says is very true, my friend. You are far too near this scene; and although, perhaps, no regular army could reach this place before you received timely warning, yet the Indian forerunners may be upon you at any moment; your house may be in flames and you and your children massacred ere any one could come to give you aid. The troops of our country are far away; and no force is between you and Horicon, but a small number of our Mohawk brethren, who are not as well pleased with England as they have been."

Mr. Prevost turned his eyes towards Lord H----, and the young Englishman replied to Mr. Gore at once, saying, with a quiet inclination of the head,--

"On one point you are mistaken, sir. Lord Loudon has returned, and there is now a strong force at Albany. I passed through that city lately, and I think that, by the facts which must have come to his knowledge, General Montcalm will be deterred from pushing his brutal incursions farther this year, at least. Before another morning shines upon us, he may receive some punishment for his faithless cruelty."

"If not here, hereafter," said the missionary. "There is justice in heaven, sir, and often it visits the evil-doer upon earth. That man's end cannot be happy. But I fear you will not give us aid in persuading your friend here to abandon, for a time, his very dangerous position."

"I know too little of Mr. Prevost's affairs," replied Lord H----, "to advise either for or against. I know still less, too, of the state of the country between this and the French line. Perhaps, in a day or two, I may know more, and then, as a military man myself, I can better tell him what are the real dangers of his situation. At all events, I should like to think over the matter till to-morrow morning, before I offer an opinion. From what was said just now, I infer that the Hurons and the French having gone back, there can be no immediate peril."

Mr. Gore shook his head, and the Indian chief remained in profound and somewhat dull silence, seeming not very well pleased at the result of the discussion.

A few minutes after, the evening meal was brought in, and to it the Black Eagle did ample justice; eating like an European with a knife and fork, and displaying no trace of the savage in his demeanour at the table. He remained profoundly silent, however, till the party rose, and then, taking Mr. Prevost by the hand, he said,--

"Take counsel of thine own heart, my brother. Think of the flower that grows up by thy side--ask if thou wouldst have it trodden down by the red man's moccassin; and listen not to the Cataract, for it is cold."

Thus saying, he unrolled one of the large skins, which lay at the side of the room, and stretched himself upon it to take repose.

Edith took Otaitsa by the hand, saying--"Come, Blossom: you shall be my companion as before." Walter, retiring the moment after, left Lord H----and his host to consult together with Mr. Gore.

CHAPTER IX

Were any one inclined to doubt the wonderful harmony which pervades all the works of God, from the very greatest to the very least, he might find a collateral, if not a direct, proof of its existence in the instinctive inclination of the mind of man to discern, in the external world of Nature, figurative resemblances and illustrations of the facts, the events, and the objects of man's moral being and spiritual existence. Not an hour of the day--not a season of the year--not a change in the sky, or on the prospect--not a shade falling over the light, nor a beam penetrating the darkness--but man's imagination seizes upon it to figure some one or other of the moral phenomena of his nature, and at once perceives and proclaims a harmony between material and immaterial things. The earliest flower of the spring (the shade-loving violet) images to the mind of most men a gentle, sweet, retiring spirit. The blushing rose, in its majesty of bloom, displays the pomp and fragrance of mature beauty. The clouds and the storms give us figures for the sorrows, the cares, and the disasters of life; and the spring and the winter, the dawning and the decline of day, shadow forth to our fancy youth and old age; while the rising sun pictures our birth into this life of active exertion, effort, toil, glory, and immortality; and the night, with the new dawn beyond it, the grave, and a life to come.

It was in the old age of the year, then--not the decrepit old age, but the season of vigorous, though declining, maturity; and in the childhood of the day--not the infancy of dawn, where everything is grey and obscure, but the clear, dewy childhood, where all is freshness, and elasticity, and balm--that three travellers took their way onward from the house of Mr. Prevost along a path which led toward the north-east.

Two other persons watched them from the door of the house, and two negro-men and a negro-woman gazed after them from the corner of the building, which joined on to a low fence, encircling the stable and poultry-yard, and running on round the well-cultivated kitchen garden.

The negro-woman shook her head, and looked sorrowful and sighed, but said nothing; the two men talked freely of the imprudence of "master" in suffering his son to go upon such an expedition.

Mr. Prevost and his daughter gazed in silence till the receding figures were hidden by the trees. Then the master of the house led Edith back, saying--

"God will protect him, my child. A parent was not given to crush the energies of youth, but to direct them."

In the meanwhile, Lord H---- and his guide--Captain Brooks, according to his English name, or Woodchuck in the Indian parlance--followed by Walter Prevost, made their way rapidly, though easily, through the wood. The two former were dressed in the somewhat anomalous attire which I have described in first introducing the the worthy captain to the reader; but Walter was in the ordinary costume of the people of the province of that day, except inasmuch as he had his rifle in his hand, and a large leathern wallet slung over his left shoulder; each of his companions, too, had a rifle hung across the back by a broad leathern band; and each was furnished with a hatchet at his girdle, and a long pipe, with a curiously-carved stem, in his hand.

Although they were not pursuing any of the public provincial roads, and they were consequently obliged to walk singly, the one following the other, yet Woodchuck, who led the way, had no difficulty in finding it, or in proceeding rapidly.

We are told by an old writer of those days, who, unlike many modern writers, witnessed, with his own eyes, all he described, that the Indian trails, or footpaths, were innumerable over that large tract of country which the Five Nations called their "Long House," crossing and re-crossing each other in every different direction: sometimes almost lost where the ground was hard and dry; sometimes indenting, by the repeated pressure of many feet, the natural soil to the depth of thirty-six or forty inches.

It was along one of these that the travellers were passing; and although a stump here and there, or a young tree springing up in the midst of a trail, offered an occasional impediment, it was rarely of such a nature as to retard the travellers in their course, or materially add to their fatigues.

With the calm assurance and unhesitating rapidity of a practised woodsman, Brooks led his two companions forward without doubt as to his course. No great light had he, it is true; for though the sun was actually above the horizon, and now and then his slanting rays found their way through some more open space, and gilded their pathway, in general the thick trees and underwood formed a shade, which, at that early hour, the light could hardly penetrate; and the sober morning was still dressed almost in the dark hues of night.

"Set your steps in mine," said Woodchuck, speaking in a whisper over his shoulder to Lord H----, "then we shall be real Ingians. Don't you know that when they go out on the war-path, as they call it, each man puts down his foot just where his leader put down his before. So, come dog, come cat, no one can tell how many went to Jack Pilbury's barn."

"But do you think there is any real danger?" asked Lord H----.

"There is always danger in a dark wood and a dark eye," answered Woodchuck, with a laugh; "but no more danger here than in Prevost's cottage of either the one or the other, for you or for Walter. As for me, I am safe anywhere."

"But you are taking strange precautions where there is no danger," observed Lord H----, who could not banish all doubts of his wild companion: "you speak in whispers, and advise us to follow all the cunning devices of the Indians, in a wood which we passed through fearlessly yesterday."

"I am just as fearless now as you war then, if you passed through this wood," answered Brooks, in a graver tone; "but you are not a woodsman, major, or you'd understand better. We who, five days out of the seven, are surrounded by enemies, or but half-friends--just like a man wrapped up in a porcupine skin--are quite sure that a man's worst enemy and greatest traitor is in himself. So, even when a wise man is quite safe, he puts a guard upon his lips, lest that traitor should betray him; and as for his enemies, knowing there is always one present with him, he takes every care that his everlasting fancy can hit upon, lest more should come suddenly upon him. What I mean, sir, is, that we are so *often* in danger, that we think it best to act as if we were *always* in it; and, never knowing how near it may be, to make as sure as we can that we keep it at a distance. You cannot tell that there is not an Ingian in every bush you pass; and yet you'd chatter as loud as if you were in my lady's drawing-room. But I, though I know there is ne'er a one, don't speak louder than a grasshopper's hind legs, for fear I should get into the habit of talking loud in the forest."

"There is some truth, my friend, I believe, in what you say," returned Lord H----; "but I hear a sound growing louder and louder as we advance. It is the cataract, I suppose.

"Yes, just the waterfall," answered the other, in an indifferent tone. "Down half a mile below, Master Walter will find the boat that will take him to Albany. Then you and I can snake up by the side of the river till we have gone as fur as we have a mind to. I shouldn't wonder if we got a shot at somewhat on four, as we run along; a moose, or a painter, or a look-severe, or something of that kind. Pity we haven't got a canoe, or a batteau, or something to put our game in."

"In Heaven's name, what do you call a look-severe?" asked Lord H----.

"Why, the French folks call it a *loup-cervier*," answered Brooks. "I guess you never saw one. But he is not as pleasant as a pretty maid in a by-place, is he, Master Walter? He puts himself up into a tree, and there he watches, looking fast asleep, but with the devil that is in him moving every joint of his tail the moment he hears anything come trotting along; and when it is just under him, down he drops upon it plump, like a rifle-shot into a pumpkin."

The conversation then fell off into a word or two spoken now and then, and still the voice of the waters grew louder and more loud, till Lord H---- could hardly hear his own footfalls. The more practised ear of Brooks, however, caught every sound; and at length he exclaimed:--"What's alive? Why are you cocking your rifle, Walter?"

"Hush!" said the lad; "there is something stealing in there behind the laurels. It is an Indian, I think, going on all fours. Look quietly out there."

"More likely a *bee*ar," replied Woodchuck, in the same low tone which the other had used--"I see, I see. It's not a *bee*ar either; but it's not an Ingian. It's gone--no, there it is agin. Hold hard!--let him climb. It's a painter. Here, Walter, come up in front--you shall have him. The cur smells fresh meat. He'll climb in a minute. There he goes. No, the crittur's on again. We shall lose him if we don't mind. Quick, Walter! spread out there to the right. I will take the left, and we shall drive him to the water, where he must climb. You, major, keep right on a head--mind take the middle trail all along, and look up at the branches, or you may have him on your head. There, he's a bending south. Quick, Walter, quick!"

Lord H---- had as yet seen nothing of the object discovered by the eyes of his two companions, but he had sufficient of the sportsman in his nature to enter into all their eagerness; and, unslinging his rifle, he followed the path, or trail, along which they had been proceeding, while Walter Prevost darted away into the tangled bushes on the right, and Woodchuck stole more quietly in amongst the trees on his left. He could hear the branches rustle, and, for nearly a quarter of a mile, could trace their course on either side of him by the various little signs of now a waving branch, now a slight sound. Once, and only once, he thought he saw the panther cross the trail, but it was at a spot peculiarly dark, and he did not feel at all sure that fancy had not deceived him.

The roar of the cataract in the mean time increased each moment; and it was evident to the young nobleman that he and his companions on their different courses were approaching close and more closely to some large stream towards which it was the plan of good Captain Brooks to force the object of their pursuit. At length, too, the light became stronger, and the blue sky and sunshine could be seen through the tops of the trees in front, when suddenly, on the right, he heard the report of a rifle, and then a fierce snarling sound, with a shout from Walter Prevost.

Knowing how dangerous the wounded panther is, the young officer, without hesitation, darted away into the brush to aid Edith's brother; for, by this time, it was in that light that he generally thought of him; and the lad soon heard his approach, and guided him up by the voice, calling--"Here, here!" There was no alarm or agitation in his tones, which were rather those of triumph; and, a moment after, as he caught sight of his friend's coming form, he added--"He's a splendid beast. I must have the skin off him."

Lord H---- drew nigh, somewhat relaxing his speed when he found there was no danger, and in another minute he was by the side of the lad who was just quietly re-charging his rifle, while at some six or seven yards' distance lay a large panther, of the American species, mortally wounded, and quite powerless for evil, but not yet quite dead.

"Keep away from him--keep away!" cried Walter, as the young nobleman approached. "They sometimes tear one terribly even at the last gasp."

"Why, he is nearly as big as a tiger," said Lord H----.

"He is a splendid fellow," answered Walter, joyfully. "One might live a hundred years in England without finding such game."

Lord H---- smiled, and remained for a moment or two, till the young man's rifle was re-loaded, gazing at the beast in silence.

Suddenly, however, they both heard the sound of another rifle on the left, and Walter exclaimed--

"Woodchuck has got one too."

But the report was followed by a yell very different from the snarl or growl of a wounded beast.

"That's no panther's cry," exclaimed Walter Prevost, his cheek turning somewhat pale; "what can have happened?"

"It was a human utterance," said Lord H----, listening, "like that of some one in sudden agony. I trust our friend, the Woodchuck, has not shot himself by accident."

"It is not a white man's cry," said Walter, bending; his ear in the direction from which had come the sounds. But all was still; and the young man raised his voice, and shouted to their companion.

No answer was returned; and Lord H----, exclaiming, "We had better seek him at once, he may need help," darted away towards the spot whence his ear told him the shot had come.

"A little more to the right, my lord, a little more to the right," said Walter; "you will hit on a trail in a minute" Then, raising his voice again, he shouted "Woodchuck! Woodchuck!" with evident alarm and distress.

He was right in the supposition that they should soon find some path, for they struck an Indian trail, crossing that on which they had been previously proceeding, and leading in the direction in which they wished to go. Both then hurried on with greater rapidity, Walter running rather than walking, and Lord H---- following, with his cocked rifle in his hand.

They had not far to go, however; for the trail soon opened upon a small piece of grassy savanna, lying close upon the river's edge; and in the midst of it they beheld a sight which was terrible enough in itself, but which afforded less apprehension and grief to the mind of Lord H---- than to that of Walter Prevost, who was better acquainted with the Indian habits and character.

About ten yards from the mouth of the path appeared the powerful form of Captain Brooks, with his folded arms leaning on the muzzle of his discharged rifle. He was as motionless as a statue; his brow contracted; his brown cheek very pale, and his eyes bent forward upon an object lying upon the grass before him. It was the body of an Indian weltering in his blood. The dead man's head was bare of all covering, except the scalp-lock. He was painted with the war colours; and in his hand, as he lay, he still grasped the tomahawk, as if it had been raised, in the act to strike, the moment before he fell.

To the eyes of Lord H----, his tribe or nation was an undiscovered secret; but certain small signs and marks in his garb, and even in his features, showed Walter Prevost at once that he was not only one of the Five Nations, but an Oneida.

The full and terrible importance of the fact will be seen by what followed.

CHAPTER X

For a few minutes, the three living men stood silent in the presence of the dead; and, then Walter exclaimed, in a tone of deep grief, "Alas, Woodchuck! what have you done?"

"Saved my scalp," answered Brooks, sternly, and fell into silence again.

There was another long pause; at last, Lord H----, mistaking in some degree the causes of the man's strong emotion, laid his hand upon the hunter's arm, saying, "Come away, my friend! Why should you linger here?"

"It's no use," answered Woodchuck, gloomily; "he had a woman with him, and it will soon be known all through the tribe."

"But for your own safety," said Walter, "you had better fly. It is very sad, indeed. What could make him attack you?"

"An old grudge, Master Walter," answered Brooks, seating himself deliberately on the ground, and laying his rifle across his knee. "I knew the crittur well--the Striped Snake they called him, and a snake he was. He tried to cheat and rob me, and I made it plain to the whole tribe. Some laughed and thought it fair; but old Black Eagle scorned and rebuked him, and he has hated me ever since. He has been long watching for this, and now he has got it."

"Well, well," returned Walter, "what's done cannot be undone. You had better get away as fast as you can; for Black Eagle told me he had left three scouts behind, to bring us tidings in case of danger, and we cannot tell how near the others may be."

"This was one of them," answered Brooks, still keeping his seat, and gazing at the Indian; "but what is safety to me, Walter? I can no more roam the forests, I can no more pursue my way of life; I must go into dull and smoky cities, and plod amongst thieving, cheating crowds of white men. The rifle and the hatchet must be laid aside for ever; the forest grass must know my foot no more. Flowers and green leaves, and rushing streams, and the broad lake, and the mountain top, are lost and gone--the watch under the deep boughs, and by the silent water. Close pressed amidst the toiling herd, I shall become sordid, and low, and filthy, as they are; my free nature lost, and gyves upon my spirit. All life's blessings are gone from me; why should I care for life?"

There was something unusually plaintive, mournful, and earnest in his tones, and Lord H---- could not help feeling for him, although he did not comprehend fully the occasion of his grief.

"But, my good friend," he said, "I cannot perceive how your having slain this Indian in your own defence can bring such a train of miseries upon you. You would not have killed him, if he had not attacked you."

"Alas for me! alas for me!" was all the answer that the poor man made.

"You do not know their habits, sir," said Walter, in a low voice; "they must always have blood for blood. If he stays here, if he ever returns, go where he will in the Indian territory, they will track him, they will follow him day and night. He will be amongst them like one of the wild beasts whom we so eagerly pursue from place to place, with the hatchet always hanging over his head. There is no safety for him, except far away in the provinces beyond those towns that Indians ever visit. Do persuade him to come away and leave the body. He can go down with me to Albany, and thence make his way to New York or Philadelphia."

For some minutes Brooks remained deaf to all arguments; his whole thoughts seemed occupied with the terrible conviction that the wild scenes and free life which he enjoyed so intensely were, with him, at an end for ever.

Suddenly, however, when Lord H---- was just about to abandon, in despair, the task of persuading him, he started up as if some new thought struck him; and, gazing first at Walter and then at the young officer, he exclaimed,--

"But I am keeping you here, and you too may be murdered. The death-spot is upon me, and it will spread to all around. I am ready to go. I will bear my fate as I can, but it is very, very hard. Come, let us be gone quick. Stay, I will charge my rifle first. Who knows how soon we may need it for more such bloody work?"

All his energy seemed to have returned in a moment, and it deserted him not again. He charged his rifle with wonderful rapidity, tossed it under his arm, and took a step as if to go. Then for a moment he paused, and, advancing close to the dead Indian, gazed at him sternly.

"Oh, my enemy!" he cried, "thou saidst thou wouldst have revenge, and thou hast had it, far more bitter than if thy hatchet had entered into my skull, and I were lying there in thy place."

Turning round as soon as he had spoken, he led the way back along the trail, murmuring, rather to himself than to his companions,--

"The instinct of self-preservation is very strong. But better for me had I let him slay me. I know not how I was fool enough to fire. Come, Walter, we must get round the falls, where we shall find some bateaux that will carry us down."

He walked along for about five minutes in silence; and then suddenly looked around to Lord H----, exclaiming,--

"But what's to become of him? How is he to find his way back again? Come, I will go back with him; it matters not if they do catch me and scalp me. I do not like to be dogged, and tracked, and followed, and taken unawares. But I can only die at last. I will go back with him as soon as you are in the boat, Walter."

"No, no, Woodchuck, that will not do," returned the lad; "you forget that if they found you with him, they would kill him too. I will tell you how we will manage it. Let him come down with us to the point; then there is a straight road up to the house, and we can get one of the bateaux-men to go with him and show him the way, unless he likes to go on with me to Albany."

"I cannot do that," replied Lord H----, "for I promised to be back at your father's house by to-morrow night, and matters of much importance may have to be decided. But I can easily land at the point, as you say--whatever point you may mean--and find my way back. As for myself, I have no fears. There seem to be but a few scattered parties of Indians of different tribes roaming about, and I trust that anything like general hostility is at an end for this year at least."

"In Indian warfare, the danger is the greatest, I have heard, when it seems the least," observed Walter Prevost; "but from the point to the house, some fourteen or sixteen miles, the road is generally safe, for it is the only one on which large numbers of persons are passing to and from Albany."

"It will be safe enough," said Woodchuck; "that way is always quiet, and, besides, a wise man and a peaceful one could travel at any time from one end of the Long House to the other without risk--unless there were special cause. It is bad shooting we have had to-day, Walter; but still I should have liked to have the skin of that painter; he seemed to me an unextinguishable fine crittur."

"He was a fine creature, and that I know, for I shot him, Woodchuck," said Walter Prevost, with some pride in the achievement. "I wanted to send the skin to Otaitsa; but it cannot be helped."

"Let us go and get it now," cried Woodchuck, with the ruling passion strong in death; "'tis but a step back. Darn those Ingians! Why should we care?"

But both his companions urged him forward; and they continued their way through the woods skirting the river for somewhat more than two miles, first rising gently to a spot where the roar of the waters was heard distinctly, and then descending to a rocky point, midway between the highest ground and the water level, where a small congregation of huts had been gathered together, principally inhabited by boatmen, and surrounded by a stout palisade. One of the most necessary parts of prudence in any body of settlers, was to choose such a site for their dwelling-place as would command a clear view of an approaching stranger, whether well or ill disposed; and the ground round this little hamlet had been cleared on all sides of every tree and shrub that could conceal a rabbit. Thus situated on the top of the eminence nearest to the water, it possessed an almost panoramic view, hardly to be surpassed in the world.

That view, however, had one principal object. On the left, at about four hundred yards' distance, the river of which I have spoken came thundering over a precipice of about three hundred feet in height. Whether worn by the constant action of the waters, or cast into that shape by some strange geological phenomenon, the rock over which the torrent poured had assumed the form of a great amphitheatre, scooped out, as it were, in the very bed of the river, which, flowing on in a mighty stream, fell over the edge at various points; sometimes in an immense green mass, sometimes in a broad and silvery sheet, sometimes in a dazzling line of sparkling foam; all the streams meeting about half-way down, and thundering and boiling in a dark abyss, which the eye from above could hardly fathom. Jutting masses of gray rock protruded themselves in strange fantastic shape about, around, and below, the chasm; and upon these, wherever a root could cling, or a particle of vegetable earth could rest, a tree, a shrub, or a flower had perched itself. The green boughs waved amidst the spray; the dark hemlock contrasted itself, in its stern grandeur, with the white, agitated waters; and the birch and the ash, with their waving branches, seemed to sport with the eddies as they leaped along.

At the foot of the precipice was a deep, whirling pool, unseen, however, from the spot where the travellers stood; and from this issued, first narrow and confined, but then spreading out gradually, between the decreasing banks, a wide and beautiful river, which, by the time it circled the point in front of the travellers, had become as calm and glossy as a looking-glass, reflecting for their eyes the blue sky and the majestic clouds which were now moving slowly over it.

The bend taken by the river shaped the hilly point of ground on which the travellers stood into a small peninsula, about the middle of the neck of which was the boatman's little hamlet which I have mentioned; and nearly at the same distance as the falls from the huts, though more than a mile and a half by the course of the stream, was a piece of broad, sandy shore, on which the woodman had drawn up ten or twelve boats, used sometimes for the purposes of fishing, sometimes for the carriage of peltries to the towns lower down; and goods and passengers returning.

Thence onward, the course of the river could be traced for eight or ten miles, flowing through a gently undulating country, densely covered with forest, while to the east and north rose up some fine blue mountains, at the distance, probably, of thirty miles.

The scene at the hamlet itself had nothing very remarkable in it. There were women sitting at the door, knitting and sewing; men lounging about, or mending nets, or making lines; children playing in the dirt, as usual, both inside and outside the palisade. The traces of more than one nation could be discovered in the features, as well as on the tongues, of the inhabitants; and it was not difficult to perceive, that here had been congregated, by the force of circumstances, into which it is not necessary to inquire, sundry fragments of Dutch, English, Indian, and even French, races, all bound together by a community of object and pursuit.

The approach of the three strangers did not in any degree startle the good people from their idleness or their occupations. The carrying trade was then a very good one, especially in remote places where travelling was difficult; and these people could always make a tolerable livelihood, without any very great or continuous exertion. The result of such a state of things is always very detrimental to activity of mind or body; and the boatmen, though they sauntered round Lord H---- and his companions, divining that some profitable piece of work was before them, showed amazing indifference as to whether they would undertake it or not.

But that which astonished Lord H---- the most, was to see the deliberate coolness with which Woodchuck set about making his bargain for the conveyance of himself and Walter to Albany. He sat down upon a large stone within the enclosure, took a knife from his pocket, a piece of wood from the ground, and began cutting the latter into small splinters, with as tranquil and careless an air as if there were no heavy thought upon his mind, no dark memory behind him, no terrible fate dogging him at the heels.

But Woodchuck and Walter were both well known to the boatmen; and though they might probably have attempted to impose upon the inexperience of the lad, they knew they had met their match in the shrewdness of his companion, and were not aware that any circumstance rendered speed more valuable to him than money.

The bargain, then, was soon concluded; but Captain Brooks was not contented till he had stipulated also for the services of two men in guiding Lord H---- back to the house of Mr. Prevost. This was undertaken for a dollar atpiece; and then the whole party proceeded to the bank of the river, where a boat was soon unmoored, and Walter and his companion set forth upon their journey; not, however, until Lord H---- had shaken the former warmly by the hand, and said a few words in the ear of Captain Brooks, adding:--

"Walter will tell you more, and how to communicate with me."

"Thank you, thank you," replied the hunter, wringing his hand hard. "A friend in need is a friend indeed; I do not want it, but I thank you as much as if I did. But you shall hear if I do; for somehow I guess you are not the man to say what you don't mean."

After seeing his two companions row down the stream for a few yards, the nobleman turned to the boatmen who accompanied him, saying--

"Now, my lads, I want to make a change of our arrangements, and to go back the short way by which we came. I did not interrupt our good friend Woodchuck, because he was anxious about my safety. There are some Indians in the forest, and he feared I might get scalped. However, we shot a panther there, which we couldn't stay to skin, as their business in Albany was pressing. Now, I want the skin, and am not afraid of the Indians--are you?"

The men laughed, and replied in the negative, saying that there were none of the red men there, except four or five Oneidas, and some Mohawks; but they added that the way, though shorter, was much more difficult and bushy, and, therefore, they must have more pay. Lord H---- was less difficult to deal with than Captain Brooks, and the bargain was soon struck.

Each of the men then armed himself with a rifle, and took a bag of parched corn with him, and the three set out. Lord H---- undertook to guide them to the spot where the panther lay; and not a little did they marvel at the accuracy and precision with which his military habits of observation enabled him to direct them step by step. He took great care not to let them approach the spot where the Indian had been slain, but, stopping about a quarter of a mile to the south, led them across the thicket to within a very few yards of the object he was in search of. It was soon found when they came near the place, and about half an hour was employed in taking off the skin and packing it up for carriage.

"Now," said Lord H----, "will you two undertake to have this skin properly cured, and dispatched by the first trader going west to the Oneida village?"

The men readily agreed to do so, if well paid for it, but of course required further directions, saying there were a dozen or more Oneida villages.

"It will be sure to reach its destination," said Lord H----, "if you tell the bearer to deliver it to Otaitsa, which I believe means the Blossom, the daughter of Black Eagle, the Sachem. Say that it comes from Walter Prevost."

"Oh ay," answered the boatmen, "it shall be done; but we shall have to pay the man who carries it."

The arrangement in regard to payment was soon made, though it was somewhat exorbitant; but to insure that the commission was faithfully executed, Lord H---- reserved a portion of the money, to be given when he heard that the skin had been delivered. He little knew the consequences which were to flow from the little act of kindness he was performing.

The rest of the journey passed without interruption or difficulty, and at an early hour of the evening the young nobleman stood once more at the door of his countryman's house.

CHAPTER XI

The return of Lord H---- without his guide and companion, Captain Brooks, caused some surprise in Mr. Prevost and his daughter, who had not expected to see any of the party before a late hour of the following evening.

Not choosing to explain, in the presence of Edith, the cause of his parting so suddenly from the hunter, the young nobleman merely said that circumstances had led him to conclude that it would be advisable to send Woodchuck in the boat with Walter to Albany; and his words were uttered in so natural and easy a tone, that Edith, unconscious that her presence put any restraint upon his communication with her father, remained seated in their pleasant little parlour till the hour for the evening meal.

"Well, my lord," said Mr. Prevost, after the few first words of explanation had passed, "did you meet with any fresh specimen of the Indian in your short expedition?"

The question might have been a somewhat puzzling one for a man who did not want to enter into any particulars; but Lord H---- replied with easy readiness--

"Only one. Him we saw but for a moment, and he did not speak with us."

"They are a very curious race," observed Mr. Prevost, "and albeit not very much given to ethnological studies, I have often puzzled myself as to whence they sprang, and how they made their way over to this continent."

Lord H---- smiled.

"I fear I cannot help you," he said. "My profession, you know, my dear sir, leads one much more to look at things as they are than to inquire how they came about. It strikes me at once, however, that in mere corporeal characteristics the Indian is very different from any race I ever beheld, if I may judge by the few individuals I have seen. The features are very different from those of any European or Asiatic people that I know of, and the frame seems formed for a combination of grace and power almost perfect. Our friend the Black Eagle, for instance; compare him with a Yorkshire or Somersetshire farmer, and what a contrast you would find! Habits could not have produced the difference, at least if they sprang from an Eastern stock, for the tribes of the desert are as free and unrestrained, as much used to constant exercise and activity; but I should be inclined to fancy that climate may have something to do with the matter, for it has struck me that many of the people I have seen in the provinces have what I may call a tendency toward the Indian formation. There is a length and suppleness of limb, which to my eyes has something Indian about it."

"Bating the grace and dignity," said Edith, gaily, "I do think that what my father would call the finest specimens of the human animal are to be found among the Indians. Look at our dear little Otaitsa, for instance, can anything be more beautiful, more graceful, more perfect, than her whole face and form?"

Lord H---- smiled, and slightly bowed his head, saying,--

"Now, many a fair lady, Miss Prevost, would naturally expect a very gallant reply; and I might make another without a compliment in good cool blood, and upon calm, mature consideration. I am very poorly versed, however, in civil speeches, and therefore I will only say that I think I have seen white ladies as beautiful, as graceful, and as perfect, as your fair young friend, together with the advantage of a better complexion. But, at the same time, I will admit that she is exceedingly beautiful, and not only that, but very charming, and very interesting too. Hers is not exactly the style of beauty I admire the most; but certainly it is perfect in its kind, and my young friend Walter seems to think so too."

A slight flush passed over Edith's cheek, and her eyes instantly turned towards her father. But Mr. Prevost only laughed, saying,--

"If they were not so young, I should be afraid that my son would marry the Sachem's daughter, and, perhaps, in the end, take to the tomahawk and the scalping-knife. But, joking apart, Otaitsa is a very singular little creature. I never can bring myself to feel that she is an Indian--a savage, in short. When I hear her low, melodious voice, with its peculiar song-like intonation, and see the grace and dignity with which she moves, and the ease and propriety with which she adapts herself to every European custom, I have to look at her bead-embroidered petticoat, and her leggins, and her moccasins, before I can carry it home to my mind that she is not some very high-bred lady of the court of France or England. Then she is so fair, too; but that is probably from care, and the lack of that exposure to the sun which may, at first, have given and then perpetuated the Indian tint. To use an old homely expression, she is the apple of her father's eye, and he is as careful of her as of a jewel, after his own particular fashion."

"She is a dear creature," said Edith, warmly; "all soul, and heart, and feeling. Thank God, too, she is a Christian, and you cannot fancy, my lord, what marvellous stores of information the little creature has. She knows that England is an island in the middle of the salt sea; and she can write and read our tongue nearly as well as she speaks it. She has a holy hatred of the French, however; and would not, for the world, speak a word of their language; for all her information, and a good share of her ideas, come from our friend, Mr. Gore, who has carried John Bull completely into the heart of the wilderness, and kept him there perfect in a sort of crystallized state. Had we but a few more men such as himself amongst the Indian tribes, there would be no fear of any wavering in the friendship of the Five Nations. There goes an Indian now past the window. We shall have him in here in a moment, for they stand upon no ceremony--and he is speaking to Antony, the negro boy. How curiously he peeps about him! He must be looking for somebody he does not find."

Lord H---- rose and went to the window, and, in a minute or two after, the Indian stalked quietly away, and disappeared in the forest.

"What could he want?" said Edith. "It is strange he did not come in. I will ask Antony what he sought here."

And, going to the door, she called the gardener boy up, and questioned him.

"He want Captain Woodchuck, missy," replied the lad. "He ask if he not lodge here last night. I tell him yes; but Woodchuck go away early this morning, and not come back since. He 'quire very much about him, and who went with him. I tell him Massa Walter and de strange gentleman, but both leave him soon--Massa Walter go straight to Albany, strange gentleman come back here."

"Did he speak English?" asked Edith.

"Few word," replied the negro. "I speak few word Indian. So patch 'em together make many, missy."

And he laughed with that peculiar unmeaning laugh with which his race are accustomed to distinguish anything they consider witty.

The whole conversation was heard by the two gentlemen within. On Mr. Prevost it had no effect, but to call a sort of cynical smile upon his lips; but the case was different with Lord H----. He saw that the deed which had been done in the forest was known to the Indians; that its doer had been recognized, and that the hunt was up; and he rejoiced to think that poor Woodchuck was already far beyond pursuit.

Anxious, however, to gain a fuller insight into the character and habits of a people of whom he had as yet obtained only a glimpse, he continued to converse with Mr. Prevost in regard to the aboriginal races; and learned several facts which by no means tended to decrease the uneasiness which the events of the morning; had produced.

"The Indians," said his host, in answer to a leading question, "are, as you say, a very revengeful people; but not more so than many other barbarous nations. Indeed, in many of their feelings and habits they greatly resemble a people I have heard of in central Asia, called Affghans. Both, in common with almost all barbarians, look upon revenge as a duty imperative upon every family and every tribe. They modify their ideas, indeed, in case of war; although it is very difficult to bring about peace after war has commenced; but if any individual of a tribe is killed by another in time of peace, nothing but the blood of the murderer can satisfy the family or the tribe, if he can be caught. They will pursue him for weeks and months, and employ every stratagem which their fertile brains can suggest to entrap him, till they feel quite certain that he is entirely beyond their reach. This perseverance proceeds from a religious feeling; for they believe that the spirit of their dead relation can never enter the happy hunting-grounds till his blood has been atoned by that of the slayer."

"But if they cannot catch the slayer," asked Lord H----, "what do they do then?"

"I used a wrong expression," replied Mr. Prevost. "I should have said the blood of some other victim. It is their duty, according to their ideas, to sacrifice the slayer. If satisfied that he is perfectly beyond their power, they strive to get hold of his nearest relation. If they cannot do that, they take a man of his tribe or nation, and sacrifice him. It is all done very formally, and with all sorts of consideration and consultation; for in these bloody rites they are the most deliberate people in the world, and the most persevering also."

Lord H---- mused gravely for some moments without reply, and then turned the conversation in another direction. It certainly was not gay; but it was, to all appearance, cheerful enough on his side; for this world is a strange teacher of hypocrisy in all its various shades, from that which is the meanest and most detestable of vices to that which is dignified by its motives and its conduct almost to a virtue. God forbid that I should ever, for a moment, support the false and foul axiom that the end can justify the means. But it is with all evil things as with deadly poisons. There are occasions when, in small portions, they may, for certain diseased circumstances, become precious antidotes. Had man remained pure, perfect, and upright, as he came from the bands of his Creator--had he never doubted God's word, disobeyed his commandments, tasted of that which was forbidden--had disobedience never brought pain and death--had blood never stained the face of earth, and pain in all its shapes followed in the footsteps of sin--there would, indeed, have never been any occasion or any circumstances in which it would have been needful, honourable, or kind for man to hide one feeling of his heart from his fellow-beings. But in this dark, corrupted world, where sickness and sorrow, care, distress, and death surround, not only ourselves, but those who are dearest to us, and hem us in on every side, how often is it needful to hide from those, even, whom we love the best and trust the most, the anxieties which imagination suggests, or to which reason and experience give birth; to conceal, for a time, even the sad and painful facts of which we are cognizant; to shut up our sorrow and our dread in our own bosom, till we have armed and steeled the hearts of those we love better than ourselves, to resist or to endure the evil which is preying on our own.

A few days earlier, Lord H---- might plainly and openly have told all the occurrences of the morning in the ears of Edith Prevost; but sensations had been springing up in his breast, which made him more tender of her feelings, more careful of creating alarm and anxiety; and he kept his painful secret well till after the evening meal was over, and she had retired to her chamber. Then, however, he stopped Mr. Prevost just as that gentleman was raising a light to hand to his guest, and said--

"I am afraid, my good friend, we cannot go to bed just yet. I have something to tell you, which, from all I have heard since it occurred, appears to me of much greater importance than at first. Whether anything can be done to avert the evil consequences or not, I cannot tell; but, at all events, it is as well that you and I should talk the matter over."

He then related to Mr. Prevost all the events of the morning, and was sorry to perceive that gentleman's face assuming a deeper and deeper gloom as he proceeded.

"This is most unfortunate indeed," said Mr. Prevost at length. "I quite acquit our poor friend Brooks of any evil intent; but to slay an Indian at all so near our house, and especially an Oneida, was most unlucky. That tribe, or nation, as they call themselves, has, from the strong personal regard, I suppose, which has grown up accidentally between their chief and myself, always shown the greatest kindness and friendship towards myself and my family. Before this event, I should have felt myself, in any of their villages, as much at home as by my own fireside, and I am sure that each man felt himself as secure on any part of the lands granted to me as if he were in his own lodge. But now their blood has stained my very mat, as they will call it, and the consequences no one can foresee. Woodchuck has himself escaped. He has no relations or friends on whom they can wreak their vengeance."

"Surely," exclaimed Lord H----, "they will never visit his offence on you or yours."

"I trust not," replied Mr. Prevost, after a moment's thought; "yet I cannot feel exactly sure. They will take a white man for their victim--an Englishman--one of the same nation as the offender. Probably it may not matter much to them who it is; and the affectionate regard which they entertain towards us may turn the evil aside. But these Indians have a sort of fanaticism in their religion, as well as we have in ours; the station and the dignity of the victim which they offer up enters into their consideration-- they like to make a worthy and an honourable sacrifice, as they consider it; and, just as this spirit moves them or not, they may think that any one will do for their purpose, or that they are required by their god of vengeance to immolate some one dear to themselves, in order to dignify the sacrifice."

"This is, indeed, a very sad view of the affair, and one which had never struck me," replied Lord H----. "It may be well to consider, my dear sir, what is the best and safest course. I must now tell you one of the objects which made me engage your son to carry my despatches to Albany. It seemed to me, from all I have learned during my short residence with you, especially during my conference with Sir William Johnson, that the unprotected state of this part of the country left Albany itself, and the settlements round it, unpleasantly exposed. We know that on a late occasion it was Dieskau's intention, if he had succeeded in defeating Sir William and capturing Fort George, to make a dash at the capital of the province. He was defeated; but there is reason to believe that Montcalm--a man much his superior both in energy and skill--entertained the same views, although we know not what induced him to retreat so hastily after his black and bloody triumph at Fort William Henry. He may seize some other opportunity; and I can perceive nothing whatsoever to oppose his progress, or delay him for an hour, if he can make himself master of the few scattered forts which lie between Carrillon or Ticonderoga. In these circumstances, I have strongly urged that a small force should be thrown forward to a commanding point on the river Hudson, not many miles from this place, which I examined as I came hither--with an advanced post or two, still nearer to your house. My own regiment I have pointed out as better fitted for the service than any other; and I believe that if my suggestions are adopted, as I doubt not they will be, we can give you efficient protection. Still I think," continued the nobleman, speaking more slowly and emphatically, "that, with two young people so justly dear to you--with a daughter so beautiful, and every way so charming; and so gallant and noble a lad as Walter, whose high spirit and adventurous character will expose him continually to any snare that may be set for him, it will be much better for you to retire with them both to Albany; at least till such time as you know that the spirit of Indian vengeance has been satisfied, and that the real peril has passed."

Mr. Prevost mused for several minutes, and then replied:--

"The motives you suggest are certainly very strong, my lord; but I have strange ways of viewing such subjects, and I must have time to consider whether it is fair and right to my fellow-countrymen, scattered over this district, to withdraw from my share of the peril which all who remain would have to encounter. Do not argue with me upon the subject to-night. I will think over it well; and doubt not that I shall view the plan you have suggested with all the favour that paternal love can afford. I will also keep my mind free to receive any further reasons you may have to produce. But I must first consider quietly and alone. There is no need of immediate decision; for these people, according to their own code, are bound to make themselves perfectly sure that they cannot get possession of the actual slayer before they choose another victim. It is clear from what the Indian said to the negro boy, that they know the hand that did the deed, and they must search for poor Brooks first, and practise every device to allure him back before they immolate another. Let us both think over the matter well, and confer to-morrow."

Thus saying, he shook hands with Lord H----, and they retired to their several chambers with very gloomy and apprehensive thoughts.

CHAPTER XII

There are hours in the life of man when no actual grief oppresses him--when there is no imminent peril near--when no strong passion wrings his heart; and yet those hours are amongst the most dark and painful of his whole existence. They come on many occasions, and under various circumstances--often when some silent voice from within warns him of the instability of all human joy, and a gray shadow takes the place of the sunshine of life--often when the prophetic soul, seeing in the distant horizon a cloud no bigger than a man's hand, foretells the hurricane and the tempest that is to sweep away his brightest hopes for ever.

Such hours were those of Mr. Prevost during a great part of the night which succeeded his parting with Lord H----. He slept but little for several hours, and, though he knew not why, a gloomy, oppressive fancy seized upon him, that his household would be the one to suffer from the event which had lately passed.

The want of sleep in the earlier part of the night protracted the slumbers of the morning. He was usually the first person up in the house, and enjoyed many an hour of study or of thought before even the negroes were stirring. But this morning he was aroused by a distant knocking at the huts where the outdoor servants slept, and then by a repetition of the same sound at the door of the house itself.

Rising hastily, he got down in time to see the door opened by old Agrippa, and found a man on horseback bearing a large official-looking letter, addressed to Major-General Lord H----.

It proved to be a despatch from Sir William Johnson, requesting both Lord H---- and Mr. Prevost to attend a meeting of some of the chiefs of the Five Nations, which was to be held at Johnson Castle on the Mohawk in the course of the following day. Though the distance was not very great, the difficulty of travelling through that part of the country made it necessary to set out at once, in order to reach the place of rendezvous before night.

"I will mount my horse as soon as it can be got ready," said Lord H----, when he had read the letter and shown it to Mr. Prevost. "I suppose, in existing circumstances, you will not think it advisable to accompany me?"

"Most certainly I will go with you, my lord," replied his host. "As I said last night, the danger, though very certain, is not immediate. Weeks, months, may pass before these Indians feel assured that they cannot obtain possession of the actual slayer of their red brother; and, as many of the Oneidas will probably be present at this 'talk,' as they call it, I may, perhaps (though it is very doubtful), gain some insight into their thoughts and intentions. I will take my daughter with me, however, for I should not like to leave her here altogether alone. Her preparations may delay us for half-an-hour; but we shall have ample time, and the horse of the messenger, who will act as our guide, must have some little time to take rest and feed."

Edith was all gaiety and satisfaction at the thought of the expedition before her. She knew many of the Indians well; was acquainted with their habits and manners, and was a great favourite with several of the chiefs; but she had never been present at any of their great meetings, and the event before her had all the recommendation of novelty. The keen observer before whom she stood drew from her active eagerness an inference, partially true, though carried, perhaps, a little too far, that she was not in reality well satisfied with her residence in the wilderness--that it was oppressive to her, and that, though she might studiously conceal her distaste for such solitude, she was very glad to seize an opportunity of escaping from it to busier scenes.

However that might be, she was ready the first. A very brief time was spent at breakfast, and then the whole party set out on horseback, followed by a negro leading a packhorse, and preceded by the messenger of Sir William Johnson.

It was customary in those days in all lands for every gentleman to go armed with the sword at least; and in those parts of America which bordered upon the Indian territory, few people thought of going forth for any distance without a rifle as a protection, not alone against any hostile natives, but against wild beasts, which were then somewhat numerous. Mr. Prevost, the messenger, and the negro, were all thus armed; but Lord H----, who had hitherto worn nothing but the common riding-suit in which he had first presented himself, except in his unfortunate expedition with Captain Brooks, had now donned the splendid uniform of a major-general in the British service, and was merely armed with his sword and pistols in the holsters of his saddle.

Thus equipped, and mounted on a horse full of life and spirit from a four days' rest, he was certainly as gallant-looking a cavalier as ever presented himself to lady's eyes. But, to say sooth, his military station and his military dress were no great recommendation to Edith; for it is sad to say, but too true, that officers in the English army in those days had made themselves anything but popular or well esteemed in the American provinces. A more simple and more virtuous state of society certainly existed in the northern portion of the New World than in any part of the Old; and, coming from a luxurious and vicious scene to a completely different state of things, the English officer, despising the simpler habits of the people, displayed no slight portion of insolence and presumption, and carried to excess the evil habits which should have been disgraceful in any country. A great change has since come over his manners and character in almost every respect; but at that period he was notorious in the colonies for blasphemy, drunkenness, and depraved morals.

Thus, to be a military man was, as I have said, no great recommendation in the eyes of any lady who possessed self-respect, but in the case of Lord H---- it served to heighten the good qualities which were apparent in him, by showing him in a favourable contrast to the great body of his comrades. He swore not; in eating and drinking he carried moderation to abstemiousness; and in manners, though firm, easy, and self-possessed, there was not the slightest touch of overbearingness or presumption. Occasionally his tone was grave, almost to sternness; but at other times it was mild, and even tender; and there was something peculiarly gentle as well as bright in his smile and in his eyes.

The journey passed without incident. Deep woods succeeded each other for many miles, but not without interruption. Every now and then a bright stream would come dancing along in its autumnal freshness, and then the road would circle the edge of a small lake, sweet, and calm, and beautiful, reflecting the blue sky and the over-hanging branches of the pine and hemlock. At places where the maple grew, the forest would be all in a glow, as if with the reflection of some vast unseen fire; and then again, where the road passed through a deep valley, all would be dark, and sombre, and gloomy.

No Indian villages were passed, and not a human being was seen for seventeen or eighteen miles; though here and there a small log-hut, apparently deserted, testified to the efforts of a new race to wrest their hunting-grounds from an earlier race--efforts too soon, too sadly, too cruelly, to be consummated.

The softer light of early morning died away, and then succeeded a warmer period when the heat became very oppressive; for in the midst of those deep forests, with no wind stirring, the change from summer to winter is not felt so rapidly as in more open lands.

About an hour after noon Mr. Prevost proposed to stop, rest the horses, and take some refreshment; and a spot was selected where some fine oaks spread their large limbs over a beautifully clear little lake or pond, the view across which presented peeps of a distant country, some blue hills, at no very great elevation, appearing above the tops of the trees. It was a calm and quiet spot; and, while resting there for an hour, the conversation, as is generally the case, was tinged by the influence of the scene.

Mr. Prevost himself, though past the age when impressions of any kind are most readily received, had preserved much of the fresh and plastic character of youth, and gave himself up to any train of thought that might be suggested by circumstances. A casual word led his mind away from those drier topics on which he was often pleased to dwell, to friendship and to love; and he and Lord H---- discussed for some time a number of subjects which rarely arise between an elderly man and one in early middle age. Of the two, strange to say, Mr. Prevost, in dealing with such topics, seemed the most enthusiastic and fanciful. He would play with them, he would embellish them, he would illustrate them, as if he had been a young lover, with his imagination freshly kindled by the torch of the blind god. But in the little said by Lord H---- there was a depth, and a strength, and an earnestness, which more than made up for the lack of figurative adornment.

Edith said little--nothing, in truth, that bore upon the subject; but perhaps she did not think--perhaps she did not feel--the less. It must be a strange thing to a young girl's ears, I have often thought, when first in her presence are discussed, by the cool, fearless tongues of men, those deep sympathies, those warm affections, those tender and absorbing passions--like the famous Amreeta cup, good or evil, life or death, according to the spirit in which they are received--which form for her the keynote of the whole harmonies of her nature, the foundation of life's happiness or woe, the talisman of her whole destiny. Must she not shrink and thrill, as would the idolater at seeing profane and careless hands sport with the image of his god?

Needless, perhaps vain, were it to try and look into that young girl's heart. Suffice it, she was silent, or very nearly so--suffice it, that she thought and felt in her silence. Was it that the portals of a new world were opened to her, full of beauty and of interest, and that she stood on the threshold, gazing in voiceless awe?

At the end of an hour, the party again mounted, and pursued their way, still through forests and valleys, across streams, and by the side of lakes, till at length, just as the evening sun was reaching the horizon, a visible change took place in the aspect of the country; spots were seen which had been cultivated, where harvests had grown and been reaped; and then a house gleamed here and there through the woodland, and blue wreaths of smoke might be seen rising up. Tracks of cart-wheels channelled the forest path; a cart or waggon was drawn up near the road side; high piles of firewood showed preparation against the bitter winter; and everything indicated that the travellers were approaching some new but prosperous settlement.

Soon all traces of the primeval woods, except those which the little party left behind them, disappeared, and a broad tract of well-cultivated country spread out before them, with a fine river bounding it at the distance of more than a mile. The road, too, was comparatively good and broad, and half-way between the forest and the river, that road divided into two, one branch going straight on, and another leading up the course of the stream.

"Is Sir William at the Hall, or at his castle?" asked Mr. Prevost, raising his voice to reach the ears of his guide, who kept a little in front.

"He told me, sir, to take you to the Hall if you should come on, sir," replied the messenger. "There is a great number of Indians up at the castle already, and he thought you might, perhaps, not like to be with them altogether."

"Probably not," returned Mr. Prevost, drily; and they rode on upon the direct road, till, passing two or three smaller houses, they came in sight of a very large and handsome edifice, built of wood, indeed, but somewhat in the style of a European house of the eighteenth century.

As they approached the gates, Sir William Johnson himself, now in full costume of an officer of the British army, came down the steps to meet and welcome them; and little less ceremonious politeness did he display, in the midst of the wild woods of America, than if he had been, at the moment, in the halls of St. James's. With stately grace, he lifted Edith from her horse, greeted Lord H---- with a deferential bow, shook Mr. Prevost by the hand, and then led them himself to rooms which seemed to have been prepared for them.

"Where is my friend Walter?" he asked, as he was about to leave Mr. Prevost to some short repose; "what has induced him to deny his old acquaintance the pleasure of his society? Ha, Mr. Prevost, does he think to find metal more attractive at your lonely dwelling? Perhaps he may be mistaken; for, let me tell you, the beautiful Otaitsa is here--here, in this very house; for our good friend Gore has so completely Anglified her, that, what between her Christianity, her beauty, and her delicacy, I believe she is afraid to trust herself with four or five hundred red warriors at the castle."

He spoke in a gay and jesting tone; and every one knows the blessed facility which parents have of shutting their eyes to the love affairs of their children. Mr. Prevost did not, in the least, perceive anything in the worthy general's speech, but a good-humored joke at the boyish fondness of his son for a pretty Indian girl; and he hastened to excuse Walter's absence by telling Sir William that he had been sent to Albany on business by Lord H----. He then inquired, somewhat anxiously, "Is our friend the Black Eagle here, with his daughter?"

"He is here on the ground," replied Sir William, "but not in the house. His Indian habits are of too old standing to be rooted out like Otaitsa's, and he prefers a bear-skin and his own blue blanket to the best bed and quilt in the house. I offered him such accommodation as it afforded; but he declined with the dignity of a prince refusing the hospitality of a cottage."

"Does he seem in a good humour to-day?" asked Mr. Prevost, hesitating whether he should tell Sir William, at a moment when they were likely to be soon interrupted, the event which had caused so much apprehension in his own mind; "you know he is somewhat variable in his mood."

"I never remarked it," replied the other. "I think he is the most civilized savage I ever saw; far more than King Hendrick, though the one, since his father's death, wears a blue coat, and the other does not. He did seem a little grave, indeed; but the shadows of Indian mirth and gravity are so faint, it is difficult to distinguish them."

While these few words were passing, Mr. Prevost had decided upon his course, and he merely replied,--

"Well, Sir William, pray let Otaitsa know that Edith is here. They will soon be in each other's arms, for the two girls love like sisters."

A few words sprang to Sir William Johnson's lips, which, had they been uttered, might, perhaps, have opened Mr. Prevost's eyes, at least, to the suspicions of his friend. He was on the eve of answering, "And, some day, they may be sisters." But he checked himself, and nothing but the smile which should have accompanied the words made any reply.

When left alone, the thoughts of Mr. Prevost reverted at once to more pressing considerations.

"The old chief knows this event," he said to himself; "he has heard of it--heard the whole, probably. It is wonderful how rapidly intelligence is circulated amongst this people from mouth to mouth!"

He was well nigh led into speculations regarding the strange celerity with which news can be carried orally, and was beginning to calculate how much distance would be saved in a given space, by one man shouting out the tidings to another afar off, when he forced back his mind into the track it had left, and came to the conclusion, from a knowledge of the character of the parties, and from all he had heard, that certainly the Black Eagle was cognizant of the death of one of his tribe by the hand of Captain Brooks, and that probably--though not certainly--he might have communicated the facts, though not his views and purposes, to his daughter, whose keen eyes were likely to discover much of that which he intended to conceal.

CHAPTER XIII

A curious and motley assembly was present that night in the halls of Sir William Johnson. There were several ladies and gentlemen from Albany: several young military men, and two or three persons of a class now extinct, but who then drove a very thriving commerce, and whose peculiar business it was to trade with the Indians. Some of the latter were exceedingly well-educated men; and one or two of them were persons, not only of enlightened minds, but of enlarged views and heart. The others were mere brutal speculators, whose whole end and object in life was to wring as much from the savage, and give as little in return, as possible.

Besides these, an Indian chief would, from time to time, appear in the rooms, often marching through in perfect silence, observing all that was going on with dignified gravity, and then going back to his companions at the castle. Amongst the rest was Otaitsa, still in her Indian costume, but evidently in gala dress, of the finest cloth and the most elaborate embroidery. Not only was she perfectly at her ease, talking to every one, laughing with many; but the sort of shrinking, timid tenderness which gave her so great a charm in the society of the few whom she loved, had given place to a wild spirit of gaiety, little in accordance with the character of her nation.

She glided hither and thither through the room; she rested in one place hardly for a moment; her jests were as light, and sometimes as sharp, as those of almost any Parisian dame; and, when one of the young officers ventured to speak to her somewhat lightly as the mere Indian girl, she piled upon him a mass of ridicule that wrung tears of laughter from the eyes of one or two elder men standing near.

"I know not what has come to the child to-night," said Mr. Gore, who was seated near Edith in one of the rooms; "a wild spirit seems to have seized upon her, which is quite unlike her whole character and nature-- unlike the character of her people, too, or I might think that the savage had returned notwithstanding all my care."

"Perhaps it is the novelty and excitement of the scene," observed Edith.

"Oh, no," answered the missionary; "there is nothing new in this scene to her; she has been at these meetings several times during the last two or three years, but never seemed to yield to their influence as she has done to-night."

"She has hardly spoken a word to me," said Edith; "I hope she will not forget the friends who love her."

"No fear of that, my dear," replied Mr. Gore. "Otaitsa is all heart, and that heart is a gentle one. Under its influence is she acting now; it throbs with something that we do not know; and those light words, that make us smile to hear, have sources deep within her--perhaps of bitterness."

"I think I have heard her say," remarked Edith, "that you educated her from her childhood."

"When first I joined the People of the Stone," replied the missionary, "I found her there, a young child of three years old. Her mother was just dead; and, although her father bore his grief with the stern, gloomy stoicism of his nation, and neither suffered tear to fall nor sigh to escape his lips, I could see plainly enough that he was struck with grief such as the Indian seldom feels, and never shows. He received me most kindly; made my efforts with his people easy; and though I know not to this hour whether with himself I have been successful in communicating blessed light, he gave his daughter altogether up to my charge, and with her I have *not* failed. I fear in him the savage is too deeply rooted ever to be wrung forth, but I have made *her* one of Christ's flock, indeed."

It seemed, as if by a sort of instinct, that Otaitsa discovered she was the subject of conversation between her two friends. Twice she looked round at them from the other side of the room, and at length glided across, and seated herself beside Edith. For a moment she sat in silence there; and then, leaning her head gracefully on her beautiful companion's shoulder, she said, in a low whisper--

"Do not close thine eyes this night, my sister, till thou seest me."

Having thus spoken, she started up, and mingled with the little crowd again.

It was still early in the night when Edith retired to the chamber assigned for her; for, even in the most fashionable society of those times, people had not learned to drive the day into the night, and make morning and evening meet. Her room was a large and handsome one; and though plainly, it was sufficiently furnished. No forest, as at her own dwelling, intercepted the beams of the rising moon; so she sat and contemplated the ascent of the queen of night, as she soared grandly over the distant trees.

The conduct of Otaitsa during that evening had puzzled Edith, and the few whispered words had excited her curiosity; for it must not be forgotten that Edith was altogether unacquainted with the fact of one of the Oneidas having been slain by the hands of Captain Brooks, within little more than two miles of her own abode. She proceeded to make her toilet for the night, however, and was almost undressed when she heard the door of her room open quietly, and Otaitsa stole in, and cast her arms around her.

"Ah, my sister," she exclaimed, "I have longed to talk with you." Seating herself by her side, she leaned her head again upon Edith's shoulder, but remained silent for several minutes.

The fair English girl knew that it was better to let her take her own time, and her own manner, to speak whatever she had to say; but Otaitsa remained so long without uttering a word, that an indefinable feeling of alarm spread over her young companion. She felt her bosom heave, as if with struggling sighs; she even felt some warm drops, like tears, fall upon her shoulder; and yet Otaitsa remained without speaking; till at length Edith said, in a gentle and encouraging tone,--

"What is it, my sister? There can surely be nothing you should be afraid to utter to my ear."

"Not afraid," answered Otaitsa; and then she relapsed into silence.

"But why do you weep, my sweet Blossom?" said Edith, after pausing for a moment or two, to give her time to recover her composure.

"Because one of your people has killed one of my people," answered the Indian girl sorrowfully. "Is not that enough to make me weep?"

"Indeed!" exclaimed Edith. "I am much grieved to hear it, Blossom; but when did this happen, and how?"

"It happened only yesterday," replied the girl, "and but a little towards the morning from your own house, my sister. It was a sad day!--it was a sad day!"

"But I trust it was none near and dear to thee, Blossom, or to the Black Eagle," said Edith, putting her arms around her, and trying to soothe her.

"No, no," answered Otaitsa; "he was a bad man, a treacherous man, one whom my father loved not. But that matters little. They will have blood for *his* blood."

The truth flashed upon Edith's mind at once; for, although less acquainted with the Indian habits than her brother or her father, she knew enough of their revengeful spirit to feel sure that they would seek the death of the murderer with untiring eagerness, and she questioned her sweet companion earnestly as to all the particulars of the sad tale. Otaitsa told her all she knew, which was, indeed, nearly all that could be told. The man called the Snake, she said, had been shot by the white man Woodchuck, in the wood to the north-east of Mr. Prevost's house. Intimation of the fact had spread like fire in dry grass through the whole of the Oneidas, who were flocking to the meeting at Sir William Johnson's castle, and from them would run through the whole tribe.

"Woodchuck has escaped," Otaitsa said, "or would have been slain ere now; but they will have his life yet, my sister,"--and then she added slowly and sorrowfully, "or the life of some other white man, if they cannot catch the one."

Her words presented to Edith's mind a sad and terrible idea--one more fearful in its vagueness and uncertainty of outline than in the darkness of particular points. That out of a narrow and limited population, some one was foredoomed to be slain--that out of a small body of men, all feeling almost as brethren, one was to be marked out for slaughter--that one family was to lose husband, or father, or brother, and no one could tell which-- made her feel like one of a herd of wild animals, cooped up within the toils of the hunters.

Edith's first object was to learn more from her young companion; but Otaitsa had told almost all she knew.

"What they will do I know not," she said; "they do not tell us women. But I fear, Edith, I fear very much; for they say our brother Walter was with Woodchuck when the deed was done."

"Not so, not so," cried Edith; "had he been so, I should have heard of it. He has gone to Albany, and had he been present I am sure he would have stopped it if he could. If your people tell truth, they will acknowledge that he was not there."

Otaitsa raised her head suddenly, with a look of joy, exclaiming,--

"I will make her tell the truth, were she as cunning a snake as he was; but yet, my sister Edith, some one else will have to die if they find not the man they seek."

The last words were spoken in a melancholy tone again; but then she started up, repeating,--

"I will make her tell the truth."

"Can you do so?" asked Edith; "snakes are always very crafty."

"I will try at least," answered the girl; "but oh, my sister, it were better for you, and Walter, and your father too, to be away. When a storm is coming, we try to save what is most precious. There is yet ample time to go; for the red people are not rash, and do not act hastily, as you white people do."

"But is there no means," asked Edith, "of learning what the intention of the tribe really is?"

"I know of none," replied the girl, "that can be depended upon with certainty. The people of the Stone change no more than the stone from which they sprang. The storm beats upon them, the sun shines upon them, and there is little difference on the face of the rock. Yet let your father watch well when he is at the great talk, to-morrow. Then, if the priest is very smooth and soft-spoken, and if the Black Eagle is stern and silent, and wraps his blanket over his left breast, be sure that something sad is meditated. That is all that I can tell you--but I will make this woman speak the truth if there be truth in her, and that, too, before the chiefs of the nation. Now, sister, lie down to rest. Otaitsa is going at once to her people."

"But are you not afraid?" asked Edith. "It is a dark night, dear Blossom. Lie down with me, and wait till the morning sunshine."

"I have no fear," answered the Indian girl; "nothing will hurt me. There are times, sister, when a spirit possesses us, that defies all and fears nothing. So has it been with me this night. The only thing I dreaded to face was my own thought, and I would not suffer it to rest upon anything till I had spoken with you. Now, however, I have better hopes. I will go forth, and I will make her tell the truth."

Thus saying, she left Edith's chamber, and, in about an hour and a half, she stood beside her father, who was seated near a fire kindled in one corner of the court attached to a large house, or rather fort, built by Sir William Johnson on the banks of the Mohawk, and called by him his Castle. Round the Sachem, forming a complete circle, sat a number of the head men of the Oneidas, each in that peculiar crouching position which has been rendered familiar to our eyes by numerous paintings. The court and the castle itself were well nigh filled with Indians of other tribes of the Five Nations; but none took any part in the proceedings of the Oneidas but themselves.

The only stranger who was present in the circle was Sir William Johnson. He was still fully dressed in his British uniform, and seated on a chair in an attitude of much dignity, with his left hand resting on the hilt of his sword. With the exception of that weapon, he had no arms whatever, and indeed it was his custom to sleep frequently in the midst of his red friends utterly unarmed and defenceless. The occasion seemed a solemn one, for all faces were very grave, and a complete silence prevailed for several minutes.

"Bring in the woman," said Black Eagle, at length; "bring her in, and let her speak the truth."

"Of what do you accuse her, Otaitsa?" asked Sir William Johnson, fixing his eyes upon his beautiful guest.

"Of uttering lies to the Sachem and to her brethren," answered Otaitsa. "Her breath has been full of the poison of the snake."

"Thou hearest," said Black Eagle, turning to a woman of some one or two-and-twenty years of age. "What sayest thou?"

"I lie not," answered the woman, in the Indian tongue. "I saw him lift the rifle, and shoot my brother dead."

"Who did it?" asked Black Eagle, gravely and calmly.

"The Woodchuck," answered the woman; "he did it. I know his face too well."

"Believe her not," rejoined Otaitsa. "The Woodchuck was ever a friend of our nation. He is our brother. He would not slay an Oneida."

"But he was my brother's enemy," answered the woman; "there was vengeance between them."

"Vengeance on thy brother's part," retorted the old chief; "more likely he to slay the Woodchuck, than the Woodchuck to slay him."

"If she have a witness, let her bring him forward," said Otaitsa. "We will believe her by the tongue of another."

"I have none," cried the woman, vehemently. "I have none; but I saw him kill my brother with my own eyes, and I cry for his blood."

"Didst thou not say that there were two white men with him?" asked Otaitsa, raising up her right hand. "Then in this thou hast lied to the Sachem and thy brethren, and who shall say whether thou speakest the truth now?"

A curious sort of drowsy hum ran round the circle of the Indians; and one old man said--"She has spoken well."

The woman in the meanwhile stood silent and abashed, with her eyes fixed upon the ground; and the Black Eagle said, in a grave tone,

"There was none."

"No," said the woman, lifting her look firmly, "there was none; but I saw two others in the wood hard by, and I was sure they were his companions."

"That is guile," said Black Eagle, sternly. "Thou didst say that there were two men with him, one the young, pale-face Walter, and the other a tall stranger; and thou broughtest a cloud over our eyes, and madest us think that they were present at the death."

"Then methinks, Black Eagle," said Sir William Johnson, using their language nearly as fluently as his own, "there is no faith to be put in the woman's story, and we cannot tell what has happened."

"Not so, my brother," answered Black Eagle. "We know that the Snake was slain yesterday, before the sun had reached the pine tops. We believe, too, that the Woodchuck slew him, for there was enmity between them, and the ball which killed him was a large ball, such as we have never seen but in that man's pouch."

"That is doubtful evidence," said Sir William, "and I trust my brother will let vengeance cease till he have better witnesses."

The Indians remained profoundly silent for more than a minute; and then the old man who had spoken once before, replied--

"If our brother will give us up Woodchuck, vengeance shall cease."

"That I cannot do," answered Sir William Johnson. "First, I have no power; secondly, he may be tried by our laws; but I will not lie to you. If he can show he did it in self-defence, he will be set free."

Again there was a long silence; and then Black Eagle rose, saying--

"We must take counsel."

His face was very grave; and as he spoke, he drew the large blue blanket which covered his shoulders over his left breast with the gesture which Otaitsa had described to Edith as indicating some dark determination. Sir William Johnson marked the signs he saw, and was too well acquainted with the Indian character to believe that their thirst for blood was at all allayed; but neither by expression of countenance nor by words did he show any doubt of his red friends, and he slept amongst them calmly that night, without a fear of the result.

At an early hour on the following morning, all the arrangements were made for the great Council or "Talk" that was about to be held. Some large arm-chairs were brought forth into the court. A few soldiers were seen moving about, and some negro servants. A number of the guests from the Hall came up about nine o'clock, most of them on horseback; but when all were assembled, the body of white men present were few and insignificant compared with the multitude of Indians who surrounded them. No one showed or entertained any fear, however, and the conference commenced and passed off with perfect peace and harmony.

It is true that several of the Indian chiefs, and more especially King Hendrick as he was called, the son of the chief who had been killed near Port George a year or two before, made some complaints against the English government for neglect of the just claims of their red allies. All angry feeling, however, was removed by a somewhat large distribution of presents; and, after hearing everything which the Indians had to say, Sir William Johnson rose from the chair in which he had been seated, with Lord H---- and Mr. Prevost on either side, and addressed the assembly in English, his speech being translated, sentence after sentence, by an interpreter, according to his invariable custom when called upon to deal publicly with the heads of the Five Nations.

The whole of his address cannot be given here; but it was skilfully turned to suit the prejudices and conciliate the friendship of the people to whom he spoke. He said that their English father, King George, loved his red children with peculiar affection; but that, as his lodge was a long way off, he could not always know their wants and wishes. He had very lately, however, shown his great tenderness and consideration for the Five Nations, by appointing him, Sir William Johnson, as Indian agent, to make known, as speedily as possible, all that his red children desired. He then drew a glowing picture of the greatness and majesty of the English monarch, as the Attotarho, or chief leader of a thousand different nations, sitting under a pine-tree that reached to the sky, and receiving every minute messages from his children in every part of the earth.

A hum of satisfaction from the Indians followed this flight of fancy; and then the speaker went on to say that this great chief, their father, had long ago intended to do much for them, and still intended to do so, but that the execution of his benevolent purposes had been delayed and impeded by the machinations of the French, *their* enemies and *his*, whom he represented as stealthily lying in wait for all the ships and convoys of goods and presents which were destined for his Indian children, and possessing themselves of them by force or fraud. Rich as he might be, he asked how was it possible that their white father could supply all their wants, when he had so many to provide for, and when so many of his enemies had dug up the tomahawk at once. If the chiefs of the Five Nations, however, he said, would vigorously aid him in his endeavours, King George would speedily drive the French from America; and, to show his intention of so doing, he had sent over the great chief on his right hand, Lord H----, and many other mighty warriors, to fight side by side with their red brethren. More, he said, would come over in the ensuing spring; and with the first flower that blossoms under the hemlock-trees, the English warriors would be ready for the battle, if the Indian chiefs there present would promise them cordial support and co-operation.

It must not be supposed that, in employing very exaggerated language, Sir William had any intention of deceiving. He merely used figures suited to the comprehension of his auditors; and his speech gave the very highest satisfaction. The unusually large presents which had been distributed--the presence and bearing of the young nobleman who accompanied him, and a natural weariness of the state of semi-neutrality between the French and English, which they had maintained for some time, disposed the chiefs to grant the utmost he could desire; and the conference broke up with the fullest assurance of support from the heads of the Iroquois tribes--assurances which were faithfully made good in the campaigns which succeeded.

CHAPTER XIV

All was pleasant ease at the house of Sir William Johnson, from which the stateliness of his manner did not at all detract; for, when blended with perfect courtesy, as an Irishman, perhaps better than any man, can blend it, stateliness does not imply restraint.

The conference with the Indians had not ended until too late an hour for Mr. Prevost and his companions to return to his dwelling on the day when it took place; and, as Walter was not expected with the answers to Lord H----'s despatches for at least two days more, the party were not unwilling to prolong their stay till the following morning. Several of the guests, indeed, who were proceeding to Albany direct, set out at once for their destination, certain of reaching the well-inhabited parts of the country before nightfall; and it was at one time proposed to send a letter by them to young Walter Prevost, directing him to join his father at the Hall.

The inconveniences which so frequently ensue upon deranging plans already fixed caused this scheme to be rejected; and while her father, Lord H----, and their host, wandered forth for an hour or two along the banks of the beautiful Mohawk, Edith remained at the Hall, not without hope of seeing Otaitsa present herself with some intelligence.

The Indian girl, however, did not appear, and gloomy thoughts thronged fast upon poor Edith. She strove to banish them; she schooled herself in regard to the folly of anticipating evils only possible; but who ever mastered completely those internal warnings of coming peril or woe which as often come to cloud our brightest days, as to darken the gloom of an already tempestuous sky. Edith's chief companion was an old lady, nearly related to Sir William, but very deaf and very silent; and she had but small relief in conversation.

In the meantime, the three gentlemen and a young *aide-de-camp* pursued their way amongst the neat farmhouses and mechanics' shops which had gathered round the Hall. Mr. Prevost gave way to thoughts apparently as gloomy as those which haunted his daughter, but in reality not so; for his was a mind of a discursive character, which was easily led by collateral ideas far away from any course which it was at first pursuing; and, though he had awoke that morning full of the considerations which had engaged him during the preceding day, he was now busily calculating the results of the meeting which had just been held, and arriving at conclusions more just than were reached by many of the great statesmen and politicians of the time.

Lord H----, on his part, paid no little attention to the demeanour and all the proceedings of their host. The character of his mind was the exact reverse of that of Mr. Prevost, attaching itself keenly to one object, and being turned from its contemplation with difficulty. His thoughts still dwelt upon the consequences which were likely to ensue from the death of the Oneida by the hands of Captain Brooks, without anything like alarm, indeed, but with careful forethought for those who, in a few short days, had won for themselves a greater share of the warm affections which lay hidden in his heart than he often bestowed upon any one.

As they quitted the door of the house, a mere trifle called his attention to something peculiar in the conduct of Sir William Johnson, and led him to believe that the mind of that officer was not altogether at ease, notwithstanding the favourable result of the meeting with the Indians.

After they had taken a step or two on their way, Sir William paused suddenly, turned back, and ordered a servant to run up to the top of the hill, and there watch till he returned.

"Mark well which paths they take," he said, without specifying the persons of whom he spoke, "and let me hear if you see anything peculiar."

The man seemed to understand him perfectly; and Lord H---- watched everything with the utmost attention. In the course of their ramble, not less than nine or ten persons came up at different times, and spoke a word or two to Sir William Johnson. First a negro, then a soldier, then an Irish servant, then another white man, but with features of a strongly-marked Indian character. Each seemed to give some information in a few words uttered in a low tone, and each departed as soon as he had spoken, some with a brief answer, some with none.

The evening which succeeded their walk passed somewhat differently from the preceding one. Fewer persons were present; the conversation was more general and intimate, and Sir William Johnson, seating Edith at the old-fashioned instrument which, in those days, supplied the lack of pianofortes, asked for a song which, it seems, he had heard her sing before. She complied without any hesitation, with sufficient skill and management of her voice to show that she had been well taught, but with tones so rich, so pure, and so melodious, that every sound in the room was instantly hushed, and Lord H---- approached nearer and nearer to listen.

Music, I suppose, may be considered as the highest language--the language of the heart and spirit. Mere words can only reach or convey a very limited class of ideas, the distinct and the tangible; but music can convey the fine, the indistinct, the intangible shades of feeling and of thought which escape all other means of expression. It is only, however, to those who understand the language; but Lord H---- was full, not only of the love, but of the science of music; and he drew closer and closer to Edith, as she sang, and, at length, hung over her, with his face turned away from the other guests in the room, and bearing, written on it, feelings which he hardly yet knew were in his heart.

Sir William Johnson was standing on the other side of the beautiful girl's chair; and, as she concluded one of the stanzas, he raised his eyes suddenly to the face of Lord H----, with a look of great satisfaction. What he saw there made him start, and then smile, for the characters written on the nobleman's countenance were too plain to be mistaken, and Sir William, who was not without his share of worldly wisdom, at once divined that Edith Prevost was likely to be a peeress of England.

"What a fine musician she is!" exclaimed the older general to Lord H----, after he had conducted Edith to her former seat, but before the enthusiasm had subsided; "one would hardly expect to find such music in these wild woods of America."

"She is all music," said Lord H----, in an absent tone, and then added, rousing himself, "but you must not attribute such powers and such perfections, altogether, to America, Sir William, for I find that Miss Prevost was educated in Europe."

"Only till she was fourteen," replied the other; "but they are altogether a most remarkable family. If ever girl was perfect, it is herself. Her father, though somewhat too much given to dream, is a man of singular powers of mind; and her brother Walter, whom I look upon almost as a son, is full of high and noble qualities and energies, which, if he lives, will certainly lead him on to greatness."

"I think so," returned Lord H----. And there the conversation dropped for the time.

The rest of the evening passed without any incident of notice; and by daybreak on the following morning the whole household were on foot. An early breakfast was ready for the travellers, and nothing betrayed much anxiety on the part of their host, till the very moment of their departure. As they were about to set forth, however, and just when Edith appeared in her riding-habit, or Amazon, as it was then called, and the hat, with large floating ostrich plumes, usually worn at that time by ladies when on horseback--looking lovely enough, it is true, to justify any compliment--Sir William took her by the hand, saying, with a gay and courteous air,--

"I am going to give you a commission, my fair Hippolyta, which is neither more nor less than the command of half-a-dozen dragoons, whom I wish to go with you for a portion of the way, partly to exercise their horses on a road, which is marvellously cleared of stumps and stones, for this part of the country, partly to examine what is going on a little to the north-east, and partly to bring me the pleasant intelligence that you have gone, at least half way to your home in safety."

Lord H---- looked in his face in silence, and Edith turned a little pale, but said nothing. Mr. Prevost, however, went directly to the point, saying, "You know of some danger, my good friend; you had better inform us of all the particulars, in order that we may be upon our guard."

"None whatever, Prevost," answered Sir William, "except the general perils of inhabiting an advanced spot on the frontiers of a savage people, especially when anything has occurred to offend them. You know what we talked about yesterday morning. The Oneidas do not easily forgive; and, in this case, they will not forgive. But I have every reason to believe that they have taken their way homeward for the present. My people traced them a good way to the west, and it is only from some chance stragglers that there is any danger."

Mr. Prevost mused, without moving to the door, which was opened for them to depart, and then said, in a meditating kind of tone, "I do not think they will attack any large party, Sir William, even when satisfied that they cannot get hold of the man who has incensed them. These Indians are a very cunning people, and they often satisfy even their notions of honour by an artifice, especially when two duties, as they consider them, are in opposition to one another. Depend upon it, after what passed yesterday, they will commit no act of national hostility against England. They are pledged to us, and will not break their pledge. They will attack no large party, nor slay any Englishman in open strife, though they may kidnap some solitary individual, and, according to their curious notions of atonement, make him a formal sacrifice, in expiation of the blood shed by another."

"You know the Indians well, Prevost," said Sir William Johnson, gravely; "marvellously well, considering the short time you have been amongst them."

"I have had little else to do than to study them," responded the other, "and the subject is one of great interest. But do you think I am wrong in the view I take, my good friend?"

"Quite the contrary," replied Sir William, "and that is the reason I send the soldiers with you. A party of eight or ten will be perfectly secure; and I would certainly advise that, for the next two or three months, or till this unlucky dog, Brooks, or Woodchuck as he is called, has been captured, no one should go any distance from his home singly. Such a party as yours might be large enough. I am not sure that my lord's red coat, which I am happy to see he has got on to-day, might not be sufficient protection; for they will not risk anything which they themselves deem an act of hostility against the English government. Still, the soldiers will make the matter more secure till you have passed the spot where there is any chance of their being found. I repeat, I know of no peril; but I would fain guard against all, where a fair lady is concerned." And he bowed gracefully to Edith.

Little more was said; and taking leave of their host, Mr. Prevost's party mounted their horses, and set out, followed by a corporal's guard of dragoons, a small body of which corps was then stationed in the province of New York, although, from the nature of the country in which hostilities had hitherto been carried on, small opportunity had as yet been afforded them of showing their powers against an enemy. Nor would there have been any very favourable opportunity for so doing in the present instance, even had Mr. Prevost and his companions been attacked; for though the road they had to travel was broad and open, compared to an ordinary Indian trail, yet, except at one or two points, it was hemmed in with impervious forests, where the action of cavalry would be quite impossible, and under the screen of which a skilful marksman might bring down his man, himself unperceived.

Sir William Johnson was nevertheless sincere in saying that he believed the very sight of the English soldiers would be quite sufficient protection. The Indians, he knew right well, would avoid anything like a struggle or a contest, and would more especially take care not to come into collision of any kind with the troops of their British allies. It was likely that they would depend entirely upon cunning to obtain a victim wherewith to appease their vengeance; but on this probability he did not choose altogether to rely. He saw his friends depart, however, with perfect confidence, as the soldiers went with them; and they proceeded without seeing a single human being after they quitted his settlement, till they reached the shores of the small lake near which they had halted on their previous journey, and where they again dismounted to take refreshment.

It was a very pleasant spot, and well fitted for a resting-place; nor was repose altogether needless, though the distance already travelled was not great either for man or horse. But the day was exceedingly oppressive, like one of those which come in what is called the Indian summer, when the weather, after many a frosty day, becomes suddenly sultry, as if in the middle of June, and the air is loaded with thin yellow vapour, well deserving the term of "smoky," usually given to it on the western side of the Atlantic. Yet there was no want of air; the wind blew from the south-east, but there was no freshness on the breeze. It was like the Sirocco, taking away strength and firmness from all it breathed upon; and the horses, after being freed from the burden they bore, stood for several minutes with bent heads and heaving sides, without attempting to crop the forest grass beneath the trees.

Thus repose was sweet, and the look of the little lake was cool and refreshing. The travellers lingered there somewhat after the hour at which they had proposed to depart, and it was the negro who took care of the luggage who first warned them of the waning of the day.

"Massa forget," he said, "sun go early to bed in October. Twelve mile to go yet, and road wuss nor dis."

"True, true," replied Mr. Prevost, rising. "We had better go on, my lord, for it is now past two, and we shall barely reach home by daylight. I really think, corporal," he continued, turning to the non-commissioned officer, who had been seated with his men hard by, enjoying some of the good things of life, "that we need not trouble you to go farther. There is no trace of any Indians, or indeed of any human beings, in the forest, but ourselves. Had there been so, my good friend Chundo, here, would have discovered it, for he knows their tracks as well as any of their own people."

"Dat I do, massa," replied the negro, to whom he pointed. "No Ingin pass dis road since yesterday, I swear."

"My orders were to go to the big blazed Basswood-tree, sir, four miles farther," observed the soldier, in a firm but respectful tone, "and I must obey orders."

"You are right," said Lord H----, pleased with the man's demeanour. "What is your name, corporal?"

"Clithero, my lord," replied the man, with a military salute--"Corporal Clithero."

Lord H---- bowed his head; and the party, remounting, pursued their way. The road, however, as the negro had said, was more difficult in advance than it had been nearer to Sir William Johnson's settlement, and it took the whole party an hour to reach the great Basswood-tree, which had been mentioned, and which was marked out from the rest of the forest by three large marks upon the bark, hewn by some surveyor's axe when the road had been laid out. There the party stopped for a moment or two, and with a few words of thanks, Mr. Prevost and his companions parted from their escort.

"How dim the air along the path is!" ejaculated Lord H----, looking on; "and yet the sun, getting to the west, is shining right down it through the valley. One could almost imagine it was filled with smoke."

"This is what we call a smoky day in America," replied Mr. Prevost; "but I never knew the Indian summer come on us with such a wind."

No more was said on that matter at the time; and, as the road grew narrower, Mr. Prevost and the negro, as best acquainted with the way, rode first, while Lord H---- followed by Edith's side, conversing with her in quiet and easy tones; but with words which sometimes caused the colour to vary a little in her cheek.

These words were not exactly words of love. Write them down, and they might have very little meaning--less application; but all things have such a harmony throughout the universe, that everything separated from its accessories means nothing, or worse than nothing. His tones, I have said, were low and easy; but they were tender, too. His words were not words of love, but they had a fire in them that nothing but love could give; and the contrast between the low, easy tone, and that rich, glowing language, added all that was needful to give them the meaning of the heart, rather than the meaning of dictionaries. He spoke of her singing the night before, and of music in general; he spoke of the beauties of the scenery, the tints of the landscape; he spoke of the old world and the new, and society and solitude. But it mattered not; whatever he spoke of, he thought of Edith Prevost, and there was something that showed her he did so.

Thus they went on for some four miles farther; and the evening was evidently closing round them rapidly, though no ray had yet passed from the sky. Suddenly Mr. Prevost drew in his rein, saying, in a low but distinct voice to the negro, "What is that crossing the road?"

"No Ingin," cried the negro, whose eyes had been constantly bent forward.

"Surely there is smoke drifting across the path," said Mr. Prevost, "and I think I smell it also."

"I have thought so for some time," said Lord H----, who was now close to them with Edith. "Are fires common in these woods?"

"Not very," answered Mr. Prevost, "but the season has been unusually dry. Good heavens! I hope my fears are not prophetic: I've been thinking all day of what would become of the Lodge if the forest were to take fire."

"We had better ride on as fast as possible," said the nobleman; "for then, if the worst happens, we may be able to save some of your property."

"We must be cautious, we must be cautious," returned the other in a thoughtful tone. "Fire is a capricious element, and often runs in directions the least expected. I have heard of people getting so entangled in a burning wood as not to be able to escape."

"O yes," cried the negro; "when I were little boy, I remember quite well, Massa John Bostock, and five other men wid him, git in pine wood behind Albany, and it catch fire. He run here and dere, but it git all round him, and roast him up black as I be. I saw dem bring in what dey fancied was he, but it no better dan a great pine stump."

"If I remember," observed Lord H----, "we passed a high hill somewhere near this spot where we had a fine clear view over the whole of the woody region round. We had better make for that at once. The fire cannot yet have reached it, if my remembrance of the distance is correct; for though the wind sets towards us, the smoke is as yet anything but dense. It may be miles off, even beyond your house."

"Pray God it be so!" ejaculated Mr. Prevost, spurring forward; "but I fear it is nearer."

The rest followed as quickly as the stumps and the fallen trees would let them; and at the distance of half a mile began the ascent of the hill to which Lord H---- had alluded. As far as that spot the smoke had been growing denser and denser every moment; apparently pouring along the valley formed by that hill and another on the left, through which valley, let it be remarked, the small river in which Walter had been seen fishing by Sir William Johnson, but now a broad and very shallow stream, took its course onwards toward the Mohawk. As they began to ascend, however, the smoke decreased, and Edith exclaimed, joyfully,--

"I hope, dear father, the fire is farther to the north."

"We shall see, we shall see," said Mr. Prevost, still pushing his horse forward. "The sun is going down fast; and a little haste will be better on all accounts."

In about five minutes more the summit of the hill was reached, at a spot where, in laying out two roads which crossed each other there, the surveyors had cleared away a considerable portion of the wood, leaving, as Lord H---- had said, a clear view over the greater part of the undulating forest country, lying in the angle formed by the upper Hudson and the Mohawk. Towns have now risen up; villages are scattered over the face of the land; rich fields of wheat and maize, gardens, orchards, and peaceful farmhouses, greet the eye wherever it is turned from the summit of that hill; but it was different then. With the few exceptions of a small pond or lake, a rushing stream, or a natural savanna of a few hundred acres, it was all forest; and the only sign of man's habitation which could be descried at any time was the roof and chimneys of Mr. Prevost's house, which, in general, could be discerned rising above the trees, upon an eminence a good deal lower than the summit which the travellers had reached. Now, however, the house could not be seen.

The sight which the country presented was a fine but a terrible one. On the one side, the sun, with his lower limb just dipped beneath the forest, was casting up floods of many-coloured light, orange and purple, gold, and even green, upon the light fantastic clouds scattered over the western sky; while above, some fleecy vapours, fleeting quickly along, were all rosy with the touch of his beams.

Onward to the east and north, filling up the whole valley between the hill on which they stood, and the eminence crowned by Mr. Prevost's house, and forming an almost semi-circular line, of some three or four miles in extent, was a dense, reddish-brown cloud of smoke, marking where the fire raged, and softening off at each extreme into a bluish grey. No general flame could be perceived through this heavy cloud; but, ever and anon, a sudden flash would break across it, not bright and vivid, but dull and half obscured, when the fierce element got hold of some of the drier and more combustible materials of the forest. Once or twice, too, suddenly, at one point of the line or another, a single tree, taller, perhaps, than the rest, or more inflammable, or garmented in a. thick matting of dry vine, would catch the flame, and burst forth from the root to the topmost branch like a tall column of fire; and here and there, too, from what cause I know not--perhaps, from an accumulation of dry grass and withered leaves, seized upon by the fire and wind together--a volley of bright sparks would mingle with the cloud of smoke, and be thrown up, for a moment, to the westward.

It was a grand, but an awful, spectacle; and, as Mr. Prevost gazed upon it, thoughts and feelings crowded into his bosom, which even Edith herself could not estimate.

CHAPTER XV

"Look, look, Prevost!" cried Lord H----, after they had gazed during one or two minutes in silence; "the wind is drifting away the smoke; I can see the top of your house; it is safe as yet--and will be safe," he added, "for the wind sets somewhat away from it."

"Not enough," said Mr. Prevost, in a dull, gloomy tone. "The slightest change, and it is gone. The house I care not for; the barns, the crops, are nothing. They can be replaced, or I could do without them; but there are things within that house, my lord, I cannot do without."

"Do you not think we can reach it?" asked Lord H----. "If we were to push our horses into the stream, we might follow its course up, as it seems broad and shallow, and the trees recede from the banks. Are there any deep spots in its course?"

"None, massa," replied the negro.

"Let us try, at all events," exclaimed Lord H----, turning his horse's head; "we can but come back again, if we find the heat and smoke too much for us."

"My daughter!" ejaculated Mr. Prevost, in a tone of deep, strong feeling; "my daughter, Lord H----!"

The young nobleman was silent. The stories he had heard that day, and many that he had heard before, of persons getting entangled in burning forests, and never being able to escape--which, while, in the first enthusiasm of the moment, he thought only of himself and of Mr. Prevost, had seemed to him but visions, wild chimeras--assumed a terrible reality, as soon as the name of Edith was mentioned; and he would have shuddered to see the proposal adopted, which he had made only the moment before. He was silent, then; and Mr. Prevost was the first who spoke.

"I must go," he said, with gloomy earnestness, after some brief consideration--"I must go, let what will betide."

He relapsed into silence again, and there was a terrible struggle within his bosom, which the reader cannot, even in part, comprehend, without having withdrawn for him that dark curtain which shades the inmost secrets of the heart from the cold eyes of the unobservant world. He had to choose whether he would risk the sacrifice of many things dearer to him than life itself, or go through that fiery gulf before him--whether he would take that daughter, far dearer than life, with him, exposing her to all the peril that he feared not for himself, the scorching flame, the suffocating smoke, the falling timber--or whether he should leave her behind him, to find her way in darkness, and through a forest perhaps tenanted by enemies, to a small farmhouse, seven or eight miles off, where resided some kind and friendly people, who would give her care and good attendance. Then came the question--for the former was soon decided--whom he should leave with her. Some one was needed with himself, for, in the many, many perils that environed his short path, he could hardly hope to force his way alone, unaided. Lord H---- might have been his most serviceable companion in one view; for his courage, his boldness, his habits of prompt decision, and his clearness of observation, were already well and publicly known.

But then, to leave Edith alone in that dark night, in that wild wood, with nothing but a negro for her guide; a man shrewd and clear-witted, keen and active enough, yet with few moral checks upon his passions, few restraints of education or honour, and still fewer of religion and the fear of God. It was not to be thought of. In Lord H---- he felt certain he could trust. He knew that, in scenes as dangerous to the spirit as any he could go through would be to the body, he had come out unfallen, unwounded, untouched. He had the reputation and the bearing of a man of honour and a gentleman; and Mr. Prevost felt that the man must be base, indeed--low, degraded, vile, who, with such a trust as Edith on his conscience, could waver even in thought.

Such considerations pressed upon him heavily--they could not be disposed of by rapid decision; and he remained for two or three minutes profoundly silent. Then, turning suddenly to Lord H----, he said,--

"My lord, I am going to entrust to you the dearest thing I have on earth, my daughter--to place her under the safeguard of your honour--to rely for her protection and defence upon your chivalry. As an English nobleman, of high name and fame, I do trust you without a doubt. I must make my way through that fire by some means--I must save some papers, and two pictures, which I value more than my own life. I will take my good friend Chando here with me. I must leave you to conduct Edith to a place of safety."

"Oh, my father!" cried Edith; but he continued to speak without heeding her.

"If you follow that road," he continued, pointing to the one which led southward, "you will come, at the distance of about seven miles, to a good-sized farmhouse on the left of the road. Edith knows it, and can show you the way up to it. The men are most likely out, watching the progress of the fire; but you will find the women within; and good and friendly they are, though homely and uneducated. I have no time to stop for further directions. Edith, my child, God bless you! Do not cloud our parting with a doubt of Heaven's protection. Should anything occur--and be it as He wills--you and Walter will find at the lawyer's at Albany all papers referring to this small farm, and to the little we still have in England. God bless you, my child, God bless you!"

Thus saying, he turned and rode fast down the hill, beckoning the negro to follow him.

"Oh, my father, my father!" cried Edith, dropping her rein and clasping her hands together, longing to follow, yet unwilling to disobey. "He will be lost--I fear he will be lost!"

"I trust not," said Lord H----, in a firm, calm tone, well fitted to inspire hope and confidence. "He knows the country well, and can take advantage of every turning to avoid the flame. Besides, if you look along what I imagine to be the course of the stream, you will see a deep undulation, as it were, in that sea of smoke, and, when the wind blows strongly, it is almost clear. He said, too, that the banks continued free from trees."

"As far as the bridge and the rapids near our house," replied Edith; "after that, they are thickly wooded."

"But the fire has evidently not reached that spot," observed the young nobleman; "all the ground within half a mile of the house is free at present. I saw it quite distinctly a moment ago, and the wind is setting this way."

"Then can we not follow him?" asked his fair companion imploringly.

"To what purpose?" returned Lord H----; "and besides," he added, "let me call to your mind the answer of the good soldier, Corporal Clithero, just now. He said he must obey orders, and he was right. A soldier to his commander; a child to a parent; a Christian to his God, have, I think, but one duty--to obey. Come, Edith, let us follow the directions we have received. The sun is already beneath the forest edge; we can do no good gazing here; and although I do not think there is any danger, and believe you will be quite safe under my protection, yet, for many reasons, I could wish to place you beneath the shelter of a roof and in the society of other women as soon as may be."

"Thank you much," she answered, gazing up into his face, on which the lingering light in the west cast a warm glow; "you remind me of my duty, and strengthen me to follow it. I have no fear of any danger, with you to protect me, my lord--it was for my father only I feared. But it was wrong to do so even for him. God will protect us all, I do hope and believe. We must take this way, my lord." And with a deep sigh she turned her horse's head upon the path which her father had pointed out.

There is no situation in which good feeling shows itself more brightly than in combat with good feeling. It may seem a paradox; but it is not so. Lord H---- did not at that moment like to hear Edith Prevost call him by his formal title. He would fain have had her give him some less ceremonious name. Nay, more, he would have gladly poured into her ear, at that moment of grief and anxiety, the tale of love which had more than once during their ride been springing to his lips, and which he fondly fancied, with man's usual misappreciation of woman's sensitiveness, might give her support and comfort--for by this time he felt sure that, if he rightly appreciated her, she was not indifferent towards him. But he remembered that she was there a young girl, left alone with him, at night, in a wild forest--a precious trust to his honour and his delicacy; and he struggled hard and manfully to govern every feeling, and regulate every word. What if a degree of growing tenderness modulated his tone?--what if the words "Miss Prevost," were uttered as if they should have been "Edith?"--what if the familiar expression of "my dear young lady," sounded almost as if it had been, "dear girl?" We must not look too closely, or judge too hardly. There was but enough tenderness to comfort, and not alarm--just sufficient familiarity to make her feel that she was with a friend, and not a stranger.

No general subject of conversation could, of course, be acceptable at that moment; only one topic had they to discuss. And yet Lord H---- made more of that than some men would have made of a thousand. He comforted, he consoled; he raised up hope and expectation. His words were full of promise; and from everything he wrung some illustration to support and cheer.

If he had appeared amiable in the eyes of Edith, in the quiet intercourse of calm and peaceful hours, much more so did he appear to her now, when the circumstances in which she was placed called forth all that was kind and feeling in his heart, naturally gentle, though it had been somewhat steeled by having to struggle and to act with cold and heartless men in scenes of peril and of strife.

A few moments after they left the summit of the hill, and began the more gentle descent which stretched away to the south-east, the last rays of the sun were withdrawn, and night succeeded; but it was the bright and sparkling night of the American sky. There was no moon, indeed; but the stars burst forth in multitudes over the firmament, larger, more brilliant, than they are ever beheld even in the clearest European atmosphere, and they gave light enough to enable the two travellers to see their path. The wind still blew strongly, and carried the smoke away; and the road was wide enough to show the starry canopy overhanging the trees.

Lord H---- lifted his hand, and, pointing to one peculiarly large orb which glittered not far from the zenith, said in a grave but confident tone, "The God who made that great, magnificent world, and who equally created the smallest emmet that runs along our path--who willed into being innumerable planetary systems with their varied motions, and perfected the marvellous organization of the most minute insect, must be a God of love and mercy, as well as of power; and is still, I do believe, acting in mercy in all that befalls us here on earth."

"I believe and trust so too," answered Edith; "yet there are times and seasons when, in our blindness, we cannot see the working of the merciful, in the mighty hand, and the heart sinks with terror for want of its support. Surely there can be no sin in this. Our Divine Master, himself, when in our mortal nature, on the cross, exclaimed, in the darkest hour, '*My God, my God, why hast thou forsaken me!*'"

Obliged to go very slowly, but little progress had been made in an hour, and, by the end of that time, a strong odour of the burning wood and a pungent feeling in the eyes showed that some portion of the smoke was reaching them.

"I fear the wind has changed," said Edith; "the smoke seems coming this way."

"The better for your father's house, dear lady," answered Lord H----. "It was a change to the westward he had to fear; the more fully east, the better."

They fell into silence again; but in a minute or two after, looking to the left of the road, where the trees were very closely set, though there was an immense mass of brushwood underneath, Lord H---- beheld a small solitary spot of light, like a lamp burning. It was seen and hidden, seen and hidden again, by the trees as they rode on, and must have been at about three or four hundred yards' distance. It seemed to change its place, too; to shift, to quiver; and then, in a long winding line, it crept slowly round and round the boll of a tree, like a fiery serpent, and, a moment after, with flash, and crackling flame, and fitful blaze, it spread flickering over the dry branches of a pitch-pine.

"The fire is coming nearer, dear Miss Prevost," said Lord H----, "and it is necessary we should use some forethought. How far, think you, this farmhouse is now?"

"Nearly four miles," answered Edith.

"Does it lie due south?" asked her companion.

"Very nearly," she replied.

"Is there any road to the westward?" demanded the young nobleman, with his eyes still fixed upon the distant flame.

"Yes," she answered; "about half a mile on, there is a tolerable path made along the side of the hill, on the west, to avoid the swamp during wet weather, but it rejoins this road a mile or so farther on."

"Let us make haste," said Lord H---- abruptly; "the road seems fair enough just here, and I fear there is no time to lose."

He put his hand upon Edith's rein as he spoke, to guide the horse on, and rode forward, perhaps somewhat less than a quarter of a mile, watching with an eager eye the increasing light to the east, where it was now seen glimmering through the trees in every direction, looking through the fretted trellis-work of branches, trunks, and leaves, like a multitude of red lamps hung up in the forest. Suddenly, at a spot where there was an open space or streak, as it was called, running through some two or three hundred yards of the wood, covered densely with brush, but destitute of tall trees, the whole mass of the fire appeared to view; and the travellers seemed gazing into the mouth of a furnace. Just then, the wind shifted a little more, and blew down the streak: the cloud of smoke rolled forward; flash after flash burst forth along the line as the fire caught the withered leaves on the top of the bushes: then the bushes themselves were seized upon by the fire, and sent flaming far up into the air.

Onward rushed the destroying light, with a roar, and a crackle, and a hiss--caught the taller trees on either aide, and poured across the road right in front.

Edith's horse, unaccustomed to such a sight, started and pulled vehemently back; but Lord H----, catching her riding-whip from her hand, struck him sharply on the flank, and forced him forward by the rein. But again the beast resisted.

Not a moment was to be lost; time wasted in the struggle must have been fatal; and casting the bridle free, he threw his right arm round her light form, lifted her from the saddle and seated her safely before him. Then striking his spurs into the sides of his well-trained charger, he dashed at full speed, through the burning bushes, and in two minutes had gained the ground beyond the fire.

"You are saved, dear Edith," he said,--"you are saved!"

He could not call her Miss Prevost then; and, though she heard the name he gave her, at that moment of gratitude and thanksgiving it sounded only sweetly on her ear.

I have not paused to tell what were Edith's thoughts and feelings when she first saw the fire hemming them in. They were such as the feelings of any young and timid woman might be at the prospect of immediate and terrible destruction.

As always happens, when any of the stern events of Fate place before us an apparent certainty of speedy death--when the dark gates between the two valleys seem to be reached, and opened to let us pass--when the flood, or the fire, or the precipitous descent, or any other sudden casualty, seems ready to hurry us in an instant into eternity, without dimming the sight of the mind, or withering the powers of reason and of memory, as in the slow progress of sickness or decay--as always happens, I say, in such cases, Edith's mind passed rapidly, like a swallow on the wing, over every event of her past existence; and thoughts, feelings, hopes, joys, griefs, cares, expectations, regrets, rose one after the other to the eye, presented with the clearness and intensity which will probably appertain in a future state to all the things done in the flesh. Every memory, too, as it rose before her, seemed to say, in a sad and solemn tone, "We are gone for ever!"

It is terrible to part with life--with all its joys, ay, and even with its cares--at the bright season of hope and happiness; to have the blossom broken off the bough of life, before the fruit can form or ripen; and Edith felt it as much as any one could feel it. But it is only necessary to allude to her feelings, in order to contrast them with the joy and gratitude she felt when the moment of peril had passed away.

"Thank God, thank God!" exclaimed Edith; "and oh, my lord, how can I ever show my gratitude to you?"

Lord H---- was silent for a moment, and then said, in a low tone--for it *would* be spoken:--

"Dear Edith, I have no claim to gratitude; but if you can give me love instead, the gratitude shall be yours for life. But I am wrong, very wrong, for speaking to you thus, at this moment, and in these circumstances. Yet there are emotions which force themselves into words, whether we will or not. Forget those I have spoken, and do not tremble so, for they shall not be repeated till I find a fitter occasion--and then they shall immediately. Now, dear Edith, I will ride slowly on with you to this farmhouse; will leave you there with the good people; and, if possible, get somebody to guide me round another way, to join your father, and assure him of your safety. That he is safe, I feel confident; for this very change of wind must have driven the fire away from him. Would you rather walk? for I am afraid you have an uneasy seat, and we are quite safe now; the flames all go another way."

From many motives, Edith preferred to go on foot, and Lord H---- suffered her to slip gently to the ground. Then, dismounting himself, he drew her arm through his, and, leading his horse by the bridle, proceeded along the road over the shoulder of the hill, leaving the lower-road, which the flame still menaced, on their left.

Edith needed support, and their progress was slow, but Lord H---- touched no more upon any subject that could agitate her, and at the end of about an hour and a half, they reached the farmhouse, and knocked for admission.

There was no answer, however; no dogs barked; no sounds were heard; and all was dark within. Lord H---- knocked again. Still all was silent; and, putting his hand upon the latch, he opened the door.

"The house seems deserted," he said. Then, raising his voice, he called loudly to wake any slumbering inhabitant who might be within.

Still no answer was returned; and he felt puzzled, and more agitated . than he would have been in the presence of any real danger. No other place of shelter was near; he could not leave Edith there, as he had proposed; yet the thought of passing a long night with her in that deserted house produced a feeling of indecision, chequered by many emotions which were not usual to him.

"This is most unlucky!" he ejaculated. "What is to be done now?"

"I know not," replied Edith, in a low and distressed tone. "I fear, indeed, the good people are gone. If the moon would but rise, we might see what is really in the house."

"I can soon get a light," rejoined Lord H----; "there is wood enough scattered about to light a fire. Stay here in the doorway, while I fasten my horse, and gather some sticks together. I will not go out of sight."

The sticks were soon gathered, and carried into the large kitchen into which the door opened directly. Lord H----'s pistols, which he took from the holsters, afforded the means of lighting a cheerful fire on the hearth; and, as soon as it blazed up, a number of objects were seen in the room, which showed that the house had been inhabited lately, and abandoned suddenly. Nothing seemed to have been carried away, indeed; and amongst the first things that were perceived, much to Edith's comfort, were candles, and a tin lamp of Dutch manufacture, ready trimmed. These were soon lighted; and Lord H----, taking his fair companion's hand in his, and gazing fondly on her pale and weary face, begged her to seek some repose.

"I cannot, of course," he said, "leave you here, and join your father, as I proposed just now; but, if you will go upstairs, and seek some room, where you can lock yourself in, in case of danger, I will keep guard here below. Most likely, all the people of the house have gone forth to watch the progress of the fire and may return speedily."

Edith mused, and shook her head, saying,--

"I think something else must have frightened them away."

"Would you have courage to fire a pistol in case of need?" asked Lord H----, in a low tone.

Edith gently inclined her head, and he then added,--

"Stay, I will charge this for you again."

He then reloaded the pistol, the charge of which he had drawn to light the fire, and was placing it in Edith's hand, when a tall, dark figure glided into the room with a step perfectly noiseless. Lord H---- drew her suddenly back, and placed himself before her; but a second glance showed him the dignified form and fine features of Otaitsa's father.

"Peace!" exclaimed the old chief. "Peace to you, my brother!"

And he held out his hand to Lord H----, who took it frankly. Black Eagle then unfastened the blue blanket from his shoulders, and threw it round Edith, saying,--

"Thou art my daughter, and art safe. I have heard the voice of the cataract, and its sound was sweet. It is a great water, and a good. The counsel is wise, my daughter. Go thou up, and rest in peace. The Black Eagle will

The Black Eagle | 115

watch by the cataract till the eyes of morning open in the east. The Black Eagle will watch for thee, as for his own young; and thou art safe."

"I know I am when thou art near, my father," said Edith, taking his brown hand in hers; "but is it so with all mine?"

"If I can make it so," answered Black Eagle. "Go, daughter, and be at peace. This one, at least, is safe also; for he is a great chief of our white fathers, and we have a treaty with him. The man of the Five Nations who would lift his hand against him is accursed."

Edith knew that she could extract nothing more from him, and, her mind somewhat lightened, but not wholly relieved, she ascended to the upper story. Lord H---- seated himself on the step at the foot of the stairs; and the Indian chief crouched down beside him. But both kept a profound silence; and, in a few minutes after, the moon, slowly rising over the piece of cleared ground in front, poured in upon their two figures as they sat there, side by side, in strange contrast.

CHAPTER XVI

There was the fate of another connected with the events of that night, of whom some notice must be taken, from the influence which his destiny exercised over the destinies of all. With greater promptness and celerity than had been expected from him, even by those who knew him best, Walter Prevost had executed the business entrusted to him, and was ready to set out from Albany, a full day, at least, before his return had been expected by his family. Fortune had favoured him, it is true. He had found the commander-in-chief in the city, and at leisure. A man of a prompt and active mind had readily appreciated the promptitude and activity of the lad; and his business had been despatched as readily as circumstances permitted.

A boat sailing up the Hudson with some stores and goods for traffic was found to convey him a considerable way on his journey; and he was landing at a point on the western bank of the river, some seventeen miles from his father's house, at the very moment that Mr. Prevost, Lord H----, and Edith, were mounting by the side of the little lake to pursue their journey.

The way before him was rough and uneven, and the path somewhat intricate; but he thought he knew it sufficiently to make his way by it, before sunset, to a better known part of the country, and he hurried on with youthful confidence and vigour. His rifle in his hand, his knapsack on his shoulder, and a good large hunting-knife in his belt, with great agility of limbs and no small portion of bodily vigour, he would have proved no contemptible opponent in the presence of any single enemy. But he never thought of enemies; and all in his bosom was courage, and joy, and expectation.

Whatever great cities, and camps, and courts might have offered, Albany, at least, a small provincial capital, filled with a staid and somewhat rigid people, and only enlivened by the presence of a regiment or two of soldiers, had no attraction for him; and he was heartily glad to escape from it again, to the free life around his paternal dwelling, and to the society of his father and Edith--and Otaitsa.

Steadily he went along, climbed the hills, strode along the plain, and forded the river. The traces of cultivation soon became fewer, and then ceased; and, following resolutely the path before him, two hours passed before he halted, even to look around. Then, however, he paused for a minute or two to consider his onward course.

Two or three Indian trails crossed at the spot where he stood, one of them so deeply indented in the ground as to show that its frequent use existed from a very ancient date. Its course seemed to lie in the direction in which he wanted to go, and he thought he remembered having followed it some months before. Across it ran the settlers' way, broader and better marked out, but not very direct to his father's house; and he was hesitating which he should take, when the sound of creaking wheels, and the common cry used by ploughmen and teamsters to their cattle, showed him that some one was coming, who was likely to give him better information. That information seemed the more necessary, as the day was already far on the decline; and he had not yet reached a spot of which he could be certain.

A moment or two after, coming up the lane in the wood, as we should call it in England, appeared a heavy ox-waggon, drawn by four stout steers, and loaded with three women and a number of boxes; while by the side of the rude vehicle appeared three men on foot, and one on horseback, each very well armed, together with no less than five dogs of different descriptions.

Walter instantly recognised in the horseman the farmer who lived some ten miles to the south-west of his father's house. The farmer was a good-humoured, kindly-hearted man, honest enough, but somewhat selfish in his way; always wishing to have the best of a bargain, if it could be obtained without absolute *roguery*, yet willing enough to share the fruits of his labour or his cunning with any one who might be in need.

On the present occasion, however, he was either sullen or stupid; and it was indeed clear that both he and his male companions had been drinking quite enough to dull the edge of intellect in some degree. Those on foot went on, without even stopping the oxen to speak with their young neighbour; and the farmer himself only paused, for a moment or two, to answer Walter's questions.

"Why, Mr. Whitter," said the young gentleman, "you seem to be moving with all your family."

"Ay, ay," answered the farmer, a look of dull cunning rising to his face. "I don't like the look of things. I've had a hint. I guess there are other places better than the forest just now--though not so warm, mayhap."

"Why, what is the matter?" asked Walter; "has anything happened?"

"Oh no," answered the farmer, looking uncomfortable, and giving his bridle a little sort of jerk, as if he wished to pass on. "The forest's too full of Ingians for my notion; but as you and your father are so fond of them and they of you, there's no harm will come to you, I guess."

His manner was almost uncivil; and Walter moved out of his way without even asking the question he had intended. The man passed on; but suddenly he seemed to think better of the matter, and turning round in the saddle called out, in a voice much louder than necessary considering the distance between them--

"I say, Master Walter, if you're going home, you'd better take that deep trail to the right, I guess. It's shorter and safer; and them red devils, or some other vermin, have set fire to the wood on there. It's not much of a thing just yet, but there's no knowing how it will spread. However, if you keep to the west, you'll get on. I'm going to more civilized parts for a month or two, seeing I have got all my crops in safe."

As soon as these words were uttered, he turned and rode after his waggon; and Walter at once took the Indian trail which the other had mentioned. About half a mile farther on, for the first time, he perceived the smell of smoke; and as soon as he reached the summit of another hill beyond, the whole scene of the conflagration was before his eyes. Between the spot where he stood and his father's house stretched a broad belt of fire and smoke, extending a full mile to the north farther than he had expected from the vague account of the farmer; and the cloud of brownish vapour had rolled so far up the opposite slope, that the lad could neither see the dwelling itself, nor distinguish what spot the fire had actually reached.

Ignorant of the absence of his father and sister, and well aware how rapidly the flame extended when once kindled in a wood after a long season of dry weather, Walter's heart sank as he gazed. But he lost no time in useless hesitation. The sun was already setting, the distance was still considerable, and he resolved to break through that fiery circle, if it were possible, and reach his home at once.

Onward he plunged, then down the side of the hill; and the moment he descended the whole scene was shut out from his sight so completely that, but for the strong and increasing smell of burning pinewood, and a feeling of unnatural warmth, he would have had no intimation that a fire was raging close at hand. As he came nearer and nearer, however, a certain rushing sound met his ear, something like that of a heavy gale of wind sweeping the forest, and the smoke became suffocating; while through the branches and stems of the trees a red light shone, especially towards the south and west, showing where the fire raged with the greatest fierceness.

Breathing thick and fast, he hurried on, lighted by the flames alone, for the sun had sunk by this time, and the dense cloud of smoke which hung over this part of the wood shut out every star, till at length he reached the very verge of the conflagration. Some hundreds of acres lay before him, with trees, some fallen one over the other, some still standing, but deprived of foliage, and with masses of brushwood and long trailing parasites, all in fiery confusion and glowing with intense heat.

To proceed in that direction he felt was death. He could hardly breathe; his face seemed scorched and burning; and yet the drops of perspiration rolled heavily from his forehead. Retreating a little to escape the heat, he turned his steps northward; but by this time he had lost the trail, and was forcing his way through the brushwood, encumbered by his rifle and knapsack, when, suddenly, by the light of the fire shining through the trees, he saw a dark figure, some twenty or thirty yards before him, waving to him eagerly and apparently calling to him also. The roar and crackling of the burning wood were too loud for any other sounds to be heard, but the gestures of the figure seemed to direct him towards the south again, and obeying the signs, he soon found himself once more upon an Indian trail.

The next instant, the figure he had seen was upon the same path, and a little nearer. It was that of an Indian; but, in the smoky light, Walter Prevost could not distinguish the tribe or nation. He advanced cautiously, then, with his thumb upon the cock of the rifle; but, as soon as he was within hearing, the man called to him, in the Oneida tongue, and in a friendly tone, telling him to follow, and warning him that death lay to the westward.

Thrown off his guard by such signs of interest, the lad advanced with a quick step, and was soon close to his guide, though the man walked fast.

"Is the house burnt, brother?" asked the youth, eagerly.

"What, the lodge of the pale-face?" returned the Indian. "No--it stands fast."

"Thank God for that!" ejaculated Walter Prevost, in English.

But the words had hardly passed his lips, when he suddenly felt his arms seized; his rifle was wrested from his hands, and he himself cast backward on the ground. Two savage faces glared above him, and he expected to see the gleam of the deadly tomahawk the next instant.

"What now?" he exclaimed, in Oneida; "am I not your brother? Am I not the son of the Black Eagle--the friend of the children of the Stone?"

There was no answer; but in dead silence the Indians proceeded with rapid hands to bind his arms with thongs of deer-skin, and then, raising him on his feet, forced him to retread his steps along the very trail which had brought him thither.

CHAPTER XVII

Day broke slowly and heavily under a gray cloud, and found Lord H----
and the Indian chief still seated side by side at the entrance of the farmhouse.
A word or two had passed between them in the earlier part of the night;
but for many hours before dawn they had remained perfectly silent. Only
once, through the hours of their vigil, had the Black Eagle moved from his
seat, and that was nearly at midnight. The ears of Lord H---- had been upon
the watch, as well as his own; but, though the English nobleman heard no
sound, the chief caught a distant footfall about a quarter before twelve; and,
starting up, he listened attentively.

Then moving slowly towards the door, he stood there a few moments,
as still as a statue. Presently Lord H---- caught the sound which had moved
him, though it was exceedingly light; and the next instant another dusky
figure, not quite so tall as that of the chief, darkened the moonlight, and
threw its shadow into the doorway.

A few words then passed between the two Indians in their native
tongue, at first low and musical in tone, but then rising high in accents,
which seemed to the ear of the listener to express grief or anger. Not more
than five sentences were spoken on either part, and then the last comer
bounded away with a quick and seemingly reckless step into the forest;
and the old chief returned, and seated himself, assuming exactly the same
attitude as before.

When day dawned, however, Black Eagle rose, and said in English,--

"Now, my brother, let the voice of the Cataract awake the maiden, and I
will lead you on the way. Her horse has not yet come; but, if it have not run
with the wind or fed upon the fire, it will be here speedily."

"Do you know, then, what became of it after it broke away from us?"
asked Lord H----.

"Nay," answered the Indian, "I know not; but my steps were in yours,
from the setting sun till you came hither. I was there for your safety, my
brother, and for the safety of the maiden."

"We should often have been glad of your advice," observed Lord H----; "for we were sometimes in sore need of better information than our own."

"The man who aids himself needs no aid," answered Black Eagle. "Thou wert sufficient for the need; why should I take from thee the right to act?"

As they were speaking, the light step of Edith was heard upon the stairs; and the eyes of Black Eagle were fixed upon her, as she descended, with a look which seemed to Lord H---- to have some significance, though he could not tell exactly in what the peculiarity consisted. It was calm and grave; but there was a sort of tenderness in it, which, without knowing why, made the young nobleman fear that the Indian was aware of some evil having befallen Mr. Prevost.

His mind was soon relieved, however; for, when Edith had descended, the chief said at once,--

"Thy father is safe, my daughter. He passed through the fire uninjured, and is in his own lodge."

Edith looked pale and worn, but the words of the chief called a joyful smile upon her face and the colour back into her cheek. In answer to the inquiries of Lord H----, she admitted that she had slept hardly at all, and added, with a returning look of anxiety, "How could I sleep, so uncertain as I was of my father's safety?"

She expressed an anxious desire to go forward as soon as possible, and not to wait for the chance of her horse being caught by the Indians, which she readily comprehended as the meaning of the Black Eagle, when his somewhat ambiguous words were reported to her.

"They may catch him," she said, "or they may not; and my father will be very anxious, I know, till he sees me. I can walk quite well."

The Indian was standing silently at the door, to which he had turned after informing her of her father's safety; and Lord H----, taking her hand, inquired in a low tone if she would be afraid to stay alone with the Black Eagle for a few moments, while he sought for some food for herself and him.

"Not in the least," she answered. "After his words last night, and the throwing of his blanket round me, I am as safe with him as Otaitsa would be. From that moment he looked upon me as his daughter, and would treat me as such in any emergency."

"Well then, I will not be long," returned Lord H----; and, passing the Indian, he said, "I leave her to your care for a few moments, Black Eagle."

The Indian only answered by a sort of guttural sound, peculiar to his people; and then turning back into the house, he seated himself on the ground as before, and seemed inclined to remain in silence. But there were doubts in Edith's mind which she wished to have solved; and she said, "Is not my father thy brother, Black Eagle?"

"He is my brother," answered the Indian, laconically, and relapsed into silence.

"Will a great chief suffer any harm to happen to his brother?" asked Edith again, after considering for a few moments how to shape her question.

"No warrior of the Totem of the Tortoise dare raise a tomahawk against the brother of the Black Eagle," answered the chief.

"But is not Black Eagle the great chief of the Oneidas?" said Edith again. "Do not the people of the Stone hear his voice? Is he not to them as the rock on which their house is founded? Whither in the sky could the Oneidas soar if the Black Eagle led them not? And shall they disobey his voice?"

"The people of the Stone have their laws," replied the chief, "which are thongs of leather, to bind each Sachem, and each Totem, and each warrior. They were whispered into the roll of Wampum which is in the hand of the great medicine-man, or priest, as you would call him; and the voice of the Black Eagle, though it be strong in war, is as the song of the bobolink, when compared to the voice of the laws."

Short as this conversation may seem when written down, it had occupied several minutes; for the Indian had made long pauses; and Edith, willing to humour him by adopting the custom of his people, had followed his example.

His last reply was hardly given, when Lord H---- returned, carrying a dry and rather hard loaf, and a jug of clear, cold water.

"I have not been very successful," he said; "for the people have evidently abandoned the place, and all their cupboards but one are locked up. In that, however, I found this loaf."

"They are squirrels who fly along the boughs at the sound of danger, and leave their stores hidden," said the Black Eagle. "But dip the bread in water, my daughter; it will give you strength by the way."

Lord H---- laid the loaf down upon the table, and hurried out of the room again; but Edith had little opportunity of questioning her dusky companion further before the nobleman's return. He was absent hardly two minutes; and when he came back he led his horse behind him, somewhat differently accoutred from the preceding day. The demi-pique saddle was now covered with a pillow firmly strapped on with some leathern thongs which he had found in the house, thus forming it into a sort of pad; and the two stirrups brought to one side, stretched as far apart as possible, and somewhat shortened, were kept extended by a piece of plank passed through the irons, and firmly attached; thus presenting a comfortable rest for the feet of any one sitting sideways on the horse.

Lord H---- had done many a thing in life on which he might reasonably pride himself. He had resisted temptations to which most men would have yielded; he had done many a gallant and noble deed; he had displayed great powers of mind, and high qualities of heart in terrible emergencies and moments of great difficulty; but it may be questioned whether he had ever smiled so complacently on any act of his whole life as on the rapid and successful alteration of his own inconvenient saddle into a comfortable lady's pad; and when he brought out Edith to the door, and she saw how he had been engaged, she could not help rewarding him with a beaming smile, in which amusement had a less share than gratitude. Even over the dark countenance of the Indian, trained to stoical apathy, something flitted, not unlike a smile.

Lifting his fair charge in his arms, Lord H---- seated her lightly on the horse's back, adjusted the rest for her feet with care, and then took the bridle, to lead her on the way. The Indian chief, without a word, walked on before, at a pace with which the horse's swiftest walk could hardly keep up; and crossing the cleared land around the house, they were soon once more under the branches of the forest.

More than once the Black Eagle had to pause and lean upon his rifle, waiting for his two companions; but, doubtless, it was the difficulties of the narrow path, never made for horses' hoofs, and not the pleasure of prolonging conversation, and of gazing up, the while, into a pair of as beautiful eyes as ever shone upon mortal man, or into a face which might have looked out of heaven and not have shamed the sky, that retarded the nobleman on his way.

Six miles were at length accomplished; and then they came into the military high-road again, which led within a short distance of Mr. Prevost's cottage. During the whole journey, the Indian chief had not uttered a word; but as soon as he had issued forth from the narrow path into the more open road, he paused, and waited till Edith came up; then, pointing with his hand, he said--

"Thou knowest the way, my daughter; thou hast no more need of me; the Black Eagle must wing his way back to his own rock."

"But shall we be safe?" asked Edith.

"As in the happy hunting-grounds," replied the chief. And, turning away, he re-entered the trail by which they came.

Their pace was not much quicker than it had been in the more difficult path. The seal seemed to be taken from Lord H----'s lips. He felt that Edith was safe--nearer home, no longer left completely to his mercy and his delicacy, and his words were tender and full of strong affection; but she laid her hand gently upon his as it rested on the peak of the saddle, and with a face glowing as if the leaves of the autumn maples had cast a reflection from their crimson hues upon it, she said--

"Oh, not now, not now--for Heaven's sake spare me a little, still."

He gazed up in her face with a look of earnest inquiry; but he saw something there, either in the half-veiled swimming eyes, or in the glowing cheek, or the agitated quivering of the lip, which was enough to satisfy him.

"Forgive me," he said, in a deprecatory tone; but then, the moment after he added, with frank soldierly boldness, "Dear Edith, I may thank you now, and thank you with my whole heart; for I am not a confident fool, and you are no light coquette; and did you hesitate, you would say more."

Edith bent her head almost to the saddle-bow; and some bright drops rolled over her cheek. The companions remained silent, each communing with his and her own thoughts for a short time.

They were roused from somewhat agitated reveries by a loud and joyous call; and, looking up the ascent before them, they saw Mr. Prevost on horseback, and two of the negro slaves on foot, coming down as if to meet them. They hurried on fast. The father and daughter sprang to the ground; and oh, with what joy she felt herself in his arms!

It is a mistake to think that affection cannot be divided. Love is like the banyan tree, which increases its own volume by casting forth shoots in every direction; and each separate branch grows and strengthens by the other. At that moment--with her whole bosom thrilling with new emotions--with love for another acknowledged to her own soul--with the earnest looking forward to happiness with him,--oh, how much more strongly than ever she had felt it before, did Edith feel her love for her father! What relief, what comfort, what happiness, it was to her to find herself in those fond paternal arms!

It is unnecessary to give here the explanations that ensued. Mr. Prevost had little to tell. He had passed safely, though not without much danger and the scorching of his clothes and face, along the course of the stream, and through a small part of the thicker wood. He had found his house and all the buildings safe, and even the forest immediately around still free from the fire, and out of danger, as long as the wind remained easterly. Satisfied that his daughter would find the farmer's family, and be kindly entertained, he had felt no anxiety on her account, till about an hour before, when her horse had come back to the house with the saddle and housings scorched and blackened, and the hoofs nearly burnt off his feet. In great alarm for Edith, Mr. Prevost had set out to seek her in haste. Her tale was soon told; and again and again Mr. Prevost shook her protector's hand, thanking him earnestly for all he had done for his child.

The distance to the house was not now great; and, giving the horses to the negroes, the little party proceeded on foot, talking over the events of the last few hours. When they reached the house, there were somewhat obstreperous screams of joy from the women-servants, to see their young mistress return; and Edith was speedily carried away to her chamber for rest and refreshment. Breakfast was immediately prepared in the hall for Lord H----, who had tasted no food since the middle of the preceding day; but he ate little even now, and there was a sort of restlessness about him which Mr. Prevost remarked with some anxiety.

"My lord, you hardly taste your food," he said; "and either seem not well, or not well at ease. I trust you have no subject of grief or apprehension pressing on your mind?"

"None whatever," replied Lord H----, with a smile; "but, to tell you the truth, my dear sir, I am impatient for a few moments' conversation with you, alone; and I could well have spared my breakfast till they were over. Pray let us go into the other room, where we shall not be interrupted."

Mr. Prevost led the way, and closed the door after them, with a grave face; for, as is usual in such cases, he had not the faintest idea of what was coming.

"Our acquaintance has been very short, Mr. Prevost," said Lord H----, as soon as they were seated--feeling, indeed, more hesitation and embarrassment than he had imagined he could have experienced in such circumstances; "but I trust you have seen enough of me, taken together with what you may know by general repute, to make what I am going to say not very presumptuous."

Mr. Prevost gazed at him in perfect astonishment, unable to conceive where his speech would end; and, as the nobleman paused, he answered, "Pray speak on, my lord. Believe me, I have the highest esteem and regard for you. Your character and conduct through life have, I well know, added lustre to your rank: and noble blood has justified itself in you by noble actions. What on earth can you have to say which could make me think you presumptuous for a moment?"

"Simply this, and perhaps you *may* think me presumptuous when I have said it," replied Lord H----: "I am going to ask you to give me something, which I value very much, and which you rightly value as much as anything you possess. I mean your daughter. Nay, do not start, and turn so pale! I know all the importance of what I ask; but I have now passed many days entirely in her society,--I have gone through some difficulties and dangers with her, as you know--scenes and sensations which endear two persons to each other. I have been much in woman's society,--I have known the bright and the beautiful in many lands; perhaps my expectations have been too great--my wishes too exacting; but I never met woman hitherto who touched my heart. I have now found the only one whom I can love; and I ask her of you with a full consciousness of how much it is I ask."

Mr. Prevost had remained profoundly silent, with his eyes bent down, and his cheek, as Lord H---- had said, very pale. There was a great struggle in his heart, as there must be always in a parent's bosom in such circumstances.

"She is very young--so very young,--just seventeen!" he murmured, speaking to himself rather than to his companion.

"I may, indeed, be somewhat too old for her," said Lord H----, thoughtfully; "yet, I trust, in heart and spirit at least, Mr. Prevost, I have still all the freshness of youth about me."

"Oh, it is not that--it is not that at all," answered Edith's father; "it is that she is so very young to take upon herself both cares and duties. True, she is no ordinary girl, and perhaps if ever any one was fit at so early an age for the great responsibilities of such a state, it is Edith. Her education has been singular--unlike that of any other girl."

Mr. Prevost had wandered away, as was his custom, from the immediate question to collateral issues; and was no longer considering whether he should give his consent to Edith's marriage with Lord H----, but whether she was fit for the marriage state at all, and what effect the education she had received would have upon her conduct as a wife. The lover, in the mean time, habitually attaching himself and every thought to one important object, was impatient for something more definite; and he ventured to break across Mr. Prevost's spoken reverie, by saying--

"Our marriage would be necessarily delayed, Mr. Prevost, for some time, even if I obtain your consent. May I hope that it will be granted to me--if no personal objection exists towards myself?"

"None in the world!" exclaimed Mr. Prevost, eagerly "You cannot suppose it for a moment, my dear lord. All I can say is, that I will oppose nothing which Edith calmly and deliberately thinks is for her own happiness. What does she say herself?"

"She says nothing," answered Lord H----, with a smile; "for, though she cannot doubt what are my feelings towards her, she has not been put to the trial of giving any answer, without your expressed approbation. May I believe, then, that I have your permission to offer her my hand?"

"Beyond a doubt," replied Mr. Prevost. "Let me call her; her answer will soon be given, for she is not one to trifle with anybody."

He rose as he spoke, as if to quit the room; but Lord H---- stopped him, saying,--

"Not yet, not yet, my dear sir. She had little, if any, rest last night, and has had much fatigue and anxiety during the last twenty-four hours. Probably she is taking some repose, and I must not allow even a lover's impatience to deprive her of that."

"I had forgotten," said Mr. Prevost. "It is, indeed, true, that the dear child must need some repose. It is strange, my lord, how sorrows and joys blend themselves together in all events of mortal life. I had thought, when in years long ago I entwined my fingers in the glossy curls of my Edith's hair, and, looking through the liquid crystal of her eyes, seemed to see into the deep fountains of pure emotions in her young heart--I had thought, I say, that few joys would be equal to that of seeing her at some future day bestow her hand on a man worthy of her, to make and partake the happiness of a cheerful home. But now I find the thought has its bitter as well as sweet; and memories of the grave rise up, to cast a solemn shade over the bright picture fancy drew."

His tone dropped gradually as he spoke, and, fixing his eyes again upon the ground, he relapsed into absent thought.

Lord H---- would not disturb his friend's reverie, and, walking gently out of the room, he gave himself also up to meditation. But his reflective moods were of a different kind from those of his friend--more eager, more active; and they required some employment for the limbs, while the mind was so busy. To and fro he walked before the house, for nearly an hour, before Mr. Prevost came forth and joined him, and then the walk still continued; but the father's thoughts, though they had wandered for awhile, soon returned to his daughter, and their conversation was of Edith only.

At length, when it was nearly noon, as they turned upon the little open space of ground in front of the dwelling, the eyes of the nobleman, which had been turned more than once to the door, rested on Edith, as she stood in the hall and gazed forth over the prospect.

"The fire seems to be raging there still," she said, pointing with her fair hand over the country towards the south-west, where hung a dense canopy of smoke above the forest. "What a blessing one of our heavy autumnal rains would be!"

Lord H---- made no reply, but suddenly left her father's side, and, taking the extended hand in his, led her into the little sitting-room.

Shall we follow them thither, and listen to the words they spoke--shall we tear the veil from that young, innocent, gentle heart, and show, in the broad glare, the shy emotions only fitted to be seen by one eye beside that of God? Oh, no! They remained long together--to Mr. Prevost it seemed very long; but when Edith's lover led her to the door again, happy tears were once more in her eyes, glad blushes on her cheek; and, though the strong, manly arm was fondly thrown around her waist, she escaped from its warm clasp, and cast herself upon the bosom of her father.

"She is mine!" ejaculated Lord H----; "she is mine!"

"But none the less mine," answered Mr. Prevost kissing her cheek.

"Oh no," said Edith, "no! Always yours, my dear father--your child." And then she added, while the glowing blood rushed over her beautiful face, like the gush of morning over a white cloud, "*your* child, though his wife."

It cost her an effort to utter the word; yet she was pleased to speak it; but then, the moment after, as if to hide it from memory again, she said, "Oh, that dear Walter were here! He would be very happy, I know, and say I had come to the end of my day-dreaming."

"He will be here probably to-night," observed her lover.

"We must not count upon it," rejoined her father; "he may meet with many things to detain him. But now, my children, I will go in, and make up my journal, till the dinner hour."

Edith leaned fondly on his bosom, and whispered, "And write that this has been one happy day, my father."

Alas, alas! that the brightest sunshine and the softest sky should so often precede the day of storms! Alas, that the dark tempest-clouds should be so frequently gathering beneath the horizon all around us, when the sky above seems full of hope and promise! But so it is too often in this life. The old geographers' fancied figure of the earth was very like the earth on which human hopes are raised--a fair and even plain, with a yawning precipice all round it.

CHAPTER XVIII

The day went by; night fell; and Walter Prevost did not appear in his father's house. No alarm, however, was entertained; for, out of the wide range of chances, there were many events which might have occurred to detain him. A shade of anxiety, perhaps, came over Edith's mind; but it passed away the next morning, when she heard from the negro Chando, or Alexander (who, having been brought up amongst the Indians from his infancy, was better acquainted with their habits than any person in the house), that not a single red man had been in the neighbourhood since the preceding morning at eight o'clock.

"All gone west, missy," he said; "the last to go were old chief Black Eagle. I hear of him coming to help you, and I go out to see."

Edith asked no questions in regard to the sources of his information; for he was famous for finding out all that was going on in the neighbourhood, and, with a childlike vanity, making somewhat of a secret of the means by which he obtained intelligence; but she argued reasonably, though wrongly, that, as Walter was not to set out from Albany till about the same hour that the Indians left, he could not have fallen in with any of their parties.

Thus passed the morning, till about three o'clock; but then, when the lad did not appear, anxiety rose up, and became strong, as hour after hour went by, and he came mot. Each tried to sustain the hopes of the others; each argued against the apprehensions he himself entertained. Lord H---- pointed out that the Commander-in-Chief, to whom Walter had been sent, might be absent from Albany. Mr. Prevost suggested that the young man might have found no boat coming up the river; and Edith remembered that very often the boatmen were frightfully exorbitant in their charge for bringing any one on the way who seemed eager to proceed. Knowing her brother's character well, she thought it very likely that he would resist an attempt at imposition, even at the risk of delay. But still she was very, very anxious; and as night again fell, and the hour of repose arrived without his presence, tears gathered in her eyes, and trembled on the silken lashes.

The following morning dawned in heavy rain; a perfect deluge seemed descending from the sky. Still Lord H---- ordered his horse at an early hour, telling Edith and Mr. Prevost, in as quiet and easy a tone as he could assume, that he was going to Albany.

"Although I trust and believe," he said, "that my young friend Walter has been detained by some accidental circumstance, yet it will be satisfactory to us all to know what has become of him; and, moreover, it is absolutely necessary that I should have some communication as speedily as possible with the Commander-in-Chief. I think it likely that Walter may have followed him down the river, as he knows my anxiety for an immediate answer. I must do so too, if I find him still absent; but you shall hear from me when I reach Albany; and I will be back myself as soon as possible."

Edith gazed at him with a melancholy look, for she felt how much she needed, and how much more she might still need, the comfort of his presence; but she would not say a word to prevent his going.

The breakfast that day was a sad and gloomy meal. The lowering sky, the pouring rain, the thoughts that were in the hearts of all, banished everything like cheerfulness. Various orders were given for one of the servants to be ready to guide Lord H---- on his way, for ascertaining whether the little river were in flood, and other matters; and the course which Walter was likely to take on his return, was considered and discussed, in order that the nobleman might take the same road, and meet him, if possible; but this was the only conversation which took place.

Just as they were about to rise from table, however, a bustle was heard without, amongst the servants; and Mr. Prevost started up, exclaiming,--

"Here he is, I do believe!"

But the hope was dispelled the next instant; for a young man, in full military costume, but drenched with rain, was ushered into the room, and advanced towards Lord H----, saying, in a quiet, commonplace tone,--

"We arrived last night, my lord, and I thought it better to come up and report myself immediately, as the quarters are very insufficient, and we may expect a great deal of stormy weather, I am told."

Lord H---- looked at him gravely, as if he expected to hear something more; and then said, after a moment's pause,--

"I do not exactly understand you, Captain Hammond. You have arrived where?"

"Why, at the boatman's village on the point, my lord," replied the young officer, with a look of some surprise; "have you not received Lord Loudon's dispatch, in answer to your lordship's own letters?"

"No, sir," replied Lord H----; "but you had better come and confer with me in another room."

"Oh, George, let us hear all," exclaimed Edith, laying her hand upon his arm, and divining his motives at once; "if there be no professional reason for secrecy, let us hear all."

"Well," said Lord H----, gravely, "pray, Captain Hammond, when were his lordship's letters dispatched, and by whom?"

"By the young gentleman you sent, my lord," replied Captain Hammond; "and he left Albany two days ago, early in the morning. He was a fine gentlemanly young fellow, who won us all, and I went down to the boat with him myself."

Edith turned very pale, and Mr. Prevost inquired--

"Pray, has anything been heard of the boat since?"

"Yes, sir," answered the young officer, beginning to perceive the state of the case; "she returned to Albany the same night, and we came up in her yesterday, as far as we could. I made no inquiries after young Mr. Prevost, for I took it for granted he had arrived with the dispatches."

Lord H---- turned his eyes towards the face of Edith, and saw quite sufficient there to make him instantly draw a chair towards her, and seat her in it.

"Do not give way to apprehension," he said, "before we know more. The case is strange, undoubtedly, dear Edith; still the enigma may be solved in a happier way than you think."

Edith shook her head sadly, saying, in a low tone,--

"You do not know all, dear George--at least, I believe not. The Indians have received an offence they never forgive. They were wandering about here on the night we were caught by the fire, disappearing the next morning; and, some time during that night, my poor brother must have been--"

Tears broke off the sentence; but her lover eagerly caught at a few of her words to find some ground of hope for her--whatever he might fear himself.

"He may have been turned from his course by the burning forest," he said, "and have found a difficulty in retracing his way. The woods were still burning yesterday, and we cannot tell how far the fire may have extended. At all events, dearest Edith, we have gained some information to guide us. We can now trace poor Walter to the place where he disembarked, and that will narrow the ground we have to search. Take courage, love, and let us all trust in God."

"He says that Walter intended to disembark four miles south of the King's road," said Mr. Prevost, who had been talking earnestly to Captain Hammond. "Let us set out at once, and examine the ground between this place and that."

"I think not," remarked Lord H----, after a moment's thought. "I will ride down, as fast as possible, to the house, and gain what information I can there. Then, spreading a body of men to the westward, we will sweep all the trails up to this spot. You, and as many of your people as can be spared from the house, may come on to meet us, setting out in an hour; but, for Heaven's sake, do not leave this dear girl alone."

"I fear not--I fear not for myself," replied Edith; "only seek for Walter; obtain some news of him, and let us try to save him, if there be yet time to do so."

Covering her eyes with her handkerchief, which was wetted with her tears, Edith took no more part in what was going on, but gave herself up to bitter thought; and many and complex were the trains which it followed. Now a gleam of hope would rise up and cheer her for an instant into a belief that her lover's supposition might be correct, and that Walter might, indeed, have been cut off by the fire, and, not knowing which way it extended, might have taken a course leading far away from the house. With the hope, as ever, came the fear; and she asked herself,--

"Might he not have perished in the woods--perished of hunger--perished by the flame? But he was prompt, resolute, and accustomed, for some years, to the life of the woods. He had his rifle with him too, and was not likely to want food when that was in his hand."

But, prominent over all in darkness and dread, was the fear of Indian vengeance; and the more she thought of the probability of her brother having been entrapped by some party of the Oneidas, the more terrible grew her apprehensions, the more completely her hopes dwindled away. There were certainly Indians in the forest, she thought, at a time when Walter must have been there. With their quick sight and hearing, and their tenacity of pursuit, he was not likely to escape them; and, if once he fell into their hands, his fate seemed to her sealed. The protection promised to herself by the old chief, but not extended to her family, alarmed rather than re-assured her; and she saw nothing in Black Eagle's unwillingness to give any assurances of their safety, but a determination to take vengeance, even on those who were dear to him. As she recalled, too, all the particulars of the old chief's visit to that lonely farmhouse, and her interviews with him, an impression, at first faint, but growing stronger and stronger, took possession of her mind, that the chief knew of her brother's capture before he parted from her.

These thoughts did not indeed present themselves in regular succession, but came all confused and whirling through her mind; while the only thing in the gloomy crowd of fancies and considerations to which she could fix a hope, was the cool deliberation with which the Indians pursued any scheme of vengeance, and the slow and systematic manner with which they carried their purposes into execution.

While Edith remained plunged in these gloomy reveries, an active but not less sad consultation was going on at the other side of the room, which ended in the adoption of the plan proposed by Lord H----, very slightly modified by the suggestions of Mr. Prevost. An orderly, whom Captain Hammond had brought with him, was left at the house, as a sort of guard to Edith, it being believed that the sight of his red coat would act as an intimation to any Indians who might be in the woods that the family was under the protection of the British government.

Lord H----and the young officer set off together for the boatmen's village, whence Walter had departed for Albany, and where a small party of English soldiers were now posted, intending to obtain all the aid they could, and sweep along the forest till they came to the verge of the recent fire, leaving sentinels on the different trails, which, the reader must understand, were so numerous throughout the whole of what the Iroquois called their Long House, as often to be within hail of each other.

Advancing steadily along these small pathways, Lord H---- calculated that he could reconnoitre the whole distance between the greater river and the fire with sufficient closeness to prevent any numerous party of Indians passing unseen, at least till he met with the advancing party of Mr. Prevost, who were to search the country thoroughly for some distance round the house, and then to proceed steadily forward in a reverse course to that of the nobleman and his men.

No time was lost by Lord H---- and Captain Hammond on the road, the path they took being, for a considerable distance, the same by which Lord H---- had first arrived at Mr. Prevost's house, and, for its whole length, the same which the captain had followed in the morning. It was somewhat longer, it is true, than the Indian trail by which Woodchuck had led them on his ill-starred expedition; but its width and better construction more than made up for the difference in distance; and the rain had not been falling long enough to affect its solidity to any great extent.

Thus, little more than an hour sufficed to bring the two officers to the spot where a company of Lord H----'s regiment was posted. The primary task--that of seeking some intelligence of Walter's first movements after landing--was more successful than might have been expected. A settler, who supplied the boatmen with meal and flour, was even then in the village; and he averred truly that he had seen young Mr. Prevost, and spoken with him, just as he was quitting the cultivated ground on the bank of the river, and entering the forest ground beyond. Thus, his course was traced up to a quarter before three o'clock on the Thursday preceding, and to the entrance of a government road, which all the boatmen knew well. The distance between that spot and Mr. Prevost's house was about fourteen miles, and from the boatmen's village to the mouth of the road through the forest some six or seven.

Besides the company of soldiers, numbering between seventy and eighty men, there were at least forty or fifty stout, able-bodied fellows amongst the boatmen, well acquainted with all the intricacies of the woods round about, and fearless and daring, from the constant perils and exertions of their mode of life. These were soon gathered round Lord H----, whose rank and military station they now learned for the first time; and he found that the tidings of the disappearance of Walter Prevost, whom most of them knew and loved, excited a spirit in them which he had little expected.

Addressing a few words to them at once, he offered a considerable reward to each man who would join in searching thoroughly the whole of that part of the forest which lay between the spot where the young man was last seen and his father's house. But one tall, stout man, about forty years of age, stepped forward, and spoke for the rest, saying--

"We want no reward for such work as that, my lord. I guess there's not a man of us who will not turn out to search for young Master Walter, if you'll but leave red coats enough with the old men to protect our wives and children in case of need."

"I cannot venture, for anything not exactly connected with the service," replied Lord H----, "to weaken the post by more than one quarter its number. Still we shall make up a sufficient party to search the woods adequately, if you will all go with me."

"That we will, that we will!" exclaimed a dozen voices.

Everything was soon arranged. Signals and modes of communication and co-operation were speedily agreed upon; and the practical knowledge of the boatmen proved fully as serviceable as the military science of Lord H----, who was far too wise not to avail himself of it to the fullest extent.

With about twenty regular soldiers, thirty-seven or thirty-eight men from the village, each armed with his invariable rifle and hatchet, and a number of good, big, active boys, who volunteered to act as a sort of runners, and keep up the communications between the different parts of the line, the nobleman set out upon his way along the edge of the forest, and reached the end of the government road, near which Walter had been last seen, about one o'clock in the day.

Here the men dispersed, the soldiers guided by the boatmen; and the forest ground was entered at about fourteen different places, wherever an old or a new trail could be discovered. Whenever an opportunity presented itself, by the absence of brushwood, or the old trees being wide or far apart, the boys ran across from one party to another, carrying information or directions; and, though each little group was often hidden from the other, as they advanced steadily onwards, still it rarely happened that many minutes elapsed without their catching a sight of some friendly party, on the right or left, while whoop and hallo marked their progress to each other. Once or twice, the trails crossing, brought two parties to the same spot; but then, separating again immediately, they sought each a new path, and proceeded as before.

Few traces of any kind could be discovered on the ground; for the rain, though it had now ceased, had so completely washed the face of the earth, that every print of shoe or moccasin was obliterated. The tracks of cart-wheels, indeed, seemingly recent, and the foot-marks of a horse and some men were discovered along the government road; but nothing more, till at a spot where a large and deeply-indented trail left the highway, the ground appeared a good deal trampled by hoof-marks, as if a horse had been standing there for some little time; and under a thick hemlock-tree, at the corner of the trail, sheltering the ground beneath from the rain, the print of a well-made shoe was visible. The step had evidently been turned in the direction of Mr. Prevost's house; and up that trail Lord H---- himself proceeded, with a soldier and two of the boatmen. No further step could be traced, however; but the boatman, who had been the spokesman a little while before, insisted upon it that they must be on young Master Walter's track.

"A New York shoe," he said, "made that print, I'm sure; and depend upon it we are right where he went. Keep a sharp look under all the thick trees at the side, my lord. You may catch another track. Keep behind, boys--you'll brush 'em out."

Nothing more was found, however, though the man afterwards thought he had discovered the print of a moccasin in the sand, where it had been partly protected. But some rain had reached it, and there was no certainty.

The trail they were then following was, I have said, large and deeply worn, so that the little party of Lord H---- soon got somewhat in advance of all the others, except that which had continued on the government road.

"Stay a bit, my lord," said the boatman, at length; "we are too far ahead, and might chance to get a shot, if there be any of them red devils in the wood. I know them well, and all their ways, I guess, having been among them, man and boy, this thirty years; and it was much worse when I first came. They'll lie as close to you as that bush, and the first thing you'll know of it will be a ball whizzing into you. If, however, we all go on in line, they can't keep back, but will creep away like mice. What I can't understand is, why they should try to hurt young Master Walter; for they were all as fond of him as if he were one of themselves."

"The fact is, my good friend," replied Lord H----, in a low tone, "the day I came down to your landing last, one of the Oneidas was unfortunately killed, and we are told that they will have some white man's life in retaliation."

"To be sure they will!" rejoined the man, with a look of consternation. "They'll have blood for blood, if all of 'em die for't. But did Master Walter kill him?"

"No," replied Lord H----; "it was our friend the Woodchuck; but he did it entirely in self-defence."

"What, Brooks?" exclaimed the boatman, in much surprise. "Do let's hear about it, and I guess I can tell you how it will all go, better than any other man between this and Boston." And he seated himself on the slump of a tree, in an attitude of attention.

Very briefly, but with perfect clearness, Lord H---- related all that occurred on the occasion referred to. The boatman listened with evident anxiety, and then sat for a moment in silence, with the air of a judge pondering over the merits of a case just pleaded before him.

"I'll tell you how it is, my lord," he said at length, in an oracular tone; "they've got him, depend on't. They've caught him here in the forest. But, you see, they'll not kill him yet--no, no; they'll wait. They've heard that Woodchuck has got away, and they've kidnapped young Walter to make sure of some one. But they'll stay to see if they can't get Brooks into their clutches somehow. They'll go dodgering about all manner o' ways, and try every trick you can think of to lure him back. Very like you may hear that they've killed the lad; but don't you believe it for a good many months to come. I guess it's likely they'll set that story afloat just to get Brooks to come back; for then he'll think that they've had all they wanted, and will know that he's safe from all but the father, or the brother, or the son of the man he killed. But they'll wait and see. Oh, they're the most cunningest set of critturs that ever dived, and no doubt of it! But let's get on, for the others are up--there's a red-coat through the trees there--and they may perhaps have scalped the boy, though I don't think it's nohow likely."

Thus saying, he rose, and led the way again through the dark glades of the wood, till the clearer light of day, shining amidst the trunks and branches on before, showed that the party was approaching the spot where the late conflagration had laid the shady monarchs of the forest low. Suddenly, at a spot where another trail crossed, the soldier who was with them stooped down and picked something up off the ground, saying--

"Here's a good large knife, anyhow."

"Let me see--let me see!" cried the boatman; "that's his knife, for a score of dollars. Ay! 'Warner, London,' that's the maker; it's Walter's knife. But that shows nothing--he might have dropped it; but he's come precious near the fire, he surely would never try to break through and get himself burnt to death. If the Ingians had got him, I should have thought they'd have caught him farther back. Hallo! what are they all a-doing on there? They've found the corpse, I guess."

The eyes of Lord H---- were bent forward in the same direction; and, though his lips uttered no sound, his mind had asked the same question and come to the same conclusion. Three negroes were standing gathered together round some object lying on the ground; and the figure of Mr. Prevost himself, partly seen, partly hidden by the slaves, appeared sitting on a fallen tree, with his head resting on his hand, contemplating fixedly the same object which seemed to engage all the attention of the negroes.

Lord H---- hurried his pace, and reached the spot in a few moments. He was somewhat relieved by what he saw when he came nearer; for the object at which Mr. Prevost was gazing so earnestly was Walter's knapsack, and not the dead body of his son. The straps which had fastened it to the lad's shoulders had been cut, not unbuckled; and it was, therefore, clear that it was not by his own voluntary act that it had been cast off. It did not appear, however, to have been opened; and the boatman, looking down on it, muttered--

"No, no! They would not steal anything--not they. That was not what they wanted. It's no use looking any farther. The case is clear enough."

"Too clear!" ejaculated Mr. Prevost, in a dull, stern tone. "That man, Brooks, has saved his own life, and sacrificed my poor boy."

The tears gushed into his eyes as he spoke; and he rose and turned away to hide them. Lord H---- motioned to the negroes to take up the knapsack, and carry it home; and then advancing to Mr. Prevost's side, he took his hand, saying, in a low tone--

"There may yet be hope, my dear sir. Let us not give way to despair; but exert ourselves instantly and strenuously to trace out the poor lad, and save him. Much may yet be done--the Government may interfere--Walter may be rescued by a sudden effort."

Mr. Prevost shook his head heavily, and murmuring, "Are *all* my family destined to perish by Indians?" took his way slowly back towards his house.

Nothing more was said till he was within a quarter of a mile of his own door; but then, just before emerging from the cover of the wood, the unhappy father stopped, and took the hand of Lord H----.

"Break it to her gently," he said, in a low tone: "I am unfit. Misfortunes, disappointments, and sorrows have broken the spirit which was once strong, and cast down the energies which used never to fail. It is in such moments as these that I feel how much I am weakened. Prepare her to leave this place, too. My pleasant solitude has become abhorrent to me, and I cannot live here without a dread and a memory always upon me. Go forward, my good lord: I will follow you soon."

CHAPTER XIX

With great pain Lord H---- contemplated the task before him; but his was a firm and resolute heart; and he strode forward quickly to accomplish it as soon as possible. Fancy painted, as he went, all the grief and anguish he was about to inflict upon Edith; but Fancy hardly did her justice--for it left out of the picture many of the stronger traits of her character.

The beautiful girl was watching from the window, and at once recognized her lover as he issued from the wood alone. Her heart sank with apprehension, it is true; nevertheless, she ran out along the little path to meet him, in order to know the worst at once.

Before they met, her father came forth from the wood, slowly and heavily, with a crowd of boatmen and soldiers following in groups of six or seven at a time. With wonderful accuracy she divined the greater part of what had occurred. She instantly stopped till Lord H---- came up, and then inquired, in a low and tremulous voice,--

"Have you found him? Is he dead or living?"

"We have not found *him*, dear Edith," said Lord H----, taking her hand, and leading her towards the house; "but your father conceives there is great cause for apprehension of the very worst kind, from what we *have* found. I trust, however, that his fears go beyond the reality, and that there is still----"

"Oh, dear George, do not keep me in suspense!" ejaculated Edith. "Let me hear all at once. My mind is sufficiently prepared by long hours of painful thought. I will show none of the weakness I displayed this morning. What is it you have found?"

"His knife and his knapsack," replied Lord H----.

"He may have cast his knapsack off from weariness," said Edith, still catching at a hope.

"I fear not," replied her lover, unwilling to encourage expectations to be disappointed. "The straps of the knapsack were cut, not unbuckled; and your father has given himself up entirely to despair, although we found no traces of strife or bloodshed."

"Poor Walter!" exclaimed Edith, with a deep sigh. But she shed no tears; and walked on in silence, till they had reached the little verandah of the house. Then suddenly she stopped, roused herself from her fit of thought, and said, raising her beautiful and tender eyes to her lover's face, "I have now two tasks before me, to which I must give myself up entirely--to console my poor father, and to try to save my brother's life. Forgive me, George, if, in executing these, especially the latter, I do not seem to give so much of my thoughts to you as you have a right to expect. You would not, I know, have me neglect either."

"God forbid!" exclaimed Lord H----, warmly; "but let me share in them, Edith. There is nothing within the scope of honour and of right that I will not do to save your brother. I sent him on this ill-starred errand: to gratify me was that unfortunate expedition made through the wood; but it is enough that he is your brother, and your father's son; and I will do anything--undertake anything--if there be still a hope. Go to your father first, my love, and then let us consult together. I will see these men attended to, for they want rest and food; and I must take liberties with your father's house to provide for them."

"Do, do," she answered; "use it as your own."

And, leaving him in the verandah, she turned to meet her father.

Edith well knew that, for a time, Mr. Prevost's mind was not likely to receive either hope or consolation. All she could give him was tenderness; and Lord H----, who followed her to speak with the soldiers and boatmen, soon saw her disappear into the house with Mr. Prevost.

When he returned to the little sitting-room, Edith was not there, but he heard a murmur of voices from the room above; and, in about half an hour, she rejoined him. She was much more agitated than when she had left him; and her face showed marks of tears: not that her fears were greater, or that she had heard anything to alarm her more; but her father's deep despair had overpowered her own firmness. All the weaker affections of human nature are infectious; fear, despondency, and sorrow, peculiarly so.

Edith still felt, however, the importance of decision and action; and, putting her hand to her head with a look of bewilderment, she stood, for an instant, in silence, with her eyes fixed on the ground, seemingly striving to collect her scattered thoughts, in order to judge and act with precision.

"One of the boatmen, Edith," said Lord H----, leading her to a seat, "has led me to believe that we shall have ample time for any efforts to save your brother, if he have, as there is too much reason to fear, fallen into the hands of these revengeful Indians. The man seems to know what he talks of well, and boasts that he has been accustomed to the ways and manners of the savages from boyhood."

"Is he a tall, handsome man, with two children?" asked Edith.

"He is a tall, good-looking man," answered Lord H----; "but his children I did not see."

"If he be the man I mean," answered Edith, "he can be fully depended upon; and it may be well to ask his opinion and advice before he goes. But, for the present, George, let us consult alone. Perhaps, I can judge better than you of poor Walter's present situation. That is first to be considered; and then what are the chances, what the means, of saving him. He is certainly in the hands of the Indians,--of that I have no doubt; and I think Black Eagle knew it when he guided us through the forest. Yet I do not think he will willingly lift the tomahawk against my brother--it will only be at the last extremity, when all means have failed of entrapping that unhappy man, Brooks. We shall have time--yes, we shall certainly have time."

"Then the first step to be taken," said Lord H----, "will be to induce the Government to make a formal and imperative demand for his release. I will undertake that part of the matter; it shall be done at once."

Edith shook her head sadly.

"You know them not," she said: "it would only hurry his fate." Then, dropping her voice to a very low tone, she added--"They would negotiate and hold councils; and Walter would be slain while they were treating."

She pressed her hands upon her eyes as she spoke, as if to shut out the fearful image her own words called up; and then there was a moment or two of silence, at the end of which Lord H---- inquired if it would not be better for him to see Sir William Johnson, and consult with him.

"That may be done," replied Edith. "No man in the province knows them so well as he does; and his advice may be relied upon. But we must take other measures too. Otaitsa must be told of Walter's danger, and consulted. Do you know, George," she added, with a melancholy smile, "I have lately been inclined to think, at times, that there is no small love between Walter and the Blossom--something more than friendship, at all events."

"But, of course, she will hear of his capture, and do her best to save him," rejoined the young nobleman.

Edith shook her head, answering, "Save him she will, if any human power can do it: but that she knows of his capture, I much doubt. These Indians are wise, George, in their own opinion; and never trust their acts, their thoughts, or their resolutions, to a woman. They will keep the secret from Otaitsa, just as Black Eagle kept it from me; but she must be informed, consulted, and perhaps acted with. Then I think, too, that poor man Woodchuck should have tidings of what his act has brought upon us."

"I see not well," said Lord H----, "what result that can produce."

"Nor I," answered Edith; "yet it ought to be done, in justice to ourselves and to him. He is bold, skilful, resolute; and we must not judge of any matter in this country as we should judge in Europe. He may undertake and execute something for my brother's rescue, which you and I would never dream of. He is just the man to do so, and to succeed. He knows every path of the forest, every lodge of the Indians, and is friendly with many of them; has saved the lives of some, I have heard him say, and conferred great obligations upon many; and I believe he will never rest till he has delivered Walter."

"Then I will find him out, and let him know the facts directly," said Lord H----. "Perhaps he and Otaitsa may act together, if we can open any communication with her."

"She will act by herself, and for herself, I am sure," replied Edith; "and some communication must be opened at any risk, and all risks. But let us see the boatman, George. Perhaps he may know some one going into the Indian territory, who may carry a letter to her. 'Tis a great blessing she can read and write; for we must have our secrets too, if we would frustrate theirs."

Lord H---- rose, and proceeded to the hall, where the men whom he had brought with him were busily engaged despatching such provisions as Mr. Prevost's house could afford on the spur of the moment. The boatman he sought was soon found. Following the young nobleman into the lesser room, he entered into full conference with Edith and her lover, and again expressed the opinion that no harm would happen to young Walter Prevost for several months at the least. "They have caught some one," he said, "to make sure of their revenge; and that is all they want for the present. Now they will look for the man himself who did it, and catch him, if they can."

"Can you tell where he is to be found?" asked Lord H---- in a quiet tone.

"Why, you would not give him up to them?" asked the man, sharply.

"Certainly not," replied Lord H----; "he is in safety, and of that safety I have no right to deprive him--it would make me an accessory to the act of the savages. But I wish to see him to tell him what has occurred, and to consult him as to what is to be done."

"That's a different case," observed the man, gravely; "and if that's all you want, I don't mind telling you that he is in Albany, at the public-house called 'The Three Boatmen.' Our people who rowed him down said he did not intend to leave Albany for a week or more."

"And now, Robert," said Edith, "can you tell me where I can get a messenger to the Oneidas? I know you loved my brother Walter well; and I think, if we can get somebody to go for me, we may save him."

"I did indeed love him well, Miss Prevost," replied the man, with his firm, hard eye moistened, "and I'd do anything in reason to save him. It's a sad pity we did not know of this yesterday; for a half-breed Onondagua runner passed by and got some milk from us; and I gave him the panther's skin which you, my lord, told some of our people to send in the poor lad's name to the daughter of the old chief, Black Eagle."

Edith turned her eyes to her lover's face, and Lord H---- replied to their inquiring look, saying--

"It is true, Edith, Walter shot a panther in the wood, and wished to send the skin to Otaitsa. We had no time to lose at the moment; but, as we came back, I induced the guides to skin it, and made them promise to dry and send it forward by the first occasion."

"I strapped it on the runner's back myself," said the man whom Edith called Robert, "and also gave him the money you sent for him, my lord. He would have taken any message readily enough, and one could have trusted him. But it may be months before such another chance offers, I guess. Look here, Miss Edith," he continued, turning towards her with a face full of earnest expression, "I would go myself, but what would come of it? They would only kill me instead of your brother; for one man's as good as another to them in such cases, and perhaps he might not get off either. But I've a wife and two young children, ma'am, and it makes me not quite so ready to risk my life as I was a few years ago."

"It is not to be thought of," said Edith, calmly. "I could ask no one to go; except one partly of their own race; for I know it must be the blood of a white man they spill. All I can desire you to do, for Walter's sake and mine, is to seek for one of the Indian runners, who are often about Albany, and about the army, and send him on to me."

"You see, Miss Prevost," replied the man, "there are not so many about as there used to be, for it is coming on winter; and, as to the army, when Lord Loudon took it to Halifax, almost all the runners and scouts were discharged. Some of them remained with Webb, it is true; but a number of those were killed and scalped by Montcalm's Hurons. However, I will make it my business to seek one, night and day, and send him up."

"Let it be some one on whom we can depend," said Edith; "some one whom you have tried and can trust."

"That makes it harder still," said the man; "for, though I have tried many of them, I can trust few of them. However, I will see, and not be long about it either. But it would be quite nonsense to send you a man who might either never do your errand at all, or go and tell your message to those you don't want to hear it."

"It would indeed," said Edith, sadly, as all the difficulties and risks which lay in the way of success were suggested to her by the man's words. "Well, do your best, Robert," she said, at length, after some thought; "and, as you will have to pay the man, here is money for----"

"You can pay him yourself, ma'am," replied the boatman, bluntly. "As for taking any myself for helping poor Master Walter, that's what I won't do. When I have got to take an oar in hand, or anything of that kind, I make the people pay fast enough what my work's worth--perhaps a little more sometimes," he added, with a laugh. "But not for such work as this--no, no, not for such work as this. So good-bye, Miss Prevost--good-bye, my lord. I won't let the grass grow under my feet in looking for a messenger."

Thus saying, he quitted the room; and Edith and Lord H---- were once more left alone together. Sad and gloomy was their conversation, unchequered by any of those bright beams of love and joy which Edith had fondly fancied were to light her future hours. All was dim and obscure in the distance; and the point upon which both their eyes were fixed most intently in the dark shadowy curtain of the coming time, was the murkiest and most obscure of all. Whatever plan was suggested, whatever course of action was thought of, difficulties rose up to surround it and perils presented themselves on all sides.

Nor did the presence of Mr. Prevost, who joined them soon after, tend, in any degree, to support or to direct. He had lost all hope, at least for the time; and the only thing which seemed to afford him a faint gleam of light was the thought of communicating immediately with Brooks.

"I fear Sir William Johnson will do nothing," he said. "He is so devoted even to the smallest interest of the Government, his whole mind is so occupied with this one purpose of cementing the alliance between Britain and the Five Nations, that, on my life, I believe he would suffer any man's son to be butchered, rather than risk offending an Indian tribe."

"In his position, it may be very difficult for him to act," said Lord H----; "but it might be as well to ascertain his feelings and his views, by asking his advice as to how you should act yourself. Counsel he will be very willing to give, I am sure; and, in the course of conversation, you might discover how much or how little you have to expect from his assistance."

"But you said, my dear lord, that you were yourself going to Albany to-morrow, to see poor Brooks," observed Mr. Prevost. "I cannot leave Edith here alone."

All three mused for a moment or two, and Edith, perhaps, deepest of all. At length, however, she said--

"I am quite safe, my father: of that I am certain; and you will be certain too, I am sure, when you remember what I told you of Black Eagle's conduct to me on that fatal night. He threw his blanket round me, and called me his daughter. Depend upon it, long ere this, the news that I am his adopted child has spread through all the tribes; and no one would dare to lift his hand against me."

"Still, some precaution," said Lord H----.

But Edith interrupted him gently, saying, "Stay, George, one moment. Let my father answer. Do you not think, dear father, that I am quite safe? In a word, do you not believe that I could go from lodge to lodge, as the adopted daughter of Black Eagle, throughout the whole length of the Long House of the Five Nations without the slightest risk or danger? and, if so, why should you fear?"

"I do indeed believe you could," replied Mr. Prevost. "Oh that we could have extracted such an act from the chief towards poor Walter. What Edith says is right, my lord: we must judge of these Indians as we know them; and my only fear in leaving her here now, arises from the risk of incursions from the other side of the Hudson."

Lord H---- mused a little. It struck him there was something strange in Edith's way of putting the question to her father--something too precise, too minute, to be called for by any of the words which had been spoken. It excited nothing like suspicion in his mind; for it was hardly possible to look into the face, or hear the tones, of Edith Prevost, and entertain distrust. But it made him doubt whether she had not some object, high and noble he was sure, but beyond the immediate point, which she did not think fit as yet to reveal.

"I was about to say," he replied at length to the last words of Mr. Prevost, "that I can easily move a guard up here sufficient to protect the house; and I need not tell you, my dear sir," he continued, taking Edith's hand, "that as the whole treasure of my happiness is here, I would not advise you to leave her for an hour unless I felt sure she would be safe. I will send down by some of the men, who are still in the house, an order to Captain Hammond to march a guard here as early as possible to-morrow morning, under a trustworthy sergeant. As soon as it arrives, I will set out for Albany; and I think you can go to Johnson's Castle in perfect security."

So it was arranged, and all parties felt no inconsiderable relief when some course of action was thus decided. Effort in this world is everything. Even the waters of joy will stagnate; and the greatest relief to care or sorrow, the strongest support in danger or adversity, is effort.

CHAPTER XX

The morning of the following day broke fresh and beautiful. A bright clearness was in the sky--a brisk elasticity in the air--that had not been seen or felt for weeks. Everything looked sparkling, and sharp, and distinct. Distances were diminished; woods and hills, which had looked dim, seemed near and definite; and the whole world appeared in harmony with energy and effort. The heavy rains of the preceding morning had cleared the overcharged atmosphere, as tears will sometimes relieve the loaded breast; and when Lord H---- and Mr. Prevost mounted their horses to set out, it seemed as if the invigorating air had restored to the latter the firmness and courage of which the grief and horror of the preceding day had deprived him.

Edith embraced her father, and gave her cheek to the warm touch of her lover's lips; and then she watched them as they rode away, till the wood shut them out from her sight.

The soldiers were by this time installed in the part of the house destined for them; and some of the negroes were busy in preparing for their accommodation; but old Agrippa, and the gardener's boy, and a woman-servant, stood near, watching their master and his guest as they departed.

As soon as the little party was out of sight, however, Edith turned to Agrippa, and said,--

"Send Chando to me in the parlour; I wish to speak with him."

When the man appeared, she gazed at him earnestly, saying,--

"How far is it to Oneida Creek, Chando? Have you ever been there?"

"Ah, yes, missa, often, when I was a little boy. Why, you know, my fadder run away and live with Ingins long time, 'cause he had bad master. But Ingins cut him and thump him more nor worst massa in de world, and so he come back again. How far be it? Oh, long way; twice so far as Johnson Castle, or more--oh yes, tree time so far."

Edith knew how vague a negro's ideas of distance are, and she then put her question in a form which would get her a more distinct answer.

"Bethink you, Chando," she said, "how long it would take me to reach the lake--how long it would take any one. Consider it well, and let me know."

"You, missy, you!" cried the negro, in great astonishment; "*you* never think of going there?"

"I don't know, Chando," she replied: "it might be needful; and I wish to know how long it would take."

"Dat 'pend upon how you go, missy," returned the man. "Ride so far as Johnson Castle; but can't ride no farder. Den walk as I walk? You never do dat; and, if you do, take you five day, and walk hard too."

Poor Edith's heart sank.

"Otaitsa walks," she said, in a desponding tone; "but, it is true, she can do much that I cannot do."

"*She* walk! Oh dee no, missy," replied the negro; "she walk little bit o' way from what dey call Wood Creek, or from de Mohawk. She walk no farder. All de rest she go in canoe, sometimes on Mohawk, sometimes on lake, sometimes on creek. She come here once in tree day. I hear old Grey Buzzard, de pipe-bearer, say dat, time when de Sachem came wid his warriors."

"And can I do the same?" asked Edith, eagerly.

"Sure you can, if you get canoe," answered Chando; "but oh, missy, tink ob de Ingins. Dey kidnap Massa Walter--dey kill you too."

"There is no fear, Chando," replied Edith. "Even my father owns that I could safely go from one lodge to another through the whole land of the Five Nations, because Black Eagle has put his blanket round me, and made me his daughter."

"Massa know best," said Chando; "but, if so, why dey kidnap Massa Walter?"

"Black Eagle refused to make him his son, or my father his brother," said Edith, with the tears rising in her eyes. "But the truth, Chando, is, that I go to try if I can save poor Walter's life--I go to tell the Blossom that they hold *my* Walter, *her* Walter, a prisoner, and see whether we cannot find means to rescue him."

"I see--I see, missy," said the man, gravely; and then, after pausing for a moment, he asked, abruptly, "I go with you?"

"Some one I must have to show me the way," replied Edith. "Are you afraid, Chando?"

"Afraid!" cried the man, bursting into a fit of joyous laughter. "Oh, no, not afraid: Ingins no hurt nigger--kick him, cuff him, no scalp him, cause nigger got no scalp-lock. Ha, ha, ha! I go help save Massa Walter. He never hab no good ting, but he give Chando some. Oh, I manage all for you. We find plenty canoe--Mohawk canoe--Oneida canoe--if we say you Black Eagle's daughter going to see you sister Otaitsa. When you go, missy?"

"Very soon, Chando," replied Edith.

She then proceeded to explain to him her plan still further. She said that she wished to set out that very day, and as soon as possible, in order first to communicate the tidings of Walter's capture to Otaitsa without delay, and secondly to save her father as many hours of anxiety as possible. She did not absolutely tell the man that she had not informed her father of her intention; but he divined it well.

Nevertheless, when he heard somewhat more at large the conduct of Black Eagle towards her on the night of poor Walter's capture, he was quite satisfied of her safety, as far as the Indians were concerned. He urged her, however, to go, in the first place, to Johnson Castle, where she could procure a canoe, or even a *bateau*, he felt certain; and it was long before he comprehended her objection to that course. At length, however, his usual "I see--I see," showed that he had caught a light; and then he was soon ready with his resources.

"Den we walk to de nearest end of little pond--only tree mile," he said; "fishing canoe all ready. Next we go down little pond, and de creek, into lake; keep by nort side, and den walk to Mohawk, tree mile more. I carry canoe cross on my back. Den, Ingin or no Ingin, we get along. If missy like to take oder nigger too, we get on very fast, and he carry bundle."

"I must have one of the women with me," said Edith, in a thoughtful tone; "but which?"

The negro's countenance fell a little. He was very proud of the confidence placed in him, and he did not like to share it with a white woman. His tone, then, was rather dejected, though submissive, when he asked,--

"Do missy take white woman Sally wid her? Sally no walk--Sally no run--Sally no paddle, when Chando is tired."

"No," replied Edith, at once. "I can take no white person with me, Chando, for it would risk her life; and, even to save my poor brother, I must not lure another into such peril. One of your colour, Chando, they will not hurt; for it is a white man's blood they will have for a white man's act."

"Then take Sister Bab!" cried Chando, rubbing his hands, with the peculiar low negro chuckle. "Sister Bab walk, run, carry bundle, and twirl paddle wid anybody."

Now, Bab was a stout negro woman of about forty years of age, with a pleasant countenance, and very fine white teeth, who rejoiced in the cognomen of sister, though, to the best of Edith's knowledge, she was sister to no one in the house, at least. Her usual occupations were in the farmyard, the dairy, and the pigsty; so that Edith had not seen very much of her. But all that she had seen was pleasant; for Sister Bab seemed continually on the watch to do everything for everybody, receiving all orders even from "Massa Walter," who was sometimes a little inconsiderate, with a broad, good-humoured grin. Her constant activity and indefatigable energy promised well for an undertaking such as that in which Edith was engaged.

"Well, Chando," said the young lady, "I do not know that I could make a better choice. Send Sister Bab to me; for where dangers such as these are to be encountered, I will not take any woman without her own free consent."

"Oh, she go; I talk wid her," said Chando; "you nebber trouble yourself, missy. She go to world's end wid Miss Edith, and fight like debbel, if dere be need. I nebber saw woman so good at catching fish; she'll hook 'em out like cabbages."

"That also may be useful to us," said Edith, with a faint smile. "But send her to me, Chando; I must speak with her before we go."

The good woman, when she came, made not the slightest objection; but, on the contrary, looked upon the expedition as something very amusing, which would give her relief from the tedium of her daily labours, and at the same time afford full occupation for her active spirit. She was as ready with suggestions as Chando; told Edith everything she had best take with her; detailed all her own proposed preparations, and even begged for a rifle, declaring that she was as good a shot as "Massa Walter," and had often fired his gun when he had brought it home undischarged.

Edith declined, however, to have a rifle-woman in her train; and having told her two chosen attendants that she would be ready in an hour, retired to make her preparations, and write a few lines to her father and her lover, to account for her absence when they returned. Both letters were brief; but we will only look at that which she left for Mr. Prevost.

"My dear father," she wrote, "I am half afraid I am doing wrong in taking the step I am about to take, without your knowledge or approbation; but I cannot sit still and do nothing, while all are exerting themselves to save my dear brother. I feel that it is absolutely necessary to any hope of his safety, that Otaitsa should be informed immediately of his situation.

"It may be months before any Indian runner is found, and meanwhile my poor brother's fate may be sealed. Were it to cost my life, I should think myself bound to go; but I am the only one who can go in perfect safety, for, while promising his protection to me, and insuring me against all danger, the Black Eagle refused to give any assurance in regard to others. You have yourself acknowledged, my dear father, that I shall be perfectly safe; and I have also the advantage of speaking the Indian language well. In these circumstances, would it not be wrong--would it not be criminal--in me to remain here idle, when I have even a chance of saving my poor brother? Forgive me, then, if I do wrong, on account of the motives which lead me.

"My course is straight to the Mohawk, by the little pond and the lake, and then up the Mohawk and Wood Creek, as far as they will carry me; for, wishing to save myself as much fatigue as possible, I shall venture to take the canoe from the pond.

"I have asked Chando and Sister Bab to accompany me, as I know you would wish me to have protection and assistance on the way, in case of any difficulty. I hope to be back in six days at the furthest; and, if possible, I will send a runner to inform you of my safe arrival amongst the Oneidas.

"Once more, my dear father, think of the great object I have in view, and forgive your affectionate daughter."

When her letters were written, Edith dressed herself in a full Indian costume, which had been given her by Otaitsa; and a beautiful Indian maiden she looked, though the skin was somewhat too fair, and the hair wanted the jetty black. In the Indian pouch, or wallet, she placed some articles of European convenience, and a hunter's large knife. Then making up a small package of clothes for Sister Bab to carry, she descended to the lower story.

Here, however, she met with some impediments which she had not expected. The news of her proposed expedition had spread through the whole household, and caused almost an open revolt. The white women were in tears; old Agrippa was clamorous; and the fat black cook declared loudly that Miss Edith was mad and should not go. So far, indeed, did she carry her opposition, that the young lady was obliged to assume a stern and severe tone, which was seldom heard in Edith's voice, and command her to retire at once from her presence. The poor woman was instantly overawed, for her courage was not very permanent, and, bursting into tears, she left the room, declaring she was sure she should never see Miss Edith again.

Edith then gave all the keys of the house to old Agrippa, with the two letters which she had written. Chando took up the bag of provisions which he had prepared; Sister Bab charged herself with the packet of clothes, and Edith, walking between them, turned away from her father's house, amidst the tears of the white women, and a vociferous burst of grief from the negroes.

Her own heart sank for a moment, and she asked herself,--

"Shall I ever pass that threshold again? Shall I ever be pressed hereafter in the arms of those I so much love?"

But she banished such feelings, and drove away such thoughts; and murmuring,--

"My brother--my poor brother!" she walked on.

CHAPTER XXI

Leaving Edith to pursue her way towards the Oneida territory, and Mr. Prevost, after parting with Lord H---- at the distance of two miles from his own house, to ride on to Johnson Castle, let us follow the nobleman to Albany, where he arrived somewhat after nightfall. His first duty, as he conceived it, led him to the quarters of the commander-in-chief, where he made a brief but clear report of all that had occurred in his transactions with the Indians.

"I found," he wrote, "from information communicated by Sir William Johnson, that there was no need of any concealment; but, on the contrary, that it would be rather advantageous to appear at the meeting with the Five Nations in my proper character. The results were what I have told you. There is one other point, however, which I think it necessary to mention, and which, if imprudently treated, might lead to serious results."

He then went on to state generally the facts in regard to the death of the Indian by the hands of Woodchuck, and the supposed capture of Walter Prevost by a party of the Oneidas.

It would be uninteresting to the reader to hear the particulars of the conversation which followed. Suffice it to say that the government of the colony, in all its departments, was very well disposed to inactivity at that time, and not at all inclined to exert itself for the protection of individuals, or even of greater interests, unless strongly pressed to do so. This Lord H---- was not at all inclined to do, as he was well aware, from all he had heard, that no action on the part of the government, short of the sudden march of a large body of troops, could effect the liberation of Walter Prevost, and that to expect such a movement, which itself might be unsuccessful, was quite out of the question with the officers who were in command at the time.

His conference with the commander-in-chief being ended, he declined an invitation to supper, and went out on his search for the small inn, where he had been told he would find the man whose act, however justifiable, had brought so much wretchedness upon Mr. Prevost's family.

The city of Albany in those days (as we have reason to know from very good authority), though not numbering, by many thousands, as large a population as it now contains, occupied a space nearly as large as the present city. One long street ran by the bank of the river, to the very verge of which beautiful and well-cultivated gardens extended; and from the top of the hill down to this lower street ran another, very nearly, if not exactly, of the same position and extent as the present State Street. On the summit of the hill was the fort; and, built in the centre of the large descending street, which swept round them on either side, were two or three churches, a handsome market-place, and a guard-house. A few other streets ran down the hill in a parallel line with this principal one; and some small streets, lanes, and alleys, connected them all together.

Nevertheless, the population, as I have said, was, comparatively, very small; for, between house and house and street and street, throughout the whole town, were large and beautiful gardens, filling up spaces now occupied by buildings, and thronged with human beings.

A great part of the population was, at that time, Dutch; and all the neatness and cleanliness of true Dutch houses and Dutch streets were to be seen in Albany in those days--would we could say as much at present! No pigs then ran in the streets, to the horror of the eye and the annoyance of the passenger; no cabbage-leaves or stalks disgraced the gutter; and the only place in which anything like filth or uncleanliness was to be seen, was at the extremity of the littoral street, where naturally the houses of the boatmen and others connected with the shipping were placed, for the sake of approximating to the water. Here certainly some degree of filth existed; and the air was perfumed with a high savour of tar and tobacco.

It was towards this part of the town that Lord H---- directed his course, inquiring for the inn called "The Three Boatmen." Several times, however, was he frustrated, in his attempt to obtain information, by the ignorance of the English language shown by a great portion of the inhabitants; and the pipe was removed from the mouth only to reply, in Dutch, "I do not understand."

At length, however, he was directed aright, and found a small and somewhat mean-looking house, in which an adventurous Englishman, from the purlieus of Clare-market, had established a tavern for the benefit of boatmen. It had, in former times, belonged to a Dutch settler, and still retained many of the characteristic features of its origin. Four trees stood in line before the doors, with benches underneath them, for the convenience of those who liked to sit and poison the sweet air of the summer evenings with the fumes of tobacco.

Entering through a swing-door into the narrow, sandy passage, which descended one step from the street, Lord H---- encountered a negro tapster with a white apron, of whom he inquired if Captain Brooks were still there.

"Oh yes, massa officer," said the man, with a grin. "You mean Massa Woodchuck," he continued, showing that the good man's Indian nick-name was very extensively known. "You find him in dere, in de coffee-room." And he pointed to a door, once white, now yellow and brown with smoke, age, and dirty fingers.

Lord H---- opened the door, and went in amongst as strange and unprepossessing an assemblage of human beings as it had ever been his chance to light upon. The air was rendered obscure by smoke, so that the candles looked dim and red, and it was literally difficult to distinguish the objects round. What the odour was, it is impossible to say, for it was as complicated as the antidote of Mithridates; but the predominant smells were certainly those of tobacco, beer, rum, and Hollands gin. Some ten or twelve little tables of exceedingly highly-polished mahogany, but stained here and there by the contaminating marks of wet glasses, divided the room amongst them, leaving just space between each two to place a couple of chairs back to back.

In this small den, not less than five or six and twenty persons were congregated, almost all drinking, almost all smoking, some talking very loud, some sitting in profound silence, as the quantity of liquor imbibed, or the national characteristics of the individual, might prompt.

Gazing through the haze upon this scene, which, besides the sturdy and coarse, but active, Englishman, and the heavy, phlegmatic Dutchman, contained one or two voluble Frenchmen, deserters from the Canadas, and none of them showing themselves in a very favourable light, Lord H---- could not help comparing the people before him with the free wild Indians he had lately left, and asking himself "Which are the savages?"

At length, his eye fell upon a man sitting at a table in the corner of the room next to the window. He was quite alone, with his back turned to the rest of the men in the place, his head leaning on his hand, and a short pipe laid down upon the table beside him. He had no light before him as most of the others had, and he might have seemed asleep, so still was his whole figure, had it not been that the fingers of his right hand, which rested on the table, beat time to an imaginary tune.

Approaching close to him, Lord H---- drew a seat to the table, and laid a hand upon his arm. Woodchuck looked round, and a momentary expression of pleasure, slight and passing away rapidly, crossed his rugged features.

The next moment, his face was all cold and stern again.

"Very kind of you to come and see me, my lord," he said, in a dull, sad tone. "What do you want with me? Have you got anything for me to do?"

"I am sorry to see you looking so melancholy, captain," said Lord H----, evading his question. "I hope nothing else has gone amiss."

"Haven't I cause enough to be melancholy," said the other, looking round at the people in the room, "cooped up with a penful of swine? Come out--come out to the door. It's cold enough there; but the coldest wind that ever blew is better than the filthy air of these pigs."

As he spoke, he rose; and a little, pert-looking Frenchman, who had overheard him, exclaimed, in a bantering tone, "Why you call us pigs more nor yourself, de great hog?"

"Get out of my way, for fear I break your back," muttered Woodchuck, in a low, stern voice. "If your neck had been broken long ago, it would have been better for your country and for mine." And taking up the little Frenchman by the nape of the neck with one arm, he set him upon the table from the side of which he had just risen.

A roar of laughter burst from a number of the assembled guests; the little Frenchman spluttered his wrath, without daring to carry the expression of his indignation further; and Woodchuck strode quietly out of the room, followed by his military visitor.

"Here--let us sit down here," he said, placing himself on a bench under a leafless tree, and leaving room for Lord H---- by his side. "I am gloomy enough, my lord, and haven't I reason to be so? Here I am for life. This is to be my condition, with the swine that gather up in these pigsties of cities--suffocating in such dens as we have just left. I guess I shall drown myself some day, when I am druv quite mad. I know a man has no right to lay hands upon himself. I larnt my Bible when I was young, and know what's God's will; so I shan't do anything desperate so long as I am right here." And he laid his finger on his forehead. "No, no, I'll just take as much care of my life," he continued, "as though it were a baby I was nursing; but, unless them Ingians catch some other white man, and kill him--which God forbid-- I've got to stop here for life; and even if they do, it's more nor a chance they'd kill me too, if they got me; and when I think of them beautiful woods, and the pleasant lakes, with the picture of everything round painted so beautiful on 'em, when they are still, and the streams that go dancing and splashing along over the big black stones and the little white pebbles, seeming for all the world to sing as if for pleasure at their freedom, and the open friendly air of the hill-side, and the clouds skimming along, and the birds glancing through the branches, and the squirrels skipping and chattering, as if they were mocking everything not so nimble as themselves, I do often believe I shall go crazed to think I shall never see those things again."

Lord H---- felt for him much; for he had a sufficient portion of love in his own heart for the wilder things of nature, to sympathize in some degree with one who loved them so earnestly.

"I trust, Woodchuck," he said, "that we shall be able to find some employment for you with the army--if not with my own corps, with some other, which may give you glimpses, at least, of the scenes you love so well, and of the unconfined life you have lived so long. But I have come to consult you upon a subject of much and immediate importance, and we must talk of that the first thing."

"What is it?" asked Brooks, in an indifferent tone, fixing his eyes upon the stones of the street, faintly lighted by the glare from within the house.

Lord H---- began his account of what had happened between the Mohawk and the Hudson, with some circumlocution; for he did not feel at all sure of the effect it would produce upon his companion's mind; and the Woodchuck seemed to fall into one of those deep reveries in which one may be said to hear without hearing. He took not the slightest notice of what his noble visitor said regarding the burning of the wood or the danger of Mr. Prevost and Edith. It seemed to produce no more distinct effect than would the wind whistling in his ears. He sat calm and silent without an observation; but he grew more attentive, though only in a slight degree, when the narrator came to mention the anxiety of the family at the protracted absence of Walter.

When, at last, Lord H---- described the finding of the knife and the knapsack, and told of the conclusions to which the whole family had come, he started up, exclaiming--"What's that--what's that?" Then, after a moment's pause, he sank down upon his seat again, saying, with a groan, "They have got him--they have got him, and they will tomahawk him--the bloody, barbarous critturs! Couldn't they have chosen some more worthless thing than that?"

Pressing his hand tightly upon his forehead, as if he fancied the turbulent thoughts within would burst it, he remained for a moment or two in silence, till Lord H---- asked if he imagined they would execute their bloody purposes speedily.

"No, no," cried the man; "no fear of that; they'll take time enough, that's the worst of the savages. It's no quick rage, no angry heat, with them; no word and a blow. It's cold, bitter, long-premeditated hatred. They wouldn't have half the pleasure if they didn't draw out their revenge by the week or the month. But what's to be done now? Gracious God! what's to be done now?"

"That is precisely what I came to consult you upon," said Lord H----. "But let us talk over the matter calmly, my good friend. This is a case where grief, anger, and indignation can do nothing; but where deliberate thought, reason, and policy, even cunning such as their own (for if we could arrive at it, we should be quite justified in using it), may, perhaps, do something to save this poor boy."

"How the devil would you have me calm?" exclaimed the man, vehemently; but then, suddenly checking himself, he said, "You're right-- you're right! I am forgetting my old habits in these smoky holes. Thought, cunning, those are the only things to do with an Indian. It's tarnation hard to outwit him, but it may be done when one knows his tracks well. I can't get my brain to hold steady to-night. This story's upset all my thoughts; and I've got no consideration in me. You must give me a night and a day to think over the matter; and then I'll see what's to be done. By the Lord, Walter shan't die! Poor fellow! what should *he* die for?--However, I guess it's no use talking in that sort of manner. I must think of what's to be done-- that's the business in hand. I'll think as soon as I can, my lord; only you just tell me now all you have done, if you have done anything. As for Prevost, I don't suppose he's had time to do much; for though he is always right in the end, and no man's opinion is worth more, yet, if you touch his heart and his feelings, as you call them, his wits get all in a work, just like mine at this moment. More fool he, and I too!"

"We have done something," said Lord H----, in reply. "Mr. Prevost set out this morning to see Sir William Johnson."

"*He* is no good," growled Woodchuck, impatiently.

"I came hither to consult with you," continued Lord H----; "and we have commissioned the boatman whom they call Robert, a tall, stout man----"

"I know him--I know him," interposed Woodchuck; "passably honest- -the best of them."

"Well, we have commissioned him," resumed the nobleman, "to seek for some Indian runner, or half-breed, to carry news of this event to Otaitsa, whom Edith believes the tribe will keep in the dark in regard to the capture of Walter."

"Likely--likely," said the Woodchuck. "Miss Prevost understands them; they'll not tell the women anything, for fear they should meddle. They've a poor opinion of squaws. But the girl may do a great deal of good, too, if you can get the tidings to her. She's not as cunning as the rest of them; but she has more heart, and soul, and resolution too, than a whole tribe of Indian women. That comes of her mother being a white woman."

"Her mother a white woman!" exclaimed Lord H----.

"Ay, didn't you know that?" interrogated Woodchuck; "just as white as Miss Prevost; and quite a lady, too, she was to look at, or to speak to--though she was not fond of speaking with white men, and would draw back into the lodge whenever she saw one. I did speak to her once, though, when she was in a great fright about Black Eagle, who had gone to battle against the French; and I, happening to come that way, gave her some news of him. But we are getting astray from what's of more matter than that. The girl will save him, take my word for it, if there's strength enough in that little body to do it. But let me see. You talk of Indian runners. Where is one to be found who can be trusted? They're generally a bad set, the scum of the tribes. No real warrior would take up on such a trade. However, what's to be done? No white person can go; for they'll scalp him to a certainty, and he would give his life for Walter's, that's all. On my life, it would be as well to give the dangerous errand to some felon, as I have heard say they do in despotic countries--give criminals some dangerous task to perform; and then, if they succeed and escape, so much the better for them; if they die, so much the better for the community. But I'm getting wandering again," he continued, rising. "Now, my lord, this is no use. Give me a few hours to think; to-morrow, at noon, if you will; and then I'll come and tell you what my opinion is."

As he spoke, he turned abruptly towards the house, without any ceremonious leave-taking, and only looked round to put one more question.

"At the post, I suppose?" he said.

Lord H---- assented; Brooks entered the house, and at once sought his own chamber.

CHAPTER XXII

In a small room, under a roof which slanted not in one straight line, but made an obtuse angle in the midst of its descent, lighted alone by a horn lantern, such as was used on board the river-boats at night, sat the stout man whom we have described under the name of Woodchuck. The furniture of the chamber was of the meanest kind; a small half-tester bed, with its dull curtains of a broad red and white checked stuff; a little table jammed close against the wall; a solitary chair; a wash-stand, with the basin and its ewer both somewhat maimed; and a little looking-glass, hanging from a nail driven into the wall, with its narrow, badly-gilt frame, and its plate so distorted that, when one looked in it, the reflection seemed to be making faces at the original. Dull, with imbibing many a year's loaded atmosphere, were those faded walls; and many a guest had written upon them in pencil his own name, or the name of his sweetheart--permanent memorials of transitory tenants, like the long-cherished memories of affections gone to the grave. There were two or three rude distiches, too, and a quatrain somewhat more polished.

But the man who sat there noted none of these things. The dim light, the gloomy aspect of the apartment, might sink in upon his spirit, and render the darkness within more dark: the strange, ill-looking, double slant of the ceiling--the obtrusive two straight lines instead of one, with the blunt, unmeaning angle between them, giving an aspect of brokenness to the roof, as if it were ready to bulge out, and then crash down--might irritate without his knowing why. Still he noted them not with anything like observation. His mind was busy with things of its own--things in which feeling took a share as well as thought--and he was, if not dead, sleeping to the external world. Even his beloved woods, and streams, and fresh air, and open skies, were forgotten for the time.

He argued with himself a case of conscience hard to solve.

He was as brave a man as ever lived--had been habituated all his life to perils of many kinds, and had met them all fearlessly. Wake him in the woods at midnight, you would find him ready. Deafen his ear with the drum or the war-whoop, you could not make him start. He blinked not at the cannon's flash or the blaze of the lightning, and would have faced the fiery-mouthed platoon without a wavering step.

And yet the love of life was strong in him. He had so many joys in the bright treasury of nature; to his simple--nay, wild--tastes, there were so many pleasures in the wide world, that to part with them was hard, very hard.

He had never known how valuable earthly existence was to him till that hour, or how different a thing it is to hazard it in bold daring, or to contemplate the throwing it away in reckless passion, or disappointment, or despair, to calmly and deliberately laying it down as a sacrifice, whatever be the end, the inducement, or the duty.

What was the case of conscience he proposed to himself? Simply this: Whether he should suffer another to die for his act, or place himself not only in the peril from which he had lately escaped, but in the actual grasp of death.

Some men, of enthusiastic spirit and great constitutional fearlessness, might have decided the matter at a dash, and, with the first impulse of a furious nature, have cast themselves under the uplifted tomahawk to save their innocent friend. But he was not such; and I do not intend so to represent him. He was not a man to do anything without deliberation-- without calculating all things--though he was generous as most men, as this world goes. All his habits--the very course of his previous life--disposed him to careful forethought. Every day had had its watchfulness, every hour its precaution. The life of the woods in those days was a life of peril and preparation, where forethought might be very rapid, but was always needful.

And now he debated the question with himself:--

"Could he live on and suffer Walter Prevost to die in his place?"

There were strenuous advocates on both sides. But the love of life was the most subtle, if generosity was the most eloquent.

"Poor boy!" he thought, "why should he die for what I have done? Why should he be cut off so soon from all life's hopes and blessings? Why should his father's eyes be drowned in tears, and his sister's heart wrung with grief, when I can save them all? And he so frank and noble, too--so full of every kindly feeling and generous quality--so brave--so honest--so frank--so true-hearted! Innocent, too--innocent of every offence--quite innocent in this case!"

But then spoke self, and he reflected,--

"Am not I innocent, too?--as innocent as he is? Did I ever harm the man? Did I provoke the savage? Did I not slay him in pure self-defence? And shall I lay down the life I then justly protected at the cost of that of another human being, because a race of fierce Indians, unreasoning, blood-thirsty savages, choose to offer a cruel sacrifice to their God of revenge, and have found a victim?

"Still," he continued, taking the other side, "it is for my act the sacrifice is offered, and, if there must be a sacrifice, ought not the victim to be myself? Besides, were it that any worthless life was in jeopardy--were it that of some desperate rover--some criminal--some man without ties, or friendships, or affections--one might leave him to his fate, perhaps, without remorse. But this poor lad, how many hopes are centred in him? what will not his family lose--what will not the world? And I--what am I, that my life should be weighed against his? Is he not my friend, too, and the son of my friend--one who has always overflowed with kindness and regard towards me?"

His resolution was almost taken; but then the cunning pleader, vanquished in direct argument, suggested a self-deceit.

"It is strange," he thought, "that these Indians, and especially their chief, should fix upon one with whom they have ever been so friendly--should choose a youth whom they have looked upon as a brother, when they might surely have found some other victim. Can this be a piece of their savage cunning? They know how well I love the lad, and how much friendship has been shown me by his father. Can they have taken him only as a bait to their trap, without any real intention of sacrificing him, and only in the hope of luring me into their power?"

At first sight the supposition seemed reasonable; and he was inclined to congratulate himself that he had not precipitately fallen into the snare.

"How they would have yelled with triumph," he thought "when they found me bringing my head to the hatchet!"

But speedily his knowledge of the Indian character and habits undeceived him. He knew that in such cases they always made sure of some victim, and that the more near and dear he was to the offender, the better for their purpose--the offender himself first--a relation next--a friend next; and he cast the self-fraud away from him.

But the love of life had not yet done, though obliged to take another course, and suggest modifications. Was there no middle course to be taken?

Was it absolutely necessary that he should sacrifice his own life to save that of Walter Prevost? Could not the object be effected without his giving himself up to the savages? Might not some one else fall into their hands? Might not the lad be rescued by some daring effort? This was the most plausible suggestion of all; but it was the one that troubled him most. He had detected so many attempts in his own heart to cheat himself, that he suspected he might be deceiving himself still; and his mind got puzzled and confused with doubts.

He went to the bed, and lay down in his clothes; but he could not sleep without taking some resolution; and, rising again, he pressed his hands upon his aching temples, and determined to cast away self from the question altogether--to look upon it as if it affected some other person than Walter Prevost, and to judge accordingly.

This plan succeeded. He separated the truth from the falsehood, and came to the conclusion that it would be folly to go and give himself up to certain death, so long as there was a chance of saving his young friend by other means; but that it was right to do so if other means failed; and that neither by delay nor by rash and uncertain efforts must he risk the chance of saving him, even by the ultimate sacrifice.

He accordingly made up his mind to re-enter the Indian territory in spite of every peril; to conceal himself as best he could; to watch the Indians as he would watch a wild beast; and to be ready for any opportunity, or for any decision.

Now that his resolution was finally taken, he lay down and slept profoundly.

CHAPTER XXIII

And what was Edith's journey? Would the reader have me dwell upon the small particulars--speak of it as if she had been taking a morning's walk, and note every bird, and flower, and insect; each smooth valley or bluff rock? Or would he have me present it as a picture, as it appeared to her after it was over, massed together in its extraordinary rapidity, and seen but from one point--at the end? Let us choose the latter plan, although it would be easy to extend the pages of this work by minute descriptions and passing panoramas, such as critics love.

But it is my object only to dwell upon events which affected the ultimate fate of the principal characters, and not to labour at length upon a mere detail of incidents. In this view of the case, I might say nothing more but that it began and ended--that she arrived safely at the place of her destination. Yet that journey was to her a matter of much interest; and when it was over, she looked back upon it as a picture full of beautiful and pleasant things.

Swiftly skimming in a bark canoe over the glassy bosoms of the lakes, which reflected every hue of herb, and tree, and sky, and mountain; darting along bright and sparkling streams, sometimes beneath the overhanging canopy of boughs, sometimes under the pure blue eye of heaven; often struggling with a rapid, often having to pass along the shore to turn a waterfall; at times walking along through the glowing woods, burning with the intense colouring of autumn; at times surrounded by a number of Indians, each rendering quiet, earnest service to the adopted daughter of the great Oneida chief; at times wandering on in the dim forest with no one but her two dark attendants near; now the fierce howl of the midnight wolf sounding in her ear; now the sharp, garrulous cry of the blue jay, or the shrill scream of the wood-hawk; now beholding the Indian lodge, or castle, as the Iroquois sometimes called their dwellings; then the brown canopy of the autumn woods which covered her: such were the principal incidents of her journey.

Still under the skilful guidance, and with the eager help, of the two negroes, she went forward with extraordinary rapidity, leaving miles and miles behind her every hour. It seemed almost like a pleasant dream, or, at least, it would have seemed so, had the sad and fearful motives which led her on been ever banished from her mind. Even as it was, the quick and continued change of place and scene, the variety of the objects, the constant succession of new matters of interest, the events, small in themselves, but important to her, which occurred to facilitate or impede her progress, were all a relief to her overcharged mind; and she reached the Oneida territory less depressed than when she set out from her home.

One cause, perhaps, of the feeling of renewed strength which she experienced, was the renewal of hope from the conduct of the Indians towards her, wherever she met them. She found that even amongst the Mohawks she was recognized at once as the adopted daughter of the great Oneida chief; and it was evident that he had spread far and wide, as he returned to his own abode after the conference at Johnson Castle, the fact of his having adopted the daughter of the pale-face, Prevost. There is always something, too, in the fact of an enterprise being actually commenced, which gives spirit to pursue it to the end. While we stand and gaze at it from a distance, hesitating whether we shall undertake it or not, the difficulties are magnified--the facilities obscured: rocks and precipices rise up, threatening to our imagination; while the small paths by which they may be surmounted are unseen.

Day had yet an hour of life left when Edith approached what we find called, in the history of the times, "The Castle of the Oneidas." "Wigwam" it is customary to name all the Indian villages, giving an idea of insignificance and meanness, and a completely savage state, which the principal residences of the Five Nations did not at all merit. Most of them were very like that which Edith now approached. It was built upon a slight elevation near the lake, with a large protruding rock close to it; for the Oneidas always affected near their dwelling some object significant of their favourite appellation, "The Children of the Stone."

Around the "Castle" were high palisades, inclosing a considerable area, within which the huts of the Indians were constructed. Rising considerably above the rest, were two wooden buildings, in the erection of which European workmanship was apparent. The one was a large oblong building, regularly roofed and shingled like that of any English settler. It consisted of two stories, and in the upper one regular framed windows were to be seen. In the lower story there were none; light being admitted by the door. That lower story, however, was floored with plain pine-boards, and divided by a sort of curtain into two equal compartments.

The other building bore the appearance of a church in miniature, with a small cottage or hut attached, which was, in reality, the residence of the missionary, Mr. Gore. Around the village, or Castle, were wide, well-cultivated fields, which had evidently lately borne maize, or some other crops of grain; and let not the reader, acquainted with the habits of Indians as they are at present, be surprised to find the art of husbandry practised at this period amongst the rude denizens of the forest; for, to the shame of civilized man be it spoken, the Indians have assuredly lost much socially, and gained little religiously, by the intercourse with the white invaders of their country. The crushing weight of despondency, a sort of morbid awe of the superiority of the white race, seems to have beaten down a spirit of enterprise which formerly bid fair to regenerate the people, and to replace them in a position which they probably at one time occupied.

Such, however, as I have described, was the appearance of a large Indian village, or Castle, in the year one thousand seven hundred and fifty-seven; and we find, from the statements of many an eye-witness, that the wild hunter of the woods, the fierce combatant in the battle, was, in his calmer moments, not at all insensible to many of the advantages and comforts of civilized life. But we refused to lead them on the way; we used their blood and their energies for our service; we even bought and profited by their fierce barbarity; and, instead of giving them, while it was possible, the arts of peace and the benefits of cultivation, we furnished them with the "fire-water," we contaminated them with our vices, and degraded them morally, physically, and intellectually. Great was our offence against our fellow-man; great must be the sin in the eyes of a just God.

The forest had disappeared; all that could be seen appeared as if rolling in grey masses along the distant country. The purple light of evening, increasing in richness every moment as the day declined, spread over the whole scene, and was reflected from the bosom of the lake. Many a light canoe was skimming along over the water, many a one was lying motionless while the Indian fisherman pursued his sport. The blue smoke curled up high and straight in the calm air from the doors of several huts within the inclosure; and, from the maize-fields without, the pleasant musical sounds of children's voices were heard, as the young people of the village wandered here and there, gathering up scattered ears of corn, which had fallen in the rude reaping of the harvest. In one place even a song was heard; and, in short, the whole scene, instead of being one of rude barbarism and fierce, active passion, indicated calm domestic peace, such as is rarely pictured in the common, but exaggerated, descriptions of Indian life. It might serve my purpose better to describe it differently; but such I find it, and so it must remain.

Even Edith was surprised to find the home of Otaitsa so different from the ideas conveyed to her by the wandering traders, who, even while carrying on commercial intercourse with the tribes, were in a state of semihostility towards the Indians, representing them as bloody savages, and cheating them wherever they could.

Slowly walking on between her two negro companions--for she was tired with a longer walk than usual--Edith approached the open gates of the Castle, and met with no opposition in entering. A tall, handsome warrior passed out, fully clothed, in Indian costume, and only distinguished from civilized man by the shaved head and the painfully significant scalp-lock. His step was stately and calm; and his air grave and reserved. Twice he turned his eyes upon Edith's face with a look of evident wonder and admiration; but he took no farther notice, and passed on.

He was the only individual whom she saw on entering the village; till, after passing through many huts, where women and children were to be seen busily employed, she came in sight of the door of the chief's house, and beheld there a figure seated on the ground quietly engaged in the art of embroidery, after the fashion in which the Indian women so greatly excel. It was a figure which she knew well; and the tranquil air and easy grace, as well as the quiet, peaceful employment, showed Edith at once that she had not been mistaken in supposing that Otaitsa was altogether ignorant of the peril of one dear to them both.

As she came near, she heard that the Indian girl, in her happy ignorance, was singing a sweet but somewhat plaintive song; and, the next moment, Otaitsa, raising her eyes, beheld the three figures, and at once perceived that they were not of her people. For a moment, she did not know Edith in her Indian garb; but when she did recognize her, the emotion produced was alarm rather than joy. She felt at once that some great and important event--some occurrence full of peril or of sorrow--must have brought Edith thither. The beautiful lips parted with a tremulous motion; the large, dark eye, Indian in its colour, but European in its form, became full of anxiety; the rosy hue of her cheek, which probably had obtained for her the name of the Blossom, faded away; and paleness spread over the clear brown skin.

Starting up, however, she cast the embroidery away from her, and, springing forward, threw her arms round Edith's neck. Then, as her head rested on her fair companion's shoulder, she asked, in a whisper--

"What is it, my sister? There must be a storm in the sky--there must be lightning in the cloud! What tempest-wind has swept my sister hither? What flood of sorrow has borne Edith to Otaitsa?"

"Hush!" ejaculated Edith, in a low tone, for there were some other Indian women near. "I will tell my sister when no ears can hear but her own. There *is* tempest in the sky. A pine-tree has fallen across the threshold of my father's house; and we are sad for fear the hatchet of the woodman should lop all its green branches away. Can I speak with the Blossom speedily and in secret?"

"Instantly," answered Otaitsa. "The warriors have all gone forth to hunt, for three days, the bear and the moose. The Black Eagle is with them. There are but three men of deeds in the Castle; and why they are women now, and go not forth to the hunting with the rest, I cannot tell. But they are little within the palisade--daily they go forth, and remain absent long. Come in hither, my sister; for, though few here speak the tongue we speak, it were better not to let the wind hear us."

"Can some of the women give food and lodging to these two negroes?" asked Edith, adding, "They have been well warned, and know that a life depends upon their silence."

Otaitsa called to an elderly Indian woman, who was cooking at the door of a cabin near, and placed Chando and his companion under her charge. She then turned to Edith, saying,--

"Come, my sister."

But, before they entered the building, Edith inquired if Mr. Gore were there, saying,--

"Perhaps he might give us counsel."

"My father sent him away some days ago," answered Otaitsa; "he will not be back for a month--perhaps longer. I think he sent him to secure him from danger."

"Alas!" exclaimed Edith, "that the danger should have fallen on others!"

"Alas, alas!" cried Otaitsa.

And Edith felt her hand tremble much as she led her into the building.

CHAPTER XXIV

A staircase, rude indeed, but still a staircase, led from the more barn-like part of the building below to the upper floor; and in this respect appeared the first difference between this house--for it deserved the name--and the lodge, or Castle, of King Hendrick the younger, though both had been built by European workmen, and that of King Hendrick at the cost of the British government, which was not the case with the dwelling of the Oneida chief. As soon, however, as you reached the upper floor, the differences became more frequent and more remarkable. It was partitioned off into separate rooms, with regular doors to them.

When Edith entered the chamber of Otaitsa, she saw at once her tendency to European habits. Of rude manufacture, but still very correct as imitations, and not without a certain degree of uncouth ornament, were chairs, tables, writing materials, a bedstead and a bed; and from wooden pegs driven into the partition depended a few drawings, some coloured, some in pencil, but all very different from the gaudy daubs which, at a later period, pedlars were accustomed to take into the Indian territory as articles of barter.

As Edith's eye glanced round the room, she gleaned a general notion of all these things; but her mind was too full of deeper and sadder thoughts to suffer even curiosity to turn it from its course for a moment.

"There is no one in any other chamber here," said Otaitsa. "None comes up those stairs but myself and my father. Now, Edith, speak; for Otaitsa's heart is very heavy, and her mind misgives her sadly. Is it your father they have taken?"

"No, oh no!" answered Edith; "but one as dear."

She then went on briefly to relate all that had occurred, endeavouring to soften and prepare the way for intelligence which she feared would affect the Indian girl much. But Otaitsa darted at her own conclusions, divining the whole truth almost as soon as the words were spoken. She was far more affected than Edith had anticipated. She cast herself upon her fair companion's neck, and wept aloud.

"He was mine, Edith," she exclaimed, in the full confidence of sorrow. "He was mine--my betrothed--my loved! And they have hidden it from me--hidden it from all the Indian women here; for they knew that every one in the tribe loved him--though not as well as I. Where was the poor wanderer who passed your house with her infant on her back, who did not receive kindness from Walter Prevost?--where was the Indian girl who could say he did not treat her with as kindly gentleness as the highest white woman in the land? He was the tree which had grown up to shelter the hut of the woodman, giving him cool shade and comfort in the days of summer and of gladness, to be cut down and burnt for fire when the winter winds are singing in the bare branches. Oh, my brother--my brother! bad is the return they make thee, and hard the measure that they deal! But shall Otaitsa suffer this?" she cried, rising vehemently, and casting her arms abroad. "Shall the Black Eagle let the ravens pick out the eyes of his young in his own nest? No, my sister, no! they shall take Otaitsa's blood first--they shall shake the Blossom from the old bough that is no longer able to bear it up against the winds of Heaven. If the Black Eagle can no longer protect even his daughter's husband, let him cast away the tomahawk--let him lay down the rifle, and be a woman amongst the chiefs of his people!"

It was impossible, for some minutes, to stop Otaitsa's vehement burst of passionate sorrow; but at length Edith succeeded in somewhat calming her, beseeching her to still her agitation and anger, and to bend her whole mind to the consideration of what means could best be used to discover whither Walter had been taken, and to rescue him from the peril in which he was placed.

As soon as Otaitsa could listen, however, or rather as soon as she caught the sense of Edith's words, and appreciated their importance, it is wonderful how rapidly she became calm, stilled all the strong and struggling emotions in her heart, and directed every effort and energy of her spirit to the one great object before her. Enough of the Indian blood flowed along her veins--enough of Indian characteristics had been acquired in early youth--to give her a portion of that strong, stoical self-command which characterized the Indian warrior, rather than the woman of the race. The first burst of grief and indignation showed the woman, and perhaps, in some degree, not the pure Indian; but, the moment after, those who knew the character of the Five Nations best might have supposed her, not only a pure Indian, but a man, and a chief, so quietly did she reason upon, and ponder, the means of accomplishing her purpose. She remained at first, for two or three minutes, in perfect silence, revolving all the circumstances in her mind, and calculating every chance. Then she said,--

"The first thing, Edith, is for you to go back to your poor father--not that you are in any danger here; but it were well, if possible, that no one knew you had been with me, at least till I have discovered where they have hid our poor brother. The women here will all aid me, and never part their lips if I desire them not; for though the men think they are very shrewd in hiding the secrets of the nation from their wives and daughters, the women, when they please, can be as secret and as resolute too. At all events, whether your coming be known or not, it would be better you should go back before the chief's return. They have gone forth to hunt, they say; but whether it be the black bear, or the brown deer, or the white man, is in great doubt, dear Edith. At all events, they will not know the object of your coming. They may suspect, and probably will, that you came to inquire for your brother; but knowing that I was ignorant of his capture, and am still ignorant where they keep him, they will think you have gone back disappointed and in sorrow, and leave me unwatched to act as I will."

"But can I do nothing to aid?" asked Edith. "Remember, dearest Blossom, what it is to remain inactive and ignorant, while the fate of one so near and so dear hangs in the balance."

"You shall not remain in ignorance, dear Edith," replied Otaitsa. "With every possible opportunity (and I will find many) my sister shall know what the Blossom does, and if there be any way in which you could give help, you shall have instant tidings. At present I know not what is to be done to save our Walter from the power of the Snake. I know not even what they have decided themselves, or whether they have taken any decision; and I have much to think of, much to do. I must seek out those in whom I can place confidence; I must employ many to obtain me information; I must buy some, consult with others, and then judge what is to be done. You can rest here, my Edith, for this day; but to-morrow you must speed home again. But be sure of one thing; my tribe shall know that if Walter dies, Otaitsa will die too."

"That is no consolation," cried Edith, throwing her arms round her neck, with tears in her eyes; "oh, do not threaten anything rash, dear Blossom! Remember you are a Christian; and many things are forbidden to Christians, as a sin, which are regarded as virtues by pagan nations."

"No threat can be rash, no threat can be a sin," answered Otaitsa, "which may save a life, innocent, and good, and noble. I would not willingly offend, my sister; but my heart is open to God; and he will judge me in mercy, seeing my motives. And now, dear sister, sit you here, and I will send you food, such as we poor Indians eat. I myself may be away for a time, for there must be no delay; but I will return as soon as possible, and you shall know all that is done before you go. Do these blacks who are with you understand the Indian tongue?"

"One of them certainly does," replied Edith; "that is to say, the language of the Mohawks."

"'Tis the same," returned Otaitsa, "or nearly the same. We may have altered a little; but, amongst the Five Nations, he who speaks one tongue understands all. Is it the man or the woman? and can we trust?"

"It is the man," answered Edith; "and I do believe he can be trusted."

"Then I go," resumed Otaitsa.

And, leaving Edith, she descended to the room below, and then issued forth amongst the Indian huts, gliding from one to another, and stopping generally for a few moments at those lodges before which was to be seen a high pole, bearing the ghastly trophies with which the Indians signalized the death of an enemy.

Strange, that with one so gentle and so kind, with one taught Christianity from her youth, and imbued with many notions different from those of the rest of the people, the horrid sight of human scalps, parched by the sun and dangling in the wind produced no appearance of horror and disgust. In truth, she hardly saw them, and looked upon the pole and its cruel trophies merely as an indication that there dwelt a famous warrior of the tribe.

Edith in the meanwhile remained for some time in sad meditation. During her rapid journey from the neighbourhood of the Hudson, not more than thirty miles from Lake Horicon, to the Oneida Lake, she had had little leisure for thought. It had passed almost as a dream, full of confused objects and feelings, but with little like reflection in it.

The sun was by this time disappearing beyond the western extremity of the lake, but still sufficiently above the gently sloping ground to pour a long stream of glorious light over the placid waters; and Edith, seated near the window, gazed over the calm and beautiful scene with that solemn feeling--that echo of the voice from another world--which seems to rise in every sensitive heart at the death of each new day. Something gone! something gone to eternity! another day on its twelve golden wings taking flight to the infinite and the irrevocable, bearing with it to the dark treasury of late an infinite mass and multitude of deeds, and thoughts, and feelings, crimes, offences, virtuous acts, and little kindnesses, human charities, and human passions, wishes, hopes, joys, sorrows, disappointments, and regrets: the smiles and tears of a whole world, gone with the departing day. Sad and solemn is that feeling. It is standing by the death-bed of a friend, and seeing the faint eyes closed for ever.

For ever! No, not for ever! There is a morning for all, when another day shall dawn; and well were it for some, if the deeds of the dead day could be forgotten.

Still, although we know that another day will rise--as surely as we know that another life will come--there is a sort of hopelessness, though that is too strong a word, in seeing the sinking sun take his parting look of the world. Perhaps it is not hopelessness; but it is a something which transfuses a portion of the twilight gloom into the chambers of the heart, and dims the light of hope, though not extinguishes it.

Edith was sad--very, very sad; and she felt that gazing on that scene made her still more so. It gave her a sensation of solitariness, of helpless homelessness in a new, wild world, the tendency of which was to depress and enervate; and, saying to herself--"I will hope still; I will not despond; I will think of nothing but action and endeavour," she rose and looked about the room for something to occupy the mind and drive away impressions that seemed to crush her energies.

There were many things around which might have answered the purpose, only strange from being found in that place: several books; a small needle-book, of ancient pattern, but evidently European, and what seemed to be an old sketch-book, with a lock and clasp upon it. It evidently dated from many years before; was somewhat soiled; and on one of the sides were two or three dark spots. They were not of ink, for, through the blackness, there was a red.

Passing by these objects, Edith's eyes turned towards the sketches hanging round the room. On one in particular the reflected light from the surface of the lake streamed as it passed from the window; and Edith, going near, examined it attentively. It represented the head of a young man, apparently from seven-and-twenty to thirty years of age, and was done well, though not exactly in a masterly manner. It was merely in pencil, but highly finished; and there seemed something in it very familiar to Edith's eye. The features were generally like those of her brother Walter--so like, that, at first, she imagined that the drawing must be intended to represent his head; but the nearer view showed that it was that of a much older person; and the dress was one long gone out of fashion.

She was still gazing and puzzling herself with the questions of whence these drawings could come, and whether they could be Otaitsa's own productions, when some Indian women entered, with their noiseless tread, and placed several carved bowls, filled with different kinds of food, before her. It was all very simple; but she was much exhausted, for she had tasted nothing from an early hour of the day, and the refreshment was grateful to her. The women spoke to her, too, in the Iroquois tongue; and their sweet, low-toned voices, murmuring in the sort of sing-song of the tribes, was pleasant to her ear. It spoke of companionship.

Their words, too, were kind and friendly; and she gathered from them that Otaitsa, in order to veil the real object of her coming, had been making inquiries as to whether any one had seen Walter Prevost. They assured Edith that they had not seen him--that he could not have come into the Oneida country, or some one in the Castle must have heard of him. A pale-face amongst them was very rare, they said; but the coming of Walter Prevost, whom so many knew and loved much, would have been noised abroad immediately. They said that his absence from his home was certainly strange, but added, laughing, that young warriors would wander, as Edith would discover when she was old enough.

Thus they sat and talked with her, lighting a lamp in a bowl, till Otaitsa returned; and then they left the two friends alone together.

Otaitsa was agitated evidently, though she tried hard to hide, if not to suppress, her emotions under Indian calmness; but her agitation was evidently joyful. She laid her small hand upon Edith's, and pressed it warmly.

"I have found friends," she said; "those who will work for me, and with me: my father's sister, who knew and loved my mother, and who is supposed by some to have a charm from the Great Spirit to make men love and reverence her--the wife of the Sachem of the Bear--the young bride of the Running Deer--the wife of the Grey Wolf--the wife of Lynxfoot--and many others. All these have vowed to help me, whatever it may cost. They all know Walter: they all have called him brother; and they all are resolute that their brother shall not die. But I must first work for him myself, dear Edith," she continued. Then, clasping her hands together with a burst of joy at the hope lighted up in her young, warm heart, she exclaimed--"Oh, that I could save him all by myself!--that I might buy him from his bonds by my own acts alone--ay, or even by my own blood! Huagh! Huagh! that were joyful indeed!"

Edith could hardly raise her mind to the same pitch of hope; still, she felt more satisfied--her object was accomplished. Otaitsa was informed of Walter's danger; and the bright, enthusiastic girl was already actively engaged in the effort to deliver him. There was something, too, in the young Indian--an eagerness, an energy, unusual in the depressed women of her race, and probably encouraged by the fond, unbounded indulgence of the chief her father--which seemed to breathe of hope and success; and it was impossible to look into her eager and kindling eyes, when the fancy that she could deliver her young lover all alone took possession of her, without believing that, if his deliverance was within human power, she would accomplish it.

Edith felt that her duty so far was done, and that her next duty was towards her father, who she well knew would be painfully anxious till she returned, however confident he might have felt of her safety in the hands of the Indians, so long as there seemed no immediate chance of her being placed in such a situation. She willingly, therefore, agreed to Otaitsa's suggestion, to set out with the first ray of light on the following morning, Otaitsa promising that some Indian women should accompany her a day's journey on the way, who, by their better knowledge of the country, and their skill in the management of the canoe, would greatly facilitate her progress.

About an hour was spent in conversation, all turning upon one subject, and then the two girls lay down to sleep in each other's arms.

CHAPTER XXV

On the very same night which was passed by Edith Prevost in the great lodge of the Black Eagle, eight or ten wild-looking savages, if they could so be called, assembled apparently to deliberate upon some great and important question. The place they took for their meeting lay nearly twenty miles in a direct line from the Oneida lake, and was, even in the daylight, a scene of no inconsiderable beauty and grandeur.

At the hour of their meeting, however, which was about forty minutes after the sun went down, the surrounding objects were illuminated by a different and a more appropriate light. Their council-fire had been kindled on the top of a large flat mass of stone, in a very narrow dell or pass which separated a rugged and forest-bearing mountain from a spur of the same range, that seemed to have been riven from the parent chain by some rude and terrible convulsion of nature. Forty yards, at the widest part, was the expanse of this deep fissure; and on either side were huge masses of rock tumbled about in chaotic confusion, and blocking up the greater part of the bottom of the dell. From behind these rose the riven cliffs, rough and serrated, like the edges of two saws, the teeth of which would fit into each other if pressed together. But upon all the salient points, even where it seemed impossible for a handful of vegetable mould to rest, a tall tree had perched itself, spreading out its branches almost till they met those on the opposite side of the glen, through which no torrent rushed, neither had any spring burst forth when the earthquake rent the solid foundations of the mountain; but a dry, short turf covered all the earth accumulated below.

Between the great blocks of stone which encumbered the pass, wherever rain could penetrate, rose tall and graceful wild flowers; and, in the more open parts, the grassy carpet was freckled, in the springtime of the year, with many a curious little blossom. Tall pines and rugged hemlocks--some straight as a column, some strangely twisted and contorted--the great black oak, with innumerable other shrubs and trees, gathered wherever the banks of the dell were a little less precipitous; and, when one looked up, one perceived, by the overhanging branches, that the mountain-top was clothed with a dense covering of forest.

About half-way through the glen was the large flat stone--a sort of natural altar, on which the Indians had lighted their fire; and strange and wild was the scene, as those swarthy men, armed as if for battle, but not painted, sat around in the broad glare, each with his rifle resting on his arm, and each still and motionless as a statue hewn out of the brown rock. Up went the towering flame from the great pile of dry wood, sending a flickering light over tree and precipice; yet no one stirred, no one spoke, for several minutes. Each eye was fixed upon the fire, not as if watching it as an object of interest, but with the steady, thoughtful gaze which showed that the mind was busy with other things; and there was something very awful in that stern, cold silence.

At length, the Black Eagle began to speak, without moving from his seat--however, at least, first. His tone, too, was low and sad; though every word, in the sharp gutteral language of the Iroquois, was clear and distinct.

"For more than fifty winters," he said, "I have hovered over the land of the Oneidas; and my wing has not failed in its flight, my eyes have not been dazzled by the blaze of the sun, nor dimmed by the light of the moon. The dew has fallen upon me, and the summer's sun, and the winter's snow; and still are my feathers unruffled, and my flight as strong as in my youth. I am not a woman, that I should spare; nor a child, that I should weep. Who has seen a tear in my eye? or who has seen the tomahawk uplifted not to strike? Have I asked anything of my children, but to be the first in the battle? Have I ever forgiven the enemies of the children of the Stone? But we have made alliance with a great nation; we have taken presents from them; we have promised to live with them as brothers in the time of peace--to go to battle with them as brothers in the time of war. Our children are their children, and their children are ours. Moreover, with some of this nation our chiefs have entered into more strict bonds of friendship. We have sat by their fires, we have smoked the pipe of peace together; we are their brothers. One family came and built their lodge amongst us, swept down the forest, planted the corn-field. Their door was always open to the red man; their food was always shared with him. They said not, 'This is mine, and that is thine,' but they opened their arms and they said, 'Thou art my brother.' The children of the Stone loved them well; they were dear to the Black Eagle as his own eaglets. The mat in the house of Prevost was a pleasant resting-place to his forehead when he was tired. *His* daughter was as *my* daughter, and his son as of my blood and bone.

"A man came to his hearth whom we all know, a good man, a friend to the red man. Should my brother Prevost refuse to the Woodchuck room to burrow for one night? He went away, and, far from the house of our brother, he met an Oneida, of the Totem of the Tortoise; a man who had robbed him, and who had a lying tongue, a snake who hated him whom he had bitten. The tomahawk was bare, and the Oneida was killed; but the man took not his scalp, he sung no song of triumph over the children of the Stone. He slew him not as an enemy, but in self-defence; otherwise he would have twisted his finger in the scalp-lock, and the Oneidas would have mourned over a disgrace. It is right that there should be blood for blood; that the man who sheds the blood of the red man should die for his act; and that, if he or none of his relations could be found, some other man of his nation should be made the sacrifice.

"But what have I done that the son of my brother should be taken? Have I led you so often in the battle, have I covered my war-post with the scalps of your enemies, that the tree I planted should be rooted up when the forest is full of worthless saplings? Was there no other white man to be found in all the land, that you must take the child of him who loved and trusted us? Had a moon passed,--nay, had even a week gone by, that you might know that there was none but the beloved of the Black Eagle whom you might use for your sacrifice? Had you made sure even that you could not catch the murderer himself, and take his blood in requital of the blood he shed? Is the wisdom of our people gone by, is their cunning a thing of other days, that they could not lure the man they sought into their power, that they could not hunt down any other game, that they would not even try to find any one but the one we loved the best?

"Remember, my children, that you are not rash and hasty, like the pale-face, but that you are the children of the Stone; and though, like it, unchangeable, and strong, you should be calm and still, likewise.--I have said."

There was a pause of several minutes before any one answered; and then a man of the middle age, not so tall as the Black Eagle by several inches, but with a peculiarly cunning and serpent-like look about his eyes, rose slowly from his seat, and, standing on the very point of the rock where he was placed, said, in a hard, cold tone,--

"The Black Eagle has spoken well. We are allies of the white man. The pale-face calls us his brother. He takes our hunting-grounds. He plants corn and feeds oxen amongst us. Where our foot was free to go, is ours no longer; it is his. He has taken it from us; and he is our brother. The Black Eagle loves the pale-face. He took a pale-face for his wife, and he loves all her race. He loves their religion. His daughter is of the religion of the white man. He himself has faith in their Gods. Their Great Spirit he adores, and he has made their medicine-man his son by adoption. Is the religion of the white man the same as the religion of the children of the Stone? Is *their* Great Spirit *our* great spirit? No; for I have heard his words spoken, and they are not the words that we are taught. The white man's Spirit tell us that we shall not do that which our Great Spirit tells us to do. It bids men spare their enemies, and to forgive. Ours tells us to slay our enemies, and to avenge. Which is the true Spirit? Our own; for the pale-face does not believe in his own Spirit, nor obey his commands. He does not spare his enemies; he does not forgive; but he takes vengeance as fiercely as the red man, and against his own law. Let us, then, obey the voice of our own Great Spirit, and do according to our own customs; for the white man knows his God to be false, or he would obey his commandments.

"Now, what would the Black Eagle have? Would he have us all turn Christians? Or would he have us obey the voice of the Maneto, and follow the customs of our fathers? Have we not done according to our own law? What do our traditions tell us? They say that thou shalt appease the spirit of thy brother who is slain, by pouring out the blood of the slayer. If his blood cannot be had, then that of one of his family, or of his friends. If his family and his friends are not to be found, then that of one of his nation. Lo! now, what is the case, chiefs and warriors of the Oneidas? You have a brother slain. His soul goes to the land of spirits; but his bow and his arrows hang idly at his back. His heart is sad and desolate. He howls for food and finds none. He wanders round and round the happy hunting-grounds, and looks in in sorrow; for he must not enter till the blood of atonement has been shed. He cries to you from the other side of the grave with a great cry: 'Give me rest!' Shall his brothers give him none?--shall they let him wander, cold and hungry, amidst frost and snow within sight of the blessed region, and prevent him from entering--or shall we take the first man we find of the race of him who slew him, and by his blood, poured out upon this very stone, appease the spirit of our dead brother, and let him enter the happy hunting-grounds, where his soul may find repose?

"Ye men of the family of the Snake! ye have done well to seize upon the pale-face whom ye first found; for ye have made sure of an atonement for the blood of your brother; and how could ye know that ye could find it if ye delayed your hand or abandoned your prey. And now let the chiefs and the warriors consider whether they will still keep their brother, who is dead, hungering and thirsting for months in the cold regions, or whether they will make the atonement this very night, and open the way for him into the happy hunting-grounds.--I have said."

Again a deep silence took possession of the throng, and it was not soon broken; but the eyes of the Black Eagle moved hither and thither round the circle, watching every face; and, when he gathered by a sort of kindling look in the eyes of one of the warriors that he was about to speak, he himself interposed, rising this time to his full height, and saying,--

"The medicine-man has spoken, and he has expounded the law; but he has counselled with words contrary to the law. The medicine-man has the law in his heart; but his words are the words of foxes. He has not unfolded the roll of the law into which the words of the Maneto were whispered; but he says truly that we are to shed the blood of the murderer of our brother to appease his spirit. If we cannot find him, we are to shed the blood of some one of his near kindred; if we cannot find one of them, the blood of one of his nation. But have ye sought for the murderer, ye brethren of the Snake? Can ye say that ye have tried to catch him? Have ye had time? Will your brother, who is gone, be contented with the blood of the first pale-face ye can find, when ye might find the real murderer? Will he lap like the dog at the first pool in his way? Will he not rather say: 'Give us the only sweet water that can allay our thirst?' Would ye mutter in our ears, and make us believe music? This is not the blood of him who shed our blood. This is not the blood of his kindred. The happy hunting-grounds will not open to the slain for this blood.

"Oneidas, it is the medicine-man who beguiles you from the customs of your fathers. They say: 'Wait till ye have searched diligently. Make sure that ye offer the best atonement that ye can. Do not kill the fox because the panther has mangled the game. Do not shoot the oriole for the thing that the hawk has done.' The son of my brother Prevost is no kin of the Yengee who slew the Snake. His blood will not atone if ye can find other blood more friendly to the murderer. The eyes of the Maneto are over all; he sees that ye have not sought as ye should seek."

Some moments after he had spoken, but with a less interval than had hitherto occurred between any of the speeches, a fierce-looking young warrior arose, and exclaimed,--

"Let him die. Why should we wait? The Woodchuck is safe in the land of the Yengees. He has taken himself far from the arrow of the Oneida. There is a cloud between us and him; and we cannot see through it. The Woodchuck has no kindred. He has often declared so when he has sat by the fire, and talked of the deeds he has done. He has boasted that he was a man alone; that his father was clay, and his mother grass, and the hemlock and the oak his brothers and his sisters. Neither him can we find, nor any of his kin; but we have taken what was nearest to him--his friend and the son of his friend. This is the blood that will appease the spirit of our brother. Let him die, and die quickly. Does the Black Eagle ask if this boy was his friend? The Black Eagle knows he was; but, moreover, it may be that he himself was companion of the murderer even when he killed our brother. They went forth together to seek for some prey. Was it not the red man that the wolves hunted? They killed a panther and a man when they were both together. That we know; for there were eyes of red men near. The blood of our brother was licked up by the earth. The skin of the panther was sent by this boy, our captive, to Otaitsa, the daughter of the Black Eagle. I took it from the runner this very day. The man who brought it is near at hand. The skin is here.--I have said."

And he threw the panther's skin down before him, almost into the flame of the fire.

A buzzing murmur ran round the Indians, and the keen mind of Black Eagle soon perceived that the immediate danger of poor Walter Prevost was greatly heightened.

"Let the law be announced to us," he said. "The roll of the law is here; but let it not be read by the tongue of a fox. Let the man of ancient times read it. Let the warrior and the priest who kept it for so many years now tell us what it ordains, according to the interpretation of old days, and not according to the rashness of boys, who would be chiefs long before a scalp hangs at the door of their lodge. I can see," he cried, in a loud voice, starting up from his seat, and waving his arm, as if some strong emotion overpowered his habitual calmness,--"I can see the time coming when the intemperance of youth, and the want of respect for age and for renown, will bring low the power of the Oneidas, will crush the greatness of the Five Nations into dust. So long as age and counsel were reverenced, they were a mighty people, and the scalps of their enemies were brought from every battle-field. They were a wise people, for they listened to the voice of experience, and they circumvented their enemies. But now the voice of boys and striplings prevails. They take presents, and they sell themselves for baubles. They drink the fire-water till they are no more men--till reason has departed, and courage and strength are not in them. They use the lightning, and they play with the thunder; but the tomahawk and the scalping-knife are green rushes in their hands. Let the law be announced, then; let it be announced by the voice of age and wisdom, and let us abide by his words, for they are good."

Thus saying, he stepped across the little chasm between him and the second speaker on this occasion, and took up a heavy roll which lay beside the priest or medicine-man. It consisted of innumerable strings of shells sawn into long strips like the pendants of an ear-ring, and stained of three separate colours, black, red, and white. These were disposed in various curious groups, forming no regular pattern, yet not without order; and so many were there in this roll, that, though each was very small, the weight of the whole could not have been less than twenty or thirty pounds.

Thus loaded, and bearing this burden with the appearance of great reverence, Black Eagle carried the roll half round the circle, and laid it upon the knees of a man evidently far advanced in life: although his shaved head and long white scalp-lock showed, to an Indian eye at least, that he still judged himself fit to accompany the warriors of the tribe to battle.

The chief then slowly resumed his seat, and once more profound silence spread over the assembly. The eyes of all were, it is true, directed towards the old man whose exposition of their laws and customs was to be final; but not a limb stirred, and even the very eagerness of their gaze was subdued into a look of tranquil attention, except in the case of the young man who had spoken so vehemently, and whose relationship as a brother to the slain Indian excused, in the sight of his tribe, a good deal of unwonted agitation.

For about two minutes after receiving the roll, the old priest remained motionless, with his eyes raised towards the flame that still towered up before him, licking and scorching the branches of a hemlock tree above.

At last, his fingers began to move amongst the carved shells; and, unloosing rapidly some thongs by which the roll was bound, he spread out the seemingly tangled mass in fair order. Then, bending down his head, he seemed to listen as if for a voice.

"The law of the Oneidas cannot change," he said, at length. "It is as the will of Hawaneyoh, the Great Spirit. A white man must die for the blood spilt by a white man. But the spiller of the blood must be sought for, or our brother will still be shut out from the happy hunting-grounds. Listen not to the song of singing-birds against the young man, thou brother of the Snake. Neither do thou make trouble in the Five Nations, because the blossom of the Black Eagle's tree cannot be reached by thy hand."

The open allusion to that which he thought was one of the deep secrets of his bosom was too much for even the Indian stoicism of the brother of the Snake; and he drew his blanket or mantle over his chest, as if to hide what was within. Black Eagle, however, though probably taken as much by surprise as any one by the old man's words, remained perfectly unmoved, not a change of expression even appearing upon his rigid features, though the speaker paused for a full minute, as if to let what he had said produce its full effect.

"Remember," continued the priest, "the prophecy of the child of the sky, Tohganawatah, when our fathers, under his counsel, joined themselves together in a perpetual league, a lifetime before a pale-face was seen in the land. He said, 'When the white-throats shall come, if ye suffer dissensions among yourselves, ye shall pull down the Long House of the Five Nations, cut down the tree of Peace, and extinguish the council-fire for ever.' And wilt thou, brother of the Snake, bring this cloud upon thy people? Thou shalt search for him who spilt thy brother's blood, till the moon have changed and waxed and waned again; and then thou shalt come before Sachems of the eight Totems, and make manifest that thou hast not been able to find him or any of his kindred. Then shall the Sachems choose a pale-face for the sacrifice, and let him die the death of a warrior by the stroke of the tomahawk. But they shall make no delay; for thy brother must not be shut out from the hunters gone before, more than two moons.--Hiro, I have spoken.

"Koué, Koué! It is well!" said all the Indians present, but one; and, rising from their seats, they raised the roll of their law reverently, and one by one glided down the path which led to the opening of the dell.

CHAPTER XXVI

Slowly up the steep middle street of Albany walked the great, powerful form of the Woodchuck, about the hour of noon. He was clothed in his usual shaggy habiliments of the forest, with his rifle on his shoulder, his hatchet and his knife in his belt. But his step had none of the light activity of former times; and his face, which always had a grave and sedate air, was now covered with heavy gloom. Altogether, he was a very singular-looking man.

Though situated inland, and in one of the most central parts of the provinces, the streets of Albany from time to time presented so many strange figures of different kinds--Indians, negroes, half-breeds, scouts, soldiers, sailors, Dutchmen, Englishmen, and hunters--that the wanderer, however odd his appearance, attracted very little attention as he went. Slowly he found his way up to the gates of the fort, and easily obtained admission to the person he sought. He found him in a mere barrack-room, with the simplest possible furniture, and no ornament whatever to distinguish it as the dwelling of a man of rank. The little camp-bed in one corner of the room, the plain deal table, not even painted, at which he sat writing; the two or three hard wooden stools, without backs, were all such as might have been used in a camp, or carried with an army, without much adding to the *impedimenta*; yet there was something about the young nobleman himself which instantly informed a visitor that he was in the presence of no common man. He turned his head as Woodchuck entered, and, as soon as he perceived who it was, he nodded, saying, "Immediately, immediately," and resumed his writing.

Captain Brooks drew a stool to some distance, and fixed his eyes first of all upon the young soldier, seeming to examine his countenance and form with great care. He then turned to another person whom the room contained, and scanned him with thorough accuracy. He seemed to be an Indian, if one might judge by complexion and features; yet he was dressed like one of the followers of the British army. The sort of hunting-tunic he wore was not the ordinary Ga-ka-ah, or Indian skirt, but a mere sort of cloth frock with sleeves, fastened round his waist by a leathern belt. It was of a peculiar colour, then very much worn both by men and women, of the hue of dead leaves, and called philomot; and on his head he wore a curious sort of cap of untanned leather, much of the same hue. It was certainly a well-devised dress for the purpose of concealing a wanderer through the woods in the autumn season; but, as I have before said, it was assuredly not Indian; and the long hair, though as black as jet, with a slight shading of moustache upon the upper lip, showed that in all probability there was some white blood in his veins, though not apparent on the surface. The man had much of the Indian impassible gravity, however; and, though he must have seen that he was undergoing a very severe scrutiny by the eyes of Woodchuck, no movement of any of the muscles of the face betrayed his consciousness, and he remained still and statue-like, with his gaze turned earnestly forward upon Lord H----.

The nobleman soon concluded his letter, and, beckoning the man up, placed it in his hands with some money.

"Take that to Mr. Prevost," he said, "and tell him, moreover, that I shall myself be up to-morrow before nightfall."

"Stay a moment," interposed Woodchuck; "I may have something to say too, that will make changes. I guess the half-breed had better wait outside a bit."

"Go down to the guard-room," said Lord H----, turning to the man, "and wait there till I send to you." Then, giving an inquiring look to Woodchuck, he added, "He tells me he can reach Mr. Prevost's house this night, if he sets out at once."

"To be sure he can," answered Woodchuck. "If he's the man I believe him to be, he'd go half as fur agin."

The runner took not the slightest notice of the conversation regarding himself and his own powers, nor, indeed, of the sort of intimation of recognition uttered by Captain Brooks.

"Is not your name Proctor?" said Woodchuck, at last. "I guess it be, though you look older since I saw you."

The other merely nodded his head; and Woodchuck continued, with a sort of grunt of satisfaction,--

"That'll do; he can speak, my lord, though he never do, except at very rare times. Them Ingian devils are as silent as snakes themselves; but this man beats them all. I travelled some two hundred miles with him, ten year or more agone, and never heard the sound of his voice in the whole way but once, and then he said three words and a half, and stopped."

"I know he can speak," said Lord H----, "for he told me how long he would take to go. Go down, Mr. Proctor, as I told you, and wait in the guard-room. You shall hear from me in a minute."

"He runs like a deer," said Woodchuck, as the man left the room, "but his way is generally to trot on at a darnation swingeing sort of rate, which does not seem to trouble his shanks at all; a sort of trot, like, carries him through everything and over everything--brambles, and bushes, and hills, and stones, and rocks, land or water, all the same. I do believe he'd trot across the Hudson, without much knowing or caring what was anything. The Indians call him Mungnokah; but, as his father's father was an Englishman, we call him Proctor."

"But can he be relied upon?" asked Lord H----. "He was recommended to me very strongly by General Webb, who employed him upon some difficult services."

Woodchuck mused. "Webb's recommendation," he said, at length, "is not worth much; for what would one give for any word out of the mouth of a man who would suffer a gallant comrade to fall, and a noble garrison to be butchered, without striking one stroke, or moving one step to their assistance? But if I recollect right, this Proctor is the runner who contrived to get through Montcalm's army and all the savage devils that were with him, and carried poor Munro's despatches to Webb. What became of the other one, nobody knows; but I guess we could find his scalp, if we sought well amongst the Hurons. Yes, this must be the man, I think; and if it be, you couldn't find a better. At all events, you can trust him for holding his tongue, and that's something in a runner. He wouldn't get up words enough in ten years to tell any secret you wanted to keep. And now, general, I've come to talk with you about what's to be done; and I think we had better settle that before the man goes. He'll get to Prevost's to-night, if he stays these two hours; and I guess we can settle sooner than that, for I've thought the matter over, and made up my mind."

"And to what conclusion have you come?" asked Lord H----.

Brooks looked down, and rubbed his great hands upon his knees for a moment, as if he hesitated to give the resolution he had formed, after so painful a struggle, the confirmation of uttered words.

"Not a pleasant one," he said, at length--"not one easily hit upon, my lord, but the only one--after all, the only one. I had a sore tussle with the devil last night, and he's a strong enemy. But I beat him--manful, hand to hand. He and I together, and no one to help either of us."

The nobleman thought that his poor friend's wits were beginning to wander a little; and, to lead him back from the diabolical encounter he spoke of, he said, changing the subject abruptly, "I suppose I could send no one better than this man Proctor?"

"I'll tell you what it is, Lord H----," answered Woodchuck, "I must go myself. There's no one can save Walter Prevost but Brooks. He's the man who must do it."

"And do you think it possible?" asked Lord H----, seeing the great probability of his companion himself being captured by the Indians, and yet hesitating whether he ought to say a word to deter him from his purpose.

"I do think it possible," said Woodchuck, with a grim smile; "for you see, if these Ingians get the man they want, they can't and darn't take any other."

Lord H---- grasped the rough hand of the hunter, saying, in a tone of much feeling, "You are indeed a noble-hearted man, Captain Brooks, if I understand you rightly, to go and give yourself up to these savages, to save your young friend. Nobody could venture to propose such a thing to you, because his having fallen into their hands was not your fault, and life is dear to every one; but--"

"Stay, stay, stay!" cried Woodchuck, "don't get along too fast. You've said two or three things already that want an answer. As to life, it is dear to every one; and I myself am such a fool, that I'd rather, by a good bit, go lingering on here, amongst all this smoke, and dirt, and dull houses, and rogues innumerable, than walk up there and be tomahawked, which is but the matter of a moment after all; for them Ingians isn't long about their work, and do it completely. Howsoever, one always clings to Hope; and so I think that, if I can get up there amongst the woods and trails that I know so well, I may perhaps find out some means of saving the poor boy and my own life too; and, if I can, I'll do it, for I'm not going to throw away my life like a bad shilling. If I can't do it, why then I'll save his life, cost what it will. I shall soon know all about it, when I get up there, for the squaws are all good, kind-hearted critturs; and if I can get hold of one of them, she'll be my scout soon enough, and fish out the truth for me, as to where the boy is, and when they are going to make the sacrifice. Lord bless you, they set about these things, them Ingians, just as orderly as a trial at law. They'll do nothing in a hurry; and so I shall have time to look about me, and see what's to be done without risking Walter's life in the meanwhile. Then you see, my lord, I've got this great advantage: I shall have a walk or two in my old haunts, among them beautiful woods. The snow will be out by that time; and, to my mind, there's no season when the woods look so well, and the air feels so fresh and free, as in a wintry day, with the ground all white, and wreaths of snow upon every vine and briar, and them great big hemlocks and pines rising up like black giants all around one. Some folks don't like the winter in the woods; but I could walk on, or go on, in a sleigh through them for ever. Why, that month among the woods, if I'm not caught sooner, would be worth ever so many years in this dull, dirty place, or any other city; for Albany, I take it, is as good as most of them, and perhaps better."

"But I am afraid that in the winter your plan of getting information would not succeed very well," said Lord H----. "In the first place, the Indian women are not likely to go very far from their wigwams, amongst which you would hardly venture; and, in the next place, your feet would be easily tracked in the snow; for these Indians, I am told, are most cunning and pertinacious hunters, and will follow any tracks they see for miles and miles."

"I've dodged an Ingian afore now," said Captain Brooks, with a look of some self-importance, "and in the snow too. I've got the very snow-shoes I did it in. I can walk in my snow-shoes either way, one as well as t'other; and so I made 'em believe that I was going east when I was going west, and going west when I was going east. Sometimes I had the shoes on the right way, and sometimes the wrong, so they could make nothing of it. And they think still--for, Lord help you, they are sometimes as simple as children--that the devil must have given me a lift now and then; for when I got where the trees grew thick together, so that the branches touched, and I could catch a great bough over my head by a spring, I would get up and climb along from one to another like a bear or a squirrel, sometimes two or three hundred yards before I came down again. I saw a set of them once upon the trail; and when they came where the tracks stopped, they got gaping up into the tree with their rifles in their hands, as if they were looking after a painter; but I was a hundred yards off or more, and quite away from the right line. Then, as to the women, I've thought about that, and I've laid a plan in case I can't get hold of any of them. Now I am going to tell you something very strange, my lord. You've heard of Freemasons, I dare say?"

Lord H---- nodded his head with a smile, and Woodchuck continued--

"Well, they've got Freemasons among the Ingians--that's to say, not exactly Freemasons, but what comes much to the same thing:[1] people who have got a secret among themselves, and who are bound to help each other in good or evil, in the devil's work or God's, against their own nation, or their own tribe, or their own family; and who, on account of some devilry or other, dare not, for the soul of them, refuse what a brother asks them. It's a superstition at the bottom of it, and it's very strange; but so it is."

While he had been speaking, he had unfastened his coat at the collar, drawn his arm out of the sleeve, and bared it up above the elbow, where there appeared a small blue line tattooed on the brown skin.

"There," he said, "there's the mark!"

"You do not mean to say you are one of this horrible association?" asked Lord H----, with a grave look.

"Not exactly that," answered Woodchuck; "and as to its being a horrible association or not, that's as folks use it. It may be for bad, and it may be for good; and there are good men amongst them. I am a sort of half-and-half member, and I'll tell you how it happened. I went once in the winter up into the woods to hunt moose by a place where there's a warm spring which melts the snow and keeps the grass fresh; and the big beasts come down to drink, and, mayhap, eat too. Well, as soon as I got there, I saw that some one had been before me; for I perceived tracks all about, and a sort of stable in the snow for the moose, such as hunters often make to get a number together, and to shoot them down when they herd in it. There were moose-tracks, too, and some blood on the snow. So I thought that the Ingians had killed some, and scared the rest away.

"I was going back by another trail, when I came upon an old man lying partly against a basswood-tree, just as quiet as if he was a corpse; and I should have thought he was as dead as a stone, if I hadn't seen his shining eyes move as I passed. Never a word did he say, and he'd have lain there and died outright rather than call for help. But I went up to him, and found the old crittur had been poked terribly by a moose all about his chest and shoulders. So I built up a little hut for him with boughs, and covered it over with snow, and made it quite snug and warm. I took him in and nursed him there; and, as I was well stocked with provisions, parched corn and dry meat and such like, I shared with him.

"I couldn't leave the poor old crittur there to die, you know, my lord, and so I stayed with him all the time, and we got a couple of deer, and prime venison steaks we had of them; and at last, at the end of five weeks, he was well enough to walk. By that time we had got quite friendly together; and I went down with him to his lodge, and spent the rest of the winter with him. I had often enough remarked a blue line tattooed upon his arm; and sometimes he would say one thing about it and sometimes another, for these Ingians lie like parrots. But at last he said he would tattoo a line on my arm; and when he had done it he told me it was the best service he could render me in return for all those I had rendered him. He said that if ever I met any of the Five Nations tattooed like that, and spoke a word which he taught me, they would help me against their own fathers. He told me something about them and about their set, but he would not tell me all.

"I was quite a young lad then, and the old man died the next year, for I went to see him, and found him just at the last gasp. I have since heard a good deal about those people, however, from other Ingians, who all have a dread of them, and call them the children of the devil; so I take care not to show my devil's mark amongst them, and have never had need to use it till now."

"How will it serve you now?" asked Lord H----, not at all liking or confiding in the support of such men.

"Well, if I can get speech of one of them, even for an instant," replied Woodchuck, "I can get together a band of the only men who will go against the superstitions of their people, and help me to set the poor boy free; and they will do it, whether they be tortoises, or bears, or wolves, or snipes, or stags."

"What--what!" exclaimed Lord H----, in utter amazement. "I do not understand what you mean."

"Only names of their Totems or tribes, my lord," answered Brooks. "These Ingians are queer people. You must not judge of them or deal with them as you would other men; and these are the only critturs amongst them I could get to help me, if their habits came in the way in the least bit. Now, you know, though I may do something by myself, I may not be able to do all. If I get the boy out of the hole where they have, doubtless, hid him, I have to find out where it is first, and to make sure that we are not followed and overtaken afterwards. I would fain save my life if I can, my lord," he continued, looking up in the face of his companion with a sort of appealing look. "I think a man has a right to do that if he can."

"Assuredly," replied Lord H----; "the love of life is implanted in us by God, himself, and all which can be expected of us by our country or our fellow-men is a readiness to sacrifice it when duty requires us to do so. But now, my good friend, I have another plan to propose. It is probable that hostilities have ceased for this year; and, since I saw you last night, a small party of the scouts, which you know we always have in pay, has been put at my disposal for the very purposes we have in view. They are all acquainted with wood warfare, with Indian habits, and with the art of tracking an enemy or a friend. Would it not be better for you to have these six men with you to give you assistance in case of need? Your own life, at all events, would be more secure."

"I think not," answered Woodchuck, musingly; "they might cumber me. No, my lord, I had better go alone. As for my own life, I may as well tell you at once, I have made up my mind to lose it, or save the boy. The devil put it hard to me that it was no fault of mine he was trapped; that my life was as good to me as his was to him, and a great deal more. But, knowing that it does not do to stand parleying with that gentleman, I said, 'Peter Brooks, it is your fault; for, if you had not shot the Ingian, Walter would never have been taken. Your life is not as good to you or anybody else as his is to him and all the world. He's quite a lad, and a young lad too, with many a bright year before him. You'll never see fifty again, and what's your fag-end worth to any one?' 'Not a stiver,' answered conscience; and so I resolved to go. Now, as to these men, the scouts, some of them are capital good fellows, and might help me a great deal when once I'm in the thick of the business. But seven men can't get all together into the Oneida country without being found out, I'll tell you what, my lord; if you'll let me place them where I want, one by one, in different places, and they slip into the country quietly, one at a time, they may do good service, and not be discovered."

"Will it not be dangerous so to divide your force?" asked Lord H----.

"Ingian ways with Ingian people," answered Woodchuck. "But I don't think you understand the thing, my lord. You see, through a great part of this Ingian territory, we English have built a little fort here, and a little fort there, all the way up the shores of Ontario, where they made sad work of it last year at Oswego. Well, if I stow away these scouts at the different posts, the nearest I can to Oneida creek, they will be only at arm's length, and can stretch out their hand to help whenever they're called upon. They'll be able to get in, one by one, quite easily; for I've a great notion some of the Ingians have got a spite at Walter, and are not very likely to look for any one in his stead. If they caught me, they'd be obliged to have me; and if the scouts went all together they'd stop them, for they don't like their number; but one at a time they'll pass well enough, if they understand their business, which is to be supposed."

"I see your plan now," said Lord H----, "and perhaps you are right. You can concentrate them upon any point very rapidly. They shall be sent for, and put under your command this very day."

"No need of command," answered Woodchuck; "scouts don't like to be commanded; and if they don't help with a good will, better not help at all. Just you tell them what I'm about. Let them know that a young man's life is at stake, and they'll work well for it, if they're worth a penny. And now, my lord, you call up that man Proctor, and send him off to Prevost's house.

Call him up here--call him up here. I've got this large powder-horn which I want to send back, though it's a doubt whether the man can muster words enough to tell who it comes from, and I must get him to do so one way or another."

"I can take it to-morrow myself," said Lord H----.

But Woodchuck shook his head.

"That won't do," he said, with a shrewd look; "the runner must take it. He'll tell Prevost before some of his negroes, and the negroes will tell any Ingians that are prowling about, and so it will get round that I've left the hunting-grounds for good, and I shall slip in the more easily. Always think of everything when you can; and if you can't do that, think of as much as possible. A hunter's life makes one mighty cautious. I'm as careful as an old raccoon, who always looks nine ways before he puts his nose out of his hole."

Lord H---- called up the runner, and into his hands was delivered the powder-horn for Mr. Prevost, with Woodchuck's message repeated over and over again, and manifold injunctions not to forget it.

"Tell him I took it that unlucky day I shot the Ingian," said Woodchuck, "and I don't like to keep what's not my own. It's nearly as good as stealing, if not quite. There, Master Proctor, you can get up words enough to say that, can't you?"

The man nodded his head, and then turned to the door, without any further reply, beginning his peculiar sort of trot before he reached the top of the stairs, and never ceasing it till he arrived at the door of Mr. Prevost's house.

In the meanwhile, Lord H---- made Captain Brooks stay to partake of his own very frugal dinner, while the scouts were being collected and brought to the fort. They came about two o'clock, ready prepared, at least in part, for what was to follow; for in the little town of Albany such an adventure as that which had befallen Walter Prevost was a matter of too much interest not to spread to every house, and to be told at every fireside. Most of the men, accustomed to continual action and enterprise of various kinds, were very willing to go, with the prospect of a fair reward before them. Life was so often perilled with them, dangers and difficulties so often encountered, that existence without activity was rather a burden than otherwise. Each, probably, had his selfishness of some kind; but only one, in whom it took the form of covetousness, thought fit to inquire what was to be his recompense beyond the mere pay for this uncovenanted service.

"Your recompense will be nothing at all," answered Woodchuck, at once, without waiting for Lord H---- to speak. "I won't have you with me. The man who can try to drive a bargain when a brave boy's life is at stake is not fit to have a share with us. There, go along, and knit petticoats; you may get a dollar apiece for them. That's the sort of winter work fit for you."

The man then sullenly stalked out of the room, and all other matters were soon settled with his companions. The method of their entrance into the Oneida territory, the different routes they were to take, and the points where they were to halt till called upon, were all arranged by Woodchuck with a sort of natural military skill which was more than once displayed by many of the American people during after wars.

The part of the nobleman who was present was merely to listen, and give some letters to officers commanding different posts. But he listened well pleased and attentively, for his was a mind always eager to acquire information and direction from the experience of others; and the insight which he gained into the habits of the new people amongst whom he was might have been highly serviceable to others as well as himself, had not a sort of pedantry prevailed amongst the older officers in the British army at that time, and for many succeeding years, which prevented them from adapting their tactics to the new situations in which they were placed.

Wolfe was a splendid exception--but Wolfe was a young man, coming in the dawning of a better day; and even had he not been so, it is probable that his genius, like that of Wellington, would have shown him that he was born to *make* rules, rather than observe them.

As soon as the scouts were gone, Woodchuck rose to take his leave also; and, as Lord H---- shook him very warmly by the hand, the good man said, in a tone of strong feeling--

"Thank you, my lord, for all your kindness. You'll be glad to know I feel very happy; and I'll tell you why--I'm doing something, and I'm doing my duty."

CHAPTER XXVII

"There is a light, sir, at the Castle," said one of the servants of Sir William Johnson, entering the room where he was seated with Mr. Prevost; "it comes from the great court."

"Then they have arrived," said the officer, turning to his guest; "let us set out at once. Are the horses saddled?"

"They have been kept ready, sir, ever since the morning," replied the servant, to whom the last words were addressed.

"It is strange," said Mr. Prevost, as he followed his host towards the door of the room, "that the negro I sent to tell Edith the cause of my delay has not returned, as I told him. He might have been here four hours ago. I am growing somewhat anxious."

"Be not so, be not so!" replied Sir William. "Two or three years of forest life, my good friend, are not enough to inure a man to all the little accidents and discomforts he must meet with; and the first serious danger so shakes his nerves that they vibrate at a trifle. The man's horse may have fallen, or he may have purloined a bottle of brandy, and got drunk, or he may have missed his way, or set out late. Between this house and yours there is room for chances enough to make a moderate volume. Let us not look out for uncertain evils, when there are real ones enough around us."

"Real ones enough, indeed!" ejaculated Mr. Prevost, with a deep sigh.

A moment after, they reached the front of the stables, from which their horses were immediately brought forth; and, mounting, they set out, followed by a small party both on horseback and on foot; for Sir William, though he affected the simplicity of the Indian, was not at all averse to a little appearance of state and dignity in his dealings with his red allies. There is a certain sort of pride which clothes itself in humility; and without at all meaning to assert that the very remarkable man in question desired to make the Indian chiefs feel that his adoption of their manners was a condescension, yet it is certain that from time to time he judged it expedient--perhaps from good motives of policy--to make a somewhat ostentatious display of power and authority.

The night was exceedingly dark. The moon now rose at a very late hour; and dim clouds hid the stars from the dwellers upon earth. In such a night, and in such circumstances, the fancy even of the most stout-hearted is apt to indulge in deceits; and as the eye of Mr. Prevost wandered round, dim forms like spectres seemed to be gliding about the field of maize, cut in many places, but not yet garnered.

Not feeling certain whether imagination cheated him or not, he made no observation, and for some time Sir William Johnson was silent also; but, at length, the latter said, in a commonplace tone--

"Our good friends seem to have come in great force, probably, in consequence of the urgency of my summons. Now, be patient, Prevost, and bear with their cool, phlegmatic ways; for these people often feel the strongest sympathies and serve their friends the best when they seem the most cold and indifferent."

Mr. Prevost felt already how difficult it was to maintain that equanimity which in theory he estimated as highly as an Indian, and in practice strove for always, but not unfrequently lost. He promised, however, to leave entirely to Sir William Johnson the management of a conference with the chiefs of the Mohawk and Onondaga Nations, which had been proposed by that officer himself, for the purpose of inducing the two most powerful tribes of the Iroquois to interfere in behalf of Walter, and save him from the fate that menaced him.

Through the gate of the castle (the door of which stood open as usual, for, although it was filled with large quantities of those stores which the Indians most coveted, its safety was left entirely to the guardianship of their good faith) the two gentlemen entered the large courtyard, which, on this occasion, was quite deserted, the weather being cold enough now to render some shelter agreeable even to an Indian. From the open door of the great hall, which stretched along the larger part of the whole building, came forth a blaze of light; and, on entering, Sir William Johnson and his companion found a number of Mohawk and Onondaga chiefs assembled, sitting gravely ranged in a semi-circle round the fire. Each was fully clothed in his garb of ceremony, and bright and brilliant were the colours displayed in the dresses and ornaments of the red men; but, as this was a peaceful occasion, their faces were destitute of paint, and the scalp-lock was concealed under the brilliant and graceful Gostoweh, or cap, in many of which was seen the plume of the white egret, used to distinguish the great chiefs of the different tribes, ever since the feathers of the famous white bird of heaven had been exhausted.

All rose with quiet, native dignity when the Indian agent and his companion entered, and a murmur of gratulation ran round while Sir William and Mr. Prevost seated themselves in two large chairs.

"This is our brother," said Sir William Johnson, pointing to Mr. Prevost.

"Hai, hai!" exclaimed the Indian chiefs. "Peace, peace! he is *our* brother."

King Hendrick then approached Mr. Prevost, dressed in his sky-blue coat of European manufacture, presented to him by the reigning monarch of England, and took his hand, saying, in a tone of friendly sympathy, and in the English tongue, "Our brother is sad. Be comforted."

He then seated himself, and the Attotarho, or grand chief of the whole confederacy, an office held by descent by the chief of the Onondaga Totem of the Bear, advanced to Walter's father, and spoke the same words in Iroquois, showing clearly that the object of the meeting was understood by the Indian leaders.

When all had arranged themselves around again, a silence of some minutes succeeded. It was painful to Mr. Prevost; for no one who has not associated with the Indians can fully comprehend the impressive--I might almost call it oppressive--effect of their exceeding stillness upon grave occasions.

At length the Attotarho said, rising to his full height, which might be almost termed gigantic, "Our father has sent for us; and we are obedient children. We are here to listen to his sweet words, and understand his mind."

Sir William Johnson then, in a speech of very great power and beauty, full of the figurative language of the Indians, related the events which had occurred in the family of Mr. Prevost, and made an appeal to his hearers for council and assistance. He represented his friend as an old tree from which a branch had been torn by the lightning; he strove to depict his desolate state; and he told a story of a panther, one of whose young ones had been carried off by a wolf, but who, on applying for assistance to a bear and a stag, recovered her young by their means. "The panther was strong enough," he said, "with the aid of the lion, to take back her young one from the wolf and to tear the wolf to pieces; but the wolf was of kin to the bear and the stag, and therefore the panther forbore."

"But the bear is slow, and the stag is not strong, when he goes against his kindred," said the Attotarho, significantly; "and the lion will never take the war-path against his allies."

The Black Eagle | 197

"Heaven forbid that there should be need!" exclaimed Sir William; "but the lion must consider his children, and the panther is his son."

Poor Mr. Prevost remained in a state of painful anxiety while the discussion proceeded in this course, wandering, as it seemed to him, round the subject, and affording no indication of any intention, on the part of the chiefs, to give him assistance; for figures, though they be very useful things to express the meaning of a speaker, are sometimes equally useful to conceal it.

At length he could bear it no longer, and, forgetting his promise to Sir William Johnson, he started up with all the feelings of a father strong in his heart, and appealed directly to the Indians in their own tongue, which he had completely mastered, but in a style of eloquence very different from their own, and, perhaps, the more striking to them on that account.

"My child!" he exclaimed, earnestly, "give me back my child! Who is the man amongst the Five Nations whom he has wronged? Where is the man to whom he has refused kindness or assistance? When has his door been shut against the wandering red man? When has he denied to him a share of his food or of his fire? Is he not your brother and the son of your brother? Have we not smoked the pipe of peace together? and has that peace ever been violated by us? I came within the walls of your Long House trusting to the truth and the hospitality of the Five Nations. I built my lodge amongst you in full confidence of your faith and of your friendship. Is my hearth to be left desolate, is my heart to be torn out, because I trusted to the truth and honour of the Mohawks, to the protection and promises of the Onondaga, because I would not believe the songs of the singing-bird, that said, 'They will slay thy children before thy face?' If there be fault or failing in me or mine towards the red man in any of the tribes--if we have taken aught from him--if we have spoken false words in his ear--if we have refused him aught that he had a right to ask--if we have shed any man's blood,--then slay *me*; cut down the old tree at the root, but leave the sapling. If we have been just and righteous towards you--if we have been friendly and hospitable--if we have been true and faithful--if we have shed no man's blood, and taken no man's goods,--then give me back my child. To you, chiefs of the Five Nations, I raise my voice; from you I demand my son, for a crime committed by one of the league is a crime committed by all. Could ye find none but the son of your brother to slay? Must ye make the trust he placed in you the means of his destruction? Had he doubted your hospitality--had he not confided in your faith--had he said, 'the lightning of the guns of Albany and the thunder of her cannon are better protection than the faith and truth of the red man,'--ye know he would have been safe. But he said: 'I will put my trust in the hospitality of the Five Nations; I will become their brother. If there be bad men amongst them, their chiefs will protect me, their Attotarho will do me justice. They are great warriors, but they are good men. They smite their enemies, but they love their friends.' If, then, ye are good men--if ye are great warriors--if ye are brothers to your brother--if ye are true to your friends--if ye are fathers yourselves,--give me back my son."

"Koué, koué!" cried the Indians, in a sad tone, more profoundly affected by the vehement expression of a father's feelings than Sir William Johnson had expected; but the moment that the word was uttered which, according to the tone and rapidity with which it is pronounced, signifies either approbation and joy, or sympathy and grief, they relapsed into deep silence.

Sir William Johnson, though he had been a good deal amazed and alarmed at Mr. Prevost taking upon himself to speak, and fearful lest he should injure his own cause, now fully appreciated the effect produced; and would not add a word to impair it.

At length, King Hendrick arose, and said, in a grave and melancholy tone--

"We are brothers; but what can we do? The Oneidas are our brethren also. The Mohawks, the Oneidas, the Onondagas, the Cayugas, and the Senecas are separate nations, though they are brethren and allies. We are leagued together for common defence, but not that we should rule over each other. The Oneidas have their laws, and they execute them; but this law is common to all the nations, that if a man's blood be shed, except in battle, the man who shed it must die. If he cannot be found, one of his nearest kin must be taken. If he have none, one of his tribe or race. The same is it with the Mohawk as with the Oneida. But in this thing the Oneidas have done as the Mohawks would not have done. They have not sought diligently for the slayer, neither have they waited patiently to see whether they could find any of his kindred. The Oneidas have been hasty. They have taken the first man they could find. They have been fearful like the squirrel; and they keep their prisoner lest, in the time of need, they should not find another. This is unjust. They should have first waited, and searched diligently, and should not have taken the son of their brother till they were sure no other man could be found. But, koué, koué! what is to be done? Shall the Mohawk unbury the hatchet against the Oneida? That cannot be. Shall the Mohawk say to the Oneida: 'Thou art unjust?' The Oneida will answer,--'We have our laws and you have yours: the Mohawk is not the ruler of the Oneida: repose under your own tree; we sit upon a stone.' One thing perchance may be done," and a very slight look of cunning intelligence came into his face; "subtlety will sometimes do what force cannot. The snake is as powerful as the panther. I speak my thought; and I know not if it be good. Were my brother, the Attotarho, to choose ten of the subtlest serpents of his nation, and I to choose ten of the subtlest of mine, they might go unpainted and unarmed, and, creeping through the woods without rattle or hiss, reach the place where the young man lies. If there be thongs upon his hands, the breath of a snake can melt them. If there be a door upon his prison, the eyes of a snake can pierce it. If there be a guard, the coil of the snake can twine around him; and many of the Oneida chiefs and warriors will rejoice that they are thus friendly forced to do right, and seek another. I speak my thought; I know not whether it is good. Let those speak who know; for no nation of the Five can do aught against another nation alone, otherwise we break to pieces like a faggot when the thong bursts."

Thus saying, he ended, sat down, and resumed his stillness; and, after a pause, as if for thought, the Attotarho rose, addressing himself directly to Mr. Prevost, and speaking with a great deal of grave dignity.

"We grieve for you, my brother," he said, "and we grieve for ourselves. We know that our great English father, who sits under the mighty pine-tree, will be wrath with his red children; but let him remember, and speak it in his ears, that the Mohawk and the Onondaga, the Seneca and the Cayuga, are not to blame for this act. They say the Oneidas have done hastily, and they will consult together, around the council-fire, how thou mayest best be comforted. Haste is only fit for children. Grown men are slow and deliberate. Why should we go quickly now? Thy son is safe; for the Oneidas cannot, according to their law, take any sacrifice, except the life of the slayer, till they be well assured that he, the slayer, cannot be found."

Mr. Prevost's lip quivered with emotion as if about to speak; but Sir William Johnson laid his hand upon him, saying, in a quick whisper, "Leave him to me." And the Onondaga proceeded.

"We will do the best that we can for our brother; but the meadow-lark has not the strength of the Eagle, nor the fox of the panther; and if we should fail, it would not be the fault of the Mohawks or the Onondagas.--I have said."

Sir William Johnson then rose to reply, seeing that the Attotarho sought to escape any distinct promise, and judging that, with the support of King Hendrick, a little firmness might wring something more from him.

"My brother, the Attotarho," he said, "has spoken well. The Five Nations are leagued together in peace and in war. They take the scalps of their enemies as one man. They live in brotherhood. But my brother says that if the Oneida commits a crime, the Mohawk and the Onondaga, the Seneca and the Cayuga, are not guilty of the act, and therefore deserve no wrath. But he says at the same time, that if the man named Woodchuck slays a red man, Walter Prevost, the brother of the red man, must die for it. How is this? Have the children of the Five Nations forked tongues? Do they speak double words? If the Onondagas are not guilty of what the Oneidas do, neither is Walter Prevost guilty of what the pale-face Woodchuck does. May the Great Spirit forbid that your great father, near the rising of the sun, should deal unjustly with his red children, or be wrath with them for acts done by others; but he does expect that his children of the Five Nations will show the same justice to his pale-face children; and, unless they are resolved to take upon themselves the act of the Oneidas, and say their act is our act, that they will do something to prevent it. My brother says that haste is for children; and true are his words. Then why have the Oneidas done this hasty thing? We cannot trust that they will not be children any more, or that, having done this thing hastily, they will not hastily do worse. True, everything should be done deliberately; we should show ourselves men, if we want children to follow our example. Let us take counsel then fully, while we are here together. The council-fire burns in the midst of us; and we have time enough to take thought calmly. Here I will sit till I know that my brothers will do justice in this matter, and not suffer the son of my brother to remain in the hands of those who have wrongfully made him a prisoner. Yes, truly, here I will sit to take counsel with the chiefs, till the words of wisdom are spoken, even although the sun should go five times round the earth before our talk were ended. Have I spoken well?"

"Koué! Koué!" exclaimed a number of voices; and one of the old Sachems rose, saying, in slow and deliberate tones,--

"Our white brother has the word of truth and resolution. The Oneida has shown the speed of the deer, but not the wisdom of the tortoise. The law of the Oneida is our law; and he should have waited at least one moon, to see if the right man could be found. The Oneida must be in trouble at his own hastiness. Let us deliver him from the pit into which he has fallen; but let us do it with the silent wisdom of the snake, which creeps through the grass where no one sees him. The rattlesnake is the most foolish of reptiles; for he talks of what he is going to do beforehand. We will be more wise than he is; and, as our thoughts are good, we will keep them for ourselves. Let us only say, the boy shall be delivered, if the Mohawks and the Onondagas can do it; but let us not say how, for a man who gives away a secret deprives himself of what he can never recover, and benefits nothing but the wind.--I have said."

All the assembled chiefs expressed their approbation of the old man's words, and seemed to consider the discussion concluded. Mr. Prevost, indeed, was anxious to have something more definite; but Sir William

Johnson nodded his head significantly, saying, in a low tone, "We have done as much,--nay, more, than we could expect. It will be necessary to close our conference with some gifts, which will be, as it were, a seal upon our covenant."

"But have they entered into any covenant?" rejoined Mr. Prevost. "I have heard of none made yet on their part."

"As much as Indians ever do," answered Sir William Johnson; "and you can extract nothing more from them with your utmost skill."

He then called some of his people from without into the hall, ordered the stores to be opened, and brought forth some pieces of scarlet cloth, one of the most honourable presents which could be offered to an Indian chief. A certain portion was cut off for each, and received with grave satisfaction. Mats and skins were then spread upon the floor in great abundance. Long pipes were brought in, and handed round; and, after having smoked together in profound silence for nearly half an hour, the chiefs stretched themselves upon the ground, and composed themselves to rest.

Sir William Johnson and his guest, as a mark of confidence and brotherhood, remained with them throughout the night, but retired to the further end of the hall. They did not sleep so soon as their dusky companions. Their conversation, carried on in low tones, was, nevertheless, eager and anxious; for the father could not help still feeling great apprehension regarding the fate of his son; and Sir William Johnson was not altogether without alarm regarding the consequences of the very determination to which he had brought the chiefs of the Mohawks and Onondagas. Symptoms of intestine discord had of late been perceived in the great Indian confederacy. They had not acted on the behalf of England with the unanimity which they had displayed in former years; and it was the policy of the British Government by every means to heal all divisions and consolidate their union, as well as to attach them more and more firmly to the English cause. Although he doubted not that whatever was done by the chiefs with whom he had just been in conference, would be effected with the utmost subtlety and secrecy, yet there was still the danger of producing a conflict between them and the Oneidas in the attempt, or causing angry feeling even if it were successful; and Sir William, who was not at all insensible to the value of his government's approbation, felt some alarm at the prospect before him.

He and Mr. Prevost both slept at length; and the following morning saw the chiefs dispersing in the gray dawn of a cold and threatening day.

CHAPTER XXVIII

The snow was falling fast; the early snow of Northern America. The woods had not yet parted with all the splendour of their autumnal foliage; and the rivers still sang along their beds, confined, indeed, and narrowed in their channel by a ledge of thin ice along their banks, but still gay and sparkling. The air, however, was raw and cold; the ground hard beneath the tread; the sky dark and lowering; and the flakes rested unmelted on the earth, covering rapidly the green grass and the brown leaves.

Otaitsa stole forth from the shelter of the great lodge, passed amongst the huts around, and out into the fields through the opening in the palisade. She was going where she wished not her steps to be traced, and she knew that the fast-falling snow would speedily fill up every foot-print. Quietly and gracefully she glided on till she reached the edge of the deep wood, and then along a little-frequented trail, till, at the distance of about half a mile, her eyes, keenly bent forward, perceived something brown crouching still and motionless under cover of a young hemlock, the branches of which nearly swept the ground.

As the Blossom approached, a head, covered with glossy black hair, rolled up behind, was raised above a little bush which partly hid the woman's figure; and, coming nearer, Otaitsa asked, in a low voice,--

"Did he pass?"

"No," answered the young maiden to whom she spoke; "it was Apukwa, the medicine-man."

Otaitsa waved her head sadly to and fro, saying, "I understand." Then, speaking to the girl again, she said, "Now back to the castle, through the brush there to the other trail, and then home."

Her own walk was to be longer; and on she went, with the same gliding step, till, about half a mile further, she turned a little out of the path to the right; and there, concealed amongst the bushes, she found an old woman of her tribe, to whom she put the same question, and received nearly the same answer.

"Thou art cold, my mother," said Otaitsa, unfastening her mantle, and throwing it over the old woman; "get thee back with the step of a mole through the most covered ways thou canst find. How far on is the other?"

"More than a mile," replied the old woman; "close at the foot of the rocks."

Otaitsa made no reply, but hastened forward to a spot where some abrupt, but not very elevated, crags rose up out of the midst of the wood. For a moment there seemed no one there; and the trail at that spot divided into two, one running to the right, and the other to the left, at the very base of the rocks.

Otaitsa gazed cautiously about. She did not dare to utter a sound; but at length her eye fixed upon a large mass of stone tumbled from the bank above, crested and feathered with some sapling chestnuts. It seemed a place fit for concealment; and, advancing over some broken fragments, she was approaching carefully, when again a head was raised, and a hand stretched out beckoning to her.

Still she trod her way cautiously, taking care not to set her foot on prominent points where the trace might remain, and contriving, as far as possible, to make each bush and scattered tree a screen. At length she reached her companion's place of concealment, and crouched down behind the rock, by the side of a young woman a few years older than herself.

"Has he passed?" asked Otaitsa. "Which way did he take?"

"To the east," replied the other; "to the rising sun; but it was not the brother of the Snake. It was Apukwa, the Bull-rush; and he had a wallet with him, but no tomahawk."

"How long is it since he passed?" asked the Blossom, in the same low tone which they had hitherto used.

"While the crow would fly a mile," answered the young woman. "Has my husband yet come back?"

"Not so," replied Otaitsa; "but let us both go, for thou art weary for thy home, my sister, and I am now satisfied. Their secret is mine."

"How so?" inquired the other; "canst thou see through the rock with thy bright eyes, Blossom?"

"The cunning medicine-man goes not to pray to his Maneto," answered Otaitsa, "nor to converse with his Hawenergo. Neither does he wander forth to fulfil his fasts in the solitude to the east. Yet he will find no dry deer's-flesh there, my sister; nor any of the fire-water he loves so well. But away there, where I have gathered many a strawberry when I was young, there is a deep rift in the rock, where you may walk a hundred paces on flat ground with the high crags all around you. The wild cat cannot spring up, and the deer winks as he looks down. It has but a narrow entrance, for the jaws of the rock are but half open; and I know now where they have hid my brother. That is enough, for this night, to Otaitsa."

"And what wilt thou do next?" asked her companion.

"Nay, I know not," answered the Blossom. "The sky grows darker--the night is coming on, and we must follow the setting sun if we would not have Apukwa see us. We have yet time, for the gloomy place he goes to is two thousand paces further. Come. Be assured, dear sister, I will call for thy aid when it is needful; and thou wilt as soon refuse it as the flower refuses honey to the bee. Step carefully in the low places, that they see not the tracks of thy feet."

Thus saying, Otaitsa led the way from their place of concealment with a freer air (for she knew that Apukwa had far to go), but with as cautious a tread as ever, lest, returning before the night had fully fallen, he should see the foot-prints in the snow.

They had been gone about ten minutes, when, creeping silently down along the trail from the east, the medicine-man appeared at the furthest corner of the rock within sight; but he was not alone. The Indian, whom they called the brother of the Snake, was with him. The latter, however, remained at the point where he could see both ways, while Apukwa came swiftly forward. At the spot where the trail separated, he paused, and looked earnestly down upon the ground, bending his head almost to his knees. Then he seemed to track something along the trail towards the Indian Castle; and then, turning back, walked slowly up to the rock, following exactly the path by which the two women had returned.

At length he seemed satisfied; and, quickening his pace, he rejoined his companion.

"Thou art right, brother," he said. "There were two. What dimmed thine eyes that thou canst not tell who they were?"

"I was far," answered the other; "and there is shadow upon shadow."

"Was not one Otaitsa?" asked the medicine-man, slowly. "Could the brother of the Snake fail to know the Blossom he loves to look at?"

"If my eyes were not hidden, it was not she," replied his companion. "Never did I see the great Sachem's daughter go out, even when the sun has most fire, without her mantle round her. This woman had none."

"Which woman?" asked Apukwa; "thou saidst there were two."

"One came, two went," replied the other Oneida; "but the second could not be the Blossom, for she was tall. The other might have been, but she had no mantle, and she seemed less than Black Eagle's daughter--more like Koya, the daughter of the Bear. What were the print of the moccassins?"

"The snow falls fast; and covers up men's steps, as time covers the traditions of our fathers," replied the medicine-man; "they were not clear, brother. One was bigger than the other, but that was all I could see. Yet I scent the Blossom in this thing, my brother. The worshipper of the God of the pale-faces would save the life of the pale-face, had he made milk of the blood of her brother. She may love the boy too well, as her father loved the white woman. She has been often there, at the lodge of Prevost, with the pale-face priest or her father--very often; and she has stayed long. That trail she likes to follow better than any other; and the Black Eagle may think that his Blossom is a flower fit to grow by the lodge of the Yengees, and too beautiful for the red man. Has not my brother dreamed such dreams? has not his Maneto whispered to him such things?"

"He has," answered the brother of the Snake, in a tone of stern meaning; "and my tomahawk is sharp. But we must take counsel on this with our brethren, to make sure that there be no double tongues amongst us. How else should these women see our tracks, when we have covered them with leaves?"

It is probable that this last expression was used figuratively: not actually to imply that a precaution, very common amongst Indians, had been taken in this case; but that every care had been used to prevent a discovery, by the women of the nation, of any part of the proceedings in regard to poor Walter Prevost.

"My tongue is single," said the brother of the Snake; "and if I had a double tongue, would I use it when my enemy is under my scalping-knife? Besides, am I not more than my brother?"

And, baring his arm, he pointed with his finger to that small blue stripe which Woodchuck had exhibited on his own arm to Lord H---- in Albany.

"My brother listens with the ears of the hare," said Apukwa. "The Honontkoh never betray each other. But there are young men with us who are not of our order. Some are husbands, some are lovers; and with women they are women. Yet we must be watchful not to scatter our own herd. There must be no word of anger; but our guard must be made more sure. Go thou home to thine own lodge; and to-morrow, while the East is still white, let us hold council in the wigwam further down the lake. The home wind is blowing strong, and there will be more snow to cover our trail."

Thus saying, they parted for the night.

But the next morning early, from one of the small fortified villages of the Indians some miles from their great Castle, no less than six young men set out at different times, and took their way separately through the woods. One said to his wife, as he left her,--

"I go to hunt the moose." And one to his sister, "I go to kill the deer." And another told his squaw the same story; but she laughed, and answered,--

"Thou art careful of thy goods, my husband. Truth is too precious a thing to be used on all occasions. Thou keepest it for the time of need."

The man smiled, and patted her cheek, saying,--

"Keep thine own counsel, wife; and when I lie to thee, seem not to know it."

CHAPTER XXIX

In the chain of low cliffs which ran at the distance of four or five miles from the Oneida village, and to which, probably, at one time the waters of the lake had extended, was a deep cleft or fissure in the hard rock, fourteen or fifteen yards in width at its widest part, and narrower at the mouth than in the interior. One of the rocks, at the time I speak of, though large masses have fallen since, and a good deal altered the features of the scene, abutted considerably over its base, and projected so far as almost to touch the opposite crag, giving the mouth of the fissure somewhat the appearance of a cave. On either side, the walls of this gloomy dell were perpendicular-- in some places even overhanging; and at the end, where it might have been expected to slope gradually away to the upland, the general character of the scene was merely diversified by a break fifteen or sixteen feet from the ground, dividing the face of the crag nearly into two equal parts. Beneath this ledge was a hollow of four or five feet in depth, rendering ascent from that side impracticable.

It is probable that at some time in the long, unknown past of America a river poured here over the edge of the cliff, wearing away the solid rock by its continued action; and, as in the case of Niagara, carrying the cataract further and further back with each succeeding year, but without diminishing the precipitancy of the fall. The stone was of a loose and friable nature, breaking, by all the various accidents of the seasons, into strange and uncouth forms; and altogether the place, rarely if ever visited by the sun, would have been one of the most dim and gloomy that can be conceived, had not some light feathery shrubs and trees perched themselves upon several prominent points, especially where the ledge I have mentioned marked out the former site of the cascade.

Underneath that ledge, at the time referred to, had been hastily constructed a small hut or Indian lodge, formed of stakes driven into the ground, and covered over skilfully enough with bark, branches, and other materials of the forest. A door had apparently been brought for it from some distance; for it was evidently old, and had strange figures painted on it in red. Across this door was fixed a great bar, which would indeed have been very useless, had not the stakes forming the walls of the hut been placed close together, rendering it in reality much stronger than an ordinary Indian lodge.

On the day after Otaitsa's expedition, mentioned in the preceding chapter, sixteen or eighteen Oneidas of different ages, but none of them far advanced in life, gathered round the mouth of the cleft, and conversed together for several minutes, in low tones, and with their usual slow and deliberate manner. At the end of their conference, one seated himself on a stone near the entrance, two advanced into the chasm, and the rest dispersed themselves in different directions through the woods.

The two who advanced approached the hut, following each other so closely that the foot of each trod in the step of the other; and when they reached the lodge, the foremost took down the bar and opened the door, suffering the light to enter the dark chamber within. The spectacle which that light displayed was a very painful one.

There, seated on the ground, with his head almost bent down to his knees, his brown hair falling wild and shaggy over his face, his dress soiled, and in some parts torn, and his hands thin and sallow, sat poor Walter Prevost, the image of despair. All the bright energies of his eager, impetuous nature seemed quelled; the look of happy, youthful enjoyment was altogether gone; and with it the warm hopes and glowing aspirations, the dreams of future happiness or greatness, of love, and joy, and tenderness. The sunshine had departed; the motes of existence no longer danced in the beam.

He lifted not his head when the Indians entered; still and impassible as themselves, he sat without movement or word; the very senses seemed dead in the living tomb where they had confined him. But the sight touched them with no pity.

Grazing at him with a curious, cunning, serpent-like look, Apukwa placed before him a wallet which he carried, containing some dried deer's-flesh and parched Indian corn; and, after having watched him for a moment without a change of countenance, he said, in a cold tone--"There is food--take it and eat."

As if the sound of his hated voice had startled the youth from a death-like sleep, Walter sprang suddenly to his feet, exclaiming,--

"Why should I eat, to prolong my misery? Slay me! Take thy tomahawk and dash my brains out! Put an end to this torment, the most terrible that thy fiend-like race have ever devised!"

The Black Eagle | 209

The two Indians laughed with a low, quiet, satisfied laugh.

"We cannot slay thee," said the brother of the Snake, "till we know that thy pale-face brother who killed our brother, cannot be found to take thy place."

"He is far beyond your power," cried Walter vehemently; "he will never be within your grasp. I helped him to escape; I delivered him from you. Slay me, slay me, dogs of Indians! Your hearts are wolves' hearts; you are not men, you are women who dare not use a tomahawk. You are the scoff of your enemies. They laugh at the Oneidas; they spit at them. They say they are children, who dare not kill an enemy till the old men say, 'Kill him.' They fear the rod of their chief. They are like hares and rabbits, that tremble at the sound of the wind."

It was in vain that he tried to provoke them. They only seemed to enjoy his agony, and the bitter words that it called forth.

"Eat and drink," said Apukwa coldly, as soon as Walter became silent; "for we are going to tie thee. We must hunt the deer, we must grind the corn--we cannot watch thee every day, till the time of the sacrifice comes. Eat and drink, then; for here are the thongs."

Walter glared at him for a moment, and then snatched up a gourd filled with water, which the brother of the Snake had brought, and drained it with a long and eager draught. He then cast it from him, and stood still and stern before them, saying,--

"I will disappoint you. Henceforth I will eat no more. Tie me if you will. I can fast as well as you Indians."

The two men looked in each other's faces, apparently puzzled how to act; for, if he kept his resolution, their object would, indeed, be frustrated. The death of their kinsman, according to their superstition, required blood; and by starvation the prisoner would escape from their hands. Still, they dared not disobey the decision of the chiefs.

A slight sign seemed to pass between them; and, taking hold of the poor lad somewhat roughly, they bound both his hands and feet, twining the stout thongs of deer-skin round and round, and through and through, in what seemed inextricable knots. He stood quite still and passive; and, when they had done, cast himself down upon the ground again, turning his face from them. The two men gazed at him for a moment or two, and then, leaving the hut in silence, replaced the bar.

For some time after they were gone, Walter lay just as he had fallen. The dead apathy of despair had taken possession of him; life, thought, feeling, were a burden. The many days which had passed in that dull, dark, silent abode were rapidly producing on his mind that effect which solitary confinement is said too often to occasion. The transition is easy from anxiety, grief, fear, through melancholy and gloom, to despair and madness. Oh, man, never shut out hope from thy fellow-creature! or, if it must be so--if crime requires relentless punishment--then, whatever a false philanthropy would say, give thou death when thou takest away this world's hope, for then thou openest the gate of the grave to a brighter light than that which is extinguished. The All-seeing Eye beams with mercy as well as light.

He lay in that death-like stillness for several hours; and there came not a sound of any kind during all that time, to relieve the black monotony of the day. His ear, by suffering, had been rendered painfully acute; but the snow fell noiselessly; the wild animals were in their coverts or in their dens; the very wind had no breath.

Suddenly there was a sound. What was it? It seemed like a cracking branch far up above his head. Then a stone rolled down and rattled over the bark roof, making the snow slip before it. Another crashing branch, and then a silence, which seemed to him to last for hours.

"Some panther or catamount," he thought, "in the trees above." And he laid his half-raised head down again upon the ground.

No! There were fingers on the bar. He heard it move. Had the Indians come back to urge the food upon him? The touch upon the bar, however, seemed feeble, compared with theirs. It lifted the heavy log of wood slowly, and with difficulty. Walter's heart beat--visions came over his mind--hope flickered up; and he raised himself as well as he could into a sitting posture. From the ground he could not rise, for his hands were tied.

Slowly and quietly the door opened; the light rushed in, and, in the midst of its blaze, stood the beautiful figure of the Blossom, with her head partly turned away, as if in the act of listening. Her long wavy hair, broken from its band, and spotted with the white snow, fell almost to her feet. But little was the clothing that she wore: no mantle, no over-dress, nothing but the Indian woman's embroidered shirt, gathered round her by a belt, and leaving the arms and legs bare. Her hands were torn and bloody; her bright face and brow scratched by the fangs of the bramble; but still to Walter Prevost, as she stood listening there, it was the loveliest sight his eyes had ever rested on.

Thus, for a moment, she listened; then gazed into the hut, sprang forward, cast her arms around his neck, and wept as she had never wept before.

"My brother--my husband!" she exclaimed, leaning her forehead on his shoulder, "Otaitsa has found thee at length!"

He would fain have cast his arms around her; he would fain have pressed her to his heart; he would fain have told her that he could bear death, or even life, or any fate, for such love as hers. But his hands were tied, and his tongue was powerless with emotion.

A few moments passed in silence; and then Otaitsa said,--

"The cruel wolves have tied thee; but Otaitsa will give thee freedom."

In an instant, her small, delicate fingers were busy with the thongs; and with the rapidity of thought they were all untied, and hands and feet were both loose; but, as she worked, the blood dropped from her fingers on his wrists, and while he held her to his heart with--oh, how fond, how warm an embrace! he said,--

"Thou bleedest, my Blossom. Oh! Otaitsa, what hast thou risked, what hast thou encountered for Walter's sake?"

"But little, my beloved," she answered; "would it were ten times more, to prove my love. What! they have put meat within thy sight, and tied thy hands to make thee die of famine, with food before thee! Out on the cruel monsters!"

"No, no, my Otaitsa," returned Walter, "I would not eat. I wished to die. I knew not that an angel would come to cheer and help me."

"And to deliver thee too, my Walter," answered Otaitsa, with a bright smile. "I trust it is certain, my beloved. By the way *I* came, by that way *you* can go."

"How came you?" asked Walter, seating her beside him, and pressing her closer with his arm to the bosom on which she leaned. "I thought it was impossible for any one to reach me, so hidden is this place, so close the watch they kept. It must have been very perilous for thee, my Blossom. Art thou not hurt?"

"Oh, no," she answered; "nor was the peril really great. God gave me wings to fly to thee. Love bore me up. But let me tell thee how I came. I have a friend, the wife of one of thine enemies, a young bride to whom his heart is open as the lake. From her I heard of all their plans; how they have filled the wood below the rocks with watchers; how they have set guards on every trail. They never dreamed that from the morning-side a way could be found down over the rock into this dell. I pondered over the tidings, and remembered that, when I was a little happy child, I clambered some way down by the aid of shrubs and crevices in search of fruit; and I laid my plan against theirs. I took two ropes, which I had woven long ago, of the tough bark of the moose-plant; and, making a wide circle round, I reached the upland above the cliffs. My only trouble was to find the exact spot from that side; for I knew that there was a cloud between me and thy enemies, and that I walked unseen. At length, however, I found the rock overlooking the chasm. I cast off all burdens, all that the brambles or branches might snatch at; and, with the ropes wound round me, came down as far as I could find safe footing. There was a tree, a small tree, on the pinnacle; and I tried it before I trusted it. One branch broke; but the root and stump stood firm, griping the rock fast. To them I fixed the end of one rope, and easily swung down to a point below where there was a larger, stronger tree. A stone, however, slipped from under my foot, and fell rattling down. Round the strong tree I twisted the rope again, and thus reached the very ledge overhead; but there, as there had been noise and some crashing of the branches, I stood for a while hidden behind the bushes, to make sure that I was not discovered. At length, however, I was satisfied; and now the other rope was a friend to give me help. I fastened it to the first, knotted it into tight loops, and thus, aiding hands and feet with sometimes the aid of a projecting stone, and sometimes a small shrub, came slowly down. By the same way I shall return, my love; and by it, too, my Walter must go back this night to his own people."

"Why not with you now?" asked Walter eagerly. "Let Otaitsa go with me, and, whenever we reach my father's house, become my wife indeed. Oh, how gladly will he fold her to his heart! how fondly will Edith call her sister!"

"It cannot be, beloved," she answered. "I came to save him I love--to save him who is the husband of my heart, but not to abandon my father till he gives me to you; and, besides, there would be none to help us. This night you must climb by the ropes and boughs up to the top of the cliff, when, as near as you can reckon, there have been six hours of darkness. At the top you will find people waiting. They are but women, yet they all love you, and me likewise; and they have sworn by their Great Spirit, that if it cost their lives they will set you free. Each will help you in some way. One has a canoe upon the creek--another knows the deepest woods on the Mohawk side, and can guide you well. Others will lead you down Wood Creek to Sir William Johnson's Castle, where you are safe. Eat now, my beloved; for you must have strength, and Otaitsa must leave you soon. Before she goes, she must tie your hands again, lest your enemies come ere the night; but she will tie them in such a sort, that with your teeth you can undraw the knot; and she will loosen the fastening of the bar, so that even a weak hand can push it out."

She had hardly uttered the words, when a low, mocking laugh came upon their ears, and two or three dark forms shadowed the doorway. Otaitsa instantly started to her feet, and drew a knife from the belt around her waist.

"Stand back," she cried aloud, in the Iroquois tongue, as the men glided in. "I am your great chief's daughter; and the blood of the Black Eagle will not bear a touch."

"We touch thee not, Blossom," answered Apukwa. "Thou shalt go free; for the Black Eagle is a great chief, a mighty warrior, reverenced by his people. But our prisoner we keep; and though thou hast loosened his bands, we can fasten them again. Put thy tomahawk in thy belt, brother of the Snake. It must taste no blood here, though it is hungry, I know well. He shall die; but not now."

As he spoke, he thrust his arm between the younger Indian and Walter, who had cast himself before Otaitsa as if for one desperate struggle, if he saw any violence offered to her. The words of the medicine-man, however, quieted him on that score; and it was but too plain that all resistance on his part would be in vain. A few hours before, he had sought death as a boon; but the coming of the Blossom had changed all his thoughts and feelings, had relighted hope, and restored firmness and constancy. He was willing to live on for the chances of what some other day might bring; the love and self-devotion of that beautiful creature made existence seem too valuable to cast away the slightest chance of its preservation. He suffered them to bind him then, while Otaitsa turned away her head, and struggled against the tears that sought to rise. It cost her a great effort; but resolution triumphed; and, with a lofty air very different from the tenderness of her demeanour a few moments before, she waved her hand for the Indians to make way, saying--

"Unworthy Oneidas! I go to carry my own tale to my father's feet; to tell him that, with his own blood warm in my heart, I came hither to save my brother, my lover, my husband; and to warn him that the tomahawk which falls on that beloved head severs the chain of Otaitsa's life. But fear not, Walter," she continued, turning towards him, "fear not, my beloved. Live, and laugh thine enemies to scorn. Thou shalt be delivered yet, let these men do what they will. It is written on high, that thou shalt not perish by their hands."

Thus saying, she left the hut; and, followed closely by two of the Oneidas, pursued her way back towards the Castle.

When she reached the gate of the palisade, she at once perceived a good deal of commotion and activity within, though none but women, youths, and children were to be seen.

"Where is the Black Eagle?" she asked of the first woman whom she met. "Has he returned to the lodge?"

"He returned with forty warriors," replied the other, in a grave tone; "painted himself for battle, and has gone forth upon the war-path, taking with him every warrior he could find."

"Against whom?" asked Otaitsa in as calm a tone as she could assume, but with her heart beating fast.

"We do not know," replied the woman sadly; "but a tale spread, coming out of darkness through which none could see, that the Black Eagle had gone against our brethren the Mohawks and Onondagas. It was said they had unburied the hatchet, and cut down the tree of peace, before the door of the Oneidas."

Otaitsa clasped her hands together, bent her head, and took some steps towards the door of the lodge. Then, turning to the two men who had followed her, she said, bitterly--"And ye were absent when the Black Eagle called for warriors? Ye were right; for ye are women, and have only courage to torment a captive."

Thus saying, she passed on with a quiet step into the lodge; and there, where no eye could see her, gave way in tears to all the sad and bitter feelings of her heart.

CHAPTER XXX

Through the wide-spread woods which lay between the extensive territory occupied by the Mohawks and the beautiful land of the Oneidas, early on the morning of the day some of the events of which have been already recorded, a small troop of Indians glided along in their usual stealthy manner. They were in their garments of peace. Each was fully clothed according to the Indian mode; and the many-coloured mat of ceremony hung from their shoulders, somewhat encumbering them in their progress. They took the narrow trails; yet it was not so easy for them to conceal themselves, if such was their object, as it might have been in another dress, and at another time; for, except when passing a still brilliant maple, or a rich brown oak, the gaudy colouring of their clothing showed itself strongly against the dark evergreens or the white snow.

The party had apparently travelled from night into day; for, as soon as the morning dawned, the head man of the file stopped, and, without changing his position, and thus avoiding the necessity of making fresh prints in the snow, conversed over his shoulder with those behind him. Their conversation was brief, and might be translated into modern English thus:

"Shall we halt here, or go on farther? The day's eyes are open in the east."

"Stay here till noon," said an elder man behind him. "The Oneidas always go to their lodge in the middle of the day. They are children. They require sleep when the sun is high."

Another voice repeated the same advice; and, springing one by one from the trail into the thicket, they gathered together under a wide-spreading hemlock, where the ground was free from snow, and seated themselves in a circle beneath the branches. There they passed their time nearly in silence. Some food was produced, and also some rum--the fatal gift of the English; but very few words were uttered, and the only sentences worth recording were--

"Art thou quite sure of the spot, brother?"

"Certain," answered the one who had been leading; "the intelligence was brought by an Albany runner, a man of a true tongue."

From time to time, each of the different members of the group looked up towards the sky; and at length one of them rose, saying,--

"It is noon; let us onward. We can go forward for an hour, and then shall be near enough to reach the place, and return while the shadows are on the earth."

"We were told to spread out and enter by several trails," said the elder man of the party.

"It is not needful now," observed the one who seemed the leader; "when it can all be done between sun and sun."

His words seemed conclusive; and they resumed the path again, walking on stealthily in a single file as before. They had gone about three miles more, when a wild, fearful yell, such as no European would believe a human throat could utter, was heard near upon their right. Another rose up on their left, the instant after, and then another in their front. Each man stopped in breathless silence, as if suddenly turned to stone; but each with the first impulse had laid his hand upon his tomahawk. All listened for a repetition of the well-known war-whoop, and each man asked himself what such a sound could mean in a land where the Indians were all at peace amongst themselves, and where no tidings had been received of a foreign foe; but no one uttered a word, even in a whisper, to the man close to him.

Suddenly, a single figure appeared upon the trail before them,--tall, powerful, commanding; one well known to all there present. It was that of the Black Eagle, now feathered and painted for battle, with his rifle in his hand, and his tomahawk ready.

"Are ye Mohawks?" he demanded, as he came nearer. "Are we brethren?"

"We are Mohawks and brethren," replied the leader of the party; "we are but wandering through the forest, seeking to find something which has been lost."

"What is it?" asked Black Eagle, somewhat sternly; "nothing is lost that cannot be found. Snow may cover it for a time; but when the snow melts, it will come to light."

"It is a young lad's coat," said the cunning Mohawk; "but why is Black Eagle on the war path? Who has unburied the hatchet against the Oneidas?"

"The Black Eagle dreamed a dream," replied the chief, round whom numerous Oneidas, fully equipped for war, had by this time gathered; "and in his dream he saw ten men come from the mid-day into the land of the Oneida, and ten men from the side of the cold wind. They wore the garb of peace, and called themselves brothers of the children of the Stone. But the eyes of the Black Eagle were strong in his dream, and he saw through their bosoms, and their hearts were black; and a voice whispered to him, they come to steal from the Oneida that which they cannot restore, and to put a burden upon the children of the Stone that they will not carry."

"Was it not the voice of the singing bird?" asked the young Mohawk chief. "Was the dream sent by the bad spirit?"

"I know not," answered the Black Eagle. "Say ye! But the Black Eagle believed the dream, and, starting up, he called his warriors round him, and he sent Lynx-eyes, the Sachem of the Bear, to the north, and led his own warriors to the south, saying, 'Let us go and meet these ten men, and tell them, if they be really brethren of the Oneida, to come with us and smoke the pipe of peace together, and eat and drink in our lodges, and return to their own land when they are satisfied; but, if their hearts are black and their tongues double, then let us put on the war-paint openly, and unbury the long-buried hatchet, and take the war-path like men and warriors, and not creep to mischief like the silent copperhead.'"

The last words were spoken in a voice of thunder, while his keen black eye flashed, and his whole form seemed to dilate with indignation.

The Mohawks stood silent before him; and even the young chief who had shown himself the boldest amongst them, bent down his eyes to the ground. At length, however, after a long pause, he answered--

"The Black Eagle has spoken well; and he has done well, though he should not put too much faith in such dreams. The Mohawk is the brother of the Oneida: the children of the Stone and the men of blood [2] are one, though the Mohawk judges the Oneida hasty in deeds. He is a panther that springs upon his prey from on high, before he sees whether it be not the doe that nourished his young. He forgets hospitality--"

The eyes of the Black Eagle flashed fiercely for a moment; but then the fire went out in them, and a grave, and even sad look succeeded.

The young man went on boldly, however, saying--"He forgets hospitality. He takes to death the son of his brother, and sheds the blood of him who has eaten of the same meat with him. He waits not to punish the guilty, but raises his tomahawk against his friend. The Five Nations are a united people: that which brings shame upon one, brings it upon all. The Mohawk's eyes are full of fire, and his head bends down, when men say, 'The Oneida is inhospitable: the Oneida is hasty to slay; and repays faith, and trust, and kindness, by death.' What shall we say to our white father beyond the salt waters, when he asks us, 'Where is my son Walter, who loved the Oneidas, who was their brother, who sat by their council-fire and smoked the pipe of peace with them?' Shall we say, 'The Oneidas have slain him, because he trusted to the hospitality of the Five Nations, and did not fly?' When he asks us, 'What was his crime? and did the Oneidas judge him for it like calm and prudent men?' shall we answer, 'He had no crime, and the Oneidas took him in haste without judgment. He was full of love and kindness towards them--a maple tree overrunning with honey for the Oneidas; but they seized him in haste, when, in a few moons, they could have found many others?' If we say thus, what will our great father think of his red children? Black Eagle, judge thou of this; and, when thou dreamest another dream, see thou forked-tongued serpents hissing at the Five Nations, and ask, 'Who made them hiss?'--I have spoken." [3]

The feelings excited by this speech in all the Oneida warriors who heard it, would be difficult to describe. There was much anger; but there was more shame. The latter was certainly predominant in the breast of Black Eagle. He put his hand to his shoulder, as if seeking for his mantle to draw over his face; and, after a long pause, he said--

"Alas, that I have no answer! Thou art a youth, and my heart is old. My people should not leave me without reply before a boy. Go in peace. I will send my answer to him who sent thee; for our brethren, the Mohawks, have not dealt well with us in using subtlety. There are more of you, however. Let them each return to his home; for the children of the Stone are masters of themselves."

"Of us there are no more than thou seest," returned the young man.

Black Eagle gazed at him somewhat sternly, and then answered--

"Six men have entered the Oneida lands from this side, since morning yesterday, by separate ways. Let them go back. We give them from sun to sun, and no one shall hurt them. But if they be found here after that, their scalps shall hang upon the war-post."

Thus saying, he turned and withdrew with his warriors, while the young Mohawk and his companions glided back through the woods towards their own district, almost as silently as they came.

The returning path of the great Oneida chief was pursued by him and his companions with a slow and heavy tread. Not a word was spoken by any one; for deep grief and embarrassment were upon each; and all felt that there was much justice in the reproof of the young Mohawk. They had come forth with feelings of much indignation and anger at the intelligence which had been received of the interference of other tribes in the affairs of the Oneida people, and they still felt much irritation at the course which had been pursued; but their pride was humbled, and their native sense of justice touched by the vivid picture which had been given of the view which might be taken by others, of their conduct towards Walter Prevost. They knew, indeed, that that conduct was mainly attributable to one family of one Totem; but they felt that the shame fell upon the whole nation, and would be reflected to a certain degree upon the confederacy generally.

Nothing grieved or depressed the Indian so much as the sense of shame. It was produced, of course, by very different causes from those which affected a European: still it was very powerful; and Black Eagle felt that, in the case of Walter Prevost, the customs of his own people had been violated by his hasty seizure; and that he himself, the chief of the nation, was in some degree responsible in the eyes of all men for an act which he had permitted, if he had not done.

At this time, while the confederacy of the Five powerful Nations remained entire, and a certain apprehensive sense of their danger from the encroachments of the Europeans was felt by all the Indian tribes, a degree of power and authority had fallen to the great chiefs which probably had not been accorded to them in earlier and more simple times. The great chief of the Mohawks called himself King, and in some degree exercised the authority of a monarch. Black Eagle, indeed, assumed no different title than the ordinary Indian appellation of Sachem; but his great renown, and his acknowledged wisdom, had perhaps rendered his authority more generally reverenced than that of any other chief in the confederacy. The responsibility, therefore, weighed strongly upon him; and it was with feelings of deep gloom and depression that he entered the great Oneida village shortly before the hour of sunset.

The women and children were all assembled to see the warriors pass; all, excepting Otaitsa, who sat before the door of Black Eagle's great lodge, with her head bent down under an oppressive sense of the difficulties and dangers of her coming task.

Black Eagle saw her well, and saw that she was moved by deep grief; but he gave no sign even of perceiving her; and, moving slowly and with an unchanged countenance to the door, he seated himself beside her, while his warriors ranged themselves around, and the women and young people formed another circle beyond the first. It was done without concert and without intimation; but all knew that the chief would speak before they parted.

Otaitsa remained silent, in the same position, out of reverence for her father; and, after a pause, the voice of Black Eagle was heard, saying,--

"My children, your father is grieved. Were he a woman, he would weep. The reproach of his people, and the evil conduct of his allies, would bring water into the eyes that never were moist. But there is a storm upon us--the heaviest storm that ever has fallen. The waters of our lake are troubled, and we have troubled them ourselves. We must have counsel. We must call the wisdom of many men to avert the storm. Let, then, three of my swiftest warriors speed away to the heads of the eight tribes, and tell them to come hither before the west is dark to-morrow, bringing with them their wisest men. Then shall my children know my mind, and the Black Eagle shall have strength again."

He paused; and Otaitsa sprang upon her feet, believing that intelligence of what she had done had reached her father's ears.

"Ere thou sendest for the chiefs, hear thy daughter."

Black Eagle was surprised; but no sign of it was apparent on his face. He slowly bowed his head; and the Blossom went on:--

"Have I not been an obedient child to thee? have I not loved thee, and followed thy lightest word? I am thy child altogether. Thou has taken me often to the dwelling of the white man, because he is of my kindred. Thou hast often left me there, whilst thou hast gone upon the war-path, or hunted in the mountains. Thou hast said, 'They are of our own blood. My wife-- my beloved--was of high race amongst the pale-face people of the east; the daughter of a great chief. I served her in the day of battle, and she became mine; and true and faithful, loving and just, was the child of the white chief to the great Sachem of the Oneidas. Shall I keep her daughter from all communication with her kindred?' Young was I,--a mere child,--when first thou tookest me there; and Edith was a sister, Walter a brother to me. They both loved me well, and I loved them; but my love for the brother grew stronger than for the sister, and his for me. We told our love to each other; and he said--'When I am old enough to go upon the war-path, I will ask the Black Eagle to give me Otaitsa; and the red chief and the white chief shall again be united, and the bonds between the Oneidas and the English people shall be strengthened.' And we dreamed a dream that all this would be

The Black Eagle | 221

true; and pledged ourselves to each other for ever. Now what have I done, my father? The brethren of the Snake and the chief Apukwa, contrary to the customs of the Oneida, seized upon my betrothed, carried off my husband captive within four days after their brother was slain by a white man, but not by my Walter. It is not for me to know the laws of the Oneidas, or to speak of the traditions of our fathers; but in this, at least, I knew that they had done evil: they had taken an innocent man before they had sought for the guilty. I found the place where they had hid him. I climbed to the top of the rock above the chasm: I descended the face of the precipice. I tied ropes to the trees for his escape. I loosened the thongs from his hands and from his feet; and I said, 'This night thou shalt flee, my husband, and escape the wrath of thine enemies.' All this I did; and what is it? It may be against the law of the Oneidas, but it is the law of a woman's own heart, placed there by the Great Spirit. It is what my mother would have done for thee, my father, hadst thou been a captive in the hands of thine enemies. Had I not done it, I should not have been thy child; I should have been unworthy to call the Black Eagle my father. The daughter of a chief must act as the daughter of a chief. The child of a great warrior must have no fear. If I am to die, I am ready."

She paused for a moment; and Black Eagle raised his head, which had been slightly bowed, and said, in a loud, clear voice--

"Thou hast done well, my child. So let every Indian woman do for him to whom she is bound. The women of the children of the Stone are not as other women. Like the stone, they are firm; like the rock, they are lofty. They bear warriors for the nation. They teach them to do great deeds."

"Yet bear with me a little, my father," rejoined Otaitsa; "and let thy daughter's fate be in thy hand before all the eyes here present. Apukwa and the brethren of the Snake had set a watch, and stole upon me and upon my white brother, and mocked thy daughter and her husband, and bound his hands and feet again, and said that he should die."

It is rare that an Indian interrupts the speech of any one; but the heart of the chief had been altogether with Otaitsa's enterprise; and he now exclaimed, with great anxiety--"Then has he not escaped?"

"He has not," replied Otaitsa; "it went as I have said. Walter Prevost is still in the hands of the brethren of the Snake, and of Apukwa; and he is not safe, my father, even until the nation shall have decided what shall be his fate. When the nation speaks," she continued, emboldened by her father's approbation, "then will Otaitsa live or die; for I tell thee, and I tell all the warriors here present, that if my husband is slain for no offence by the hand of an Oneida, the daughter of the chief dies too."

"Koué, koué!" murmured the chiefs, in a low, sad tone, as they gazed upon her, standing in her great beauty by her father's side, while the setting sun looked out from beneath the edge of the snow-cloud, and cast a gleam of rosy light around her.

"He is not safe, even till the word is spoken," said Otaitsa: "for they are bad men that hold him. They took him contrary to our customs. They despise our laws. They are Honontkoh, and fear nothing but the tomahawk of the Black Eagle. They drink blood. They slay their mothers and their brethren. They are Honontkoh!"

A murmur of awe and indignation at the hated name of the dark secret order existing amongst the Indians, but viewed with apprehension and hatred by all the nobler warriors of the tribes, ran round the circle; and Black Eagle rose, saying--

"Let them be examined; and, if the stripe be found upon them, set honest men to guard the lad. To-morrow, at the great council, we will discuss his fate; and the Great Spirit send us dreams of what is right! Come with me, my child. The Blossom is ever dear."

Thus saying, he turned and entered the lodge.

CHAPTER XXXI

The promise of the sunset was verified. The succeeding day dawned bright and clear. The wind had shifted to the south-west; and, as frequently happens in the American autumn, the cold and icy breath of the north-east had been succeeded by a wind as soft and gentle as the warmest sigh of spring. In large masses, the snow fell from the boughs of the hemlock and the pine; the white surface of the earth's covering glistened as if with shining scales, as the upper surface began to melt; and, drop after drop, the water trickled from the extreme boughs of the trees, till the fully-risen sun sent the snow away dissolved into the streams and into the lake. It was like the recovery of the mind from sorrow, under the bright influence of happier days.

Only here and there, a patch of snow was still seen upon the tops of the hills, or in the more shady parts of the forest; only here and there upon the sky lingered the fragment of a cloud; but, instead of the dark, heavy, gray mass which had palled the heavens on the preceding day, that cloud was as light and soft as the down of the swan.

About two o'clock, several long lines of Indian chiefs and warriors might be seen approaching the great Oneida village. Soon after, a great fire was lighted before the door of the principal lodge; and, as on the preceding evening, the warriors were ranged in a circle round, and the women and children in another beyond.

The great chief, dressed in all the glittering finery of the Indian peace-costume, with feathers, and red and white head-dress, and crimson mantle, and embroidered shirt, and over-dress, and medals innumerable hanging round his neck, took the seat of honour with a grave dignity such as few civilized monarchs have ever, after the greatest study, been able to attain. He wore no warlike weapons; nothing but a single knife appeared in his girdle; and in his hand he carried the richly-ornamented calumet, or pipe of peace.

Close behind her father sat Otaitsa, with her heart greatly troubled, less perhaps with fear than with expectation. The Black Eagle had been kind and tender with her when they were alone together. He had held her to his heart with a display of fondness such as an Indian rarely shows openly to his child. He had listened to the whole tale of her love for Walter Prevost without a word of disapprobation or reproach; and sometimes even a playful smile had come upon his dark stern face as her words recalled the memory of feelings experienced in youth--like a well-remembered song heard again after a long lapse of years. Instead of reprehending her attempt to deliver Walter, he commended it highly.

"It was thy part, my child," said he; "thou shouldst have been a boy, Otaitsa; the warrior's spirit is in the maiden's bosom."

But when she came to speak of her lover's fate--to plead, to sue, to entreat--the stern, grave coldness of the Indian chief returned; and though she could see that he was full of fixed resolves, she could in no degree discover what they were. The explanation of them she knew was now to come; and it may be imagined, with what eager and intense interest she listened for every word.

There was, of course, some little confusion as the multitude took their places; but it was soon hushed, and then a deep silence ensued. The great pipe was lighted, and sent from hand to hand till it had passed all round the circle; and then, and not till then, Black Eagle rose and spoke.

"Have my words been heard?" he asked; "have my warriors examined whether any of the dark and infernal order of the Honontkoh are amongst us."

He seated himself again as soon as he had made the inquiry; and, after a moment's pause, two middle-aged warriors who had been with him on the preceding day rose, and took a step forward, while one of them said,--

"We have heard thy words, and examined. The brother of the Snake, Apukwa the medicine-man, and the Flying Squirrel, are Honontkoh. The stripe is upon them, and upon none else."

"It is well," said the chief, rising again. "Bring forward that man who was taken at our Castle-door last night."

Half-a-dozen young men sprang upon their feet, and speedily brought from the door of a neighbouring lodge the half-breed runner, Proctor, whom we have seen with Brooks and Lord H----, at Albany. He had a calumet in his hand, the sign of a peaceful mission; and he showed no fear, for he knew that his life would be respected, although he had learned by this time that the Oneidas had been greatly excited by some acts referring to the very object of his mission.

Standing in the midst, then, as calm and collected as he had been in the fort at Albany, he hardly gave a glance around the circle, but looked straight, with a cold and inexpressive countenance, at the chief before whom he was placed.

"What hast thou to say?" demanded Black Eagle.

The man remained silent, although there was an evident movement of his lips as if to speak.

"Fear not," said Black Eagle, mistaking the ineffectual effort to speak for a sign of apprehension, although it really proceeded from an habitual unwillingness to hear the sound of his own voice; "thou shalt go in safety, whatever be thy message. Art thou dumb, man? Is thy tongue a stone?"

"I am not dumb--I am not afraid," said the runner, with a strong effort. "Great chiefs in Albany send me to say, 'Give us the boy.'"

There he stopped, for it had cost him much to utter so many words.

"Were they war chiefs?" demanded Black Eagle, aloud.

The man nodded his head, and Black Eagle asked--

"Did they threaten the Oneidas? Did they say they would unbury the hatchet?"

The runner shook his head; and the chief asked--

"What did they say, then, would befall us if we refused to comply?"

"Shame!" replied Proctor, aloud.

Black Eagle suddenly drew his mantle over his face.

A low murmur spread around, like the hum of a hive of bees. When it had subsided, the chief again rose, and with an air of grave, sad dignity, looked round upon his people.

"Ye have heard, O children of the Stone," he said, in a rich, clear, deep-toned voice, "what the chiefs of the pale-faces say of the Oneida nation; and there are warriors here who were with me yesterday, when our brethren, the Mohawks, reproached me with treachery and inhospitality towards our pale-face brother, Prevost; and the Black Eagle had nothing to answer. Ye know the history. Why should I sing again the song of yesterday? A man of our nation was slain by one of the Yengees; and the brethren of the dead man seized upon the son of Prevost, who is also *our* son, without searching for him who had spilt the blood. This was contrary to the custom of the Five Nations. But they say the man was not to be found--he was already beyond our territory; and we must take the first we can find to appease the spirit of our brother. Now Prevost is a good man, loved by all the Five Nations, a brother to the red man, a friend who trusted us. So hard do the Mohawks and the Onondagas think this deed, that they have dealt subtly with the Oneidas, and striven to rescue our captive from our hands by the crooked ways of the serpent. The pale-face chiefs, too, have sent men into our land, and think darkly of the Oneidas. But the Black Eagle saw what they did, and spread his wings and drove them forth. He had no answer for the reproaches of the Mohawks or of the Yengees. He will give them both their answer this day by the messenger; and the children of the Stone will thereby know his mind. Let them say if it be good."

Then turning to Proctor, he stretched out his hand towards the south, saying--

"When thou goest hence, two of my warriors shall go with thee to the Castle of the Mohawk, and thou shalt say, 'Why hast thou dealt subtly with the Oneida? If thou hadst aught against him, why didst thou not send a messenger of peace to tell thy brother thy mind? or why didst thou not appeal to the great council of the Five Nations to judge between thee and him? If thou wilt unbury the hatchet, and cut down the tree of peace, and bring trouble into the Five Nations, that the pale-face may prevail and our Long House be pulled down to the ground, paint thy face, and dance the war-dance, and come upon the battle-way; but follow not the trail of the serpent, to steal unperceived into thy brother's land.'"

A murmur of approbation followed this bold speech; but the next moment the chief continued, still addressing Proctor, and saying--

"When thou hast thus spoken to the Mohawk, thou shalt go on to the pale-face chiefs at Albany, and to them thou shalt say, 'The children of the Stone have heard your message. They are the children of the great King. He is their father and they love him; but the Oneidas have their own laws, and are led by their own chiefs. They take the war-path against your enemies as against their own; and ye are glad in the day of battle when they fight the Frenchmen by your side. It is sweet to them that you have used no threats; and they would not have their white brother think darkly of them. They love, too, the chief, Prevost. They love his son as a brother; but one of their own children has been slain by one of yours, and their law must be fulfilled. His spirit must not be shut out from the happy hunting-grounds. They will mourn as a whole nation for Walter Prevost; but Walter Prevost must die, unless the murderer be taken. Thus says the Black Eagle, the great chief of the Oneida nation; he who has taken a hundred scalps of his enemies, and fought in fifteen battles with your foes and his. Give us up the murderer if ye would save the boy. He is in your land: you can find him. Do justly by us in this matter, and walk not in the trail of the fox to deceive us, and to save from us our captive.'"

Then pausing for an instant, he somewhat lowered his voice, but spoke the succeeding words very slowly and distinctly, in order that every syllable might not only be impressed upon the mind of the man he addressed, but be clearly heard and comprehended by all the people around.

"Thou shalt say, moreover, to our brethren, the pale-face chiefs at Albany, 'The Black Eagle finds that Walter Prevost has fallen into the hands of bad men, men who are not to be trusted, dealers in dark things, vultures whose heads are bare, but whose hearts are covered. The Black Eagle will take the boy from their hands, and will treat him well, and keep him in safety till the hour come. As ye have said that the Oneidas are hasty, that they do rashly, that they have not sought as they ought to seek--for six moons will Black Eagle keep the lad in peace, as his own son, to see whether ye will give him up the murderer of an Oneida. But, as the chief would slay his own son, if the laws of his people required it at his hands, so will he and the chiefs of his nation slay Walter Prevost, if, in six moons, ye do not give him up the murderer. He shall die the death of a warrior, with his hands unbound, and, as Black Eagle knows the spirit that is in him, he is sure he will die as a warrior should.' This thou shalt say to the English chiefs; let them look to it; the fate of the boy depends upon their counsel. Give him a roll of wampum for his reward, and let him go in peace."

His commands were immediately obeyed, and the half-breed runner removed from the circle.

Then, turning to the warriors without reseating himself, the chief demanded--

"Have I said well?"

The usual words of approbation followed, repeated by almost every voice present; and then Black Eagle resumed, in a sterner tone, saying--

"And now, my children, what shall be done to the Honontkoh? I have already removed the captive from their hands; for they are a people without faith. They live in darkness, and they wrap themselves in a shadow. They take their paths in deceit, and we see blood and dissension follow them. Already have they raised against us the wrath of our brethren of the Five Nations; they have brought the yellow cloud of shame upon the Oneidas. They have well nigh severed the threads which hold the roll of our league together. They have laid the hatchet to the root of the tree which we and our English father planted. I say, let them go forth from amongst us. The Totem of the Tortoise casts them forth. We will not have our lodges near their lodges. They shall not dwell within our palisade. Let them betake themselves to the darkness of the forest, and to the secret holes of the rock; for darkness and secrecy are the dwelling-places of their hearts. Or let them go, if they will, to the deceitful Hurons, to the people beyond Horicon, and fight beside the deceitful Frenchmen. With us they shall not dwell; let them be seen no more amongst us.--Is my judgment good?"

A general cry of approbation followed; the council broke up, and the warriors commenced wandering about, those who came from a distance seeking hospitality in the neighbouring lodges; for the great lodge itself could not afford room for all.

To her own little chamber, Otaitsa retired at once; and, barring the door, went down upon her knees, to offer up thanksgiving and prayer-- thanksgiving, for hope is ever a blessing--prayer, for danger was still before her eyes. Safe for the next six months she knew Walter would be, in the careful custody of her father; but she still prayed earnestly that her mother's God would find some way of deliverance, for the sake of Him who died to save mankind.

CHAPTER XXXII

More than five months had passed, months of great trouble and anxiety to many. The usual tragedies of life had been enacted in many a house, and in many a home: the dark, ever-recurring scene of death and suffering and grief had passed through the dwellings of rich and poor. Many a farce, too, in public and private, had been exhibited to the gaze; for, in the history of each man and of all the world, the ridiculous and the grand, the sad and the cheerful, stand side by side in strange proximity.

The woods, blazing in their autumnal crimson when last we saw them, had worn and soiled, in about a fortnight, the glorious vestments of the autumn, and cast them to the earth; and now they had put on the green garments of the summer, and robed themselves in the tender hues of youth. The rivers and the streams, bound in icy chains for many a month, now dashed wildly and impetuously along in the joy of lately-recovered freedom, and, swollen by the spring rains, in some places became torrents; in some places, slowly flooded the flat land, marching over the meadows like a vast invading army.

The beasts of the forest were busy in their coverts, the birds in the brake, or on the tree-top; the light clouds skimmed along the soft blue sky; and the wind tossed the light young branches to and fro in its sport. Everything was gay and active on the earth, and over the earth; everything spoke of renewed life, and energy, and hope.

To the fancy of those who have not seen it, the vast primæval forest presents an idea of monotony; and certainly, when seen from a distance, it produces that impression on the mind. Looming dark and sombre, thick and apparently impenetrable, over upland and dell, over plain and mountain, it conveys a sensation of solemnity by its very sameness; and, though the first sight is sublime, its long-continued presence is oppressive. But penetrate into its depths, and you will find infinite variety; now the dense, tangled thicket, through which the panther and the wild cat creep with difficulty, and into which the deer cannot venture; now the quaking morass, unsafe to the foot, yet bearing up the tamarach or cedar, with its rank grasses, its strangely-shaped leaves, and its rich and infinitely varied flowers; now the wide grove, extending for miles and miles, with the tall bolls of the trees rising up distinct and separate, and with little or no brushwood hiding the carpet of dry pine-spindles and cones on which they stand; then the broad savanna, with its grass knee-high, green and fresh and beautiful, and merely a tree here and there to shelter some spot from the sun, and cast a soft blue shadow on the natural meadow; and then again, in many spots, a space of ground where every characteristic of the forest is mingled--here thick and tangled brush, there a patch of open green, here the swamp running along the brook-side, there the sturdy oak or wide-spreading chestnut, standing far apart in reverence for each other's giant limbs, shading many a pleasant slope, or topping the lofty crag.

It was under one of these large trees, on a high bank commanding the whole prospect round for many and many a mile, and in the eastern part of the province of New York, that three red men were seated in the early summer of 1758. A little distance in advance of them, and somewhat lower down the hill, was a small patch of brush, composed of fantastic-looking bushes, and one small blasted tree. It formed, as it were, a sort of screen to the Indians' resting-place from all eyes below, yet did not in the least impede their sight as it wandered over the wide forest world around them. From the elevation on which they were placed, the eye of the red man, which seems, from constant practice, to have gained the keenness of the eagle's sight, could plunge into every part of the woods around where the trees were not actually contiguous. The trail, wherever it quitted the shelter of the branches; the savanna, wherever it broke the outline of the forest; the river, where it wound along in its course to the ocean; the military road from the banks of the Hudson to the head of Lake Horicon; the smallest pond, the little stream, were all spread out to view as if upon a map.

Over the wide, extensive prospect the eyes of those three Indians wandered incessantly, not as if employed in searching for some definite object, the direction of which, if not the precise position, they knew, but rather as if they were looking for anything which might afford them some object of pursuit or interest. They sat there nearly two hours in the same position; and during the whole of that time not more than four or five words passed between them.

At length they began to converse, though at first in a low tone, as if the silence had its awe even for them. One of them pointed with his hand towards a spot to the eastward, saying, "There is something doing there."

In the direction to which he called the attention of his companions was seen spread out, in the midst of the forest and hills, a small, but exquisitely beautiful lake, seemingly joined on to another, of much greater extent, by a narrow channel. Of the former, the whole extent could not be seen; for, every here and there, a spur of the mountain cut off the view, and broke in upon the beautiful waving line of the shore. The latter was more distinctly seen, spread out broad and even, with every little islet, headland, and promontory, marked clear and distinctly against the bright, glistening surface of the waters.

Near the point where the two lakes seemed to meet, the Indians could descry walls, and mounds of earth, and various buildings of considerable size; nay, even what was probably the broad banner of France, though it seemed but a mere whitish spot in the distance.

At the moment when the Indians spoke, coming from a distant point on the larger lake, the extreme end of which was lost to view in a sort of indistinct blue haze, a large boat or ship might be seen, with broad white sails, wafted swiftly onward by a cold north-easterly wind. Some way behind it, another moving object appeared--a boat likewise, but much more indistinct; and, here and there nearer in shore, two or three black specks, probably canoes, were darting along upon the bosom of the lake, like water-flies upon the surface of a still stream.

"The pale-faces take the war-path against each other," said another of the Indians, after gazing for a moment or two.

"May they all perish!" exclaimed the third. "Why are our people so mad as to help them? Let them fight, and slay, and scalp as many of each other as they can, and then the red men tomahawk the remainder."

The other two uttered a bitter malediction, in concert with this fierce, but not impolitic, thought; and then, after one of their long pauses, the first who had spoken, resumed the conversation, saying--

"Yet I would give one of the feathers of the White Bird to know what the pale-faces are doing. Their hearts are black against each other. Can you not tell us, Apukwa? You were on the banks of Horican yesterday, and must have heard the news from Corlear."

"The news from Albany matters much more," answered Apukwa. "The Yengees are marching up with a cloud of fighting-men; and people know not where they will fall. Some think Oswego; some think Ticonderoga. I am sure that it is the place of the Singing Waters that they go against."

"Will they do much in the war-path?" asked the brother of the Snake; "or will the Frenchman make himself as red as he did last year, at the south end of Horicon?"

"The place of the Singing Waters is strong, brother," replied Apukwa, in a musing tone, "and the Frenchmen are great warriors; but the Yengees are many in number, and they have called for aid from the Five Nations. I told the Huron who sold me powder, where the eagles would come down; and I think he would not let the tidings slumber beneath his tongue. The great-winged canoes are coming up Corlear very quick; but I think my words must have been whispered in the French chief's ear, to cause them to fly so quickly to Ticonderoga."

A faint, nearly-suppressed smile came upon the lips of his two companions as they heard of this proceeding; but the younger of the three said--

"And what will Apukwa do in the battle?"

"Scalp my enemies," replied Apukwa, looking darkly round.

"Which is thine enemy?" asked the brother of the Snake.

"Both," answered the medicine-man, bitterly; "and every true Honontkoh should do as I do; follow them closely, and slay every man that flies, be his nation what it may. So long as he be white, it is enough for us. He is an enemy; let us blunt our scalping-knives on the skulls of the pale-faces. Then, when the battle is over, we can take our trophies to the conqueror, and say, 'We have been upon thy side.'"

"But will he not know?" suggested the younger man; "will he listen so easily to the song?"

"How should he know?" asked Apukwa, coldly. "If we took him red men's scalps, he might doubt; but all he asks is white men's scalps, and we will take them. They are all alike, and they will have no faces under them."

This ghastly jest was highly to the taste of the two hearers; and, bending down their heads together, the three continued to converse for several minutes in a whisper. At length, one of them said--

"Could we not take Prevost's house as we go? How many brothers did you say would muster?"

"Nine," answered Apukwa; "and our three selves make twelve." Then, after pausing for a moment or two in thought, he added, "It would be sweet as the strawberry and as easy to gather; but there may be thorns near it. We may tear ourselves, my brothers."

"I fear not," returned the brother of the Snake; "so that I but set my foot within that lodge, with my rifle in my hand, and my tomahawk in my belt, I care not what follows."

"The boy's to die," rejoined Apukwa; "why seek more in his lodge at thine own risk?"

The other did not answer; but, after a moment's pause, he asked--"Who is it has built the lodge still farther to the morning?"

"One of the workers of iron," answered Apukwa, meaning the Dutch. "He is a great chief, they say, and a friend of the Five Nations."

"Then no friend of ours, my brother," responded the other speaker; "for though it be the children of the Stone who have shut the door of the lodge against us, and driven us from the council-fire, the Five Nations have confirmed their saying, and made the Honontkoh a people apart. Why should we not fire that lodge too, and then steal on to the dwelling of Prevost?"

"Thy lip is thirsty for something," said Apukwa. "Is it the maiden thou wouldst have?"

The other smiled darkly; and, after remaining silent for a short space, answered--

"They have taken from me my captive; and my hand can never reach the Blossom I sought to gather. The boy may die, but not by my tomahawk; and, when he does die, I am no better, for I lose that which I sought to gain by his death. Are Apukwa's eyes misty, that he cannot see? The spirit of the Snake would have been as well satisfied with the blood of any other pale-face; but that would not have satisfied me."

"Yet making Prevost's house red will not gather for thee the Blossom," answered Apukwa.

The third and younger of the Indians laughed, saying----

"The wind changes, Apukwa, and so does the love of our brother. The maiden in the lodge of Prevost is more beautiful than the Blossom. We have seen her thrice since this moon grew big; and my brother calls her the Fawn, because she has become the object of his chase."

"Thou knowest not my thought," said the brother of the Snake, gravely. "The maiden is fair, and she moves round her father's lodge like the sun. She shall be the light of mine, too; but the brother of the snake forgets not those who disappoint him; and the boy Prevost would rather have seen the tomahawk falling, than know that the Fawn is in his lodge."

The other two uttered that peculiar humming sound by which the Indians sometimes intimate that they are satisfied; and the conversation which went on between them related chiefly to the chances of making a successful attack upon the house of Mr. Prevost. Occasionally, indeed, they turned their eyes towards the boats upon Lake Champlain, and commented upon the struggle that was about to be renewed between France and England. That each party had made vast preparations was well known, and intelligence of the extent and nature of those preparations had spread far and wide amongst the tribes, with wonderful accuracy as to many of the details, but without any certain knowledge of where the storm was to break.

All saw, however, and comprehended, that a change had come over the British government; that the hesitating and doubtful policy which had hitherto characterized their military movements in America was at an end; and that the contest was now to be waged for the gain and loss of all the European possessions on the North American continent. Already was it known amongst the Five Nations, although the time for the transmission of the intelligence was incredibly small, that a large fleet and armament had arrived at Halifax, and that several naval successes over the French had cleared the way for some great enterprise in the north. At the same time, the neighbourhood of Albany was full of the bustle of military preparation; a large force was already collected under Abercrombie for some great attempt upon the lakes: and from the west news had been received that a British army was marching rapidly towards the French posts upon the Ohio and the Monongahela.

The Indian nations roused themselves at the sound of war; for, though some few of them acted more regularly in alliance with one or the other of the contending European powers, a greater number than is generally believed cared little whom they attacked, or for whom they fought, or whom they slew; and were, in reality, but as a flock of vultures spreading their wings at the scent of battle, and ready to take advantage of the carnage, whatever was the result of the strife.

CHAPTER XXXIII

We must now return to the scene in which this narrative commenced. But oh, how changed was the aspect of all things from that which the house of Mr. Prevost presented but five short months before! The father and the daughter were there alone. The brother no longer glanced about the house with his blithesome air and active energies; and the thought of him and of his fate hung continually like a dark shadow over those to whom he was so dear. They were not wholly without comfort, they were not wholly without hope; for, from time to time, renewed assurances came to them from many a quarter that Walter would still be saved. Yet time wore on, and he was not delivered.

When one speaks of five months of uncertainty, it seems a long and tedious period, and it would be so if it were all one blank; but there are a thousand little incidents--incidents external and internal--that fill up the time, and make it pass wonderfully soon, especially if fear predominates over hope.

Didst thou ever sit up, reader, with the sick or dying through the livelong night? In contemplation, it seems an awful task of long endurance to watch there with the eternal battle going on in your breast between the only two deathless passions--the only two which may be called the immortal passions of the soul--from the fading of the evening light till the breaking of another day. And yet it is wonderful how soon, how very soon, one sees the faint blue light of dawn mingling with the sickly yellow glare of the watcher's lamp. Every thought, every expectation, is an incident. The change of breathing, the restless movement, the muttered word, the whispered comfort, the moistening of the parched lip, the smoothing of the pillow,--all are events that hurry on the time.

And so it was in the house of Mr. Prevost. Each day had its something; each hour; and although the object was always the same, or rarely varied, yet the rapid changes of thought and feeling made the time fly far more rapidly than might have been expected.

During the winter, Lord H---- visited the house very frequently; and it is probable that, had no dark cloud overshadowed the hopes as well as the happiness of all, he would have pressed for the prize of Edith's hand without delay; but he loved not the mingling of joy and sorrow. In that, at least, his view of the world, and life, and fate, was deceitful. He was not yet convinced, although he had some experience, that such a thing as unalloyed happiness, even for a few short days, is not to be found on earth--that the only mine of gold without dross lies beneath the grave.

Once, indeed, he hinted, rather than asked, that an early day might be fixed for his union with her he loved; but a tear rose in Edith's eye, and she bent down her head. Her father would have made no objection, although he still thought her very, very young to take upon her the duties of a wife. In that respect his feelings were not changed; but the loss of his son weighed heavily upon him, and, calling him away from the present, had projected his thoughts into the future. What might be Edith's fate, he asked himself, if he too should be taken from her? Any of the many accidents of life might leave her alone, and an orphan; and there is nothing which brings home so sensibly to our thoughts the unstable hold which we have upon all earthly things, so much as our tenderness for those we love.

But Lord H---- saw that it would be painful to Edith herself to become his bride as long as Walter's late was uncertain; and he said no more.

In the meantime the gathering together of the British soldiers on the Hudson and the Mohawk had, like one wave meeting another, somewhat repelled the Indian tribes. A runner, a half-breed, or one or two red men together--more frequently from the nation of the Mohawks than from any other tribe--would be seen occasionally wandering through the woods or crossing the open ground near the settler's dwelling; but they seldom approached the house; and their appearance caused no apprehension. Relations of the greatest amity had been re-established between the British authorities and the chiefs of the Five Nations; and several of the tribes were preparing to take part in the coming strife upon the side of England.

Three times during the winter the house of Mr. Prevost was visited by a single Indian of the Oneida tribe. On two occasions it was a man who presented himself; and his stay was very short. On the first occasion, Edith was alone; when, without the sound of a footfall, he glided in like a dark shadow. His look was friendly, though for a moment he said nothing. Edith, well knowing Indian habits, asked if he would take food. He answered

"Yes," in his own language; and she called some of the servants to supply him; but, before he ate he looked up in her face, saying--

"I am bidden to tell thee that thy brother shall be safe."

"Whose words do you bear?" asked Edith. "Is it the Black Eagle who speaks?"

"Nay, it is Otaitsa," replied the man.

This was all Edith could learn; for the messenger was either ignorant of more, or affected to be so; yet still it was a comfort to her. The next who came was a woman somewhat past the middle age, and by no means beautiful. She stayed long; and, with good-humoured volubility, related all that had happened immediately after Edith's visit to the Oneida castle. She dwelt upon the attempt of the Blossom to deliver her lover as she would have expatiated upon some feat of daring courage in a warrior; and though in the end she had to tell how the maiden's bold attempt had been frustrated, she concluded by saying--

"Yet he shall be safe. They shall not slay our brother."

The third time the man returned, hearing the same assurance; but, as hour after hour and day after day went by without the lad's return, or any definite news of him, hope sickened and grew faint. By this time it was known that the efforts of the Mohawks and Onondagas had been frustrated; and, moreover, it was plainly intimated by the chiefs of those two nations that they would interfere no more.

"The Oneidas have reproved us," they said, "and we had no reply. We must not make the children of the Stone hiss at our children; neither must we break the bands of our alliance for the sake of one man."

The scouts who had been put under the order of Woodchuck were recalled to the army early in the spring without having effected anything. All that had been heard at the forts showed that the young prisoner had been removed to the very farthest part of the Oneida territory, where it was impossible for any one Englishman to penetrate without being discovered by the Indians.

If, in civilized times, with a country cleared in a great degree of its forests, and with a regular organization ensuring rapid intercourse between place and place, it is possible for a man to be hidden for weeks and months from the most diligent search; how much more easy was concealment in those days, when, with the exception of a few patches of maize or other grain, the whole land was one wild tangled wood, crossed, it is true, with innumerable Indian trails, but with no direct means of communication, except by one large road, and the lakes and rivers. Search would have been in vain, even if in the political state of the country it could have been attempted; but the attempt was impossible, without rendering the whole country hostile; for the Mohawks themselves showed no inclination to suffer any considerable body of men to cross their territory, except indeed a small party of soldiers, now and then, destined to strengthen the garrisons at Oswego, or any of the regular British posts.

Of Woodchuck himself, nothing was heard, till the flowers began to spring up close upon the footsteps of the snow. It was believed that he was still in the forest; but even of this, no one was assured; and all that could with any accuracy be divined, was, that he had not fallen into the hands of the Oneidas, inasmuch as there was every reason to believe that, had such been the case, Walter's liberation would immediately have followed.

Thus matters had gone on in the household of Mr. Prevost, till about a month before the period at which I have thought best to present to the reader the three Indians seated on the hill. The snow had melted, except in a few places, where it still lay in white patches, under shelter of the darker and thicker-leaved evergreens; here and there, too, it might be seen in the shade of a steep bank; but the general surface of the country was free, and, despite, the variable character of the American spring--one day as soft as summer, and then two or three following, with the icy fang of winter in the wind, and the sky covered with low lurid clouds--the flowers were peeping out in every covert, and mingling themselves thickly with fern, and ground-pine, and hemlock, varying with many a brilliant hue the green carpet of the earth.

The day had been one of exceeding loveliness, and not without its activity too; for a party of soldiers had been thrown forward, for some object, to a spot within a mile and a half of the house; and Lord H---- had been twice there, making Edith's heart thrill, each time he appeared, with emotions so new and strange as to set her dreaming for an hour after he was gone. The evening had come, bringing with it some clouds in the western sky; and Edith, as she sat with her father, looked out from the window, with her head resting on her hand.

No one knows the full weight of a great predominant idea, till he has had to bear one up for weeks or months--no one can tell how it crushes one down, seems to resolve all other things into itself, and almost, like the giant in the child's fable, to grind one's bones to make its bread. The sweet reverie of a lover's visit had passed away, and the beautiful girl's thoughts had reverted to the subject of her brother's fate, which took hold of her the moment her mind was free from some temporary relaxation, and again chained the slave to the accustomed task.

As she gazed, she perceived a figure slowly crossing between the gardener-boy and old Agrippa, who were working in the gardens, and apparently taking its course to the door of the house. At first she did not recognise it, for it was more like an Indian than a European, and more like a bear than either. It had a human face, however; and, as it came forward, an impression, first faint, but increasing with every step it advanced, took possession of her, that it must be the man whose fatal act had brought so much wretchedness upon her family. He was very much--very sadly--changed; and, although the bear-skins in which he was dressed hid the emaciation of his form, the meagreness of his face was very evident as he came near.

Edith lifted her head from her hand, saying, "I think, my father, here is Captain Brooks approaching. Poor man! he seems terribly changed!"

Mr. Prevost started up, gazed for a moment from the window, and then hurried forth to meet him. Edith felt some doubt as to how her father would receive him; for, in the purest and the highest hearts, there is--there ever will be--one small drop of selfishness much to be guarded against. It may not poison our acts, but it too often poisons our feelings; it mingles even with candour itself, diminishing the efficacy of that most noble of virtues; and if it do not make us detract from the merit of others, it still gives some slight colouring to their acts when they are painful or disadvantageous to ourselves.

She had the happiness, however, to see her father take the wanderer kindly by the hand, and lead him towards the door. Whatever had been Mr. Prevost's feelings, the sight of Woodchuck's altered face was enough to soften them entirely. The next moment they entered the room together, and Edith extended her hand kindly to him.

"Ah, Miss Prevost, you are very good," he said, "and so is your father, too. I have not been to see you for a long time."

"That was not right of Woodchuck," said Edith; "you should have come to see us. We know all you have been trying to do for my poor brother. If you cannot succeed, it is not your fault, and we should have been glad to see you, both for your own sake, and for the sake of hearing all your proceedings as they occurred."

"Ah, but I have been far away," he answered. "I first tried to get at the poor boy from this side, and, finding that would not do, I took a long round, and came upon them from the west, but I got nothing except some information, and then I made up my mind. Them Ingians are as cunning as Satan. I have circumvented them once; but they won't let a man do it twice."

Mr. Prevost had stood listening, eager to hear anything that related to his son; but now he interrupted, saying: "We will hear more of this by-and-by, Brooks. Come into the hall and have some food; you must be hungry and tired--both, I am sure."

"No," replied Woodchuck, "I am not hungry. Tired, a little, I am, I guess, though I hav'n't walked more than forty miles; but I met a young Ingian two or three hours ago, who gave me a venison-steak off his own fire. Some rest will set all to rights."

"Take some wine, at least," said Mr. Prevost; "that will do you good; you look quite faint."

"Faint in limb, but not in heart," replied Woodchuck, stoutly. "However, I won't refuse the wine; for it was given to cheer the heart of man--as the Bible says; and mine wants cheering, though it does not want strengthening, for I'll do what I say, as I am a living man."

They took him into the hall, and persuaded him both to eat and to drink, evidently much to his benefit; for, though he did not lose the sad tone with which he spoke, his voice was stronger, and his features seemed to grow less sharp.

"And where have you been ever since this snow has been on the ground?" asked Edith, when he seemed a little revived; "you cannot, surely, have been wandering in the woods during the terribly severe weather we had in January."

"I hutted myself down," he said, "like an Ingian, or a beaver, and covered the lodge all over with snow. I planted it upon a ledge of rock, with its mouth close behind an old hemlock-tree, and made it white all over, so that they would have been worse than devils to find me; for life is sweet, Miss Prevost, even in winter time, and I did not wish to be tomahawked so long as I could help it."

"You must have had a sad, desolate time, I fear," said Mr. Prevost; "at least, till the spring came round."

The Black Eagle | 241

"I guess it warn't very cheerful," answered Woodchuck; "but that's the best way to teach one's-self not to care for what's coming. At least, I used to think so once, and to believe that if a man could only make himself very miserable in this world, he would not much care how soon he went out of it. But I've changed my opinion on that matter a little; for up there, on the side of the hill, after four or five weeks, half famished and half frozen, I did not feel a bit more inclined to die than I did a year ago, when there were few lighter-hearted men than myself. So I thought, before I did anything of the kind, knowing that there was no need of it just yet, I would just go and take a ramble among the mountains in the fine weather, like Jephtha's daughter."

His words would have been enigmas to Edith, had she not somewhat misunderstood even their obvious meaning; for Lord H----, not fully knowing the character of the man, and unwilling to excite anything like confident hope, that might ultimately be disappointed by some change of Woodchuck's feelings, had forborne to mention more of his purposes than the mere fact of his intention to peril his own life to save that of Walter Prevost. To Edith, then, the words used by Brooks seemed but to imply that he still contemplated some daring attempt to set her brother at liberty; and, in the hope, if she could learn the particulars of his scheme, to be able to procure the co-operation of Otaitsa and others in the Oneida Castle, she said,--

"You are, indeed, a good kind friend, Woodchuck; and you have, I know, already undergone great risks for poor Walter's sake. There are others labouring for him, too; and, perhaps, if we knew what you intended to do next--"

"To do next!" echoed the man, interrupting her. "Why, ha'n't I told you? I said, when I found I couldn't git in from the west, I made up my mind."

"To do what, my good friend?" said Mr. Prevost. "You certainly implied you intended to do something; but what you did not state. Now I easily understand Edith's anxiety to know your intentions; for we have obtained friends in the Oneida camp, who might give great assistance to your efforts, if we knew what they are to be. But I should tell you, my dear daughter ventured across the Mohawk country to see our dear little Otaitsa, who, like you, risked her own life to save my poor boy--God's blessing be upon her!"

The tears rose in his eyes, and he paused for a moment. But Woodchuck waved his hand, saying--

"I know all about it. I war on the bank of the creek, Miss Edith, when the Ingian woman paddled you back; and I guessed how it had all been. I said to myself, when I heard more of it two days arter. 'Her father will be mighty angry;' and so he war, I guess."

"You are mistaken, my friend," said Mr. Prevost, laying his hand on Edith's with a tender pressure. "I was not angry, though I was much alarmed; but that alarm was not of long endurance, for I was detained much more than I expected at Sir William Johnson's, and my anxiety was only protracted two days after my return. Still you have not told us your plans. If that dear girl, Otaitsa, can help us, she will do it, though it cost her life."

Woodchuck paused a moment or two in deep, absent thought, and over his rough countenance the trace of many strong emotions flitted. At length, he said, in a low, distinct voice, "She can do nothing. Black Eagle has the boy under his keen eye. He loves him well, Mr. Prevost; and he will treat him kindly. But just inasmuch as he *does* love him, he will make it a point to keep him safely, and to kill him too, if he haven't got another victim. That man should ha' been one of them old Romans I have heard talk of, who killed their sons and daughters, rather than not do what they thought right. He'd not spare his own flesh and blood--not he; and the more-he loves him, the surer he'll kill him."

Edith wept, and Mr. Prevost covered his eyes with his hands; but Woodchuck, who had been gazing down upon the table, and saw not the powerful emotions which his words had produced, proceeded, after a gloomy pause--

"He'll watch his daughter sharply too. Yet they say he praised her daring; and I guess he did, for that's just the sort of thing to strike his fancy; but he'll take care she shan't do it again. No, no. There's but one way with Black Eagle. I know him well, and he knows me, and there is but one way with him."

"What is that?" asked Mr. Prevost, in a tone of deep melancholy.

"Just to do what I intend," returned Woodchuck, with a very calm manner. "Mr. Prevost, I love my life as well as any man--a little too much, mayhap; and I intend to keep it as long as I rightly can, for there are always things wrote in that chapter of accidents that none on us can see. But I don't intend to let your son Walter--he's a good boy--be put to death for a thing of my doing. You don't suppose it. Atfirst, when the thing came fresh upon me at Albany, I felt mighty like a fool and a coward; and I would ha' skulked away into any hole just to save myself from myself. But I soon took thought, and made up my mind. Now, here you and Miss Edith have been praising and thanking me for trying to save poor Walter's life. I didn't deserve praise, or thanks either. It was my own life I was trying to save; for, if I could get him out secretly, we should both be secure enough. But I've given that up. It can't be done, and Black Eagle knows it. He knows me, too; and he's just as sure, at this blessed moment, that before the day he has appointed for Walter to die, Woodchuck will walk in and say, 'Here I am!' as he is that he's in his own lodge. Then he will have got the right man, and all will be settled. Now, Mr. Prevost--and you, Miss Edith--you know what I intend to do. To-morrow, when I'm a bit rested, I shall set out again, and take my ramble in the mountains, like Jephtha's daughter, as I said. Then, this day month, I will be here again to bid you all good-bye. Walter will have to tell you the rest. Don't cry so, there's a good girl. You're like to set me a' crying too. There's one thing more I have to ask you both, and that is, never speak another word to me about this matter--not even when I come back again. I try not to think of it at all myself, and I don't much now. If I can screw myself up, like them Ingians, I shall just walk quietly in among them as if nothing were going to happen, and say, 'Set the boy free! Here is Woodchuck himself,' and then die--not like an Ingian, but like a Christian, I trust, and one that knows he's a' doing of his duty anyhow. So now not a word more--but let us talk of something else."

CHAPTER XXXIV

An hour had passed after the conversation detailed in the last chapter, and Woodchuck had steadily and sturdily refused to pursue any further the subject of his fixed determination, although both Mr. Prevost and Edith, deeply touched, and, to say truth, much agitated, would fain have dwelt upon the topic longer. Edith felt, and Mr. Prevost argued in his own mind, that the poor man was performing a generous and self-devoted act, which no moral obligation forced upon him. They felt, too, that so noble a heart was not one which ought to be sacrificed to the vengeful spirit of the Indians; and the natural feeling of joy and satisfaction which they experienced at the apparent certainty of Walter's deliverance from death seemed to them almost a crime when it was to be purchased at so dear a price.

Woodchuck's obstinacy, however, had conquered; the subject had been changed; and, as they now sat together in the little room, to which he had led the way after speaking the last words cited, they continued, while the shades of evening gathered quickly round them, a broken sort of conversation upon topics connected with that which they had quitted, though avoiding the point which was most painfully prominent in the mind of each. They rambled a good deal indeed, though ever taking a direction which faintly showed, like the waves in the trees marking the course of a forest-path, what the mind was running on beneath the mere words.

Sometimes gazing into the embers of the fire with his feet upon the hearth, Woodchuck would talk, neither unphilosophically nor unlearnedly in the best of all learning, upon a world to come, and life immortal, and compensation beyond the grave; and, in his simplicity, his words would reach almost to the sublime. Then, at other times, they would speak of the Indians, and their habits, and their good and bad qualities; and here many of the poor man's prejudices were seen clinging to him strongly.

"They are like vermin," he would say; "and the devil himself has a share in them. I have heard people talk largely of their generosity, and all that; but I guess I've not seen much of it."

Mr. Prevost was silent, for his feelings had suffered a natural change towards the Indians; but Edith exclaimed warmly--

"We cannot say that of dear Otaitsa, at all events, Woodchuck, for she surely has a heart full of generosity and everything that is noble."

"That's nat'ral, that's nat'ral," answered Woodchuck; "that comes of the blood that is in her. For that matter, Black Eagle has some fine things about him--he's the best of them I ever saw. We used to say, whole Ingian, half devil; but I think in his case it must have been quarter devil, and that's saying a good deal for so fierce a man as he in battle. They say he has scalped more enemies than all his tribe put together; especially in that war down upon the Pennsylvania side some nineteen years ago, when some of our people foolishly took part with the Mohaguns."

Mr. Prevost started, and Woodchuck went on, saying,--"He has good things about him, for he always makes his people spare the women and children, which is what them Ingians seldom think of. A scalp's a scalp to them, whether it has got long hair on it or only a scalp-lock. But, as I was saying, the Blossom has got all that is good in him, and all that was good in her mother, poor thing! and that was a mighty great deal."

"I have often wished," said Mr. Prevost, "that I could hear something of Otaitsa's history. Her mother, I believe, was a white woman, and I have more than once tried, when I found the Black Eagle in a communicative mood, to lead him to speak upon the subject; but the moment it was touched upon, he would wrap his blanket round him, and stalk away."

"Ay, he has never forgotten her," said Woodchuck. "He never took another wife, you know; and well he may remember her, for she was his better angel, and ruled him completely, which was what no one else could. But I can tell you all about it if you like to know; for I heard it all from an old squaw one time, and I saw the lady once too myself, and talked to her."

"I think," said Edith, thoughtfully, "that she must have been a lady; for, when I was in their lodge, I saw in Otaitsa's little chamber a great number of things of European manufacture, and of high taste."

"May not those have been procured for the dear girl by our good friend Gore?" asked Mr. Prevost; "he is a man of much taste himself."

"I think not," answered Edith; "they are evidently old, and seemed to have belonged to one person. Besides, there are a number of drawings, all evidently done by one hand--not what any one would purchase, and apparently the production of an amateur, rather than of an artist."

Mr. Prevost fell into a fit of thought, and leaned his head upon his hand; but Woodchuck said,--

"Oh, they are her mother's; beyond doubt, they are her mother's. She was quite a lady every inch of her; you could hear it in the tone of her voice; you could see it in her walk; her words too were all those of a lady, and her hand was so small and delicate, it could never have seen work. Do you know, Miss Edith, she was wonderful like you--more like you than Otaitsa; but I'll tell you all about it just as I heard it from the old squaw.

"At the time I talk of," continued he, "that's a good many years ago-- eighteen or nineteen may be--Black Eagle was the handsomest young man that had ever been seen in the tribes, they say, and the fiercest warrior too. He was always ready to take part in any war; and whenever fighting was going on, he was there. Well, the Delawares had not been quite brought under at that time by the Five Nations; and he went down with his warriors, and the Mohawks, to fight against the Mohaguns--they were Delawares too, you know; some were on the Monongahela river, just at the corner of Pennsylvania and Virginny. Our people had given some help to the Mohaguns, and they were at that time just laying the foundations of a fort, which the French got hold of afterwards, and called Fort Du Quesne.

"Well, there was an old general officer, who thought he would go up and see how the works were going on; and, as things were quiet enough just then--though it was but a calm before a storm--he took his daughter with him, and journeyed away pleasantly enough through the woods, I dare say, though it must have been slow work; for, as he intended to stay all the summer, the old man took a world of baggage with him; but, the third or fourth night after leaving the civilized parts, they lodged in an Ingian village; when, all in a minute, just as they were going to bed, down comes Black Eagle upon them, with his warriors. There was a dreadful fight in the village; nothing but screams, and war-whoops, and rifle-shots; and the Mohaguns, poor devils! were almost put out that night, for they were taken unawares, and they do say, not a man escaped alive out of the wigwam.

"At the first fire, out runs the old general from the hut, and at the same minute a rifle ball, perhaps from a friend, perhaps from an enemy, no one can tell, goes right through his heart. Black Eagle was collecting scalps all this time; but when he turned round, or came back, or however it might be, there he found this poor young lady, the officer's daughter, crying over her father. Well, he wouldn't suffer them to hurt her; but he took her away to the Oneida country with him, and gathered up all her goods and chattels, and her father's, and carried them off too, but all for her; for it seems that he fell in love with her at first sight. What, they say, made her first like him, was, that he wouldn't let his savages scalp the old man, telling them that the English were allies, and declaring that the ball that killed him had not come from an Oneida rifle.

"However that may be, the poor girl had no choice but to marry Black Eagle, though his mother said that, being a great chief's daughter, she made him promise never to have another wife; and, if ever a Christian priest came there, to be married to her according to her own fashion."

While he spoke, Mr. Prevost remained apparently buried in deep and very gloomy thought. But he had heard every word; and his mind had more than once wandered wide away, as was its wont, to collateral things, not only in the present, but in the past. It was a strange habit of his--a sort of discrepancy in his character--thus to suffer his thoughts to be turned aside by any accidental circumstance even in matters of deep interest; for, in times of action--when it was necessary to decide and do--no intellect was ever more prompt and decisive than his own, going straight forward to its object with great and startling rapidity. Where there was nothing to be done, however, where it was all a matter of mere thought, this rambling mood almost always prevailed: but still, like a stream flowing through a level country, and turning aside at every little obstacle, though pursuing its onward course towards the sea and reaching it at length, his mind, sooner or later, got back into the course from which it had deviated. When Woodchuck stopped, he raised his head and gazed at him for a moment in the face, with a look of earnest and melancholy inquiry.

"Did you ever hear her name?" he asked. "Can you tell me her father's name?"

"No," replied Woodchuck. "I had the history almost all from the old squaw, and if she had tried to give me an English name she would have manufactured something such as never found its way into an English mouth. All she told me was that the father was a great chief among the English, by which I made out that she meant a general."

"Probably it was her father's portrait that I saw at the Indian castle," said Edith. "There was hanging up in Otaitsa's room a picture that struck me more than any of the others, except, indeed, the portrait of a lady. It was that of a man in a military dress of antique cut. His hand was stretched out with his drawn sword in it, and he was looking round with a commanding air, as if telling his soldiers to follow. I marked it particularly at first, because the sun was shining on it, and because the frame was covered with the most beautiful Indian beadwork I ever saw. That of the lady too was similarly ornamented; but there was another which interested me much--a small pencil drawing of a young man's head, so like Walter, that, at first, I almost fancied dear Otaitsa had been trying to take his portrait from memory."

"Would you remember the old man's face, my child, if you saw it again?" asked Mr. Prevost, gazing earnestly at his daughter.

"I think so," answered Edith, a little confused by her father's eagerness. "I am quite sure I should."

"Wait then a moment," said Mr. Prevost, "and call for lights, my child."

As he spoke, he rose and quitted the room; but he was several minutes gone, and lights were burning in the chamber when he returned. He was burdened with several pictures of small size, which he spread out upon the table, while Edith and Woodchuck both rose to gaze at them.

"There, there!" cried Edith, putting her finger upon one, "there is the head of the old officer, though the attitude is different, and there is the lady too; but I do not see the portrait of the young man."

"Edith," said her father, laying his hand affectionately upon hers, and shaking his head, sadly, "he is no longer young, but he stands beside you, my child. That is the picture of my father, that of my mother. Otaitsa must be your cousin. Poor Jessie! we have always thought her dead, although her body was not found with that of her father. Better had she been dead, probably."

"No, no, Prevost," said Woodchuck, "not a bit of it. Black Eagle made her as kind a husband as ever was seen. You might have looked all Europe and America through, and not found so good a one. Then think of all she did, too, in the place where she was. God sent her there to make better people than she found. From the time she went, to the time she died, poor thing! there was no more war and bloodshed, or very little of it. Then she got a Christian minister amongst them--at least, he never would have been suffered to set his foot there if she had not been Black Eagle's wife. It is a hard thing to tell what is really good, and what is really evil, in this world. For my part, I think, if everything is not exactly good, which few of us would like to say it is, yet good comes out of it like a flower growing out of a dunghill; and there's no telling what good to the end of time this lady's going there may produce. Bad enough it was for her, I dare say, at first, but she got reconciled to it; so you mustn't say, it would have been better if she had died."

"It is strange, indeed," said Mr. Prevost, "what turns human fate will take! That she--brought up in the midst of luxury, educated with the utmost refinement, sought and admired by all who knew her--should reject two of the most distinguished men in Europe, to go to this wild land, and marry an Indian savage! Men talk of Fate and Destiny; and there are certainly strange turns of fortune so beyond all human calculation and regulation, that one would almost believe that the doctrine of the Fatalists is true."

"Do you not think, my dear father," said Edith, waking up from a profound reverie, "that this strange discovery might be turned to some great advantage? that Walter, perhaps, might be saved without the necessity of our poor friend here sacrificing his own life to deliver him?"

"That's like a kind, dear girl," interposed Woodchuck; "but I can tell you it's no use."

"Still," urged Edith, "Otaitsa ought to know; for Black Eagle certainly would never slay the nephew of a wife so dear to him."

"It's no use," repeated Woodchuck, almost impatiently. "Don't you know, Miss Edith, that Walter and the Blossom are in love with each other? and that's worth all the blood relationship in the world--

'Sometimes it doesn't last as long,
But, while it does, 'tis twice as strong.'

Then as to Black Eagle, he'd kill his own son, if the customs of his people required it. I guess it would only make him tomahawk poor Walter the sooner, just to show that he would not let any human feeling stand in the way of their devilish practices. No, no; much better keep it quiet. It might do harm, for aught we can tell; it can and will do no good. Let that thing rest, my dear child. It is settled and decreed. I am ready now, and I shall never be so ready again. Let me take one more look at my mountains, and my lakes, and my rivers, and my woods, and I have done with this life. Then, God in His mercy receive me into another! Amen.--Hark! there is some one coming up at a good gallop. That noble young lord, I dare say."

It was as Woodchuck supposed; and, the moment after, Lord H---- entered the room with a beaming look of joy and satisfaction in his countenance. He held a packet of considerable size in his hand, and advanced at once to Mr. Prevost, saying--

"My dear sir, I am rejoiced to present you with this letter, not alone because it will give you some satisfaction, but because it removes the stain of ingratitude from the government of the country. His Majesty's present ministers are sensible that you have not received justice; that your long services to the country in various ways--all that you have done, in short, to benefit and ameliorate your race, and to advocate all that is good and noble--have been treated with long neglect, which amounts to an offence; and they now offer you, as some atonement, a position which may lead to wealth and distinction, which, I trust, is but the step to more."

"What is it, George, what is it?" asked Edith, eagerly.

"It is, I am told," replied Lord H----, "in a letter which accompanied the packet, a commission as commissary-general of the army here, and an offer of the rank of baronet."

"Thank God!" exclaimed Edith; and then, seeing a look of surprise at her earnestness come upon her noble lover's face, a bright smile played round her lips for a moment, and she added--"I say, thank God, George--not that I am glad my father should have such things, for I hope he will decline them both; but because the very offer will heal an old wound, by showing him that zealous exertions and the exercise of high and noble qualities are not always to be treated with neglect, forgetfulness, and contempt. He will be glad of it, I am sure, whatever his decision may be."

"Now I understand you, my own love," answered Lord H----. "With regard to the baronetcy, he shall do as he will; but I must press him earnestly to accept the office tendered to him. To decline it might show some resentment. By accepting it, he incurs no peril, and he serves his country; for, from his knowledge of the people here, of the physical features of the land and its resources, and of the habits and feelings of all classes, I believe no man could be found, with one or two exceptions, so well fitted for the task as himself. Ah, my good friend, Captain Brooks, how do you do? I have much wished to see you lately, and to hear of your plans."

"I am as well as may be, my lord," replied Woodchuck, wringing in his heavy grasp the hand which Lord H---- extended to him. "As for my plans, they are the same as ever--you did not doubt me, I am sure."

"I did not," returned Lord H----, gravely; and, looking down, he fell into a fit of thought. At length, looking up, he added, "And yet, my good friend, I am glad you have had time for reflection; for since we last met I have somewhat reproached myself for, at least, tacit encouragement of an act in the approval of which so many personal motives mingle that one may well doubt oneself. Forgive me, Edith--forgive me, Mr. Prevost,--if I ask our friend here if he has well considered and weighed in his mind, calmly and reasonably, without bias--nay, without enthusiasm--whether there be any moral obligation on him to perform an act which I suppose he has told you he contemplates."

"There is no forgiveness needed, my lord," replied Mr. Prevost. "I would have put the same question to him, if he would have let me. Nay, more; I would have told him--whatever I might suffer by the result--that, in my judgment, there was no moral obligation. Because he did a justifiable act, these Indians commit one that is unjustifiable upon an innocent man. That can be no reason why he should sacrifice his life to save the other. God forbid that, even for the love of my own child, I should deal in such a matter unjustly. I am no Roman, father--I pretend not to be such. If my own death will satisfy them, let them take the old tree withered at the root, and spare the sapling full of strength and promise. But let me not doom--let me not advise--a noble and honest man to sacrifice himself from a too generous impulse."

"I don't know much of moral obligations," replied Woodchuck, gravely; "but I guess I have thought over the thing as much as e'er a one of you. I have made up my mind just upon one principle, and there let it rest, in God's name. I say to myself: 'Woodchuck, it's not right, is it, that any one should suffer for what you ha' done?' 'No, it's not.' 'Well, is there any use talking of whether they've a right to make him suffer for your act or not? They'll do it.' 'No; there's no use o' talking; because they'll do it. It's only shuffling off the consequences of what you did upon another man's shoulders. You never did that, Woodchuck; don't do it now. Man might say, "It's all fair;" God might pardon it; but your own heart would never forgive it.'"

Edith sprang forward, and took both his hands, with the tears rolling over her cheeks.

"God will prevent it," she said, earnestly. "I have faith in Him. He will deliver us in our utmost need. He provided the Patriarch with an offering, and spared his son. He will find us a means of escape if we but trust in Him."

"Miss Edith," replied Woodchuck solemnly, "He may, or He may not, according to His good pleasure; but of this I am certain, that, though Christ died for our transgressions, we have no right to see any one else suffer for our doings. I have read my Bible a great deal up there on the hill-side lately--more than I ever did before, since I was a little boy--and I'm quite certain of what I'm about. It has been a comfort and a strength to me. It's all so clear--so very clear. Other books one may not understand--one can't misunderstand *that*--unless one tries very hard. And now, pray let us have an end o't here. My mind is quite made up. There is no use in saying a word more."

All the rest were silent, and Edith left the room, with: the large tears falling down her face.

CHAPTER XXXV

The great apothecary's shop of Human Vanity is filled with "flattering unctions;" and there is not a sore spot upon the heart or mind of man, which cannot there find its unguent--whether the disease proceed from a self-generated canker, or from a blow inflicted by others. The greatest, the wisest, the healthiest, the soundest-minded of mankind have all occasion to apply to this shop; and they do so now and then, under the sores of regret, and failure, and disappointment, or the wounds of superciliousness, forgetfulness, or neglect. Oh,

> "The insolence of office, and the spurns
> That patient merit of the unworthy takes,"

how often do they drive the iron into the flesh which requires that apothecary's shop to heal it!

Yet, let us not look too curiously into the motives which induced Mr. Prevost, after some hesitation and some reluctance, to accept the appointment offered to him by the government through Lord H----. It was pleasing to him to think that his merits, and the services of which he was conscious--though, be it said, not too conscious--had only been so long overlooked, not from being unapparent or forgotten, but because, in some of his views, he had differed from the ministers lately dismissed. He knew not--or, at least, he did not recollect--how easy it is to forget when one is not willing to remember; how rarely qualities are brought before the public gaze, except by interest, accident, or position--unless by impudence, arrogance, and self-sufficiency. One in ten thousand men of those who rise, rise by merit alone; though there must be some merit in almost all who rise. But the really great are like fixed stars; few of the greatest are ever near the eye; one requires a telescope to see them, and that telescope is Time.

Putting aside military chiefs, who write their names in fire, many of the greatest men of all ages have been overlooked by Fame. The author of Job is unknown; the builders of almost all great buildings of antiquity are nameless: the sculptor of the one Venus, and the one Apollo--doubtful, doubtful--never recorded in history. Then look at the fate of others. Behold

Friar Bacon and Galileo, in their dungeons; Dante proscribed and banished; Shakspeare, a mere yeoman at Stratford; Homer and Milton, blind and poor; Virgil, Petrarch, Verulam, the flatterers of a court; Newton, the Master of the Mint! Heaven and earth! what a catalogue of black spots upon the great leopard! To hardly one of them did contemporary fame ascribe a place pre-eminent. Why, it is a salve and a comfort to every fool and every driveller. No spawner of a penny pamphlet--with vanity enough--can be sure that he is not twin brother to the blind beggar of Greece.

But Mr. Prevost forgot all this. He was conscious of having laboured well and diligently in what he believed, the right path: there was in him a sense and an experience of intellectual power: he had felt, and had exercised, the capability of guiding and directing others aright; and, more than all, he had seen many a time the schemes which he had devised, the words which he had written or spoken, adopted--appropriated--filched--by others, and lauded, making the fame and the fortune of a weak, impudent, lucky charlatan, supported by interest, family, or circumstances, while the real author was forgotten, and would have been hooted had he claimed his own. This gave him some confidence in himself, independent of vanity; and be it not for us to assay the metal too closely.

He accepted the office tendered, and at once set about preparing for its duties. There was but one impediment--his anxiety for his son; for, notwithstanding every assurance, he felt that quivering doubt and fear which can only be felt by a parent when a beloved child's fate is in the balance--which all parents worthy of the name have felt, and no child can comprehend.

When Edith rose, on the day following the visit of poor Captain Brooks--somewhat later than was her custom (for the first half of the watches of the night had known no comforter)--Woodchuck was gone. He had waited for no leave-taking, and was on his road towards the mountains before the dawn of day.

It was better for all, indeed, that he should go; and he felt it: not that there was any chance of his resolution being shaken; but, as he had himself said, he wished to forget that resolution as far as possible--to think no more of his coming fate than the dark remembrance of it within his own heart forced him to think; and the presence of Mr. Prevost and his daughter--the very absence of Walter from their fireside--would have reminded him constantly of the rock on which his bark was inevitably steering. With Mr. Prevost and Edith, his presence would have had the effect of keeping up the anxious struggle between affection for Walter and a kindly sense of justice towards him. His every look, his every word, would have been a source of painful interest; and the terrible balancing of very narrowly-divided equities, when life was in the scale, and affection held the beam, would have gone on, in the mind at least, continually.

When he was gone, the agitating feelings gradually subsided. His self-sacrifice presented itself to the mind as a thing decided: the mind was relieved from a greater apprehension by a less; and a quiet melancholy, whenever his coming fate was thought of, took the place of anxious alarm. In some sort, the present and the past seemed to transpose themselves; and they almost looked upon him as already dead.

True, all fear in regard to Walter was not completely banished. There was nothing definite; there was no tangible object of apprehension; they felt perfectly certain that Woodchuck would execute his resolution; yet the heart, like an agitated pendulum, vibrated long after the momentum had ceased. It grew quieter and quieter by degrees, however, on the part of Mr. Prevost: a change of thought and of object did much. All his preparations had to be made for the proper execution of the office he had undertaken; he had more than once to go to Albany, and on each occasion he took his daughter with him. Each change had some effect; and both he and Edith recovered a certain degree of cheerfulness, at least in general society. It was only in the quiet and the silent hours, when either was left alone--when those intervals took place during which sleep refuses to visit the eye--when all external sounds are still--when all external sights are absent, and the mind is left alone with thought, and nothing but thought, for its companion,--it was only then that the fears, and the anxiety, and the gloom returned.

Every moment that could be spared from military duties was passed by Lord H---- at Edith's side, whether in her own home or in the city. People remarked his attentions, and commented on them as usual; for no publicity had been given to their engagement, and the good-humoured world thought fit to judge it strange that a young nobleman of such distinction should be so completely captivated by the daughter of a simple gentleman like Mr. Prevost.

Their comments affected the two lovers little, however. They were thinking of themselves, and not of the world; and though the happiest hours of Lord H---- were those in which, at her father's quiet hermitage, he could pass a brief space in wandering with her alone through the beautiful scenery round, or sitting with her under the verandah, gazing out upon the prospect and watching the advance of summer over the forest world, still he was happy by her side anywhere; and her demeanour in society, her grace, her beauty, as compared with others, only served to render him proud and happy in his choice.

Thus passed nearly three weeks; by which time the bustle of active preparation, the marching of several regiments towards the north, and signs of activity in every department, gave notice to the inhabitants of Albany that some important military movement was about to take place. The fife and drum, and the lumbering roll of the cannon, were daily heard in the quiet streets. Boats were collecting on the river; parades and exercises occupied the greater part of every day; scouts and runners were seen hurrying about in different directions; and clouds of Indians, painted and feathered for the war-path, hovered round the city, and often appeared in the streets.

Lord H---- had advanced with his whole regiment to the neighbourhood of Sandy Hill; other bodies of troops were following; and the Commissary-General, whose active energy and keen intelligence surprised all who had only known him as a somewhat reserved and moody man, had advanced to a spot on the Hudson where a small fort had been built at the commencement of what was called the King's Road, to see with his own eyes the safe delivering and proper distribution of the stores he had collected. Long ranges of huts were gathered round the fort, which was judged so far within the English line as to be a place of perfect security; and many a lady from Albany, both young and old, had gathered together there to see the last of husband, brother, or father, before they plunged into the forest and encountered the coming strife.

Here everything was done as usual to smooth the front of war, and conceal its ugly features; and certainly after the arrival of Lord H----, with his regiment and the wing of another, the scene was brilliant and lively enough. Bright dresses, glittering arms, military music, fluttering flags, and prancing chargers were beheld on every side; and gay and lively talk, only interrupted now and then by the solemn words of caution or direction from anxious heart to anxious heart, hid, in a great degree, the deeper, stronger, sterner feelings that were busy underneath.

In all such expeditions, amidst the bustle and excitement, there come lapses of quiet inactivity, especially before the first blow is struck. Some accident causes a delay; some movements have not been combined with sufficient accuracy; one party has to wait for another, and is left unoccupied. Thus was it in the present instance. A small but important division of the army, to be accompanied by a large body of Indians, was retarded by a deficiency of boats; and the news arrived that two days must elapse before they could reach the fort.

A superior officer was now present; and both Lord H---- and Mr. Prevost felt that it would be no dereliction of duty to seek leave of absence in order to visit once more the house of the latter, and personally escort Edith to the place where she was to remain till the object of the expedition was accomplished.

The same day it was first made known what the object of that expedition was. The word "Ticonderoga" was whispered through the encampment, running from the general's quarters through every rank down to the private soldier. A strange sort of feeling of joy spread throughout the force; not that many knew either the importance of the object or the state of the place, but simply that all were relieved from an uncertainty.

The comment of Lord H---- was very brief. He had, indeed, long known the fact now first published; but, as he told it to Edith while seating her on her horse to set out, he said--

"The place is luckily near; and the business will soon be brought to an end, my love." A something indefinable in his heart made him add, mentally, "one way or another."

But he gave no utterance to the gloomy doubt; and the little party rode away.

CHAPTER XXXVI

A calm, quiet evening, with the wind at south, the sun setting red in clouds, and a gray vapour stealing over the sky, with every prospect of a coming storm, and yet everything still and sober in solemn tranquillity, often puts me in mind of those pauses in the busy course of life which precede some great and decisive event. It is very strange, too, but I have remarked that it not unfrequently happens that such an aspect of external nature comes, as it, were, to harmonize with our feelings when we take a brief pause upon the brink of great events, destined to bring fruition or disappointment to all the hopes of life.

Such an evening was that which Lord H---- and Edith and Mr. Prevost spent together at the house where so many of these scenes have been laid, after quitting Fort Edward in the morning. Their journey had passed quite peaceably; they had encountered no human being but a few bands of friendly Indians, going to join the army; and the ride, as every one knows, was, and still is, a very beautiful one. It had occupied hardly four hours, and thus the principal part of the day had been spent in tranquillity in a scene endeared to all.

Mr. Prevost had retired to his room to write, and Lord H---- and Edith sat together in front of the house gazing out towards the setting sun. There are few things really sublime on earth; but amongst the most sublime are those moments when we sit beside a fellow-being so linked to us by love that our existence seems but as a part of his or hers, our hopes, our fears, our happiness, our joy, identified; and yet, in the course of mortal fate, the approach of some dark hour of parting keeps ever whispering in our ear, "Ye are not truly one. Though mingling every thought and feeling; though heart beat with heart, and mind walk with mind; though each breast is open to the other, as to the eyes of conscience and of God; though linked and bound by every aspiration and by every sentiment, ye are two, and ye must sever." The sensation is very painful, but it is sublime in its intensity; and such were the sensations of Edith and her lover as they sat there and watched the setting sun.

They talked of many things, some not at all connected with the circumstances of the present or the future; they feared to dwell upon them too long, and they often sought relief in indifferent topics; still the coming hour was vaguely present to the mind of each. It was like sitting near a waterfall, with the quiet, melancholy murmur of the cataract mingling harmoniously, but sadly, with every other sound.

"I trust, dear Edith, that we shall see it together," said Lord H----, speaking of the distant land where they both had birth. "Many a lovely thing is to be met with in the old world, both in nature and in art; and though I love these beautiful scenes well, and enjoy as much as any one the magnificence of unadorned Nature, yet methinks that is no reason why we should not appreciate to the full all that is fine or lovely, though of a different kind and character. It is the narrow-minded man--the man of an uncapacious soul, who suffers one sort of excellence alone to take possession of his taste or heart. Beauty and goodness are infinitely varied; and though I may love some aspects best, yet I trust ever to be capable of deriving pleasure from each and all."

"But you have seen all these things, George," she answered; "will it not weary you to go over them all again, with so untutored a companion as myself?"

He gazed at her for a moment, with a look of earnest affection, and gently pressed the hand he held in his.

"I take a new light with me, Edith," he replied; "a light that will give new loveliness to everything that is beautiful. I have often thought, my beloved, that to see our own sensations,--I mean happy ones, enjoyment, admiration, satisfaction,--reflected from the mind of one so dear as you are to me, must be like beholding a lovely scene reflected from the bosom of a calm lake, where every fair feature and bright hue acquires a magic lustre, and a brightness greater in the borrowed image than even in the tangible reality. These are happy dreams, Edith; let us trust to renew them some few weeks hence; and then, whenever this campaign is over, I will quit this busy, perilous game of war, if Edith will then be mine, and realize the visions we love so well. In the meanwhile, dear one, as every one who goes into battle encounters certainly some peril, let us speak a word of the future, in case the worst should befall. You will remember me, Edith, I am sure, if I should not return. I do not think you will ever love any other so well; but, remember, I am not so selfish in my love as to wish you to sacrifice the whole comfort and happiness of a life to the memory of one departed. Be happy when and in what way you can; consult your own feelings solely. And I do believe that, if spirits can look down on earth when parted from this frail body, your happiness, however it is attained, will add to mine; for I cannot think, that, when we quit this earth, we carry the selfishness of clay along with us."

The tears swam in Edith's eyes, and gemmed the long black lashes round them; but they ran not over.

"I have but one wish on earth, George," she answered, "when I think of the chances that you mention. It is, that I may not survive you even an hour. If I had not known it could not be, I would have asked to go with you, in the hope that, if you are to fall, one hour might take us both."

Lord H---- smiled sadly, and shook his head.

"That might entail greater sorrows still," he rejoined, "and in no sense could it be, my Edith. No soldier should have his wife with him. While in the field, he should be detached as much as possible from every thought but that of duty. I doubt, indeed, that he should have any tie to earth whatever, except those which God imposed upon him at birth. This is one reason why I shall quit the army. I am less fit to be a soldier than I was; but I should be utterly unfit if I thought you were in peril. From all apprehension on that score I go free. I felt some uneasiness, indeed, while I thought that you were to remain alone here with none but the servants round you. As matters are arranged at present, however, you would be quite safe with Colonel Schneider and his wife. Besides, his servants, and the host of workmen employed in finishing his house and all the other works he has going on, will prove a little body-guard in itself."

"I should have felt myself perfectly secure here," returned Edith; "for the familiar aspect of all things round gives a sort of confidence which I could feel nowhere else. These Schneiders I hardly know; but, if you and my father are better satisfied, I am content to be with them. What hour are we to set out to-morrow?"

"Between one and two o'clock," replied Lord H----, "will be quite time enough. The distance is but six miles, and your father and I can very well escort you thither, and reach Fort Edward before night."

"I am glad of that," answered Edith. "To-morrow is the day that poor Captain Brooks is to be here. I should much like to see him once more, and I hope that he will arrive before we go. If not, I must tell the servants to provide for him well, and show him every kindness. Oh, George, is it not terrible to think of his encountering such a fate? The very idea of providing his last meals for him when going to a voluntary death, makes my heart sink with horror and regret."

"The only choice is between him and poor Walter," answered Lord H----; "and we must not forget that this act of Woodchuck's has not been pressed, or even asked, by us. He judges, and judges rightly, I think, that it would be ungenerous to allow Walter to suffer for his acts; and, though I would not urge him to adopt the course he has chosen, I certainly would say nothing to dissuade him."

"His self-devotion only makes it more terrible," returned Edith, "at least in my eyes; and yet I cannot help hoping," she continued, looking up inquiringly in her lover's face, "that something may occur--why should I not say that something will be provided?--to rescue them both, without this awful sacrifice."

Lord H---- would say nothing to quell a hope which he thought would give comfort; yet he did not share it, for his faith was less than Edith's--man's faith always is less than woman's.

Not many minutes more passed before Mr. Prevost rejoined them, speaking to one of the servants, as he entered, in a calm but rapid tone, and giving various orders and directions for the morrow. Although not likely to be exposed so much as if entrusted with a military command, some danger, of course, attended the mere fact of his accompanying the army; and he had spent the last hour or two in making many arrangements in view of probable death. Though a man of a quick imagination and susceptible temperament, death had never had any great terrors for him. He was personally, constitutionally, courageous; and in whatever aspect or under whatever circumstances he contemplated the mere passing from one life to another, he could not bring his mind to fear it. Yet, strange to say, he was in some respects of an apprehensive turn of mind. He feared difficulty, he feared disgrace, he feared the slightest imputation on his honour or his character; he was exceedingly apprehensive when any danger menaced those he loved. Thus, as far as he himself was concerned, he had sat down that day to contemplate his own death as calmly as any other event inseparable from life; but when the thought of Edith and Walter, and their future fate, mingled with his reflections, his courage was shaken, and he felt much agitated. He had pursued his task steadily, however; had arranged all things so as to leave neither obscurity nor difficulty in his affairs; and then, casting all sombre thoughts from him, came down and joined his daughter and his friend below, with a tranquil, nay, a cheerful face.

All the proceedings of the following day were then definitely arranged. After an early and hasty dinner, he and Lord H----, with the four mounted men who accompanied them, and Edith's old travelling companion,

Chando, were to escort her to the dwelling of Colonel Schneider, the new house built that spring even further in the wild than that of Mr. Prevost, and of which the Indians on the hill had spoken. There, leaving her at once, the two gentlemen were to return to the camp, which they calculated upon reaching before nightfall. Vain arrangements,--vain preparations! How continually are we frustrated, even in the smallest and most insignificant plans, by that obdurate, over-ruling will of Fate!

The night passed quietly, day dawned, and, while Edith was dressing, she saw from her window the expected figure of Woodchuck, walking towards the door with a firmer tread and more resolute and easy bearing than he displayed when he had last appeared. On descending, she found him talking with her father and Lord H---- with perfect calmness and ease. His look was firm and self-possessed; his air was bold, though tranquil; and he seemed to have gained health since she saw him. Edith was almost tempted to believe that some happy change of circumstances had taken place; but his first words dispelled the illusion.

"No, I thank you, Mr. Prevost," he said, "I must go on. I'll just take some breakfast with you, and then begin my march. I have calculated well my time, and I should like to have a day or two to come and go upon. It doesn't do to push things to the last. I guess I shall reach Johnson Castle to-night. Then, mayhap, I shall get a lift up the river in a canoe; but, at all events, even if I am obliged to foot it all the way, I shall be in time."

Mr. Prevost looked down, and fell into thought, while Woodchuck advanced to Edith, shook hands with her, and spoke upon indifferent subjects. She now remarked that he was dressed in different guise from that which he had assumed during the winter. A light brown hunting-shirt, loose in the body and the sleeves, seemed to be his principal garment; and in the belt which bound it round him was stuck the tomahawk and scalping-knife of an Indian. His rifle stood in one corner of the room. On his head he wore a fur cap as usual; a pouch and powder-horn, with moccassins on his feet, completed his equipment.

"Well, general," he said, turning to Lord H----; "I saw some of your people as I came up the river. There had been a fuss about bateaux, but I showed them how they could find some; for a set of knaves, more French than English at their hearts, had drawn a crowd of them up the creek. So Abercrombie and the rest are all up at Fort Edward by this time."

Lord H---- looked towards Mr. Prevost; but he was still in thought, and only roused himself to lead the way into the hall to breakfast. Woodchuck ate heartily; but to touch a single mouthful was a hard task for each of the other three. While still at the table, however, the sound of horses' feet galloping up to the door was heard; and Lord H----, starting up, looked out of the window. A young officer and a trooper of dragoons were at the door; and the moment the former saw Lord H----, he handed him a letter in at the window, dismounting and entering soon after. By this time, the despatch had been read both by the young nobleman and Mr. Prevost; and the latter exclaimed, "This is most unfortunate! An immediate recall, Edith. We must not delay a moment, for the march commences to-morrow at daybreak. Get ready as fast as possible, my love; we will see you safely to Colonel Schneider's and then gallop back to the Fort."

"Excuse me for observing," said the young officer, "that the order is peremptory. Of course, his lordship will judge for himself; but I only follow General Abercrombie's commands, in saying that he wishes not a moment's delay."

"But, my daughter, sir, my daughter," said Mr. Prevost.

The young gentleman bowed stiffly, but made no answer; and the countenance of Lord H---- was very grave.

"Surely," said Mr. Prevost, "'twould be no great disobedience of orders to see my daughter safely to the house of my friend, Colonel Schneider, a distance of not more than six miles."

"Which would take nearly two hours to go and come," said the young officer drily; "at least over roads such as these. But you and his lordship are the best judges. I do not presume to dictate; I only convey to you the commander-in-chief's orders."

"Leave her to my care, Prevost," said Woodchuck, starting up. "I will see her safe. It's all in my way. Some of the servants can go with us, and there is no danger."

"I am in no fear, indeed, my dear father," said Edith; "do not risk a censure. I shall be quite safe with our friend here."

"I believe, indeed, you will," said Lord H----; "otherwise, I myself should be tempted to disobey. But the terms of this despatch are so pressing, that, unless there were immediate and positive peril, I think we are bound to return to camp at once."

He spoke aloud, and very gravely; but then, advancing to Edith's side, he added a few words in a lower tone. Mr. Prevost walked up and joined in their consultation--a sufficient indication, it might have seemed, that they wished, for a few moments' privacy. Woodchuck understood, and walked quietly to the door; for natural delicacy of feeling is but the reality of that of which politeness is the shadow. But the young officer, who was of that coarse, common stuff of which martinets are ultimately made, still kept his ground, till Lord H----, somewhat provoked, turned round and said,--

"Captain Lumley, you will have the goodness to return to head-quarters, and inform the commander-in-chief that his orders shall be punctually obeyed."

The young man paused a moment with a look of surprise and discontent; and a moment or two after, when he passed Woodchuck at the door of the house, he was muttering,--

"Without asking me to take any refreshment!"

His murmurs were, perhaps, natural; for those who concede least to the feelings of others invariably exact most for their own.

It is true, Lord H----, occupied with thoughts that engrossed him altogether, dismissed the *aide-de-camp* without remembrance of his needs as well as without any feeling of resentment, and omitted a courtesy which no resentment assuredly would have curtailed. But the young man, swelling with indignation and offended dignity, mounted sullenly, and proceeded but slowly on his way. He had not gone one-half the distance, however, between Mr. Prevost's house and Fort Edward, when Lord H---- and the commissary passed him at great speed; and he did not reach head-quarters till half an hour after they had announced their own return.

CHAPTER XXXVII

The storm, prognosticated from the red aspect of the setting sun on the night before, had not descended when Edith Prevost left the door of her father's house. No raindrops fell, no wind even stirred the trees; and it was only a sort of misty obscurity to the westward which gave token, to eyes well acquainted with the forest, that the promise of the preceding sunset would yet be fulfilled. Overhead, all was clear and blue; and the sun, though some white haze hung round its broad disk, was powerful for the season of the year.

Edith's companions were only Chando the negro, the good woman Sister Bab, whose kindness, faithfulness, and intelligence had all been tried, and Woodchuck, who refused to take a horse from the stable, but set out on foot by Edith's side.

"You can't canter a step of the way, Miss Edith," he said; "so I can keep up with you, I guess; for the road, such as it is, is better fitted for two feet than four."

As she turned from the door, tears were in Edith's eyes, arising from many a mingled source. She had seen her father and him whom she loved as well, though differently, depart suddenly to danger and to battle. Her brother was far away, and she could not help thinking him still in peril. Not only was the future of all uncertain--for so the future of every one is--but the uncertainty was dark, and, as it were, more tangible than is generally the case with the dim, misty approach of the coming time. There was not only a cloud, but the cloud was threatening.

Nor was this all. There are times in the course of almost every life, when some little event, some marking point in the journey of existence, causes the mind to pause and review the past--to compare the present state with a state gone by. It is rarely that the contemplation has not something painful in it, both on account of the heart's self-deceit and waywardness, which teaches us always to estimate gains less than losses; and, also, because in our warfare with the world (except in very early youth) the gains, however highly we may estimate them, are, as in all other warfares, really less than the losses. We may have attained that which we desire; but, nine times out of ten, we find that we have over-appreciated the object; and, when we come to sum up the cost in health, happiness, purity of mind, exertion, care, anxiety, and all the pieces of coin with which man purchases success, we frequently find that we have bought the victory too dear--that that which we have obtained was not worth all we have exchanged for it.

The moment of departure from her father's door was one of those pausing-places of the mind for Edith Prevost. She did not cast her thoughts far back: she took in but a little range; six months was the limit. But she remembered how calmly happy she had been in that dwelling six months before. Her father, her brother, were both there with her; sweet natural affections had garlanded the doorposts, and tranquil hours of unagitated enjoyment had been the sunshine of her path. All that was necessary, much that was superfluous, she had possessed; and if she, as all other mortal beings, had not been absolutely content--if she, like every other girl, had felt a want, a vacancy of the heart, a capability of love unexercised, which neither filial nor fraternal affection could supply,--still it had been but a vague, indefinite feeling that there was something more in life than she had yet known--one crowning blessing not yet possessed. She had been very happy, though there had been the one thing wanting.

Now, that one thing had been attained--Heaven knows without her seeking it. She loved, and was beloved. But, oh! how sadly changed was all the rest! Her brother afar, with a dark fate hanging over him--her father gone upon a path of peril. And love, what had love left her? Anxiety, keen, terrible anxiety, which might well counterbalance for some portion, at least, of all the sweetness of the bright blessing.

She mused sadly, gazing down upon the horse's neck, and hardly seeing or thinking of the way she took. In the mean time, Woodchuck trudged on by her side, with his head erect, his face lifted towards the sky, his pace steady and assured. Edith suddenly and almost unconsciously turned her eyes towards him. There was a tranquil elevation in his countenance, a lofty resolution in his look, which gave her thoughts, in a moment, another direction. She was parting from a well-loved home and cherished associations, with some clouds hanging over her, with some anxieties dogging her path, but with a probability of soon returning, and with many a sweet promise of future happiness. Yet she was sad and downcast. Woodchuck was marching onward, wittingly and voluntarily, to a certain and terrible death; and yet his march was tranquil, firm, and resolute. She felt ashamed of her tears. Nay more, as thought ran on, she said to herself,--

"There is something more in life, something higher, nobler, grander than any human passion, than any mortal enjoyment, than any mere earthly peace, can give--something that comes from Heaven to aid and support us in our struggles here below. My poor companion knows and feels that he is doing his duty, that he is acting according to the commandment of his God; and he is calm and firm in the presence of death, and in the separation from all earthly things. And I--what have I to suffer, what have I to fear, in comparison with him?"

She made a great effort; she shook off her sadness; she wiped the tears from her eyes, and said a few words to Woodchuck in a quiet tone. He answered briefly to her actual words, but then turned at once to the feelings which he believed to be in her heart.

"Ah, Miss Prevost," he said, "it's a sad thing for a young lady like you to part, for the first time, with those she loves when they are going to battle; and I don't know that a woman's heart ever gets rightly accustomed to it. But it don't do to love anything too well in this world--no, not even one's own life. It's a sad stumbling-block, both in the way of our duty and our happiness. Not that I'd have people keep from loving anything. That would never do. They wouldn't be worth having if they couldn't love their friends, and love them very well; but, I guess, the best way is to recollect always, when we've got a thing, that it is but a loan--life itself, all the same as everything else. It's all lent, and all will be recalled; only, you see, my dear young lady, we've got a promise that, if we use what we've had lent to us well, it shall be given to us for ever hereafter, and that should always be a comfort to us. It is to me."

A slight sigh followed his words, and he walked on in silence for a minute or two, probably pursuing the course which he had laid down for himself in his very excellent philosophy, of marching on straight to a high object, and casting from him all thought of the unavoidable sufferings of the way. Soon after, he looked up to the sky, and said,--

"It's getting wonderfully black out there. I should not wonder if we had a flaw of wind and a good soaking rain. I say, Master Chando, put that bear-skin over the young lady's baggage, and hold the horse better in hand, or you'll have him down amongst these stumps. You ride better than you lead, my friend."

The negro grinned at him, but did as he was directed; and, a few minutes after, they issued out of the wood upon a small open space of ground extending over the side of a slight eminence. The view thence was prolonged far to the westward in a clear day, showing some beautiful blue hills at the distance of eight or nine miles. Those hills, however, had now disappeared; and in their place was seen what can only be called a dense black cloud, although those words give a very inadequate idea of the sight which presented itself to Edith's eye. It was like a gigantic wall of black marble, with a faint, white, irregular line at the top. But this wall evidently moved, coming forward with vast rapidity, although, where the travellers were, not a breath of air was felt. On it rushed towards them, swallowing up everything in its own obscurity. Each instant some tree, some undulation of the ground, some marking object in the prospect, disappeared in its deep gloomy shadow; and for a few moments Edith sat still upon her horse, gazing in awe and even in terror. Woodchuck himself seemed for an instant overpowered; but then he caught Edith's rein, and turned her horse, exclaiming,--

"Back, Miss Prevost, back, as fast as possible! That's the blackest cloud I ever see in all my days. There, there, to the east'ard! Get under them big old hemlocks. Keep away from the pines and the small trees. A tree had need to have been fastening to the ground for a hundred years to stand what's coming."

As he spoke, he ran fast on by the side of Edith's horse till they reached the edge of the wood, and there he checked her progress.

"Not too far in; not too far in! You must be ready to jump out if you find that these old fellows begin crashing."

He then left her bridle, and walked carefully round several of the trees, examining their trunks and roots with a very critical eye, to ascertain that they were firmly fixed and not decayed; and then, approaching Edith again, he held out his hand, saying,--

"Jump down! Here's one will do. He must ha' stood many a hard storm and bitter blast, and p'r'aps will bear this one too; for he's as sound as when he started up a little twig out of the ground, before the eye of any mortal man now living winked in the sunshine--ay, or his father's either. Here, Chando, take the horses and grip them all tight, for depend upon it they'll caper when the wind and rain come. Now, my dear, put yourself on this side of the tree, keep close to him, and listen well. You may find him shiver and sway a bit, but don't mind that, for he's not so tall as the rest, and twice as stout; and what makes me trust him is, that in some storm his head has been broken off, and yet his feet have stood stout. He won't catch so much wind as the others, and I think he'd stand it if he did. But if you hear him begin to cranch, jump clear out here to the left into the open ground. He'll fall t'other way. If you keep close, the branches won't strike you when they fall, and the rain won't get at you; for it's taking a long sweep."

The next moment, it came. The wind, blowing with the force of a hurricane, rushed over the valley below; the leaves were torn off, the small twigs, with their umbrageous covering, were carried aloft into the air and scattered; a few large drops of rain fell; and then the whole force of the tempest struck the hill-side and the more open forest where Edith stood. In an instant, the scene of confusion and destruction was indescribable. The gusts seemed to hiss as they passed through the boughs of the trees and between the tall stems. Large branches were torn off and scattered far; the young pines and birches bent before the force of the storm. As in the case of war and pestilence, the weak and the sickly and the young and the decayed suffered first and most. Wherever the roots had not got a firm hold of the ground--wherever the thawing of the spring, or the heavy rains, had washed away the earth or loosened it--the trees came thundering and crashing down, and the din was awful; the howling wind, the breaking branches, the falling tree, all joining in the roar; and the pattering rain, rustling and rushing amongst the withered leaves left by the winter, became at length thicker and more dense, till it seemed as if a river was falling down from the sky, hardly separated into drops, rather than a fertilizing shower passing over the landscape.

Edith gazed round her in affright, for she could, as Woodchuck had predicted, feel the enormous but low-stemmed hemlock against which he had placed her tremble and quiver with the blast; and a number of large trees hard by were rooted up, and cast prostrate, bearing the turf and earth in which they had stood, up into the air; while, here and there, some more firmly fixed in the ground, but defective higher up, snapped in the midst, and the whole upper part was carried many yards away. But, though she gazed, little was the distance she could see, so thick and black was the covering of the sky; while all around, what between the close-falling deluge and a sudden mist rising up from the earth, the sort of twilight that the storm-cloud left, was rendered hazy and still more obscure.

The two negroes, as usual with that race, were clamorous and excited, adding the noise of their tongues to the roar of the tempest; but the horses, contrary to the expectation of Woodchuck, seemed cowed and paralyzed by fear. Instead of attempting to break loose and rush away, they merely turned from the wind and rain; and with hoofs set firm, and drooping heads, abode the storm, with now and then a shivering thrill, showing the terror that they felt. Woodchuck himself stood silent close by Edith, leaning his strong shoulder against the tree, and, with his eyes bent down upon the ground, seemed to lose himself in heavy thought. A man who has parted with the world and the world's hopes, is tempest-proof.

After the first rush of the storm, there came a lull: and then another fierce roar, and more falling trees and crashing branches. The whole forest swayed and bent like a feather in a breeze, and down came the torrents from the sky more furiously than ever. But, in the midst of all, Woodchuck started, leaned his head a little on one side, and seemed to listen, with his eyes fixed upon vacancy.

"What is the matter?" asked Edith, alarmed by his look.

"I thought I heard a footfall," he answered.

"In the roar of such a storm!" exclaimed Edith. "It must have been some falling branch."

He only smiled for an answer; but still he listened, and she could see him lift his arm a little from the lock of his rifle on which it had been tightly pressed, and look down upon it to see that it was dry.

The next moment, however, he resumed his ordinary attitude, and said, in a quiet tone,--

"It's all nonsense, however. The Indians are all quiet and friendly on this side of the lake. But you see, Miss Prevost, I have been for so many months on the watch every minute, not knowing whether I should not feel the scalping-knife or the tomahawk the next, that I have got over-wary. The Mohawks are all on the move about here, and no Hurons or any other of our enemies would venture across, except in a large body, to fight a regular battle. It must have been the tread of some friendly Ingian I heard, though they don't usually leave the trail, except when they've some object in view."

"But is it possible you could hear anything distinctly amidst this awful noise?" asked Edith. "Are you sure you were not mistaken?"

"Oh no, I'm not like to be mistaken," answered Woodchuck. "One's ears get sharp with continual listening. I'm pretty sure it was a foot I heard, and a man's foot too. It seemed to me as if it had slipped off a loose stone, hidden under the leaves, and come down harder, perhaps, than he expected. But that's no proof that he meant mischief, for they've all got those cat-like sort of ways, creeping about silently, whether there's 'casion for it or not; and, as I said just now, they're all friendly here on this side of Horicon."

A few moments' silence succeeded; the wind once more swelled up, raged for a minute or two, and then fell again a little; and Woodchuck, putting out his head from beyond the shelter of the great trunk, observed, "It seems to me to be getting a little clearer there to the west'ard. I guess it won't last more nor half an hour longer."

Almost as he spoke, from every side but that which opened upon the hill, came a yell, so loud, so fierce, so fiend-like, that, ere she knew what she was doing, Edith, under the sudden impulse of terror, darted at once away from the tree into the open space, and ran a few steps, till her long riding-dress caught round her feet, and she fell upon the grass. At the same instant, she felt a strong arm seize her by the shoulder, and heard the rattle of a rifle; and, turning her head in mute terror, she beheld the gleaming eyes and dark countenance of an Indian, rendered more hideous by the half-washed-off war-paint, bending over her. His tomahawk was in his right hand; her last hour seemed come; but so sudden, so confounding, had been the attack, that she could not collect her ideas. She could not speak, she could not think, she could not pray. The weapon did not fall, however; and the savage dragged her up from the ground, and gazed upon her, uttering some of the uncouth exclamations of his people, in tones of satisfaction, and even merriment.

One hurried glance around for help, showed Edith that all hope for help was vain; and no words can describe her horror at the scene she saw. At the moment when she looked round, a tomahawk, in the hands of a gigantic Indian, was falling on the head of the poor negro Chando, and the next instant a wild shrieking yell told that his agony was come and gone. Woodchuck, hatchet in hand, was battling for life against another savage, and seemed nearly, if not quite, his match; but eight or ten more Indians were rushing up, yelling like wolves as they came; and, in the midst of the struggle, while the hatchets were playing and flashing round the heads of the combatants, a young and active Indian sprang upon the poor hunter from behind, and threw him backwards on the earth.

Woodchuck lay perfectly still and motionless, gazing up at the tomahawk lifted over his head; but, at that instant, the young Indian put his arm upon his companion's naked breast, and pushed him violently back, with a loud exclamation in the Iroquois tongue. Then, seizing the hand of Woodchuck, he pulled up the sleeve of his hunting-shirt, and pointed to a blue stripe tattooed upon his arm.

The lifted hand and tomahawk of the other sunk slowly by his side; and Woodchuck sat up, and gazed around him, but without attempting to rise altogether from the ground.

Five or six of the Indians came quietly up; and, some kneeling, some bending down, gazed upon the blue line, while the savage who had seized upon Edith, dragged her forward to the spot, and, still holding her fast, gazed likewise. Several quick and muttered words succeeded amongst their captors, a few only of which Edith heard and understood.

"It's the sign! it's the sign!" cried one. Then came a sentence or two that escaped her ear; and then another vociferated, "Ask him! ask him!"

One of the Indians next seated himself on the ground before Woodchuck, spread out his hands like a fan, and addressed some words to him, which Edith, notwithstanding her perfect knowledge of the Iroquois language in most of its dialects, did not in the least comprehend. The answer of

Woodchuck was equally unintelligible to her; and the only word which she caught was "Honontkoh."

The moment he had spoken, two of the Indians placed their hands under his arms, and raised him from the ground. They took the precaution of disarming him entirely; and then, gathering round, they talked quickly and eagerly in low tones. But now they spoke a language which Edith understood; and, though she did not catch all that was said, she heard enough to show her that they were discussing what was to be done with herself and Woodchuck, whom, it seemed to her, that from some cause they recognized as a brother.

Suddenly, the savage who held her pressed his fingers tighter upon her arm, exclaiming aloud, in a fierce, angry voice,--"She is mine! I will dispose of her as I please!"

"No one will oppose the brother of the Snake," said another and older man. "Scalp her when thou wilt; where canst thou carry her if thou dost not slay her?"

"Let us all go to the other side of Corlear, Apukwa," said the man who held her. "I will take her with me; she shall cook my venison for me; 'twas for this I brought you hither."

"What! shall we become women amongst the Hurons?" demanded Apukwa.

"No," replied the brother of the Snake; "there are many of our tribe and order there, men of our own nation, outcasts like ourselves. We will become, like them, warriors of the great French king, and fight against the accursed Yengees."

"But how shall we cross?" asked Apukwa.

"There are canoes in plenty," replied the other. "Besides, our Canada brethren are here close at hand, at Che-on-de-ro-ga. They will give us help."

A silent pause succeeded; and then Woodchuck, having recovered from the confusion which perhaps the suddenness of the attack, perhaps the violence of his fall, had produced, stretched forth his arm, and addressed them after their own fashion.

"Are we not brothers?" he said; "are we not all Honontkoh? are we not all bound by the dreadful name to aid each other even unto blood and death? I demand, therefore, ye who have lifted the hatchet against us unjustly, to set me and this maiden free; to make our feet as the feet of the panther, to go whither we will. I have spoken the terrible words; I have uttered the dreadful name; the sign of the order is in my flesh, and ye dare not refuse."

A look of doubt and hesitation came over the faces of the Indians; and Apukwa inquired,--

"Whither wouldst thou go, my brother? We have all sworn the oath, in the presence of the dark Spirit, that we will aid one another, and that each of the Honontkoh will defend another of the order, though he should have eaten fire or shed his brother's blood. Thou hast shed our brother's blood, for we know thee, though we knew not that thou wert of our order. But we are Honontkoh, and we will keep the oath. We will defend thee, we will assist thee. But whither wouldst thou go?"

"I go," answered Woodchuck, with unfortunate frankness and truth, "I go to lay down my life for your brother's life. I go to the castle of the Oneidas, to say, 'Woodchuck is here! Let the hatchet fall upon the old tree, and let the young sapling grow up till its time be come. I killed the Snake; take the blood of him who slew him, and set the boy Walter free.' As for this maiden, she is mine; I have adopted her. I claim her as brother claims from brother. Ye cannot be Honontkoh and take her from me. If ye be true to our order, give her into my hand and let us go."

While he thus spoke, the countenances of the Indians round betrayed no mark of any emotion whatever, though many and varying feelings were undoubtedly busy in their breasts.

As he ended, however, a slight and somewhat scornful smile came upon the cunning face of Apukwa, and he replied,--

"We cannot let our brother go on such an errand. It would be contrary to our laws. We are bound to defend and protect him, and must not let him make wind of his life. The yellow leaf falls of itself from the bough; the green leaf is torn off by the tempest. We must preserve our brother's life, though the young man perish."

Edith's eyes wept fast with the bitterest drops of despair; but Apukwa went on.

"As for the maiden, we will hear and judge more another day. Thou sayest thou hast adopted her. We will hear how, for we know her to be the daughter of the pale-face Prevost. If she be the prize of the brother of the Snake, the brother of the Snake must have her. But if she be thy daughter, she is thine. Let her be with thee till we have heard all, and judged. We have not room now; for time goes fast, and we are near danger. The pale-faces are to the rising and the setting sun, towards the cold and towards the soft wind. The Honontkoh is the enemy of the pale-face, the abandoned of the Mohawk, and the outcast of the Oneida. Take the maiden in thy hand, and go on towards the rising sun. We come with thee as thy brethren, and will preserve thy life."

Woodchuck gave an anxious glance at Edith's face, and said, in a low voice, and in English,--

"We can't resist, but we may outwit them. Come on for the present, for I guess it may be no better. I will shed my blood for *you*, my dear, if I cannot for your brother."

Taking her hand, he led her on towards the north-east, preceded by one and followed by five or six Indians, who, according to their usual cautious plan, walked singly one after the other, well knowing that their prisoners could not escape them. Several remained upon the spot for a few minutes longer, engaged in stripping the pack-horse of all that he carried, and taking the saddles and bridles of the other horses, which they knew would be valuable in the eyes of the French.

All this was done with extraordinary rapidity, and then the last party followed the first into the depth of the wood.

By this time, the wind had considerably abated, though it still rained hard. The moment after the Indians had departed, however, the leaves and branches of a large flower-covered bush of the calmia, growing under a low, spreading hemlock, moved gently, and the next instant a black face protruded. After one hasty glance around, the whole form of the negress, Sister Bab, was drawn slowly out from the bush; and, running from tree to tree with silent speed, she stopped not till she caught sight again of the retiring Indians, and then followed them quietly and cautiously on their way towards Champlain.

CHAPTER XXXVIII

The stillness of death pervaded the great lodge of the Oneidas; and yet it was not vacant. But Black Eagle sat in the outer chamber alone. With no eye to see him--with none to mark the traces of those emotions which the Indian so carefully conceals from observation, he gave way, in a degree at least, to feelings which, however sternly hidden from others, wrought powerfully in his own heart. His bright blue and scarlet apparel, feathers and belt, medals and armlets, were thrown aside; and, with his head bowed, his face full of gloomy sadness, and all the strong muscles of his finely-proportioned figure relaxed, he sat like an exquisite figure of grief sculptured in porphyry. No tear, indeed, bedewed his eyelids; no sigh escaped his lips; but the very attitude bespoke his sorrow, and there was something awfully sad in the perfect unvarying stillness of his form.

Oh, what a terrible strife was going on within! Grief is ten times more terrible to those who concentrate it in the heart, than to those who pour it forth upon the wide air.

The door of the lodge opened. He started, and instantly was himself again: the head upright, the face clear, the aspect active and dignified.

"Where hast thou been, my child?" asked the chief, gazing on his daughter as she entered, with feelings mingled of a thousand strong emotions,--parental love, fond admiration, pity, regret, and manifold memories.

"Where thou hast permitted me to go, my father," she answered, with a smile so bland and sweet that a momentary suspicion crossed her father's mind.

"Thou dost not forget thy promise, my Blossom," he said, in a tone as stern as he ever used to her.

"Oh no, my father," answered Otaitsa; "didst thou ever know me do so? To see him, to be with him in his long captivity--to move the rock between us, and to let some light into his dark lodge--I promised that if thou wouldst let me stay with him even a few hours each day, I would do naught, try naught, for his escape. Otaitsa has not a double tongue for her own father.

Is Black Eagle's eye dim, that it cannot see his child's heart? Her heart is in his hand."

"How fares the boy?" asked her father. "Is there sunshine with him, or a cloud?"

"Sunshine," said Otaitsa, simply. "We sat and talked of death. It must be very happy."

The chief gazed at her silently for a few moments, and then asked-- "Does *he* think so too?"

"He makes *me* think so," answered the Blossom. "Must it not be happy where there is no weeping, no slaughter, no parting of dear friends and lovers; where a Saviour and Redeemer is ever ready to mediate even for those who do such deeds as these?"

"The Great Spirit is good," said Black Eagle thoughtfully; "the happy hunting-grounds are ever ready for those who die bravely in battle."

"For those who do good," returned Otaitsa, with a sigh; "for those who spare their enemies, and show mercy to such as obey the voice of God in their own hearts, and are merciful and forgiving to their fellow-men."

Black Eagle smiled. "A woman's religion," he said. "Why should I forgive my enemies? The voice of God you speak of in my heart teaches me to kill them; for, if I did not, they would kill me."

"Not if they were Christians too," said Otaitsa. "The voice of God tells all men to spare each other, to love each other; and if every one obeyed it, there would be no such thing as enemies. All would be friends and brethren."

Black Eagle mused, for a moment or two, and then answered, "But there *are* enemies, and therefore I must kill them."

"That is because men obey the voice of the Evil Spirit, and not that of the Good," rejoined the Blossom. "Will my father do so? Black Eagle has the voice of the Good Spirit in his heart. He loves children, he loves his friends, he spares women, and has taught the Oneidas to spare them. All this comes from the voice of the Good Spirit. Will he not listen to it further?"

Her parent remained lost in thought; and, believing that she had gained something, Otaitsa went on to the point nearest to her heart.

"The Black Eagle is just," she said; "he dispenses equity between man and man. Is it either just, or does it come from the voice of the Good Spirit, that he should slay one who has done good and not harm? that he should kill a man for another man's fault? Even if it be permitted to him to slay an enemy, is it permitted to slay a friend? If the laws of the Oneidas are unjust, if they teach faithlessness to one who trusted them, if they are contrary to the voice of the Good Spirit, is not Black Eagle a great chief, who can change them, and teach his children better things?"

Her father started up, and waved his hand impatiently.

"No more," he said, "no more. When I hear the voice of the Good Spirit, and know it, I will obey it. But our laws came from Him, and I will abide by the sayings of our fathers."

As he spoke, he strode to the door of the lodge, and gazed forth, while Otaitsa wept in silence. She saw that it was in vain to plead further, and, gliding up to her parent's side, she touched his arm reverently with her hand.

"My father," she said, "I give thee back the permission to see him, and I take back my promise. Otaitsa will not deceive her father; but the appointed hour is drawing on, and she will save her husband if she can. She has laid no plan with him, she has formed no scheme, she has not spoken to him of safety or escape. She has deceived Black Eagle in nothing: but now she tells him that she will shrink from nothing, no not from death itself, to save her brother Walter."

"Koué, Koué! my Blossom," ejaculated the chief, in a tone of profound melancholy. "Thou canst do nothing." Then, raising his head suddenly, he added, "Go, my daughter; it is well. If thy mother has made thee soft and tender as a flower, thy father has given thee the courage of the eagle. Go in peace; do what thou canst; but thou wilt fail."

"Then will I die!" exclaimed Otaitsa.

And gliding past him, she sought her way through the huts.

The first door she stopped at was partly covered with strange paintings, in red and blue colours, representing, in rather grotesque forms, men, and animals, and flowers. She entered, at once, without hesitation; and found, seated in the dim twilight before a large fire, the old priest who had spoken last at the council of the chiefs in the glen. His ornaments bespoke a chief of high degree; and several deep scars in his long, meagre limbs showed that he had been known in the battle-field. He did not even look round when the Blossom entered, but still sat gazing at the flickering flame, without the movement of a limb or feature. Otaitsa seated herself before him, and gazed at his face in silence, waiting for him to speak.

At the end of not less than five minutes, he turned his head a little, looked at her, and asked--

"What would the Blossom with the Old Cedar-tree?"

"I would take counsel with wisdom," replied the girl. "I would hear the voice of the warrior who is just, and the great chief who is merciful. Let him whom my mother reverenced most after her husband amongst the children of the Stone, speak words of comfort to Otaitsa."

She then, in language which, in rich imagery, and even in peculiarities of style, had a striking resemblance to the Hebrew writings, poured forth to him all the circumstances of Walter's capture, and of their love and plighted faith; and, with the same arguments which we have seen already used, she tried to convince him of the wrong and injustice done to her lover.

The old man listened with the usual appearance of apathy; but the beautiful girl before him gathered that he was much moved at heart, by the gradual bending down of his head till his forehead nearly touched his knees.

When she ceased, he remained silent for several moments, according to their custom; and then raised his head, saying,--

"How can the Old Cedar help thee? His boughs are withered, and the snows of more than seventy winters have bent them down. His roots are shaken in the ground, and the first blast of the tempest will lay him low. But the law of the Oneidas is in his heart: he cannot change it or pervert it. By thine own saying, it is clear that the Good Spirit will do nothing to save this youth. The young warrior is the first they lay hands on. No means have been found for his escape. No pale-face has come into the Oneida land, who might be made to take his place. All thine efforts to rescue him have been seeds that bore no fruit. If the Good Spirit wished to save him, he would provide a means. I have no counsel; and my heart is dead, for I loved thy mother as a child. She was to me as the evening star coming from afar to shine upon the night of my days; but I have no way to help her child, no words to give her comfort. Has not the Black Eagle a sister who loved thy mother well, who has seen well-nigh as many winters as I have, and who has a charm from the Great Spirit? Her lodge is even now filled with wise women of the tribe, taking counsel together as to this matter of the young chief. All love him well, except the dark and evil Honontkoh: all would save him, whether men or women of the nation, were not the law of the Oneida against him. Go to her lodge, then, and with her take counsel; for the Cedar-tree is without words."

CHAPTER XXXIX

The lodge of Black Eagle's sister was next in size and importance to that of the chief himself, and on it, too, some European skill had been expended. Though on a somewhat smaller scale, it was very much such another building as that which has been described by a writer of those times as the palace of a celebrated chief of the Mohawks. In a word, "It had the appearance of a good barn, divided across by a mat hung in the middle." It was only of one story, however; but the workmen who had erected it a good many years before, on their return from the completion of Fort Oswego, had added a door of European form, with a latch and a brass knob, which greatly increased its dignity in the eyes of the tribe.

The possessor of this mansion, who was held in great reverence all through the Oneida nation, and was supposed to have communication with the spiritual world, had obtained, I know not how, the name of the Grey Dove, although her features by no means displayed the characteristic meekness of the bird from which she derived her appellation, but bore a considerable resemblance to those of her brother, which certainly well accorded with his name.

When Otaitsa approached the door, she found it fastened, and she knocked twice with her hand before it was opened. A young girl then peeped out, and, seeing the Sachem's daughter, gave her admission at once into the outer apartment. The space on that side of the large mat which formed the partition was vacant; but a murmur of voices came from the division beyond, and a light shone through the crevices between the mat and the wall.

The feelings of Otaitsa's heart were too powerful to leave any timidity in her bosom; and, although she shared in some degree the feelings with which the other Oneidas regarded the Grey Dove, she advanced at once, drew back the corner of the mat, and entered the chamber beyond.

The scene was neither of a beautiful nor of a very solemn character; nevertheless, there was something very striking in it. Seated around a large fire in the middle, were a number of the elder women of the tribe, whose features and forms, once, perhaps, fair and lovely, had lost almost every trace of beauty. But their lineaments were strongly marked, and had, in many instances, a stern and almost fierce expression. Their eyes, jetty black, and in most cases as brilliant as in early youth, shone in the light of the fire like diamonds; and, in many an attitude and gesture, appeared much of that grace which lingers longer with people accustomed to a free and unconfined life, than with those of rigid and conventional habits.

Outside of the first and elder circle, sat a number of the younger women, from fifteen or sixteen years of age, up to five or six and twenty. Many of them were exceedingly beautiful; but the figures of their elder companions shaded them mostly from the glare of the fire, and it was only here and there that one of those countenances could be discovered which might offer, in many of the Indian tribes, fit models for painter or sculptor.

Seated, not on the ground like the rest, but on a small low settle at the further side of the inner circle, appeared Black Eagle's sister, gorgeously dressed almost entirely in crimson, with anklets and bracelets of gold, and innumerable glittering ornaments round her neck. She was much older than her brother. Her hair, almost as white as snow, was knotted up behind on the ordinary roller, without any decoration. Her features were aquiline, and much more prominent than those of Black Eagle; and her eyes were still keen and bright.

The moment they lighted upon Otaitsa, the exclamation burst from her lips,--

"She is come! the Great Spirit has sent her! Stand there in the midst, Blossom, and hear what we have resolved."

Otaitsa passed between two of the younger and two of the elder women, taking her place between the inner circle and the fire; and wonderfully bright and beautiful did she look, with the flame flashing upon her exquisite form and delicate features, and lighting up a countenance full of strong enthusiasm and pure emotion.

"Thy child hears thy words," she said, without pause or hesitation; for it must be remarked that the stoical gravity which prevailed at the conferences of the chiefs and warriors was not thought necessary among the women of the tribes. "What has the Grey Dove to say to the daughter of her brother?"

"The boy must not die!" exclaimed the old woman, in a firm and decided tone. "It is not the will of the Great Spirit; or, if he die, there shall be wailing in every lodge, and mourning amongst the children of the Stone. Art thou willing, Otaitsa, child of the Black Eagle, daughter of the Flower of the East, to do as we do, and to obey my voice?"

Otaitsa gazed round the circle, and saw a stern and lofty determination written on every countenance. Her own heart was not one to quail at any undertaking, known or unknown; and the only thing which could have deterred her from taking the pledge proposed, was the spirit of Christianity. But it must not be supposed that the Christianity of the Indian girl, notwithstanding all the labours of her missionary friend, was pure and unmixed with the characteristics of her people. All the daily habits of life, all that she saw, all that she heard around her, mingled the notions and the feelings of the Indian with the doctrines and the sentiments of the Christian. The first impulse was always Indian; the rectifying principle nearly Christian.

After gazing round them for an instant, she answered, "I am; I will do what thou sayest to save him, even unto death."

"She has said!" cried the old woman. "Now then, Blossom, this is thy task; thou shalt watch eagerly as a fox upon the hill-side, and bring word to me of the exact day and hour when the sacrifice is to be offered. Every one must watch."

"But how shall I discover?" asked Otaitsa. "The warriors tell not their secrets to women. The Black Eagle hides his thoughts from his daughter; he covers his face with a cloud, and wraps his purposes in shadows from our eyes."

"By little signs shalt thou know," returned the Grey Dove. "Small clouds prognosticate great storms. When thou seest any change, mark it well. If his head droops, and his eye seeks the ground more than common, bring or send the tidings unto me. If he be silent when he should speak, and hears not the words thou utterest--if he gazes up to the heaven as if he were seeking to know the changes of the weather, when all is clear--and if he looks at the tomahawk as it hangs upon the beam, with a dull and heavy eye--be sure the time is coming."

Otaitsa gave a wild start, and exclaimed,--

"Then it is this night! for all the signs you mention have been present. When I entered the lodge, his head was bowed down, and his eyes were fixed upon the ground. He was very sad. He heard me; but his thoughts seemed to wander. When he stopped my petition, and turned towards the door, his eyes rested gloomily on the hatchet; and when he stood without, they were lifted to the sky, as if looking for stars in the daytime. It is to-night! it is to-night! Oh, what shall be done?"

"Nay," answered the Grey Dove, with a kindly look, "it is *not* to-night. Be comforted, my child. Not until to-morrow, at the hour of twilight, will the six moons have passed; and the Black Eagle speaks no word in vain. He will not lift the tomahawk a moment before the hour; but to-morrow will be the time, after the sun has set. The pale-faces have taken the war-path against each other; and the allies of the Black Eagle have called upon him to take wing, and help them. They have bade him paint himself for the battle, and come forth with his warriors. He has waited but for this; and now we know the day and the hour, for he will not tarry."

Otaitsa still trembled; but her mind was much relieved for the moment. She knew her father well, and she saw the truth of what the Grey Dove said.

"How shall we stay him?" she inquired. "The Black Eagle bends not in his way like a serpent; he goes straight upon his path like a bird in the air. He hears not the voice of entreaty; his ears are stopped against the words of prayer. You may turn the torrent as it rushes down after the melting of the snow, or the rock as it falls from the precipice; but you cannot arrest the course of the Black Eagle, or turn him from his way."

"Be firm and constant," said the Grey Dove. "We are in the hands of the Great Spirit. Watch your father closely, Otaitsa, all to-morrow, from the mid-day till the setting sun--from the setting sun till the dawn, if it be needful. The moment he goes forth, come thou to me at the lodge of the Lynx, by the western gate of the palisade; there shalt thou find me with others. I know that thy young heart is strong, and that it will not quail. Watch carefully, but watch secretly. See if he take the tomahawk in his belt, and if his face be gay or gloomy. Mark every sign, and bring the news to me."

"They may go by the other gate, and steal round," said one of the women in the inner circle. "I will set my daughter, now waiting without, to watch that gate, and bring us tidings. She is still and secret as the air of night, and has the foot of the wind."

"It is good," said the Grey Dove, rising. "Let us all be prepared, for the boy must not die."

No more was said; for the old prophetess fell into one of those deep and solemn reveries, from which all present knew she could not easily be wakened, and which probably had acquired for her the reputation of conversing with the spirit-world.

One by one, slowly and silently, the women stole out of the lodge, dispersing in various directions the moment they quitted the door. Otaitsa remained till the last, in the hope that the Grey Dove would speak again, and afford her some further information of her plans; but the old woman remained silently gazing on the fire, with her tall figure erect and stiff, and probably perfectly unconscious of the departure of the others, till at length the Blossom followed the rest, and returned quietly to the great lodge.

The following day became dark and stormy about three o'clock in the afternoon. A sharp, cold wind succeeded to the mild breath of spring; and the Indians generally remained assembled round their fires, leaving the wide place within the palisade very nearly deserted.

Shortly before sunset, one Indian woman crept quietly forth, and took her way towards a hut near the eastern entrance of their village. Another followed very speedily; and before twilight had ended, and night begun, no less than twelve stood beneath the roof, with the Grey Dove in the midst of them. It was too dark for any one to see the face of another; for the night had fallen heavily and thick, and a blanket was stretched across the entrance. But the Grey Dove felt them one after another with her hands, asking a question of each, to which she seemed to receive a satisfactory answer.

"The thirteenth is not here," she said; "but she will come, and her heart will not fail."

A dead silence fell over them all after these words were spoken; that sort of stern, heavy, solemn silence which not unfrequently precedes the execution of some strong and terrible resolution. Yet, of those twelve, there were several gay and lively girls, as well as women fallen into the decline of life. Nevertheless, all were as still as death. The volatile lightness of youth, as well as the garrulity of old age, was hushed.

Suddenly, after they had waited about twenty minutes, the blanket was pushed aside, and another figure was added to the number. The voice of Otaitsa whispered--

"He is gone forth armed as if for battle; he has his tomahawk with him; his face was very sad. I saw the Old Cedar cross to the west gate, with others whom I knew in the darkness."

She spoke in eager haste, and gasped for breath; but the old woman took her by the arm, saying,--

"Be calm, be still! Now follow noiselessly. Then bend down as you pass through the maize; though, in this black night, who shall see us?"

She was the first to issue forth; then came Otaitsa; and the others followed one by one, with quick but silent steps, through the wide field of maize that swept round the palisade, and then into the neighbouring forest. Once, when they came near a spot where the polished mirror of the lake collected and cast back every ray of light that remained in the air, they caught sight of a dark file, shadowy and ghost-like as themselves, moving on at a little distance in the same direction. But it was soon lost, and the sight only served to hasten their footsteps.

Passing along a trail which cut across the neck of a little wooded promontory, they suddenly came in sight of the lake again, and, by its side, a low Indian hut, marked out plainly against the surface of the water. When within about thirty yards, the Grey Dove halted, whispered a word or two to those who followed, and then, bending down, crept closer to the lodge.

"Oh, let us hasten," whispered Otaitsa. "They are already there; I hear my father speaking."

"Hush, hush! be still!" ejaculated the old woman in the same tone. "The Black Eagle will do nothing hastily; it is for him a solemn rite. Let me first get near; then follow, and do what I do."

CHAPTER XL

It was a sad and weary day to poor Walter Prevost, for he was without his consolation. The time of his long imprisonment, indeed, had been less burdensome than might have been supposed, although, during the first two or three weeks, many a fruitless effort to escape had wearied his spirits. He learned, however, that escape was impossible; he was too closely and too continually watched. There was nothing to prevent his quitting the hut; but the moment he did so, whether night or day, he was met by two or three armed Indians. They were kind and courteous to him, though they suffered him not to bend his steps in the direction of their castle, or village, nor to approach the lake, to the banks of which many a canoe was moored. Sometimes one of them would take him to hunt; but two or three others followed, and never separated from his side. They were not fond of speaking of his probable fate, and generally avoided the subject with true Indian skill; but once a young warrior, less experienced than the rest, related to him the messages which the great chief had sent by the runner Proctor, and Walter learned the decision regarding his own fate, and the chances on which it hung. That young Indian was never seen near him more. It was evident that he was looked upon as having betrayed counsel, and that he had been removed.

But, about that time, the greatest solace and balm he could receive was afforded him. Otaitsa suddenly appeared in the hut, and told him that, by promising to make no personal effort for his rescue, and to take no advantage of the freedom granted her to facilitate his escape by his own efforts, she had obtained permission to visit him for two hours each day. She had explained to him, however, that others, in whom she trusted, were busy in his cause; and that the Grey Dove herself, on whom all her people looked with the greatest reverence, had positively assured her he should not die.

At first, their interviews were sad enough. Hope and fear kept up their battle in the heart; but in time those emotions passed away, and love and happiness were all that remained; or, if aught of fear mingled with those blessings, it was but enough, as it were, to sanctify their intercourse, to purify it of some portion of earthly passion, so that, even while they sat twined in each other's arms, their conversation would often be of death and future life, and happiness unmingled. She often called him "husband" to her father; but it was always "brother" when they were there alone.

Day after day, beneath the sunshine or the cloud, over the snow or the green earth, Otaitsa visited the hut. But she had grown anxious as the days rolled on. She had not calculated the time accurately; but she knew the appointed day was near, and Walter was not delivered. She accused herself of folly in having trusted to others; though she saw not how, watched as he was, his deliverance could be effected by herself. But she resolved now to bestir herself, and, if she lost her life in the attempt, to make one last great effort to set him free.

Such was her resolution on the preceding day, when, on parting with him, she whispered in his ear, lest any one should be listening without,--

"I shall not come to you again, my brother, till I come to save you. I know not how it will be; but, if I fail, Walter will not be long in heaven ere Otaitsa seeks him there."

He hardly believed she could keep her resolution of abstaining from at least one more interview. But the weary day passed by; the Indians who brought him food and fire appeared and disappeared; the rain fell heavily; the wind shook the hut; and Otaitsa did not come.

At length, the night began to fall, stern, gloomy, dark; a rayless sunset, a brief twilight, and then utter blackness. His spirit sank low indeed; his heart felt heavy and oppressed: he bent him down, stirred up the embers of his fire, piled more wood upon it, and kindled a bright, cheerful blaze. But it had no effect in raising his spirits or warming his heart. All within him was cheerless.

He sat and gazed into the fire, and thought of his absent home, and of the pleasant days of youth, and of the sweet dreams he had once cherished--the hopes that hung like faded pictures upon the wall of memory. A thousand little incidents, a thousand delightful recollections, came back upon him, while he sat and meditated, as if merely to make life more dear; when, suddenly, on the other side of the hut, a dark figure crossed the firelight, and then another, and another, and another, till they numbered six. They were all chiefs, and men of lofty mien; but stern, and grave, and silent. They seated themselves in a semicircle at the very further part of the hut, and for several minutes remained profoundly still.

He understood at once what it meant. The last hour of life was come; and the dead, heavy sinking of the heart which the aspect of death suddenly presented to an unprepared and unexcited mind, was the first sensation. True, the door stood at a little distance, on his right hand, and they were at the other end of the hut, with no one between him and the means of egress; but he knew their swiftness of foot and deadly aim too well. It was better to stay and to meet the worst there, than to fall by the thrown tomahawk in inglorious flight. He rallied his spirits: he called all his courage to his aid: he bethought him of how an Indian would die, and resolved to die boldly and calmly likewise.

Sitting still in silence, he gazed over the countenances of the chiefs, scanning their stern, hard features thoughtfully. Only two were there whom he knew; Black Eagle himself, and an old man with a white scalp-lock, whom he recollected having comforted and supported once when he found him ill and exhausted near his father's house. The others were all strangers to him: and nothing could be read upon their faces but cold, rigid determination. No passion, no anger, no emotion, could be traced; but there was something inexpressibly dreadful in gazing on those still, quiet countenances, with a knowledge of the bloody purpose of the men. To have died in battle--to have struggled with them fiercely for life--would have been nothing; but to sit there, coldly awaiting the moment of the ruthless blow, and to know that they expected it to be borne with the same quiet, stoical apathy with which it was dealt, was very, very terrible to the young European.

Yet Walter tried to nerve himself to the utmost against any sign of fear; and strove for resolution not to disgrace himself, his name, and family, even in the opinion of those wild Indians. There must have been apprehension in his eyes--in the straining eagerness with which he scanned them; but there was no other mark of alarm: not a muscle moved; the lip did not quiver; the brow was not contracted.

At length, after that long, solemn pause, the voice of Black Eagle was heard speaking low and softly.

"My son, thou must die," he said. "Thou art dear to me as a child; thy father is my brother; but thou hast drawn an evil lot, and thou must die.

The morning of thy days has been short and bright; the night comes for thee before the day is well begun. The blood of our brother who was slain must be atoned for by the blood of one of the race that slew him--the white man for the red man. We have sought in vain for the murderer of our brother, or for some one who might have been a substitute for him whom we love. Each man here would have perilled his own head to find another in thy place; but it could not be. The pale-faces took fright at the news of what had been done, and none has been found within our territory. We know that the man who did the deed has been here. We fancied that he had come generously to pay the penalty of his own act; but fear was in his heart, and twice he escaped us. He is as cunning as the fox, and as swift to flee. Now, O thou son of my brother! thou must die; for the time has gone by that was given thee in the hope of some deliverance: the hours have run swiftly and in vain; and the last has come. We know that it is the custom of thy people to sing no war-song at their death; but to pray to their Good Spirit to receive them speedily into the happy hunting-grounds. We shall not think it want of courage if thou prayest; for the son of our brother Prevost will not disgrace his name at his death. Pray, therefore, to thy God; thy prayer shall be as it were a war-song, and, strengthened by it, thou shalt die as a man and a warrior."

Walter remained silent for a moment, while a terrible struggle went on in his heart; but resolution conquered, and he rose from the ground on which he was sitting, erect and firm; and, stretching forth his hand, he said,--

"Chiefs of the Oneidas, you are unjust. At this hour of my death, I tell you, you know not equity. Your laws are not of the Good Spirit, but of the bad; for it is evil to kill an innocent man, black and dastardly to slay a helpless man who trusted you and loved you; and, if it is by your law you do it, your law is bad, and the Good Spirit will condemn it. My father came and planted his tree amongst you; we grew up,--my sister and myself,-- loving and confiding in your people. We made your tongue our tongue; and my heart became one with the heart of the daughter of your chief. Lo, now, how ye repay kindness, and love, and truth, with falsehood, cruelty, and death! You are great warriors, but you are not good men. In this last hour, I reproach you; and I tell you, with the voice of a dying man, as with the voice of one from the land of spirits, that, sooner or later, the great God of all men will make you feel that you have done an evil thing in my death."

He paused suddenly; for his eyes, turning somewhat in the direction of the door, saw a female figure enter, wrapped in the peculiar blanket or mantle of the Indian women. Another and another entered; and one by one the shadowy forms ranged themselves in line along the side of the hut, their faces but faintly seen by the flickering firelight. They were all as silent as death; and there they stood as solemn witnesses of the dreadful scene about to be enacted.

The eyes of all the chiefs were turned in the same direction as his own, and a moment or two of wonder and embarrassment passed; but then the voice of Black Eagle was raised loudly and sternly, saying,--

"Get you home to the Castle, Oneida women. This is no place for you. Meddle not with the business of warriors and of men. Dare not to intrude upon the sacrifice of atonement for our brother's blood."

"Who is it that speaks?" said the clear, shrill voice of the Grey Dove. "Is it the man of the black heart who slays the son of his brother? Who is it that dares to speak thus to her who sees the Great Spirit in her visions, and holds communion with the souls of the dead? Is it a man pure in heart and hand--a man whose purposes are good in the sight of the Great Spirit, and who is doing a deed pleasing in his sight? Is he taking the life of an enemy in the battle? Is he scalping a foe with whom he has fought and conquered? Lo, now, this is a brave deed, to slay the son of a friend, and a boy who has no power to resist. But the boy shall not die. If a pale-face has killed one of the children of the Stone, this boy has saved the life of more than one. His hand has been free, and his heart open to the Oneida, and his good deeds are more than enough to atone for the evil deeds of another. The ashes of thy pipe, Black Eagle, upon the hearth of Prevost, call out shame upon the murderer of his son."

"Get you hence, woman!" vociferated another chief. "We are not soft as water, to be turned in what course you will; we are the children of the Stone, and our heart is the rock."

"Be it so, then," cried Black Eagle's sister. "Look upon us now, oh, chiefs! We are here, your mothers, your sisters, your daughters, your wives; those you love best, those who best love you. See now what we are commanded to do by the voice of the Good Spirit. If you slay the youth, you slay us. Every lodge shall be left desolate; there shall be wailing through the village, and through the land. Now, my sisters, if their heart be a stone, let our heart be soft, and let the knife find it easily."

As she spoke, every mantle was thrown back, and every arm raised, and in every hand was seen the gleam of a knife.

Black Eagle covered his eyes with his mantle, but sat still. Walter sprang across, and cast himself at the feet of Otaitsa, exclaiming,--

"Hold, hold! for God's sake hold, my Blossom!"

"Back, back!" cried the girl, vehemently; "if thou diest, I die."

"All, all!" exclaimed the women, in the same determined tone.

At this moment, the old priest rose and stretched forth his hands.

"It is the voice of the Great Spirit," he ejaculated, in the tone of one inspired. "He speaks to us by their tongue; he tells us to forbear. The deed is evil in his sight; we must not do it. The blood of our brother is atoned for. It is the voice of the Great Spirit!"

"It is the voice of the Great Spirit--it is the voice of the Great Spirit!" exclaimed each of the chiefs. And Black Eagle, casting from him the tomahawk, took Walter in his arms, saying, in a low voice,--

"My son, my son!"

Otaitsa advanced a step towards them; but, before she reached her father, her sight grew dim, and she fell fainting at his feet.

CHAPTER XLI

The din of preparation was heard in the great castle of the Oneidas. With the first light of morning numerous small bands began to pour in, summoned secretly long before, to hold a war-council, and to march against the enemy. Before noon, larger bands began to appear, led by several of the noted warriors of the nation; and one very numerous body, coming across the lake in a little fleet of canoes, brought with them a great quantity of baggage, in the shape of tents and provisions, with women and even children.

The scene which took place when all were assembled, in number more than a thousand, is perfectly indescribable. Nor shall I attempt to give a picture of it. A long period of peace seemed only to have given the western warriors a sort of thirst for war; and their joy at the unburying of the hatchet and the march against an enemy brought forth demonstrations which, to any civilized eye, would have appeared perfectly frantic. Screaming, shouting, singing, dancing, striking the war-posts with their tomahawks, and shaking their rifles in the air, they seemed like beings possessed by some evil spirit; the quiet and grave demeanour was altogether cast aside; and the calmest and most moderate boasted outrageously of deeds done in the past, and which ought to be performed in the coming war.

About an hour after noon, however, a sudden and complete change came over the scene. In an open space before the great lodge, all the chieftains of the different Totems or tribes assembled; and the usual circle was formed around the great war-post of the Black Eagle. The younger warriors gathered in other rows, without the first; and the youths, the women, and the children, beyond them again.

One exception to the usual order took place. The great chief had, on either side of him, one of those both of whom he now called his children. Otaitsa, in her most brilliant apparel, stood upon his left; and Walter Prevost, armed and dressed like the Oneidas, with the sole difference that his head was not shaved like theirs, remained standing throughout the ceremony on his right.

As soon as all movement had ceased, and the stillness of death fell over the whole multitude, Black Eagle, in a speech of powerful eloquence, related all that had occurred on the preceding night, and justified the act of himself and the other chiefs in the eyes of the people. He said that he, himself, and five of his brethren, had been prepared to sacrifice the son of Prevost to atone for the blood of the Snake, and to satisfy the customs of the Oneidas, although each would rather have slain his own son; but that the Great Spirit had spoken by the tongue of his sister, and they had forborne.

When he had done, the Old Cedar rose, but uttered only a few words.

"It was the voice of the Great Spirit," he said; and immediately a murmur of "Koué! Koué!" ran round the assembly in confirmation of the act.

The chief then explained to his warriors why he had that day called them around him; for, although the object was already well known to all, and the news had spread that the English were marching against the French upon Lake Champlain, the Indians never acted in masses without solemn deliberation; and a war-speech, as they called it, was universally expected from their renowned leader. He dwelt at large upon the alliance between the English and the Five Nations, and upon the good faith with which the stipulations of their treaties had been maintained by the British provinces; he referred to "the talk" held some six months before, at the Castle of Sir William Johnson, skilfully mingling with his discourse the names of several persons most popular with the tribes; and he ended by exhorting his hearers to show their truth and friendship towards their English brethren, and to pour down their fiercest wrath upon the French, whom he spoke of contemptuously, as the brethren of the Hurons and the Alonquin.

The same signs of approbation followed; and many another chief added his voice, raising the passions of the warriors to the highest pitch. One especially urged them to immediate action, telling them that the Mohawks had already marched; that they were with the English army; and that the faces of the children of the Stone would be red with shame if a Mohawk brought home more scalps than an Oneida.

Some were for setting out on the instant; but this proposal was overruled, and the following morning was appointed for the march to begin, as more war-parties were expected from different districts, and some had not come fully prepared for the long journey and important enterprise.

The council was succeeded by similar scenes to those with which the day began; and it must not be concealed that in many instances the dreadful "fire-water" was employed so far as even to produce beastly intoxication. Small drums and wild instruments of music, songs of every character, from the wailing lament or the religious chant, to the fierce and boastful war-song, rose from every part of the village; and it was not till the sun had completely set, that anything like quiet and order was restored.

Paint it in what colours we will, it was a barbarous and terrible, though exciting, scene; and Walter Prevost was well pleased to hear the noise gradually die away into low murmurs, and silence begin to resume its reign.

Then came a very, very happy hour. He sat with Otaitsa alone in the great lodge while the Black Eagle wandered amongst his people without; and, for the first time since his deliverance from death, the two had an opportunity of pouring forth to each other the many feelings which had accumulated in the last four-and-twenty hours.

"At this time last night," said the youth, "I was preparing to die."

"And at this time last night," returned the girl, gazing fondly upon his face as he sat with his arm clasped fondly round her, and her head leaning on his shoulder--"and at this time last night Otaitsa was ready to die with you. I have since thought it very wrong of me, Walter; and, fearing what I did was sinful, I have prayed part of the night to God for forgiveness; and another part I have spent in praise and thanksgiving. But I believe I was mad, my beloved; for I hardly know what I did, and followed blindly what they told me to do to rescue him for whom I would have sacrificed a thousand lives. Besides, I was surrounded by my countrywomen, and you know they do not think as we have been taught to think."

"If it was an error, it was a blessed one, my own Blossom," answered Walter; "for to it I owe my life; and life, when it is brightened by Otaitsa's love, is but too precious to me. The time will come, dear one, when we shall look back upon these days but as a painful dream; and the only bright reality that will last will be the memory of my Blossom's love, and all that she has done to save and bless me."

She gazed at him believingly; for hers was not a heart to doubt, and his was not a heart to be doubted; and she then said, with a sigh--

"But you are now going to battle, to risk your life and all our happiness. Still, though it may be strange, I would not stay you, though all I have learned from good Mr. Gore should make me look upon such things with horror; and, though I would fain have you stay away from danger, I suppose the habits of the people still cling about me, even though I hold a better faith than theirs."

"Fear not, dearest, fear not," answered Walter, boldly. "No harm will happen to me, I do trust and believe; and I only leave you for a few short weeks."

"You will not leave me at all, Walter," she rejoined--"no, never more. I will go with you, if not to the battle, as near it as I can be. I have my father's leave; the warriors of my race will defend me, and I will not part with my recovered treasure any more."

"Go to my father's house," said Walter, joyfully. "It is very near the spot, and Edith will rejoice to have you with her."

Otaitsa fixed her eyes upon vacancy, and fell into a deep reverie; and an expression came into her face, which Walter had remarked more than once before.

"Do you know, my beloved," he said, "that sometimes you strike me as very like our dear Edith--especially when you look thoughtful, as you did just now."

"It is very natural," said Otaitsa, nestling closer to him. "You do not know she is my cousin. My mother was your father's sister. Hush! not a word, especially in the ears of any of the tribe. My father knows it--but he will not know it, because, among the elder people of the nation, it was held contrary to our customs that cousin should marry cousin. I asked Mr. Gore, long ago, if it were against your law; but he said 'No,' that it was neither against law nor religion. He inquired why I asked so earnestly," she added, laughing, "but I would not tell him. Come with me into my chamber, and I will show you many things belonging to my mother. Stay, I will light my lamp."

What a beautiful thing is innocence! how free, how untrammelled, how boundless! and what a sad thing is its loss, to man, and to society! Surely, that loss implies slavery of the worst kind--slavery to which we voluntarily submit--bonds that we rivet round our own hands. He who thinks no evil, because he knows of none, is the only freeman on the earth's face.

Otaitsa bent down, and lighted her lamp, and guided her lover up to her little chamber; and there they sat and turned over many a long-stored treasure, and she showed him the picture of his own father, and of her mother, and of many of their mutual kin, and drawings of fair scenes in Europe, some of which he remembered well, with others of the land in which they then were, but of spots which he had never seen. There was one, also, which had been left unfinished, of a young, sweet child; and Walter gazed first upon the infant face, and then upon the bright, happy countenance beside him, and clasped his Blossom warmly to his heart. The book, too, with the drop of blood upon it, told its own tale to both their hearts.

"And where is Mr. Gore?" he asked, at length; "he seems to have left altogether his little flock; and I am sure I should have seen him during my captivity."

"He is coming back now," said Otaitsa. "My father would not let him return before. He was afraid that the breath of the good man would melt his icy purpose. He had a power over Black Eagle that none other had. I prayed and besought in vain. But had Mr. Gore been here, he would have conquered. Black Eagle knew it, and feared; and therefore he sent him hence, and would not let him return till the day was past."

"Would that he were here now!" ejaculated Walter, earnestly.

Otaitsa asked him, why; and he answered, with a warm kiss--

"That he might unite us for ever."

A flush came upon her cheek; but the low sound of a step was heard below, and, looking down the stairs, she said--

"Is that you, my father?"

"I come," replied the chief.

And, slowly mounting the stairs, he entered the chamber where they were. His eyes roved round the room in a manner which evidently showed that it was strange to him; and then he fixed them on the pictures which lay upon the table, lighted but faintly by the lamp. At first, he seemed not to distinguish what they were; but the moment he saw them clearly, he drew his mantle over his face, and turned towards the door. He uttered no word; he shed no tear; but he descended slowly, and Walter and Otaitsa followed.

CHAPTER XLII

On that part of Lake Champlain, or Corlear, as it was called by the Indians, where, quitting the narrow basin which it occupies, from its southern extremity to some distance northward of Ticonderoga, it opens out into a broader sheet of water, and sweeps round the small peninsula of Crown Point, a large canoe was seen crossing to the Canada side, with about sixteen or seventeen persons on board. There was no attempt at concealment, no creeping along under the shelter of the banks; but boldly and openly the Indians paddled on within range of the guns of the French fort, and then directly across the bows of two large, flat-bottomed boats, or *bateaux*, accompanied by several light canoes, each containing six or seven men, which were going down the lake in the direction of Ticonderoga.

From each of the larger boats, the flag of France was conspicuously displayed; but, as the canoe above mentioned seemed bearing straight for the shore fully in possession of France, its movements for a time appeared to excite no attention. Neither the *bateaux*, nor the canoes, altered their course, the men on board the former continuing a shouted conversation in a mixed jargon, part French, part Indian, with their dusky companions in the lesser craft, who kept as nearly alongside as possible.

At length, however, it would seem some suspicion was excited. Perhaps it might have been by the sight of two figures, male and female, in the stern of the canoe, whose dress at once showed them to belong to none of the Indian tribes, and was also somewhat different from that of either the Canadian colonists, or the native French. The two parties were now within less than a hundred yards of each other, and it seemed doubtful whether the large canoes would clear the eastern boat without trouble. But suddenly a voice was raised loudly in the foremost *bateau*, and a question was put in French, as to whither the others were bound, and who they were.

The Indians were silent, for they did not understand the words addressed to them; but Woodchuck whispered to Edith, eagerly, "Answer, answer! if you can speak their jargon. Better be in the hands of French officers, than these incarnate devils."

Edith's eyes had been cast down, and were so full of bitter tears, that she had seen nothing since they left the western shore. But now she looked up, and, in an instant, her presence of mind returned. It is true, she did not speak at once, for she feared her voice would not reach the boat; but it was nearing the canoe fast; and, in a moment after, the question was repeated in a more peremptory and distinct tone.

"Tell them we are allies of the great French chief," said Apukwa, who seemed to comprehend, in some degree, the meaning of the call; "say we are going to join our Canada Father." And he glared at her, fiercely, as he spoke.

"We are English," exclaimed Edith, exerting her utmost power of voice; "we are English, and Iroquois, going I know not whither."

Instantly, at a signal from the *bateaux*, the light canoes dashed out with extraordinary rapidity; and, before any effectual effort could be made to escape, the larger canoe was surrounded, while the yells of the Hurons announced that they recognized, at length, a band of ancient enemies. With a fiend-like look at Edith, Apukwa drew his tomahawk from his belt; but, the brother of the Snake spoke some words to him in a low tone, the weapon was replaced, the men ceased to work the paddles, and every face assumed the stillness of perfect indifference.

The yells and whoops of the Hurons still continued, and their canoes came rushing nearer, so that one danger seemed only to be escaped to encounter a still greater. Their fierce faces, and dark, half-naked forms, tattooed and painted, were seen all round, and the tomahawk and the knife were brandished as if for immediate action. But one of the larger boats bore right down amongst them, and soon grappled the canoe in which Edith and her companion were. A handsomely-dressed middle-aged man stood up in the stern as it came near, and, turning to an Indian by his side, who seemed a chief, said to him in French--

"Keep your people quiet, Great Elk."

A few words were then spoken, or rather shouted, by the Indian to the others in the canoes, in a language which Edith did not at all understand, and in an instant every Huron sank down in silence, and the light skiffs lay quietly upon the water, or only moved slightly with the momentum they had already received from the paddles. Then, raising his hat and plume with an air of much grace, the French officer addressed Edith, saying--

"Will you have the goodness to explain to me, mademoiselle, who and what you are, and how you came to be in the position in which I find you?

I am sorry to be obliged to detain a lady, but you have too many men with you for me to suffer your canoe to pass."

"I am the daughter of an English gentleman," replied Edith. "I have been attacked and captured, with the friend who was escorting me from my father's house to that of Colonel Schneider; my two servants were murdered--at least, one of them I am sure was. These Indians, who are with me, are Iroquois, who are taking me forcibly across the lake towards Canada, and I have little doubt that I shall be put to death also, if you do not save me from their hands."

"This is a strange story, mademoiselle," returned the officer. "The Iroquois and your countrymen are in alliance."

"I cannot account for it," answered Edith; "they are certainly Iroquois, for they speak no other language, except a few words of English. You must ask them what is the meaning of their conduct, if you have any on board who can speak their tongue."

The officer turned once more to his Indian companion, and addressed some words to him in French; but the chief shook his head, and then, drawing his eyelids together, as if to see more distinctly, gazed into the canoe, scanning the persons of the Indians closely.

"They are Iroquois," he said, at length, in broken French; "let us scalp them."

This proposal, however, the officer did not think fit to comply with, at least for the time; and he replied with a laugh,--

"Wait a little, my friend. The Great Elk shall have scalping enough soon. We will take them ashore with us, at all events, and, perhaps, may learn more. Then, if they are really enemies, you shall exercise your skill upon them to your heart's content. The lady and her English companion, however, I claim as my prisoners.--Permit me, mademoiselle, to assist you into the boat. You will be safer here, and may trust to the honour and courtesy of a French gentleman."

"I have no fears on that score, sir," answered Edith, rising; and, with the aid of the officer and Woodchuck, she passed into the other boat, which, flat-bottomed and heavily laden, was not much higher above the water than the canoe. Woodchuck followed her closely, but not without exciting the wrath of the Honontkoh. They had sat, ever since the canoe had been grappled by the boat, with the utmost tranquillity; not a limb, not a feature had moved; and to the eye of an observer, ignorant of their habits, they would have seemed perfectly indifferent to all that was taking place. In fact, one of them appeared actually going to sleep; for the sun, which had now broken out after the storm, shone full on his face, and his eyes were closed, and his head bent. But the moment that Woodchuck put his foot over the side of the *bateau*, a yell of disappointed rage burst from every lip; and, unable to contain himself, Apukwa rose and poured forth a few words of Huron, mixed with a good deal of Iroquois.

"Hold your tongues!" exclaimed the French officer, waving his hand imperiously. "Tow them along behind us; and you, Great Elk, command your people to keep close around them, and see that they do not cut the rope, and slip away."

The orders were given as he directed, and the arrangements made; but when all was completed, and the boat was once more moving along the lake, the Indian by his side pulled the officer's sleeve, thus interrupting a speech he had just begun with a gallant air to Edith, and seemed to explain something to him in a low tone.

"Well, we shall soon find out," said the Frenchman, with a gay laugh. "If they be Iroquois, who are about to become Hurons, and take service under his Majesty, we will make them fight for us while we are going. We shall not have too many hands to help us, Great Elk, and they'll make a good reinforcement to your party. As for the lady and her attendant, I will take care of them." Then turning to Edith, with a courteous smile, he spread his *roquelaure* in a more convenient part of the boat, and assisted her to seat herself more comfortably, saying--"Mademoiselle is a great deal too charming to travel any more with such savages. But may I know the name of this gentleman? Can he not speak French?"

"Not a word, I believe," replied Edith.

"That is singular!" exclaimed the Frenchman, giving expression to the general feeling of his nation, who seem to believe that the French language is one of those blessings of God which it is strange that he should deny to any of his creatures. "What is his name?"

It instantly passed through the mind of Edith that, if she gave her good companion the name of Captain Brooks, she would be certain to cause his detention as a prisoner of war; and she therefore merely replied--"He is called Woodchuck."

"Voodchick!" exclaimed the Frenchman; "*quel drôle de nom!* Is Monsieur Voodchick in the army?"

To the question thus put, Edith could fairly answer in the negative; for Brooks, though he had seen no little fighting in his day, was merely one of those amateur soldiers, then very common in the provinces, who rarely missed an opportunity of joining some band of volunteers in times of war with France, or fighting upon their own hand, according to the Scotchman's expression, as one of the extensive class called Stragglers. They generally bore away from the field, especially if they distinguished themselves, some military title, such as captain or major, without having commanded half-a-dozen men in their lives.

After having asked his questions and settled his conduct, the French officer's next business was, of course, *politesse*; and he would fain have engaged his lovely companion in gay and lively conversation during the rest of their little voyage; but Edith, though her mind was greatly relieved to find herself freed from the power of the Honontkoh, had many a subject of melancholy contemplation to occupy her. The dark and dreary consideration of her brother's fate--the uncertainty of what might befall her father and her lover--the separation from all most dear to her--the doubt, even now, whether she might not herself be detained a prisoner amongst strangers--all these reflections tormented her beyond endurance. Moreover, the war in America had hitherto been conducted by the French upon principles the most barbarous, and the most opposed to the ordinary characteristics of that nation. The scene which succeeded the capture of Fort William-Henry was a black and damning spot, never to be obliterated from the minds of men; and although it has been put forth by an American author as the only stain upon the character of Montcalm, Mr. Cooper must surely have forgotten the violated capitulation of Oswego, the death of the gallant De la Court, and the scalping and massacre of the sick in the hospital. All that we can trust is, that these barbarities were only permitted, not encouraged. But how can we account for or excuse--how can we even palliate--the voluntary delivery of twenty of the garrison into the hands of the savages, to be tortured to death under the very eyes of the French soldiery, in direct violation of the articles of capitulation, as compensation for the loss of twenty Indians? It is a fact which has never been denied, or it would be too horrible for belief.

Edith replied briefly, therefore, to the compliments and pretty speeches of her military companion; and in the meanwhile the boat proceeded rapidly over the surface of the lake, passed Crown Point, and entered the narrow portion of Champlain, which stretches from that promontory towards the spot where the Sounding Waters, as the Indians called the outlet of Lake George, flow into the greater lake near Ticonderoga.

The French officer, somewhat baffled in his attempts to make her speak, tried his fortune with Woodchuck, but with still less success; for, to everything he said in French, he received what can hardly be called an answer in English, and generally, it must be said, not a very civil speech, as Brooks was filled with all the absurd prejudices of his country, and never uttered the word "Frenchman," without coupling it with the epithet "rascally."

The voyage was brought to a close before night fell, for the boat stopped short by a mile or two of Ticonderoga, and somewhat further to the north of the spot where the ferry now exists. The scene would have appeared beautiful had Edith's mind been free to enjoy it; for in front were seen the tops of the several bold eminences round the French fort. On the one side were those rich lands, varied at that time with scattered masses of forest, though now highly cultivated, known as the New Hampshire grants; and, to the westward, a varied country, rising gradually to the foot of the Mohigan mountains.

The spot chosen for the landing was a secluded cove in the woods, where the shelving rocks broke through the soil, and dipped gradually into the water. Boats and canoes were all speedily hauled up, and the commander of the party, with delicate attention, handed Edith out, and then gave orders to his men to follow him, which was effected with rapidity and precision. The savages, under the orders of their chief, took care of the Iroquois prisoners, and apparently, by no slight act of forbearance, resisted the great temptation to possess themselves of their scalps.

When all had disembarked, the canoes were drawn safely up under concealment of the bushes on either side, and the voyageurs pushed off, and took their way up the lake again.

"I fear, mademoiselle," said the captain of the Frenchmen, who might have amounted in number to sixty or seventy, "I must trouble you to take a somewhat fatiguing promenade of four or five miles--at least, I am told that such is the distance, for I have never been here myself, and do not know the way."

"Then are we not going to Fort Ticonderoga?" asked Edith.

"Not so," replied the officer; "we are going a little beyond, and I shall have no opportunity of detaching any party whom I could trust to send you into the fort to-night. The Indians, indeed, could be spared--at least, a sufficient number to escort you--but I should really be apprehensive, from what I know of their habits, that you might not be quite so safe in their charge as under the protection of my musketeers, with your devoted servant at their head. We will endeavour to make you as comfortable as we can for the night; and I doubt not that, early to-morrow, I shall be visited by some superior officer, who will have the honour of conveying you to the fort."

"Then am I to consider myself as a prisoner?" asked Edith, in a cold tone. "I did not know that it was the habit of French officers to make women captives."

"So," replied the Frenchman, with a graceful bow; "we ourselves are much more frequently *their* captives; but, my dear lady, within the limits of this garrison I myself have no command--am merely acting under orders, and feel myself imperatively bound to send you and your companion, Monsieur Voodchick, to the commandant of the fortress, who will act, I am sure, as he finds befitting. I only regret that I cannot do so at once; but my orders are strict, my route marked out, and I am told to hasten across this small peninsula as fast as possible without approaching the fortress. It is certainly a rather long walk; but, if you feel fatigued, I can easily make my men construct a little litter and carry you. We shall find some preparations made for us where we are going, though I am afraid not very suitable for your use."

Edith evidently saw that remonstrance was in vain; and, saying that she should prefer to walk, she took the arm of Woodchuck, and explained to him, as they went, all that had passed between her and the Frenchman.

"I guess he is going to form an ambuscade," said Woodchuck. "If so, Miss Prevost, our army must be near, and we shan't be long in their hands. I wish to Heaven I could get away from them, and had but a horse to carry me," he added, thoughtfully, and with a sigh. "But it's no use wishing. God knows his own ways best! Them Hurons look very much like as if they would eat the Oneidas before they've done. Pray God they mayn't take such a fancy to us too!"

Thus saying, he took the place which was assigned to him and Edith in the march. A number of Indians preceded, several little parties moved upon the flanks, and the small body of French infantry marched on, two abreast, for the trail was barely wide enough for that number. Woodchuck and Edith followed them, and the French officer, with the Indian whom he called the Great Elk, walked next, succeeded by the Iroquois prisoners, a large quantity of baggage borne on men's shoulders, and the remainder of the Huron auxiliaries.

It was now twilight in the forest; and, for more than an hour after darkness had fallen upon the earth, the weary and rather perilous march was continued. Once, a small stream was crossed, Woodchuck taking up his fair companion in his sturdy arms, and bearing her over like an infant. Nothing of any note occurred, except a slow and low-toned conversation in the rear, which led Edith to believe that the Iroquois, her late captors, had found some of the other band of natives with whom they could converse; but she could not distinguish anything that was said.

Weary and exhausted, the sight of a fire at length glimmering through the trees, was exceedingly pleasant to her eyes; and, a minute or two after, a scene presented itself which might have looked dreary and comfortless enough under other circumstances, but which had a cheerful and comfortable aspect, after that long and gloomy march.

The trail which they had followed terminated in a small open space, flanked on three sides by low earthworks of no very regular construction, but evidently designed by an experienced military hand. The outer surface of these works was partially concealed by a thicket; and great care had been taken not only to preserve the brambles and the large-leaved raspberry, but to fill every gap in this shrubby screen with branches of pine, and hemlock, and maple. Within these embankments the ground had, to a certain extent, been cleared, though two or three of the larger trees had been left standing, to prevent a vacancy being apparent without. About the middle of the open space, a number of rude huts had been erected of small felled trees and branches; and before one, somewhat larger than the rest, a sentinel was seen planted, who, at the moment Edith came in sight, stood motionless, presenting arms as his comrades filed into the little quadrangle. Behind the soldier, and between him and the hut, was a large, blazing fire, which threw out his dark figure sharply outlined upon the flame.

"Ah, this will do," said the French captain, in a tone of relief. "The commandant has been careful of us. Mademoiselle, I welcome you to my redoubt, and will do the best to make the evening pass pleasantly to you. Now bring in the baggage, tell the cook to get supper ready, and you, Pierrot, see that hut properly arranged for this young lady's accommodation. I calculated on sleeping upon a very comfortable bear-skin to-night; but I will most willingly resign it to you, mademoiselle, in the hope of your passing a good night's rest."

Edith would fain have declined accepting a sacrifice so enhanced; but the captain insisted, and his servant, whom he called Pierrot, at once set about the preparations for her comfort with a degree of skill and dexterity truly French. In the meantime, while Edith, sitting on the trunk of a fallen tree, waited till all was ready, and while a group of stragglers unpacked the baggage which had just been deposited from the sturdy shoulders of the bearers, the French officer called his friend the Huron chief to council; and Apukwa and the other Oneidas were brought before him, accompanied by two young Hurons, who undertook to act as interpreters. Many were the questions asked; and what between the captains' ignorance of Indian manners and the interpreter's ignorance both of French and Iroquois, the worthy officer seemed completely puzzled.

At length, however, after consulting the Great Elk in a low voice, he exclaimed,--

"Tell them that, if their tale be really true--though I've got my doubts, for I never heard of Freemasons amongst Indians before, and that must be what you mean by Honontkoh--but, if their tale be really true, they can stay here with us, and prove their devotion to the service of his Majesty Louis XV., king of France, by fighting the English at our side. They shall be sharply watched, however," he added, in a low voice, as if speaking to himself.

Apukwa heard his words translated; and then, saying something in reply, pointed to Edith and her English companion, with a look of two much meaning to be misunderstood.

"Nothing of the kind," answered the French officer, without waiting for the words which seemed about to follow. "Tell him there's but one choice: either to prove their story and their loyalty by fighting on our side, or to pass under the fire of these gentlemen." And he laid his hand upon a pile of muskets which stood close beside him.

This intimation was quite sufficient. The Honontkoh agreed to stay and fight, without any further conditions; and the Frenchman then gave strict directions, both to his own soldiers and to the Hurons, by whom they were much more likely to be efficiently obeyed, that their very doubtful allies should be kept continually in sight. He then seemed to cast all thought of the affair behind him, and turned towards Edith, who was already in the hut, saying,--

"I hope, mademoiselle, Pierrot has taken good care of you."

"With all the skill and courtesy of a Frenchman, monsieur," she answered, really pleased with the attention and almost fatherly kindness of the old soldier who had been arranging the hut.

"Then, now that you have the means of rest, it only remains to provide you with meat and drink," said the officer. "I see they have spread my table-cloth on the grass there. Will you and your friend come and partake of my fare? Pray make my words understood to him."

Woodchuck readily agreed to accept the Frenchman's hospitality; but Edith declined taking more than a little bread and some wine, alleging that she needed rest more than anything else. The French officer, however, would not be content with this, but with his own hands brought her some savory mess, which would not have disgraced a Parisian dinner-table, some choice wine, and, what was still more valuable to her, a small lamp. He then closed the hurdle-door of the hut upon her, and returned to his meal with Woodchuck, keeping up with him for half an hour a silent conversation by nods and signs, one half of which was probably unintelligible to both. The Frenchman then took possession of another hut, and invited Woodchuck to share it with him for the night.

But the stout woodsman declined any other covering than the sky; and stretching himself across Edith's door, was soon in profound slumber.

CHAPTER XLIII

We must go back, for a very short time, to the spot where Edith and her Oneida captors set out upon what proved to them an unfortunate voyage across Lake Champlain, and to the very moment after their canoe had left the shore. The Long House of the Five Nations, as they were pleased to call their territory, extended from the Great Lakes and a point far west, to the banks of the Hudson, and Lakes Horicon and Champlain; but, as is always the case in border countries, the frontier was often crossed by wandering or predatory bands, and by outlaws from the Hurons and other nations under the sway of France, or from the Iroquois tribes attached to England. The peculiar habits and laws of the Indian tribes rendered the incorporation of fugitives with other nations a very easy matter, although the language of the Five Nations would seem to be radically different from that of the tribes originally inhabiting the seaboard of America. Thus, on the western shore of Lake Champlain, not a few pure Hurons were to be found; and, indeed, that tribe, during the successful campaigns of France against England, with which what is called the French and Indian war commenced, had somewhat encroached upon the Iroquois territory, supported in their daring by the redoubted name of Montcalm.

With some of these, it would seem, Apukwa and his companions had entered into a sort of tacit alliance; and towards their dwellings they had directed their steps after their attack upon Edith and her little escort, in the expectation of readily finding a canoe to waft them over the lake. At first, they had been disappointed; for the barques which had been there the day before were gone; and when they did find the canoe in which they ultimately commenced their voyage, the avaricious old man to whom it belonged would not let them use it without a world of bargaining; and it cost them a considerable portion of the little stock of ornaments and trinkets which they had found in Edith's plundered baggage, before the Huron consented to lend that which they did not dare to take by force.

Thus, more than an hour was passed after they reached the lake-shore before they departed; and their taking their course so boldly across the bows of the French boats was more a matter of necessity than choice, although they little doubted a good reception from the inveterate enemies of England. The moment, however, that the canoe had shot out into the water, a tall, dark woman emerged from the bushes of the low point under which the skiff had lain, and began wringing her hands with every appearance of grief and anxiety.

"Oh, what will poor massa do?" she cried, in a piteous voice; "what will poor massa do? Him son killed: him daughter stolen, and Chando tomahawked. Ah, me! ah, me! what will we all do?"

Her imprudent burst of grief had nearly proved destructive to poor Sister Bab. The old Huron had turned him quietly towards a small birch-bark cabin in the forest hard by, and would never have remarked the poor negress if she had confined the expression of her cares to mere gesture; but her moans and exclamations caught the quick ear of the savage, and he turned and saw her plainly gazing after the canoe.

With no other provocation than a taste for blood, he stole gently through the trees with the soft, gliding, noiseless motion peculiar to his race; and making a circuit so as to conceal his advance, came behind the poor creature just as she beheld the canoe which bore away her young mistress, stopped and surrounded by the little flotilla of the French.

Another moment would have been fatal to her (for the Indian was within three yards), when a large rattlesnake suddenly raised itself in his path, and made him recoil a step. Whether it was the small, but never-to-be-forgotten, sound of the reptile's warning, or some noise made by the Huron in suddenly drawing back, the poor negress turned her head, and saw her danger.

With a wild scream, she darted away towards the lake. The savage sprang after with a yell; and, though old, he retained much of the Indian lightness of foot. Onward towards the shore he drove her, meditating each moment to throw his hatchet, if she turned to the right or left.

But Sister Bab was possessed of qualities which would not have disgraced any of his own tribe; and, even while running at her utmost speed, she contrived continually to deprive him of his aim. Not a tree, not a shrub, not a heap of stone, that did not afford her a momentary shelter; and of every inequality of the ground she took advantage. Now she whirled sharply round the little shoulder of the hill; now, as the tomahawk was just balanced to be thrown with more fatal certainty, she sprang down a bank which almost made the Indian pause. Then she plunged head-foremost like a snake through the thick brushwood, and again appeared in a different spot from that where he had expected to see her.

Still, however, he was driving her towards the lake, at a spot where the shores were open, and where he felt certain of overtaking her. Nevertheless, on she went to the very verge of the lake, gazed to the right and left, and, seeing, with apparent consternation, that the banks rounded themselves on both sides, forming a little bay, near the centre of which she stood, she paused for a single instant, as if in despair. The Huron sprang after with a wild whoop, grasping the tomahawk firmly to strike the fatal blow.

But Sister Bab was not yet in his power; and, with a bold leap, she sprang from the ledge into the water. Her whole form instantly disappeared; and, for at least a minute, her savage pursuer stood gazing at the lake in surprise and disappointment, when, suddenly he saw a black object appear at the distance of twenty or thirty yards, and as suddenly sink again. A few moments after, it rose once more, still further out; and then the brave woman was seen striking easily away towards the south.

Rendered only more eager by the chase, and more fierce by disappointment, the Huron ran swiftly along the shore, thinking that he could easily tire her out or cut her off; but, in sunny waters, in far distant lands, she had sported with the waves, in infancy; and, taking the chord of the bow where he was compelled to take the arc, she gained from distance what she lost in speed. So calm was she, so cool, that, turning her eyes from her pursuer, she gazed over the water in the direction where she had seen her beloved young mistress carried, and had the satisfaction of beholding the canoe in which she was towed along by one of the French boats. Why she rejoiced, she hardly knew, for her notions on such matters were not very definite; but anything seemed better than to remain in the hands of the murderers of poor Chando.

Her thoughts were still of Edith; and she asked herself,--

"Where are they taking her to, I wonder? Perhaps I may come up with them, if that red-skin would but leave off running along by the shore, and let me land, and cross the narrow point. He may run, the devil-foot! He can't catch Bab. I'll dive again. He think her drowned."

Her resolution was instantly executed; and--whether it was that her stratagem was successful, or that the Huron had less than Indian perseverance, and gave up the chase--when she rose again, she saw him turning towards the woods, as if about to go back to his lodge. But Bab had learned caution, and she pursued her way towards the small peninsula where stood the French fort of Crown Point, which, at the period I speak of, had been nearly stripped of its garrison to reinforce Ticonderoga.

She chose her spot, however, with great care; for, though in her wanderings she had made herself well acquainted with the country, she was, of course, ignorant of the late movements of the troops, and fancied that the French posts extended as far beyond the walls of the fortress as they had formerly done. A little woody island, hardly separated from the main land, covered her approach; and the moment her feet touched the shore, she darted away into the forest, and took the trail which led nearly due south. The neck of the point was soon passed; and once more she caught sight of the French boats still towing the canoe on which her thoughts so pertinaciously rested.

The short detention of the French party, and the advantage she gained by her direct course across the point, had put her a little in advance; and she ran rapidly on till she reached the mouth of the small river, now called Putnam's Creek, which, being flooded by the torrents of rain which had fallen in the earlier part of the day, made her pause for a moment, gazing at the rushing and eddying waters coming down, and doubting whether she had strength left to swim across it.

The boats, by this time, were somewhat in advance; and, when she gazed after them, she naturally came to the conclusion that they were bound for what she called, after the Indian fashion, Cheeconderoga.

Suddenly, however, as she watched, she saw their course altered; and it soon became evident that they intended to land considerably north of the fort. Running up the creek, then, till she found a place where she could pass, she followed an Indian trail through the woods lying a little to the west of the present line of road, and at length reached an eminence nearly opposite to Shoreham--a spur of Mount Hope, in fact, where she once more saw the lake just in time to catch a view of the disembarkation of the French troops and the Indians.

Notwithstanding her great strength, the poor negress was, by this time, exceedingly tired; still, that persevering love which is one of the brightest traits of her unfortunate race, carried her on.

"If I can but catch sight of them again," she thought, "before night I can carry old massa tidings of where she be."

Encouraged by this idea, she pushed on without pause. But night overtook her before she had seen any more of the party; and poor Bab's spirit began to fail. More slowly she went, somewhat doubtful of her way; and, in the solitude, the darkness, and the intricacy of the woods, fears began to creep over her which were not familiar to her bosom.

The Black Eagle | 309

At length, however, she thought she heard voices at a distance; and, a minute or two after, found herself on the banks of a small brook. She paused and listened; the voices were now distinct; and, without hesitation, she crossed, and crept cautiously along in the direction from which the sounds came. A moment or two after, the flickering of a fire through the trees attracted her attention; and more and more carefully she stole on upon her hands and knees through the low brush, still seeing the blaze of the firelight when she raised her eyes, but unable to perceive the spot whence it proceeded. A small pine cut down then met her hand as she crept along, and then a number of loose branches tossed together. And now sister Bab began to get an inkling of the truth.

"It must be what dey call an ambush," she thought; and, raising herself gently, she found that she was close to a bank of earth, over which the firelight was streaming. The sounds of voices were now distinctly heard; but she could not understand a syllable, for it seemed to her that they were speaking in two different languages, if not more, and each of them was strange to her. At one time, she fancied she heard Edith's voice; still, the language spoken was a strange one; and, although the bank of earth was not more than shoulder-high, she did not venture at first to rise to her whole stature in order to look over.

At length, however, came some words of English; and the voice which she judged to be Edith's was plainly heard, saying,--

"This gentleman is asking you, my good friend, if you will not go and take some supper with him where the people have spread a cloth yonder."

Bab could resist no more, but raised herself sufficiently to bring her eyes above the top of the breastwork, and gazed over into the little rude redoubt. On the right, and at the further part of the enclosure, were a number of Indians, seated on the ground; and, besides the fire already burning, several others were being piled up amidst the various groups of natives. Somewhat on the left, and stretching well nigh across the western side of the open space, were the French soldiers, in groups of five or six, with their arms piled near them. Other straggling parties were scattered over the ground; and two sentinels, each with musket on shoulder, appeared on the other side of the redoubt.

But the group which attracted the poor woman's chief attention was one on the left, near a spot where some small huts had been erected. It consisted of three persons--a gaily-dressed French officer, a man in the garb of a soldier, but with his weapons cast aside, and, lastly, a powerful man in a yellowish-brown hunting-shirt, whom sister Bab instantly recognized as her old acquaintance, the Woodchuck. That sight was quite enough; and, sinking again amongst the bushes, she crept slowly away to a little distance, and there lay down to meditate as to what was next to be done.

At one time she was tempted to enter the French redoubt, and remain with her young mistress. Several considerations seemed in favour of this course; and let it be no imputation upon poor Bab, that hunger, and the savoury odours which came wafted over the earthwork, were not without their influence. But then she thought,--"If I do, how will old massa ever know where missy is?"

And this remembrance enabled her to resist the strong temptation.

"I will stay here and rest till de moon get up," thought the poor woman. "I know dey must be coming up de lake by dis time, and I can catch dem before to-morrow."

To prevent herself from sleeping too long, if slumber should overtake her, she crept further out of the thick wood, and seated herself in a more open spot, with her clasped hands over her knees, but with nothing else to support her. Various sorts of fears suggested themselves to her mind, as she thus sat; but oppressive weariness was more powerful than thought, and in a few moments her head was nodding. Often she woke up at first; but then she slept more profoundly, bending forward till her forehead actually rested on her knees. It is probable, too, that she dreamed, for, in the course of the next two hours, several broken sentences issued from her lips in a low murmur. At length, however, she woke with a start, and found the moon silvering the whole sky to the eastward, though some bold heights, towering up, still obscured the face of the orb of night.

Bab sat and gazed, somewhat bewildered, and hardly knowing where she was. But the musical voice of the falling waters, which has gained for the outlet of Lake Horicon an ever-enduring name, and the grand outline of Mount Defiance seen through the trees, soon showed her that she was on that narrow point of land lying between Trout Brook and the Falls. She waited till the moon had fully risen, and then stole quietly away again, keeping a south-western course nearly up the current of the brook, and for three hours she pursued her way with a rapid and untiring foot. She had no idea of the time, and wondered if the day would never break; but the moonlight was beautifully clear, and the calm beams, as if they had some affinity with the woodland solitude, seemed to penetrate through the branches and green leaves, even more easily than was usual with the sunshine.

Bab's fears had now nearly passed away; for she knew that she must be far beyond the French and Huron posts, and could only expect to meet either with the scouts and outposts of the English army, or with parties of Indians, and she consequently went on without care or precaution.

Suddenly she found herself emerging from the wood into one of those low open savannahs, of which I have already spoken, close to the spot where the embers of a fire were still glowing. The grass was soft, and her tread was light, but the sleep of the Indian is lighter still; and, in an instant, three or four warriors started up around her.

"I am a friend, I am a friend!" cried the negress, in the Iroquois tongue. "Who are you? Mohawks?"

"Children of the Stone," replied the man nearest to her, gazing at her earnestly by the moonlight. "I have seen the Black Cloud before. Does she not dwell in the house of our brother Prevost?"

"Yes, yes!" cried Sister Bab, eagerly. "I'm his slave girl, Bab, who came to the Oneida Castle with my own missy. But now she is the prisoner of bad men; and I have escaped, tired and hungry, and am nearly dead."

"Come with me," said the Indian; "I will take thee where thou shalt have rest to comfort thee, and meat to support thee, till the Black Eagle comes. He will not be long, for he will keep the war-path night and day till he is here; and his wings are swift."

The poor woman shuddered at the name, of the terrible chief, for it was closely connected in her mind with the circumstances of her young master's fate; but, wearied and exhausted, the prospect of food and repose was a blessing, and she followed him in silence to the other side of the savannah.

CHAPTER XLIV

Sixteen thousand gallant men, led by a brave and experienced general, and supported by a fine, though not very large, park of artillery, seemed certainly sufficient for the reduction of a small fortress, not very well garrisoned, nor supplied with any great abundance of stores. But it seemed the fate of English officers in North America to adhere strictly to all ancient rules, when ancient rules could be of no service in face of a new and totally different mode of warfare, and to abandon those rules at times and in circumstances when only they could be available.

A large fleet of *bateaux* had been collected at the southern extremity of Lake George, ready to transport the troops to the destined point of attack; and a council of the most experienced officers was held on the morning of the third of July, to consider the further proceedings of the army.

All had now assembled at what was then commonly called in the province "Fort Lyman," although the name was already changed to "Fort Edward."

General Abercrombie was there in person; and a number of other officers appeared at the council likewise, whose experience in Indian warfare was superior to his own. There is much reason to believe, that had Abercrombie's own opinion been followed in acting against a French fort under French command, all the operations would have been conducted in the same manner, and upon the same system which would have guided a similar enterprise in Europe; and thus much bloodshed and some disgrace would have been spared.

It was represented to the Commander-in-Chief, however, that numerous bodies of Indians were acting upon the side of France, and that all operations carried on according to European rules had hitherto failed in America; and more than one bloody disaster was held up as a warning to his eyes, which he unhappily suffered to bias his own better judgment. In a word, as it was known that every day fresh reinforcements were being thrown into Ticonderoga, that large bodies of Indians were collected for its defence, and that preparations of every kind were in progress, it was determined that a sudden and rapid rush should be made upon the fort, and that no consideration should be put in competition with celerity of movement and boldness of attack. Lord H---- alone represented that, from what he had personally learned during the last six months, it was absolutely necessary to employ cannon, though, perhaps, with a want of proper confidence in his own reputation, he offered to lead the advanced parties, lest the opinion he expressed should seem to any one to savour of timidity.

At as early an hour as possible the march commenced along what was called the King's Road; and in high spirits regiment after regiment entered the forest, confident in their numbers and their prowess. The regular troops pursued the well-constructed causeway, while clouds of Mohawks were scattered on the flanks, sweeping the forest ground on either side. The artillery, on the heavy and clumsy carriages of that day, the tumbrils and the baggage-waggons, came lumbering in the rear, and a large crowd of stragglers followed, comprising the scouts, who might have been much more advantageously employed in the front, but who, for some reason unexplained, had very little service assigned them on the expedition. General Abercrombie and his staff, with several of the superior officers, followed slowly, well aware that the advance of the forces would meet with no opposition, at least upon the first day's march. To this group, from every quarter, came numerous messengers throughout the day; some bringing news of a fresh levy marching up from the eastern states; some from the front seeking clearer orders when any little difficulty or impediment occurred; some from Albany, with intelligence from that city or New York; and several Indian runners from the west, bearing far more important tidings from the Indian tribes, now all in movement to support their British allies.

Amongst the rest appeared the silent runner Proctor, with a letter to General Abercrombie, who, as soon as he had read it, turned to Lord H----, saying,--

"This is a communication from your friends, the Oneidas, my lord, but written by some Englishman, who signs himself 'Gore.' He states that a war-party of the nation is already on the western bank of the lake, and that the main body, under Black Eagle himself, is expected in the course of the day. I suppose we may therefore consider ourselves secure upon our left flank."

"Undoubtedly," replied Lord H----, with a look of so much anxiety, as almost to induce the Commander-in-Chief to believe that he entertained doubts which he did not choose to express.

"You *think* so, I presume," interposed Abercrombie, gazing at him.

"Entirely," replied Lord H----; "but I was in hopes of hearing some other intelligence of a private nature, concerning Mr. Prevost's son, whose alarming position amongst the Oneidas I mentioned to you, if you recollect."

"There is nothing more," said General Abercrombie, handing him the letter; "but there is the messenger. Probably he can give you some information."

Lord H---- immediately turned towards Proctor, who was running at a sort of trot by the side of the general's horse, and inquired if he had been at the Castle of the Oneidas. The man shook his head, and trotted on.

"Then where did you last come from?" asked Lord H----.

But Proctor only lifted his hand, and pointed towards the north-west.

"How many miles?" demanded the nobleman, determined to get some speech out of him.

But he lifted up his hands three times with the ten fingers spread abroad, without ever opening his lips.

"Did you hear amongst those who sent you," asked Lord H----, "any tidings of young Mr. Prevost?"

The man shook his head; but then suddenly stopped in his trot, and said, as if upon recollection,--

"They thought he had been put to death."

He paused, as if what he had said had cost him a great effort; but then added, slowly, when he saw the painful expression of the young nobleman's countenance, "They only *thought*. They did not *know*. They left before."

"Did you see or hear of a man whom you know as Woodchuck--the man you saw with me at Albany?" asked Lord H----.

But the other shook his head; and nothing more could be extracted from him. He was then sent forward to join the rear-guard; but his taciturnity gave Lord H---- good assurance that Mr. Prevost, who had gone forward, would not be pained by the terrible rumour which he bore.

The long and fatiguing march to the nearest point of Lake Horicon I need not describe. Many of the scenes recorded in the life of the gallant Putnam passed near or on the very route pursued; and the feats of daring and the escapes of that fine soldier are almost as marvellous still in our eyes as in those of the savage Indians of his own time, who supposed him to bear a charmed life. Suffice it, that, after encountering great difficulty and severe fatigue in dragging the cannon over a road which in the neighbourhood of the settled portion of the colony was good enough, but which became almost impassable near the lake, in consequence of the heavy rains, the whole army arrived in safety at the newly-constructed and yet incomplete works of Fort George, lying a little to the east of the site of ever-memorable Fort William-Henry.

By the care and diligence of the commissary-general, everything that could refresh the weary soldiers was found prepared; a fleet of one hundred and thirty-five large boats and nine hundred *bateaux* was seen lying along the shore of the lake of pure and holy waters; and hardly a head was laid down to slumber in the tents that night, which did not fondly fancy that Ticonderoga must inevitably fall.

As usual in camp, or on the march, Lord H---- dined with his soldiers, and shared their simple fare; but he passed the evening with Mr. Prevost, who had found quarters in the fort. Both were grave, but the deeper gravity was with Lord H----; for though through the mind of the elder man continually flitted painful fancies--thoughts, images, or whatever they may be called--of the fate of poor Brooks, and his lips murmured twice, almost involuntarily, the words, "Poor Woodchuck!" yet the certainty which he felt of the safety of his son, however great the sacrifice which purchased it, was a comfort--a great, a mighty consolation, although he almost reproached himself for the sensation of rejoicing, which he could not help experiencing.

Lord H----, on the contrary, felt no such certainty. Ever since his conversation with Proctor, if conversation it can be called, a gloomy feeling of apprehension had rested on him. He did not doubt poor Woodchuck in the least: he was sure that he would hold fast to his resolution. Neither had he any fears that the execution of his purpose would be delayed or prevented by any such accident as that which had in reality occurred. But he asked himself, "Might he not come too late?" They had been told the time allowed by the Oneida chief to provide a substitute for Walter, and had taken it at the European calculation of months; but, since he heard that a rumour of the young man's death was prevalent amongst the Indians, he doubted whether there had not here been a mistake. The very rumour showed that some of the natives, at least, imagined the time had expired, and implied that their calculation was different. The effect upon the mind of Edith, he knew, would be terrible, when she found that her brother might have been saved, but that his life had been lost by such a mistake.

From Mr. Prevost, he strove to hide his apprehensions as far as possible; knowing well that previous anxiety never diminishes an inevitable evil; and soon after nightfall he left him, to seek thought in his own tent.

The sky was clear and cloudless; the stars shining out with a largeness and a lustre such as European skies can never give; a light breeze stirred the waters of the lake, and made them musical along the shore; and one of the voyageurs was singing a tranquil song of home in a clear, mellow voice, as he sat in his bark. The air was mild and gentle as a morning dream: yet the whole had that solemn calmness which is always allied to melancholy. All things which, in their calmness, detach us from this untranquil earth, bring with them the feeling of parting from old friends.

Under the influence of such sensations, he went not more than a hundred steps from the gates of the fort; but seated himself upon a mass of the dark gray marble recently quarried for building, and gave himself up to the thoughts in which he would have indulged had he been in his tent. They were sadder perhaps than they had ever been before in life--without anything like presentiment, without anything like apprehension, on his own account. But new ties, new affections, tenderer sympathies, warmer hopes, than any he had yet tasted in existence, had lately grown up around him; and it is a sad fact, with man, as with states, that the more he increases his possessions--be they mundane, or be they of the heart--the more defenceless points does he expose to ever-ready enemies.

Nor was he in the fresh hey-day of life, when the down of the butterfly has never been crushed--when all is joy: the present in fruition--the future in anticipation--the past forgotten. He knew that there were sorrows: he felt that there were dangers to his peace; he was conscious how frail is the thread upon which mortal happiness is poised in the midst of the dark abyss. True, he would not have yielded the blessing of Edith's love for all that earth could give of security; still, he was well aware that his heart had now a vulnerable point to be reached by weapons which had never yet been encountered. All that touched her, touched him; and the uncertainty of Walter's fate threw a sadness over his meditations. What would have been his sensations, had he known that for Walter he need have no fear? that it was *her* fate he had to dread? But that was spared him.

He sat there long: no inclination to sleep interrupted his reveries, notwithstanding the fatigues of the day; and at length the moon rose over the high eastern hills, showing an unrivalled scene of solemn beauty. The moment the beams touched the waters, they were converted into a flood of liquid silver: the grand forms of Rattlesnake Mountain, and its fellow giants, to the east, and of that high hill now called French Mountain to the north-west, the deep gloomy woods, the walls of the fortress, picturesque in their rugged incompleteness, the tents of the sleeping army, with here and there the light of a night-Gwatcher gleaming amongst them, and the slopes of the nearer hills dotted with Indian fires, formed a scene such as the eye of man has seldom rested on; while over all poured the lustrous stream of light, calm and passionless like the look of a good, pure being cast over the troublous scene of mortal life.

Lord H---- rose; and, after gazing round him for a few moments, drinking in as it were the solemn loveliness, walked on slowly towards the blackened remains of Fort William-Henry. Little was to be seen there. Montcalm had not left his work half done; for all had been destroyed, and little beyond some irregularities in the ground, and some large detached fragments of masonry, showed where so many gallant men had fought in their country's cause, only to be slaughtered after surrender by a treacherous enemy.

By report, he knew the ground well; and after pausing for a minute or two amongst the ruins, he turned down the dark and fearful dell where the horrible massacre was perpetrated. Every rock around had echoed to the yell of the Indians, the groan of the dying soldier, or the shrieks of defenceless women and children. Every tree had seen beneath its boughs some of the deeds of horror and of blood which went to make up that great crime. The bones of hundreds were lying still unburied; and where the moonlight fell on the western side of the gorge, some portion of a woman's garment, which had caught upon a bush, was seen fluttering in the breeze.

The immediate path along which Lord H---- went, was still in profound shadow; but, suddenly, across the moonlight side, a little in advance of him, he saw, gliding along with noiseless step, a troop of eight or ten shadowy figures, looking like ghosts in the pale moonlight. So much was their colour the same as the rocks around, that you might almost fancy you saw through them, and that they were but the shadows from some other objects cast upon the broken crags as they passed.

Lord H---- stood and gazed; when suddenly the band stopped, and, comprehending that he had been perceived, he challenged them in English, judging at once that they must be a troop of friendly Indians. A deep voice replied in the same language, but with a strong Indian accent, "We are friends--children of the Stone. Can you tell us where to find Prevost?"

As he spoke, the leader of the Indians had advanced nearer down the sloping ground at the foot of the rocks, and there seemed something in his tall, powerful form, and majesty of carriage, familiar to the eyes of the young nobleman, who exclaimed, "Is that the Black Eagle?"

"It is," answered the other, whose limited knowledge of English did not suffer him to indulge in his usual figurative language. "Art not thou the Falling Cataract?"

"I am he to whom you gave that name," returned Lord H----. "But what want you with Mr. Prevost? Where is his son?"

"On yonder side of Horicon," answered the Indian chief, pointing with his hand towards the western side of the lake. "The boy is safe; be thy mind at rest."

Lord H---- took the hand he proffered, and pressed it in his; but at the same time he asked, "And poor Woodchuck--what of him?"

"I know not," answered Black Eagle; "we have not beheld him."

"That is strange," rejoined the nobleman; "he set out to deliver himself up to you, to save the young man's life."

"He is brave," answered Black Eagle; "the Good Spirit kept him away."

"Then, how was the boy delivered?" asked Lord H----. "We feared that your people would be inexorable."

"The Great Spirit spoke by the voices of the women," answered the chief. "She who sees beyond the earth in her visions, heard the voice, and told its words. It was decreed that if the boy died, our wives, our daughters, our sisters, should all die with him; and we listened to the voice, and obeyed."

"Come with me quickly," said Lord H---- eagerly; "let us carry the news to Mr. Prevost. He is here at the fort, now holding an office in our army."

"I know it," replied Black Eagle. "I have been to his lodge, and found no one but the slaves, who told me. The boy I sent on with my people; for the children of the Stone have taken the war-path for England, and a thousand warriors are on their way to the place of the Sounding Waters. He goes to fight amongst us as our son. But I must speak with Prevost before I go, for the wings of the Black Eagle are spread, perhaps, for his last flight; and who knows but he will leave his scalp on the war-post of the Huron?"

Lord H---- led the way with a quick step; and the chief and his companions followed. At the first outpost they were of course challenged;

and, strict orders having been given to admit no troop of Indians within the limits of the fort, the young nobleman and the chief proceeded alone to the quarters of Mr. Prevost. They found him still up, and busily writing orders for the following morning. When he beheld the face of Black Eagle following his noble friend, he started up, and, at first, drew back; but then, with a sudden change of feeling, he seized the warrior's hand, exclaiming, "My son lives! my son lives, or you would not be here!"

"He lives," replied Black Eagle.

He then proceeded to give the same account to Mr. Prevost which had been heard by Lord H----. The former, however, understanding the Indian better, soon drew from him, partly in English, and partly in Iroquois, the whole particulars of Walter's deliverance.

"And would you really have slain him?" asked Mr. Prevost.

"I would," replied Black Eagle, calmly and firmly. "I would have torn out my own heart, had the laws of my people required it."

The father mused for a few moments, and then said, in a thoughtful tone,--

"I believe you would. Dear Otaitsa, did she then really peril her life to save her young friend?"

"She did more," answered Black Eagle; "she was one of those prepared to go to the happy hunting-ground, with him; but I tell thee, Prevost, not the sight of my child, with the knife in her hand ready to plunge it into her own heart, made the Black Eagle pause or hesitate. It was, that we heard the voice of the Great Spirit in the words that were spoken. He only can change the laws of the Oneida, and he changed them. But now hear me, Prevost, for I must back to my people and thy son. I sent them forward towards the Sounding Waters, while I sought thee first at thy lodge, and then here; and I must join them, for they must not throw a hatchet or fire a rifle without the Black Eagle."

He had seated himself when first he entered, but now he rose, and stood erect, as if about to make a speech.

"There is a Blossom on the Black Eagle's tree," he said, "which is dear to his eyes; and thou hast a Bough on thy tree, which is dear to thee. Otaitsa is a Christian--believes in your Good Spirit. She is descended from a race of warriors, every one of whom has left a name in the hearts of his people. She is of the highest race of the highest tribe of the children of the Stone. The blood of the red man is as fine as the blood of the white. Her mother was the daughter of a great chief, and of a race as good as thine own; a race that is renowned."

Mr. Prevost bent down his head; but he knew the Indian customs too well to interrupt, and the chief went on:--

"The Blossom loves the Bough: the Bough loves the Blossom. She has purchased him; she has bought him for herself; she has offered her heart's blood for his price. Is he not hers? If the Black Eagle should never return from his war-flight--if the bullet of the French should break his wing, or the arrow of the Huron pierce his heart, will his brother Prevost bind the Blossom and the Bough together as the white men bind them, and as the Christian people unite those who love? Will he take the Blossom to his own home, and make her indeed his daughter?"

Mr. Prevost rose, and threw his arms round the chief, saying,--

"Thou art my brother; I will do as thou hast said; and may the Good Spirit deal with me as I deal with thee in this matter! *Thy* daughter is *my* daughter; *my* son is *thy* son. But thou knowest not, perhaps----"

Black Eagle raised his hand, saying, in Iroquois,--

"Forbear! I know what I know; thou knowest what thou knowest. We may believe much that it is not right to prove. Silence is a good thing when secrets are dangerous. Now go I to my people with my heart at rest."

And, without more words, he glided out of the room.

CHAPTER XLV

Day dawned brightly and clearly over the wild woods, the green savannahs, the streams, the lakes, and mountains that lay between Horicon, or Lake George, and the small chain of Indian lakes. The advanced party of the Oneidas were up, and bustling with the earliest beam--bustling, but in their quiet manner. All were actively clearing away every trace of their sojourn from the face of the savannah as far as possible, and preparing to betake themselves to the shade of the neighbouring woods; but Sister Bab was still sound asleep.

Amongst those who have travelled much over that part of the country, there may be some who remember a beautiful and rich green meadow, extending for about a third of a mile from its inland extremity to the shores of Horicon. It has now--and it is not much altered since the time I speak of--a sloping ground, well covered with wood, to the northward of this grassy plot; and on the south is, a rocky but still well-wooded bank, in which several small caves are to be observed.

In one of these caves lay the negress, on the morning I have just mentioned; and though the Indians moved about in different directions, and removed a large iron pot of European workmanship which had been placed near the entrance of the cavern, the good woman, in the sleep of fatigue and exhaustion, showed no sign whatever of waking.

Few had been the explanations which she had given on the preceding night. She was too weary to indulge in her usual loquacity; and the Indian sat quietly before her, after having supplied all that she required, seeing her eat and drink, but putting no questions.

Now, however, he approached the hollow in the rock; and, after gazing at her for an instant as she lay, he moved her with his moccassined foot. She started up and rubbed her eyes, looking round with evident wonder; but the Indian said,--

"Get up, and follow into the woods, if thou wouldst see the Black Eagle. We must leave the ground that has no shadow, now that the day has come."

"Ah me!" cried Sister Bab, "what shall I do for my poor Missy? She is a prisoner with the French, not more than a few miles hence; and, what is worse still, the Woodchuck is with her, and all our people said he was going to give himself up to save Massa Walter."

Quietly and deliberately, the Indian seated himself on the ground, and remained silent for a moment or two. He then asked, without the slightest appearance of interest,--

"Where is the daughter of Prevost? Is she at the castle of the Sounding Waters?"

Sister Bab replied, "No;" and, as far as she could describe it, explained to her companion where Edith was, and gave him no very inaccurate notion of the sort of field-work on which she had stumbled the night before. Still not a muscle of the man's face moved; and he merely uttered a sort of hum at this intelligence, sitting for full two minutes without uttering a word.

"What can we do, brother, to save them?" asked Sister Bab at length, "I don't think there's any danger either to Missy or Massa Woodchuck, because the young man in the blue coat seemed very civil; but then, if Massa Woodchuck not get away, your people will kill Massa Walter. For six months will be over very soon."

"Six moons have grown big and small since the Black Eagle spoke," said the Indian gravely; "but we will see whether there be not a trail the prisoners can tread. You must get up quickly, and walk before me, but without noise, to where you left them like a cloud upon the mountain-side."

"It's a long way," said the poor woman; "and my feet are all cut and torn with yesterday's ramble."

"We will give thee moccassins," answered the Indian. "The way is not long, even to the house of the Sounding Waters, if you keep the trail straight. Thou must show me, if thou wouldst save Prevost's daughter. Her fate is a toppling stone upon the edge of a precipice. A wind will blow it down. The French Hurons do not spare women. Come, get thee up; eat, and talk not. I must know this place, and that quickly."

The last words were spoken somewhat sternly; and Sister Bab rose up, and followed to one of the little groups of Indians, where she seated herself again, and ate some cakes of maize and dried deer's-flesh, while the chief who had been speaking with her held a consultation with several of the other warriors. Not much time was allowed her for her meal, for in less than five minutes she was called upon to lead the way; and, followed by a party of five Indians, she proceeded for a mile or two, till they reached a spot where the trail divided into two. She was about to take the left-hand path, knowing that it was the one which she had followed on the preceding night; but the chief commanded her in a low voice to turn her steps upon the other, adding, "We shall come upon thy foot-prints again speedily."

So indeed it proved, for she had wandered during the night far from the direct course; and after walking on for some ten minutes, they cut into the former path again, where, to Indian eyes, the traces of a negro foot were very apparent.

Twice the same thing occurred; and thus the distance was shortened to nearly one-half of that which she had travelled on the preceding night between the little masked redoubt of the French and the Indian camping-place.

At length, the objects which Sister Bab saw around her gave warning that she was approaching the spot of which they were in search. From time to time Mount Defiance was seen towering up on the right, and the character of the shrubs and trees was changed. The first hint sufficed to make the Indians adopt much greater precautions than those which they had previously used. They spread wide from the trail, the chief leading Sister Bab with him; and slowly and noiselessly they pursued their way, taking advantage of every tree and every rock to hide behind and gaze around.

Before five minutes more were over, Sister Bab paused suddenly, and pointed forward. The Indian gazed in silence. To an unpractised eye, nothing would have been apparent to excite the slightest suspicion of a neighbouring enemy; but some of the pine branches of what seemed a low copse in front, were a shade yellower than the other trees. Besides, they did not take the forms of young saplings. They were rounder, less taper, without leaving shoot or peak.

A grin came upon the Indian's countenance; and pointing with his finger to the ground, he seemed, without words, to direct the negress to remain exactly on the same spot where she stood behind a great butternut-tree. He then looked round him for his companions; but their movements were well combined and understood. Though at some distance from each other, each eye from time to time had been turned towards him as they advanced; and the moment it was perceived that he stopped, each of the others stopped also. His raised hand brought them all creeping quietly towards him; and then, after a few whispered words, each Indian sank down upon the ground, and, creeping along like a snake, disappeared amongst the bushes.

Sister Bab found her situation not altogether pleasant. The slightest possible rustle in the leaves was heard as her red companions disappeared; but then all sounds ceased, except from time to time when the wind, which had risen a little, bore her some murmurs from the redoubt, as if of voices speaking. Once she caught a few notes of a merry air, whistled by lips that were probably soon after doomed to everlasting silence. But that was all she heard, and the stillness grew oppressive to her.

After waiting for a moment or two, she sought a deeper shelter than the butternut-tree afforded, and crept amongst some thick shrubs at the foot of a large oak. She thought her Indian companions would never return; but at length one of the red men looked out from the bushes, and then another; and both gazed around as if in search of her. Following their example, she crept forth; and the chief, approaching, beckoned her away without speaking.

When far enough off to be quite certain that no sound of voices could reach the redoubt, he stopped suddenly and gazed in her face, saying,--

"You love the daughter of the pale-face; you followed her where there was danger; will you go where there is no danger, to bear her the words of warning?"

"I will go anywhere to do her any good," answered the woman warmly. "I am not afraid of danger. I had enough of it yesterday to make me careless of it, to-day."

"Well, then," said the chief, "thou seest this trail to the left; follow it till it crosses another. Then turn to the right on the one it crosses--it is a broad trail, thou canst not miss it. It will lead thee straight into the Frenchman's ambush. They will not hurt thee. Ask for the daughter of the pale-face Prevost. Tell them thou hast passed the night in the woods seeking for her, and they will let thee stay with her. Tell her she shall have deliverance before the sun has set to-morrow; but bid her, when she hears the war-whoop and the shot of the rifle, to cast herself down flat on the ground beneath the earth-heap, if she be near at the time. She knows the Oneida people; she can tell their faces from the Hurons, though the war-paint be bright upon them. She need not fear them. Tell her secretly when no one hears; and what I tell her to do, do thou, if thou wouldst save thy life."

"But," suggested Bab, with more foresight than the Indian, "perhaps they will not keep her there till to-morrow. They may send her into the fort--most likely will."

"Bid her stay, bid her stay," said the chief; "if they force her away, I have no arm to hold her. Go on. I have said."

The negress shook her head, as if much doubting the expediency of the plan proposed; but she obeyed without further remonstrance; and walking on upon the little narrow path which the Indian had pointed out, she reached, in about a quarter of an hour, the broader trail, along which Edith had been taken on the preceding night. Turning to the right, as directed, she followed it with slow and somewhat hesitating steps, till suddenly a sharp turn brought her in sight of two sentinels, pacing backwards and forwards, and a group of Indians seated on the ground round a fire, cooking their food. Then she halted abruptly, but she was already seen: and, receiving no answer to his challenge, one of the sentinels presented his musket, as if to fire. At the same moment a voice exclaimed in French, "What's that--what's that?" and a man in the garb of a soldier, but unarmed, came forward and spoke to her.

She could make no reply, for she did not understand a word he said; and, taking her by the wrist, the man led her into the redoubt, saying to a sentinel, with a laugh,--

"It's only a black woman; did you take her for a bear?"

The next instant poor Bab beheld her young mistress quietly seated on the ground, with a pure white tablecloth spread before her, and all the appurtenances of a breakfast-table, though not the table itself; while the officer she had seen in the redoubt the night before was applying himself assiduously to supply her with all she wanted. In a moment the good woman had shaken her wrist free from the man who held it; and, darting forward, she caught Edith's hand, and smothered it with kisses.

Great was Edith's joy and satisfaction to see poor Bab still in life. It was soon explained to the French officer who she was, and how she came thither. But the object of her coming had nearly been frustrated before she had time to explain to her young mistress the promised rescue; for, ere she had been half an hour within the works, a non-commissioned officer from Ticonderoga appeared with a despatch for the commander of the party, who at once proposed to send the young lady and her dark attendant, under the officer's charge, to the fortress, expressing gallantly his regret to lose the honour and pleasure of her society, but adding that it would be for her convenience and safety.

The suggestion was made before he opened the despatch, and Edith eagerly caught at a proposal which seemed to offer relief from a very unpleasant situation. But as soon as the captain had seen the contents of his letter, his views were changed, and he explained to his young prisoner that, for particular reasons, the commander-in-chief thought it best that there should be as little passing to and fro, during the period of daylight, between the fortress and the redoubt, as possible. He would therefore, he said, be obliged to inform his superior officer, in the first place, of her being there, and of the circumstances in which she had fallen under his protection, as he termed it; adding that probably after nightfall, when the same objections would not exist, he would receive instructions as to what was to be done both with herself and companions, and with the Indians in whose power he had found her.

He then sat down to write a reply to the despatch he had received, and occupied fully half an hour in its composition, during which time all that sister Bab had to say was spoken. The very name of the Oneidas, however, awakened painful memories in Edith's breast; and, notwithstanding all the assurances she had received from Otaitsa, her heart sank at the thought of poor Walter's probable fate. She turned her eyes towards Woodchuck, who had refused to take any breakfast, and sat apart under a tree, not far from the spot where Apukwa and his companions, kept in sight constantly by a sentinel, were gathered round their cooking-fire. His attitude was the most melancholy that can be conceived; his eyes were fixed upon the ground, his head drooping, his brow heavy and contracted, and his hands clasped together on his knee. Edith moved quietly towards him, and seated herself near, saying,--

"What is the matter, my good friend?" She then added, in a low voice, "I have some pleasant news for you."

Woodchuck shook his head sadly, but made no answer; and Edith continued seeking to cheer him.

"The poor negro woman," added she, "who was with me when we were attacked, escaped the savages, it seems, and has brought an intimation that, before to-morrow's sunset, we shall be set free by a large party of the Oneidas."

"It is too late, my dear, it is too late!" ejaculated Woodchuck, pressing his hands tight together; "too late to do anything for your poor brother; it was him I was thinking of."

"But there are still four or five days of the time," said Edith, "and----"

"I've been a fool, Miss Prevost," interrupted Woodchuck bitterly; "and there's no use concealing it from you. I have mistaken moons for months. The man who brought me the news of what that stern old devil, Black Eagle, had determined, said the time allowed was six months, and I never thought of the Indians counting their months by moons, till I heard those Honontkoh saying something about it this morning. No, no! it's all useless now, it's all useless!"

Edith turned deadly pale, and remained so for a moment or two; but then she lifted her eyes to a spot of the blue sky shining through the trees above, and, with a deep sigh, ejaculated,--

"We must trust in God, then, and hope He has provided other and less terrible means. He can protect and deliver according to His will, without the aid or instrumentality of man. You have done your best, Woodchuck, and your conscience should rest satisfied."

"No, no!" he exclaimed bitterly; "if I had but thought of what I knew quite well, I should have gone a fortnight sooner, and the poor lad would have been saved. It's all the fault of my stupid mistake. A man should make no mistakes in such emergencies, Miss Edith."

He fell into a fit of thought again; and, seeing that, the attempt to comfort him was vain, Edith returned to the side of the black woman, and inquired eagerly if she had found any tidings of Walter amongst the Oneidas. Sister Bab, however, was more cautious than poor Woodchuck had been, and denied stoutly having heard anything, adding that she could not think they had done any harm to her young "massa," or they would not be so eager to help her young "missy."

The smallest gleam of hope is always a blessing; still, the day passed sadly enough to poor Edith. The commandant of the redoubt was occupied with military business which she did not comprehend, and which afforded no relief to her thoughts, even for a moment. She saw the soldiers parading, the sentinels relieved, the earthworks inspected, and the Indians harangued, without one thought being withdrawn from the painful circumstances of her own fate.

Shortly after dusk, however, the same servant who had brought the despatch in the morning, re-appeared with another letter, which the French commandant read, and then carried to Edith in the little hut where she was seated, with her lamp just trimmed and lighted.

"The Marquis of Montcalm informs Captain le Courtois that it will be greatly inconvenient to receive any additional mouths into Fort Carillon.

Should he think fit, he can send the lady who has fallen into his hands, with the English gentleman, her companion, back to Crown Point [4] or Fort St. Frederick, as early to-morrow as he thinks fit. If the lady earnestly prefers to retire to Fort Carillon at once, the Marquis of Montcalm will not be so wanting in courtesy as to refuse; but he begs to warn her that she may be subjected to all the inconveniences of a siege, as he cannot at all tell what course of operations the enemy may think fit to pursue. The Indians taken, if willing, as they say, to serve, may be usefully employed within the redoubt, but with caution, and must not be suffered to operate upon the flanks as usual."

"It is for you to say, mademoiselle," observed Monsieur le Courtois, "whether you will now go to the fort or not."

Edith, however, declined, saying that the reasons given by Monsieur de Montcalm were quite sufficient to induce her to remain till it was convenient to send her elsewhere.

Thus ended that eventful week. The following day was Sunday--a day not fit to be desecrated by human strife, but one which was destined to behold on that very spot one of those scenes which write man's shame in letters of blood upon the page of history.

CHAPTER XLVI

The day was intensely hot, the wind nearly south-west, the sky deep blue towards the horizon, but waning to a hazy gold colour in the zenith, when, at an early hour on the Saturday morning, the great flotilla of General Abercrombie got under way. One large boat, modelled like a whale-boat, and so designated in contemporary accounts, led the way with the active and energetic second in command, accompanied by a portion of his own regiment. The rest followed, spreading out in the shape of an irregular wedge over the face of the lake, and the whole steered at once directly towards the Narrows.

Fresh, and peaceful, and beautiful was the scene upon that loveliest of lakes, with the wild mountains and sweeping forests round, and myriads of graceful islands studding the golden waters like gems. Lord H---- sat somewhat reclining on his cloak, in the stern of the leading boat, with a telescope in his hand, which, however, he did not use. The scene presented to his eye had sufficient in its general features to afford pleasant occupation to the thoughts; and he strove to turn them as much as possible towards objects unconnected with his own fate, or with the fate of the expedition.

Had he misgivings? it may be asked. I cannot tell. His mind was relieved in regard to Walter's fate, and he knew nothing of the painful circumstances in which Edith was placed. On those points his mind was at rest. Nay; with a kindly heart like his, there was ground for rejoicing; yet a certain degree of melancholy mingled with all his thoughts, which he could not altogether cast off. He strove, then, to occupy his mind with the contemplation of the ever-changing picture presented by the mountain, lake, and islands, as, with a gentle, pleasant breeze, the boat sailed on--to forget the bloody business of the coming hours, the contest for which he thought he had provided as far as human foresight could reach, and to fancy himself a wandering traveller enjoying a summer's sail on holy waters. Diamond Island was soon passed, Long Island left to the eastward, and the rich narrow strip of low land extending far into the lake, and known as Long Point, was rounded by the boat in which he sat.

He gazed back to see how near the others were following, and then looked forward again. Trench Mountain, Deer-pasture Mountain, Harris's

Bay, Dunham's Bay, were left behind; and the Dome Island, rising up in the midst of the waters, like the cupola of some large submerged cathedral, was right in front. Many another little islet was seen scattered round, with that peculiar and magical effect of the hazy midsummer light, making them look hardly real.

At length, the high, precipitous cliff, known as Shelving Bock, on the one hand, and the Tongue Mountain on the other, were seen in front, announcing the approach to the Narrows: while the top of the Black Mountain appeared dark and grim over the lower land in the foreground.

More caution now became necessary, for hitherto no fear had been entertained that the sailing of the flotilla would be discovered by the enemy's scouts; but that part of the lake most frequently swept by the French boats was near at hand, and it became necessary to keep as far in shore as possible and take advantage of every headland and island as a means of concealment in order to hide the approach and number of the armament till the last moment.

The general orders having been given, Lord H---- again lay quiet, and meditated. On an active and energetic spirit, the saddest thoughts are most apt to obtrude in moments of forced tranquillity. He could not cast them off; he tried to think of everything that was happy--of Edith--of his speedy union with her who had become the brightness of his life--of pleasant days beyond the sea, far away in their peaceful native land. Still, still, through all the visions he conjured up, of hope, and happiness, and long cheerful hours, came chiming, like the tolling of a bell, the sad prophetic words of question, "Shall I ever see her more?" and he longed for the moment of landing, to shake off thought in exertion.

At length it came. The wild, strange scenery of the Buck Mountain and the Rattlesnake Dens was seen upon the left, with, stretching out in front, the low fertile sweep of land known from that day forward as Sabbath-day Point. Here, in the evening, the troops landed for refreshment; and the boats were drawn up to the southward, under cover of the banks and woods, with but a few miles further sail on the following day, ere they reached the point of attack.

Happy are the thoughtless; for, though perhaps they enjoy not so highly, and their pleasure is of a lower kind, they can take delight in each sunshiny hour that God grants them in their course through life. The brief repose, the pleasant meal, the fair and the strange things around, afforded matter for much happiness to many a light heart there during the halt of the army; but it was not so with Lord H----. He knew that the next day was to be one of great fatigue, difficulty, and exertion; and, in order that his corporeal powers might be in full activity, he lay down and tried to sleep; but sleep would not come, and he had not closed an eye, when, towards midnight, the order was given to form upon the beach and re-embark.

Every one, as well as the young nobleman, felt that to be a solemn moment. The sky was clear and bright; the stars were shining out large and lustrous; not a breeze was felt; the clear waters of the lake were smooth as a sheet of glass; the only sound that stirred the air was the tramp of the troops towards the boats, the whirring insects in the trees, and the wailing voice of the whip-poor-will.

All was conducted as silently as possible; the oars of the boats were muffled; and once more Lord H---- led the way with a few bodies of rangers in several *bateaux*. The regular troops followed in the centre of the line, and the volunteers of the provinces formed wings on either side. Stilly and silently, the flight of boats skimmed over the waters, till, after a few hours of solemn darkness, day dawned upon them, revealing to the scouts of Montcalm, upon the rocky eminences near the shore, the full blaze of the English uniforms in the innumerable boats sweeping down as if to certain conquest.

Somewhat less than an hour after, the first boat neared what is called Prisoner's Island, bore away a little to the westward, where the ground was open, touched the shore, and the young nobleman instantly sprang to land. From that day, it has borne the name of Howe's Landing. Regiment after regiment followed. The debarkation was perfectly orderly and uninterrupted, and it was evident that the French garrison of Ticonderoga, if not actually taken by surprise, was attacked much sooner than had been expected.

The number of the Indians with the army was actually small; but it was known that large parties of Mohawks, Oneidas, and even Onondagas, were hovering on the flanks, sweeping, in fact, in a crescent round that which was then considered the key of Lake Champlain.

It was nearly noon before the disembarkation was completed, and the men formed into three columns, ready for advance. The first column, however, then plunged into the woods, headed by Lord H---- in person, and pushed on for some little way unopposed, except by the difficulties of the road, which at every step became greater and greater, from the thick juniper bushes and tangled brushwood which encumbered the ground under the larger trees. The men's strength was spent in contending with these natural obstacles; and, to give them time to breathe, Lord H---- halted his corps for a moment at the first open space in the woods which they reached. He himself leaned upon the short ranger's musket which he carried in his hand, his fine, expressive countenance glowing with exercise and eagerness, and beaming encouragement upon the gallant men who followed him on what they fully believed to be the road to victory.

At that moment something was heard plunging through the thick brushwood on the left, and an Indian in his full war-costume, painted and armed, burst out into the open space, holding up a piece of paper in his hand. He darted instantly towards the commander of the column, lifting the paper high; and Lord H----, who was just upon the point of giving the order to advance again, paused and stretched forth his hand. What the man gave him was not a letter, but apparently merely a leaf torn out of a pocket-book; and the moment it was delivered, the Indian, whose eyes had been gleaming with eagerness, dropped his arms by his side, and stood as still as a statue.

Lord H---- gazed upon the paper, and beheld, written in pencil, apparently in great haste, the following words:--

"There is a masked redoubt in front, as far as I can discover, a little to the east of the brook. It is concealed by low bushes, and the gaps in the under-wood are filled up with boughs of pine. Edith is within, a prisoner. Beware! we are marching forward rapidly to take it in reverse--I mean the Oneidas.

"WALTER PREVOST."

Several of the superior officers had gathered round, and, amongst the rest, a man deservedly famous in those and succeeding times, then simply known as Major Putnam.

"We have been seen by friend, if not by enemies, Putnam," said Lord H----, handing to him the paper.

"What do you advise to be done? You are more skilled in wood warfare than I am."

"Send back the Indian," answered Major Putnam. "Let him tell his brethren to advance as speedily as possible, and help to clear the woods. Then give me a hundred rangers and a handful of Indians, and I will push on myself, and make a way for you."

"Good," said Lord H----. "Call out your men, Putnam, while I send away the Indian."

Beckoning up an interpreter, the nobleman gave their savage allies directions, telling him particularly to report the exact spot which the column had reached; and by the time this was done, and the man gone, Major Putnam had placed himself at the head of his little party, ready to dash on.

"Stay, Putnam," said Lord H----. "You command; but I go with you."

Putnam paused, and dropped the point of his sword, looking almost aghast.

"My Lord," he said, "I beg you will forbear. If I am killed, the loss of my life will be of little consequence to any one; but the preservation of your life is of infinite importance to this army."

Lord H---- laid his hand upon his arm, saying,--

"Putnam, your life is as dear to you as mine is to me. I am determined to go. Lead on."

The next moment, they dashed on at quick time along a trail which opened before them. The few Indians who accompanied the party, scattered as usual to the right and left; and, for some little way, they made good progress through the tangled wood. At length, however, all, even to the natives, became puzzled by the number of trails crossing each other, and the thick and intricate nature of the wood; still they forced their way forward, judging the direction they ought to take by the way the shadows of the trees were thrown by the sunshine. Thus, for four or five hundred yards, they pushed on without seeing an enemy, when Putnam, suddenly pointing with his sword, exclaimed,--

"There goes a Frenchman's cap--more of them--more of them! Now, gallant rangers, down with your pieces, and make your barrels ring!"

In an instant, every gun was levelled; but, at the same moment, a sharp flash ran along the trees and bushes beyond; the loud report of firearms rattled through the forest, and one of the young officers of the rangers dropped at once. Several privates fell before they could draw the trigger; and while the rest were sending a fatal volley into the wood--

"On, on!" cried Putnam; "clear the copse of them! My lord, what is the matter?"

Lord H---- stood for a moment longer without answering; then wavered for an instant on his feet, and fell back into the arms of a sergeant of the rangers.

"I knew it!" cried Putnam. "Forward, my men! Forward, forward! and avenge this noble fellow!"

CHAPTER XLVII

Very different from the array of Abercrombie's army was the march of the Oneidas through the deep woods on the western side of Lake Horicon. Far spread out, and separate from each other, they pursued a number of different trails in profound silence, and in single files of not more than twenty or thirty each; yet, with what seemed a sort of instinct, each party directed its course unerringly to one particular point. They knew the spot they were to strike--they knew the time they were to be there; and at that spot and at that time, each little band appeared with its most famous warrior at its head. Thus, in the small savannah where the poor negress, Sister Bab, had found the advance-guard of the whole nation, nearly six hundred warriors of the children of the Stone assembled on the night of Saturday.

Dressed, like themselves, with tomahawk and knife in his belt, and moccassins upon his feet, appeared Walter Prevost, distinguished from the rest by his fair skin and flowing hair. The sports of the field, the wild life he had led for several years, and even the hardships he had lately suffered, had fitted him for all the fatigues of an Indian march, and rendered a frame naturally strong extraordinarily robust and active. Ignorant of any danger to those he best loved, rejoicing in deliverance from captivity and the peril of death, and full of bright hopes for the future, his heart was light and gay, and happiness added energy to vigour. The hardy warriors with whom he marched saw, with surprise and admiration, the son of the pale-face bear difficulties and fatigues as well as themselves, and come in at the close of day as fresh and cheerful.

The fires were lighted, the rifles piled near to each separate band, and the food, which they brought with them, cooked after their manner, and distributed amongst them; but the meal was not over ere another small band joined them, and Black Eagle himself passed round the different fires till he paused by that at which Walter was seated. None of his own people had taken any notice of his approach. Once or twice one of the warriors, indeed, looked up as he went by; but no sign of reverence or even of recognition was given, till Walter, after the European fashion, rose and extended his hand.

"Thou art before me, my son," said the chief; "the wings of the Black Eagle have had far to fly. I have visited thy father's lodge, and have followed him to the new Castle at the mid-day end of Horicon."

"My father!" exclaimed Walter, in great surprise. "Was he not at his house?"

"Nay, he is a war-chief with the army," returned Black Eagle.

"Then, where is Edith?" inquired the young man. "Did you leave the Blossom with her?"

"I left Otaitsa at thy father's house," answered the chief; "but thy sister was not there."

"Where was she, then?" asked Walter, with some alarm.

"I know not," answered Black Eagle, and was silent.

"Perhaps he has taken her to Albany," rejoined the young man. "But you saw my father. How did he fare?"

"Well," answered Black Eagle; "quite well; and he gives thee to Otaitsa. The Blossom is thine."

"Then Edith is safe," said Walter, in a tone of relief; "and his mind must have been relieved about me, for he could not be well, or seem well, if either of his children were in danger."

"The red man feels as much as the white man," observed Black Eagle; "but he leaves tears and lamentations, sighs and sad looks, to women and children. Where is the Night Hawk? and where are the warriors who went with him?"

"They are on before," replied the youth. "We have not seen them; but their fires have been lighted here."

No further questions were asked by the chief; and, walking slowly away, he seated himself with those who had accompanied him, to partake of the meat they were making ready.

Few words were spoken amongst the various groups assembled there, and some twenty minutes had elapsed when one of the young men, seated at the fire with the Black Eagle, started up, and darted away towards the north like a frightened deer. No one took any notice, and several soon after composed themselves to sleep. The others sat round their fires, with their heads bent down almost to their knees; and the murmur of a few sentences, spoken here and there, was the only sound that broke the silence for nearly an hour.

At the end of that time, two young warriors on the north side of the savannah started up and listened, and shortly after, several of the Oneidas who rested in the neighbourhood of the same spot the night before, were seen coming through the long grass, and crossing the tiny brook which meandered through the midst.

Led by the young messenger who had lately departed to seek for them, they glided up to the fire of the great chief, and seated themselves beside him. The conversation then grew earnest and quick; and eager gestures and flashing eyes might have been seen.

The great body of the Oneidas took not the slightest notice of what was occurring around the council-fire of the Black Eagle; but Walter watched every look with an indefinable feeling of interest and curiosity; and, after much discussion, and many a long pause between, the chief beckoned him up, and made him sit in the circle.

"Thou art young to talk with warriors," said the Black Eagle, when he was seated. "Thy hand is strong against the panther and the deer, but it has never taken the scalp of an enemy. But the daughter of the white man Prevost is my daughter, and she is thy sister. Know then, my son, that she is in the power of the French. The Honontkoh, whom we have expelled,--they are wolves,--have taken her: they have run her down as a hungry pack runs down a fawn, and have delivered her and themselves into the hands of the enemy. The muzzles of their rifles have fire for our bosoms: their knives are hungry for our scalps. Be not a woman, who cannot hear with a calm eye, or limbs that are still; but sit and listen, and thus prove thyself a warrior in the fight."

He then went on to repeat all that he had just heard from the chief who had succoured the poor negress on the preceding night, and all that had been done since.

"The Night Hawk was right," he said, "to send word that we would deliver thy sister, for she is a daughter of the Oneida. The story, also, of the Dark Cloud is true; for the children of the Stone have caused search to be made, and they have found the horses that were lost, and the body of the man they slew. They scalped him not, it is true; for what is the scalp of a negro worth? but the print of the tomahawk was between his eyes."

"Let me have a horse," cried Walter, "and I will bring her out from the midst of them."

"The swallow flies faster than the eagle," returned the chief; "but where is his strength? Listen, boy, to the words that come forth from many years.

Thy sister must be delivered; but our brethren, the English, must know of this ambush, lest they fall into it. So, too, shall she be saved more surely. Draw thou upon paper the history of the thing, and send it to the great chief thy friend, the Falling Cataract. I will find a messenger who knows him. Then will we break in upon this ambush at the same time with the English, and the scalps of the Honontkoh shall hang upon the war-post, for they are not the children of the Stone--they spat upon their mother. One of the horses, too, shalt thou have to save thy sister out of the fight, if a thing with four feet can run easily in this forest."

"There is the great trail from the setting sun to the Place of the Sounding Waters," said the Night Hawk. "A horse can run there as well as a deer. It passes close by the back of the hiding-place of the Frenchman."

"Let me hear," said Walter, mastering his emotion, and striving to imitate the calm manner of the Indians, "let me hear where this hiding-place is, and what it is like. The white man, though he be but young, knows the ways of the white man best; and he may see light where the older eyes fail."

In language obscured by figures, but otherwise clear and definite enough, the Night Hawk described the masked redoubt of the French, and its position.

Ignorant of the ground about the fortress, Walter could form but an insufficient judgment of the spot where it was situated; but the form and nature of the work he comprehended well enough. He mused in silence a minute or two after the chief had spoken, giving the Black Eagle good hope of his acquiring in time the Indian coolness; and then he said,--

"It would be better for us, while the army attacks the redoubt in front, to take it in reverse."

"What meanest thou, my son?" asked Black Eagle; for Walter, still busy with his own thoughts, had spoken in English.

The young man explained his meaning more clearly in the Iroquois tongue, showing that, as the enemy's position was, probably, from want of time, only closed on three sides, it would be easy for an Indian party, by making a circuit, to come upon the rear of the French, unless some considerable body of natives was thrown out upon their western flank. The Night Hawk nodded his head slowly, with a look of approbation, saying,--

"The Hurons are dogs, and creep close to the heels of their master. They are all within the stones or the mounds of earth, except those watching by the side of Horicon. The Night Hawk has skimmed over the ground towards the setting sun, and there is no print of a moccassin upon the trail."

"Thou hast the cunning of a warrior when thou art calm," said Black Eagle; "and it shall be as thou hast said. We will spring upon the back of the game. But let the Falling Cataract know quickly. Hast thou the means? He will not understand the belt of wampum, and knows not the tongue of the Oneida."

"I can find means," said Walter, taking from the pouch he carried a pencil and an old pocket-book. "But where will thy messenger find him, my father?"

"He is not far," answered the chief. "He sailed to-day from the mid-day towards the cold wind, with the war-party of the English. I watched them from the Black Mountain, and they are a mighty people. They floated on Horicon like a string of swans; and their number upon the blue waters was like a flight of passage-pigeons upon the sky, when they travel westward. They landed where the earth becomes a lizard by the Rattlesnake Dens. But how long they may tarry, who shall say? Send quickly, then."

Walter had been writing on his knee while the chief spoke; and the brief note which we have already seen delivered was speedily finished. A messenger was then chosen for his swiftness of foot, and despatched at once to the point where the English army first landed.

When he returned, all was still amongst the Oneidas; and the warriors, with but few exceptions, were sleeping in the long grass. The news he brought, however, soon roused the drowsiest. The English flotilla had sailed on, he said. He had found but a solitary canoe, with a few Mohawks, who told him that the battle would be on the following morning. All the warriors were on their feet in a moment; their light baggage and arms were snatched up in haste. One party was detached to the east, to watch the movements of the army; and before half an hour had gone by, the dusky bands were once more moving silently through the dark paths of the forest, only lighted from time to time by glimpses of the moon, and directed by the well-known stars which had so often guided their fathers through the boundless wilderness.

CHAPTER XLVIII

Calm, and bright, and beautiful, the Sabbath morning broke over the woody world around Edith Prevost. Through the tall pine-trees left standing within the earthwork, the rosy light streamed sweetly; and though no birds deserving the name of songsters inhabit the forests of America, yet many a sweet short note saluted the rising day.

Edith, with the good negro woman lying near, had slept more soundly than she had hoped; but she was awake with the first ray, and rousing her dark companion, she said,--

"We must not forget that this is Sunday, Bab. Call in our good friend, Woodchuck; and we will pray before the noise and bustle of the day begins. I am sure he will be glad to do so."

"But you have no book, missy," answered the woman.

"That matters not," returned Edith; "I know almost all the prayers by heart, from reading them constantly."

Sister Bab opened the little hurdle-door, and looked round. She could not see the person she sought. Three sentinels were pacing to and fro at different points; one man was rousing himself slowly from the side of an extinguished fire; but all the rest within sight were fast asleep. It was useless for Sister Bab to ask the neighbouring sentinel any questions, and she looked round in vain.

"He has most likely gone to sleep in one of the huts," said Edith, when the woman told her Woodchuck was not to be seen; "we will not wait for him." And, closing the door again, she kneeled and prayed with the poor negress by her side.

It was a great comfort to her, for her heart that day was sad. Perhaps it was the memory of many a happy Sabbath with those she loved, and the contrast of those days with her situation at the time; perhaps it was the uncertainty of her brother's fate; and doubtless, too, the thought that every rising sun brought nearer the hour when a parent and a lover were to be exposed to danger--perhaps to death, had its weight likewise. But she was that day very sad, and prayer was a relief--a blessing.

Before she had concluded, a good deal of noise and turmoil was heard without; voices speaking sharply; calls such as Edith had not heard before; and in a moment after, the door of the hut opened, for it had no latch, and Monsieur le Courtois appeared, inquiring if she had seen anything of her English companion.

"No, indeed," replied Edith. "I sent my servant out to seek for him half an hour ago; but she could not find him, and I concluded that he was in one of the huts."

The Frenchman stamped his foot upon the ground, and, forgetting his usual politeness, uttered some hasty and angry words which implied a belief that "Mademoiselle knew where Woodchuck was," and had aided his escape. Edith drew herself up with an air of dignity, and replied,--

"You make me feel, sir, that I am a prisoner. But you mistake me greatly. I do not permit myself to speak falsely on any occasion. If he have escaped, and I trust he has, I know nothing of it."

"I beg your pardon, mademoiselle," returned the officer; "but this to me is a very serious matter. I may be subject to the severest military punishment for this unfortunate affair. It was of the utmost importance that the existence of this post should be kept a secret. The utmost precautions have been taken to keep its existence concealed, even from the forces in Fort Carillon; and now this man is at large, to bear the intelligence to the enemy. This must excuse a little heat. How he has escaped, it is impossible to divine; for I ordered him to be kept in sight by the sentinels continually, as well as the Indians who came with you. He must be worse than an Indian, for *they* are all safe and quiet enough; but he has disappeared, though the sentinel swears he passed him sleeping on the ground, under the great pine-tree, not an hour ago."

"Half an hour ago, he certainly was gone," observed Edith; "for the servant went to look for him, and could not find him."

"He may be still in the bushes," said the French officer. "I will send a party to search." And he turned from the door of the hut.

Edith followed a step or two, to see the result; but hardly had Monsieur Le Courtois given his orders, and about a dozen men issued forth--some clambering over the breastwork, some running round by the flanks--when a French officer, brilliantly dressed, rode into the redoubt, followed by a mounted soldier; and Edith retired into the hut again.

Le Courtois saluted the new-comer reverently; and the other gave a hasty glance round, saying,--

"Get your men under arms as speedily as possible. On the maintenance of this post and the *abattis* depends the safety of the fortress. I trust them to the honour of a French gentleman, and the faith of our Indian allies. Neither will tarnish the glory of France, or their own renown, by yielding a foot of ground while they can maintain it."

He spoke aloud, so as to make his voice heard all over the enclosure; but then, bending down his head till it was close to Le Courtois' ear, he added, in a low tone, almost a whisper,--

"The English are within sight. Their first boats are disembarking the troops. Monsieur de L----, with our reinforcements, has not appeared. All depends upon maintaining the outposts till he can come up. This, sir, I trust to you with full confidence, as a brave man and an experienced soldier. I must now visit the other posts. Farewell! Remember, the glory of France is in your hands."

Thus saying, he rode away; and the bustle of instant preparation spread through the little fort. The French soldiers were drawn up within the breastworks; the stores and ammunition gathered together near the centre of the open space, so as to be readily available whenever they were wanted; two parties of Hurons were placed upon the flanks, so as to be ready to rush out with the tomahawk the moment opportunity offered; next came the long lines of French muskets, and in the centre of the longest face of the breastwork were placed Apukwa and his companions, with their rifles in their hands, and a small party of French soldiers forming a second line behind them, thus insuring their faith, and rendering the fire in the centre more fierce. Their presence, indeed, was needed at the moment; for the men who had been sent out in pursuit of Woodchuck had either mistaken the order not to go far, or had lost their way; and they had not re-appeared when the whole preparations were complete.

These had taken some time, although Monsieur le Courtois had shown all the activity and precision of a thorough soldier, giving his orders rapidly, but coolly and clearly, and correcting any error as soon as made. The Indians, indeed, gave him the greatest embarrassment; for they were too eager for the fight, and never having been subjected to military discipline, were running hither and thither to the points they thought most advantageous without consideration for the general arrangements.

The Frenchman found time, however, for a few courteous words to Edith.

"I am greatly embarrassed, my dear young lady," he said, "by your presence here, as we expect to be attacked every instant. I wish to Heaven, Monsieur de Montcalm had taken you away with him; but in the hurry of the moment I did not think of it, and I have no means of sending you away now; and, besides, the risk to yourself would be still greater than staying here. I believe you are as safely posted in this hut as anywhere. It is near enough to the breastwork to be protected from the fire of the enemy; but you may as well lie down upon the bear-skin if you hear musketry."

"Could I not place myself actually under the breastwork?" asked Edith, remembering the instructions sent to her.

"Impossible," replied the officer. "That space is all occupied by the soldiers and Indians. You are better here. If we should be driven back, which God forbid, you will be safe, as you speak English, and can say who you are; but, remember, address yourself to an officer, for the canaille get mad in time of battle, and on no account trust to an Indian."

"I speak the Iroquois tongue," answered Edith.

"My dear young lady, there is no trusting them," said the officer; "friends or enemies are the same to them when their blood's hot. All they want is a scalp; and that they *will* have. It would be terrible to see your beautiful tresses hanging at an Indian's belt."

As he spoke, one of the men who had been sent forth came running up, exclaiming,--

"They are coming now, captain,--they are coming."

"Who?" demanded Le Courtois, briefly.

"The red-coats, the English," replied the man. "I saw their advance-guard with my own eyes; they are not two hundred yards' distance."

"Where are your companions?" asked Le Courtois. "We want every musket."

"I do not know," answered the man; "they have lost their way, I fancy, as I did. I saw two amongst the bushes just in front, trying to get back."

"*Sacré Dieu*, they will discover us!" said the captain.

And, running forward, he jumped upon the parapet just behind one of the highest bushes, and looked over. The next instant, he sprang down again, saying, in a low tone, to the corporal near him,--

"Stand to your arms! present! pass the word along not to fire, whatever you see, till I give the order."

At the same moment, he made a sign with his hand to the renegade Oneidas; but probably they did not see it, for their keen black eyes were all eagerly bent forward, peeping through the bushes, which now seemed agitated at some little distance. A moment after, a straggling shot or two

The Black Eagle | 343

was heard, and instantly the Honontkoh fired. The order was then given by Le Courtois, and the whole front poured forth a volley, which was returned by a number of irregular shots blazing out of the bushes in front.

Then succeeded a silence of a few moments, and then a loud cheer, such as none but Anglo-Saxon lungs have ever given.

Edith sat deadly pale and trembling in the hut; but it is not too much to say that but a small portion of her terror was for herself. The battle had begun--the battle in which father and lover were to risk life, in which, among all the human beings destined to bleed and die that day, her love singled out two, while her fancy painted them as the aim of every shot. It was of them she thought, much more than of herself.

The door of the hut was turned, as I have shown, towards the inside of the square; and Captain le Courtois had left it open behind him. But, as Edith sat a little towards one side of the entrance, she had a view, both of a great part of the square itself, and of the whole of the inner front of the western face of the redoubt, along which were posted a few French soldiers and a considerable body of Hurons.

The firing was soon resumed, but in a somewhat different manner from before. There were no longer any volleys, but frequent, repeated, almost incessant, shots, sometimes two or three together, making almost one sound. Twice she saw a French soldier carried across the open space; and laid down at the foot of a tree. One remained quite still where he had been placed; one raised himself for a moment upon his arm, and then sank down again; and Edith understood the signs full well. Clouds of bluish-white smoke then began to roll over the redoubt, and curl along as the gentle wind carried it towards the broad trail by which she had been brought thither. The figures of the Indians became indistinct, and looked like beings seen in a dream.

Still the firing continued, drawing apparently more towards the western side, and still the rattle of the musketry was mingled with loud cheers from without.

But suddenly those sounds were crossed, as it were, with a wild yell, such as Edith had heard only once in life before, but which now seemed to issue from a thousand throats, instead of a few. It came from the northwest, right in the direction of the broad trail. The French soldiers and the Hurons, who had been kneeling to fire over the breastwork, sprang upon their feet, looked round, and from that side, too, burst forth at once the war-whoop.

"O missy, missy, let us run!" cried Sister Bab, catching Edith's wrist.

"Hush, hush, be quiet!" ejaculated the young lady. "These may be friends coming."

As she spoke, pouring on like a dark torrent was seen a crowd of dusky forms rushing along the trail, emerging from amongst the trees, and spreading over the ground; and, amidst them all, a youth dressed like an Indian, and mounted on a grey horse which Edith recognized as her own. The sight confused and dazzled her. Feathers and plumes and war-paints, rifles and tomahawks and knives, grim countenances and brandished arms, swam before her like the things that fancy sees for a moment in a cloud; while still the awful war-whoop rang horribly around, drowning even the rattle of the musketry, and seeming to rend the air. Two figures only were distinct: the youth upon the horse, and the towering form of Black Eagle himself, close to the lad's side.

Attacked in flank and front and rear, the French and Hurons were broken in a moment, driven from the breastworks, beat back into the centre of the square, and separated into detached bodies. Still they fought with desperation; still the rifles and the muskets pealed; still the cheer, and the shout, and the war-whoop, resounded on the air. A large party of the French soldiery were cast between the huts and the Oneidas, and the young man on the horse strove in vain, tomahawk in hand, to force his way through.

But there are episodes in all combats; and a pause took place when a gigantic Huron rushed furiously against the Black Eagle. It may be that they were ancient enemies; but, at all events, each seemed animated with the fury of a fiend. Each cast away his rifle, and betook himself to the weapons of his race--the knife and the tomahawk; but it is almost impossible to describe, it was almost impossible to see, the movements of the two combatants, such was their marvellous rapidity. Now here, now there, they turned, the blows seeming to fall like hail, the limbs writhing and twisting, the weapons whirling and flashing round. Each was the giant of his tribe, each its most renowned warrior; and each fought for more than life--for the closing act of a great renown. But the sinewy frame of the Black Eagle seemed to prevail over the more bulky strength of his opponent; the Huron lost ground; he was driven back to the great pine-tree near the centre of the square; he was forced round and round it; the knife of the Black Eagle drank his blood, but missed his heart, and only wounded him in the shoulder.

Those nearest to the scene had actually paused in the contest for a moment to witness the fierce single combat going on; but in other parts of the square the bloody fight was still continued. For an instant, the French party in front of the huts, by desperate efforts, seemed likely to overpower the Oneidas before them. A tall French grenadier bayoneted the Night Hawk before Edith's eyes; and then, seeing the Huron chief staggering under the blows of his enemy, he dashed forward, and, not daring in the rapid whirls of the two combatants to use his bayonet there, he struck the Black Eagle on the head with the butt of his musket. The blow fell with tremendous force, and drove the great chief on his knee, with one hand on the ground. His career seemed over, his fate finished. The Huron raised his tomahawk high to strike; the Frenchman shortened his musket to pin the chief to the earth.

But, at that moment, a broad, powerful figure dropped down from the branches of the pine-tree between the Oneida and the grenadier, bent slightly with his fall, but even in rising lifted a rifle to his shoulder, and sent the ball into the Frenchman's heart. With a yell of triumph, Black Eagle sprang up from the ground, and in an instant his tomahawk was buried in the undefended head of his adversary.

Edith beheld not the end of the combat; for, in the swaying to and fro of the fierce struggle, the French soldiery had, by this time, been driven past the huts, and the eye of one who loved her was upon her.

"Edith, Edith!" cried the voice of Walter Prevost, forcing the horse forward through the struggling groups, amidst shots and shouts and falling blows. She saw him, she recognized him, she stretched forth her arm towards him; and, dashing between two parties, Walter forced the horse up to the door of the hut, and caught her hand.

"Spring up, spring up!" he cried, bending down, and casting his arms around her. "This is not half over; I must carry you away."

Partly lifted, partly springing from the ground, Edith bounded up before him; and, holding her tightly to his heart, Walter turned the rein, and dashed away through friends and enemies, trampling, unconscious of what he did, alike on the dead and the dying. The western side of the square was crowded with combatants, and he directed his horse's head towards the east, reached the angle, and turned sharp round to get in the rear of the English column, which was seen forcing its way onward to support the advance party of Major Putnam. He thought only of his sister, and pressing her closer to his heart, he said,--

"We are safe, Edith--we are safe!"

Alas, he said it too soon! One group in the square had stood almost aloof from the combat. Gathered together in the south-eastern angle, Apukwa and his companions seemed watching an opportunity for flight. But their fierce eyes had seen Walter, and twice had a rifle clanged at him from that spot, but without effect. They saw him snatch his sister from the hut, place her on the horse, and gallop round. Apukwa, the brother of the Snake, and two others, jumped upon the parapet, and scarcely had Walter uttered the words, "We are safe!" when the fire blazed at once from the muzzles of their rifles. One ball whistled by his ear, another passed through his hair; but, clasping Edith somewhat closer, he galloped on, and in two minutes after came to a spot where three or four men were standing, and one kneeling with his hand under the head of a British officer who had fallen.

Walter reined up the horse sharply, for he was almost over them before he saw them; but the sight of the features of the dead man drew the sudden exclamation from his lips of "Good God!" They were those of Lord H----. Edith's face, as he held her, was turned towards him, and he fancied that she rested her forehead on his bosom to shut out the terrible sights around. He looked down at her to see whether she had caught even a glimpse of the features of the corpse. Her forehead was resting there still; but over the arm that held her so closely to his heart Walter saw welling a dark red stream of blood. He trembled like a leaf.

"Edith!" he exclaimed, "Edith!"

There was no answer. He pushed the bright chestnut curls from her forehead; and, as he did so, the head fell back, showing the face as pale as marble. She had died without a cry, without a sound.

Walter bent his head, and kissed her cheek, and wept.

"What is the matter, sir?" said the sergeant, rising from beside the body of Lord H----. "Did you know my lord?"

"Look here!" cried Walter. It was all he uttered. But in an instant they gathered round him, and lifted Edith from the horse. The sergeant put his hand upon the wrist, then shook his head sadly, and they laid her gently by the side of Lord H----. They knew not with how much propriety,--but thus she would have loved to rest.

Thus they met, and thus they parted; thus they loved and thus they died. But in one thing they were happy; for neither, at the last hour of life, knew the other's peril or the other's fate.

CHAPTER XLIX

From the bloody field of Ticonderoga, Abercrombie retreated, as is well known, after having in vain attempted to take the inner *abattis* without cannon, and sacrificed the lives of many hundred gallant men to his own want of self-reliance.

I need dwell no more upon this painful subject; but it was a sad day for the whole army, a sad day for the whole province, and a sadder day still for one small domestic circle, when the bodies of the gallant Lord H---- and his promised bride were brought to rest for a night at the house of Mr. Prevost, before they were carried down to Albany. A party of the young nobleman's own regiment carried the coffins by turns, another party followed with arms reversed; but between the biers and the escort walked four men, with hearts as sad as any upon earth.

It may seem strange, but neither of the four shed a tear. The tall Indian warrior, though he grieved as much as if he had lost a child, had no tears for any earthly sorrow. The fountain in the heart of Mr. Prevost had been dried up by the fiery intensity of his grief. Walter had wept long and secretly, but the pride of manhood would not let him stain his cheeks in the presence of soldiers. Woodchuck's eyes were dry, too; for, during six long months, he had disciplined his heart to look upon the things of earth so lightly, that, although he grieved for Edith's fate, it was with the sort of sorrow he might have felt to see a beautiful flower trampled down by a rough foot; and bright hope mingled with the shadow of his woe--for he said to himself, frequently, "They have but parted for to-day, to meet in a happier place to-morrow."

As the procession approached the house, the servants came forth to meet it, with a young and comely girl at their head, clad in the Indian costume. She bore two little wreaths in her hand, one woven of bright spring flowers, the other of dark evergreens; and, when the soldiers halted for a moment with their burden, she laid the flowers upon the coffin of Edith, the evergreens upon the soldier's bier. Then turning, with the tears dropping from her eyes, but with no clamorous grief, she walked before them back into the house.

Some four years after, another kind of scene might be beheld at the house of Mr. Prevost. He himself sat in a great chair under the verandah, with his hair become as white as snow, and his head a good deal bowed.

Seated on the ground near him was a tall Indian chief, very little changed in appearance; grave, calm, and still severe. On the step of the verandah sat two young people; a tall, handsome, powerful man of about one-and-twenty years of age, and a graceful girl, whose brown cheek displayed some mixture of the Indian blood. On the green grass before them, with a black nurse sitting by, was as lovely a child of about two years old as ever the sun shone upon. They had gathered for her a number of pretty flowers, and she was sporting with them, with the grace and happiness that only childhood can display or know. The eyes of all were fixed upon her, and they called her Edith.

One was wanting to that party, out of those who had assembled at the door four years previously. Woodchuck was no longer there. He had gone where he longed to be. When he felt sickness coming upon him some two years after the death of Lord H----, he had left the house of Mr. Prevost, which he had lately made his home; and had gone, as he said, to wander in the mountains. There he became worse. An Indian runner came down to tell his friends that he was dying; and when Mr. Prevost went up to see him, he found him in a Seneca lodge with but a few hours of life before him.

He was glad to see the friendly face near him; and as his visitor bent over him, he said, "I am very much obliged to you for coming, Prevost, for I want to ask you one thing, and that is to have me buried in the churchyard at Albany, just beside your dear girl. I know this is all nonsense; I know that the flesh sees corruption; still I've a fancy that I shall rest quieter there than anywhere else. If ever there was an angel, she was one, and I think her dust must sanctify the ground."

It was his only request, and it was not forgotten.

FOOTNOTES

Footnote 1 : This very curious fact is avouched upon authority beyond question. The order was called that of the Honontkoh, and was generally regarded with great doubt and suspicion by the Iroquois.

Footnote 2: A name greatly affected by the Mohawks.

Footnote 3: The word "Hero," or "Hiro," "I have spoken," was so common in all the speeches of the orators of the Five Nations, that it was supposed to have given rise, in combination with the word "Koué," (an exclamation either of approbation or grief, according as it was pronounced quickly or slowly,) to the name of "Iroquois," given by the French to the Five confederate Nations.

Footnote 4: I find it stated, that the fort referred to did not receive the name of Crown Point till after its capture by the English; but it is so called by contemporary English writers.